THE SKYLARK'S SONG

Audrey Howard

'Because the road is rough and long,
Shall we despise the skylark's song?'
ANNE BRONTE, *Views of Life*

ARROW

Published by Arrow Books in 1996

5 7 9 10 8 6

© Audrey Howard 1984

First published in the United Kingdom by
Century Publishing Co Ltd 1984

Arrow Books Limited
Random House UK Limited
20 Vauxhall Bridge Road, London SW1V 2SA

Random House Australia (Pty) Limited
20 Alfred Street, Milsons Point, Sydney
New South Wales 2061, Australia

Random House New Zealand Limited
18 Poland Road, Glenfield, Auckland 10, New Zealand

Random House (Pty) Limited
Endulini, 5a Jubilee Road, Parktown 2193, South Africa

Random House UK Limited Reg. No. 954009

www.randomhouse.co.uk

A CIP catalogue record for this book
is available from the British Library

Papers used by Random House are natural,
recyclable products made from wood grown in
sustainable forests. The manufacturing processes conform to
the environmental regulations of the country of origin

ISBN 0 09 966371 6

Printed and bound in Great Britain by
Cox & Wyman Ltd, Reading, Berkshire

THE SKYLARK'S SONG

Audrey Howard was born in Liverpool in 1929 and it is from that once great seaport that many of the ideas for her books come. Before she began to write she had a variety of jobs, among them hairdresser, model, shop assistant, cleaner and civil servant. In 1981, out of work and living in Australia, she wrote her first novel, *The Skylark's Song*. She was fifty-two. This success was followed by *The Morning Tide*, *Ambitions*, *The Juniper Bush* and *Between Friends*. *The Juniper Bush* won the Boots Romantic Novel of the Year Award in 1988. She now lives in her childhood home, St Anne's on Sea, Lancashire.

In memory of my mother
who would have loved all this

Chapter One

Zoe.

Her name meant 'life', but the child sitting on the kerb, feet in the gutter, naked buttocks chill on the stone, knew only existence. Her bare grimy feet splayed in the damp spongy lichen growing through the cobblestones and her thin frame shivered, the autumn cold creeping under the tattered remnant of a dress.

It was all she wore.

Her eyes were the colour of variegated moss, changing shades subtly with the light, set in brown lashes tipped with gold, long and fine. The tangle of chestnut hair, which had known neither scissors nor comb since the day she was born, moved with the vermin it harboured, curling about her delicately shaped skull, and her baby skin was coated with layers of dirt long accumulated.

She held a piece of wood, roughly carved by an unknown hand, to her thin chest; two stick arms tenderly cradling her 'dolly', as she crooned a lullaby of her own composing.

She rocked gently in time to the melody in her head, and to the chanting of three barefoot girls she was watching as they skipped in and out of a whirling rope, one end tied to a lamp post, the other held by a fourth child who turned it fiercely.

The game was complicated and called for agility and speed, and the child drew in her breath with a hiss as a foot caught in the rope bringing the ritual of musical, rhythmical leaping to a temporary halt. With cries of derision the offender was forced to take the place of the rope-turner and the game resumed.

'One potater, two potater, three potater, four; five potater, six potater, seven potater, more,' the chorus continued, the meaning of the words long forgotten, if indeed they were ever known.

Up and down the cheerless street similar games were being played, though not all so vigorously. Poverty did not encourage such displays of energy and many of the ragged children were lethargic. Women, poorly clad, dragged down, the vacant look of the undernourished on their work-worn faces, stood in doorways, watching with little interest the activities of their offspring, too dispirited even to gossip.

As if to flaunt the destitution which touched every house, every figure in the beggarly back street, the sun shone in cruel humour, searching out every particle of dirt, every crack and mottled, scabby brick. It lay warmly on slovenly head and bedraggled form, caressing dirty skin with as much affection as it would a garden of exquisite blooms. It shone from the cloudless sky, and the shadows it cast on one side of the street were sharp. The dust raised by the barefoot girls rose in tiny, mushroom-shaped puffs as they slapped the pavement with their hard-soled feet, and floated for a moment before drifting gently to the flags again.

A ramshackle wooden cart clattered slowly by on the cobbles, the overstrained wheels leaning inwards with the weight of its load: an iron stove, a birdcage, an upturned table with huge, bulbous, elaborately carved legs, and pile upon pile of boots, shoes and worn clothing all drawn by a caricature of a horse, his head bent low. He was wheezing from tortured lungs, and his bones threatened to break through his dry, dusty, sore-encrusted hide.

'Raaaaabow, raaaabow, raaaaabow.'

The strident call of the rag-and-bone man reached every ear and penetrated every scullery of the squalid houses which lined each side of the street; women reached for hidden pennies, saved painfully, farthing by farthing, month by month, to put a pair of boots or a second- or third-hand dress on an infant about to start school.

The child moved back from her ringside seat as the

skeletal horse drew near: ironically, in her short life of stinking sewer, privy and dungheap, the smell of the beast offended her. She lowered her poor chafed backside to the filthy step of the house where she had spent the first four years of her life, and watched with interest as the women filtered from their doorways to bicker and haggle apathetically with the ragman.

The door behind her banged open and a girl came out, dragging a small boy towards the horse and cart. She had the chestnut tangle of curls and huge mossy eyes of the half-naked child on the step.

'One more word out of you, our Jamie, an' I'll give yer such a clip round the 'earole, ya won't know what bloody 'it yer, so shut yer gob. You've to 'ave boots for school.'

She gave him a vicious shove towards the cart and shouldering aside the crowd of women, began to turn over the pile of boots in her search for a pair which would roughly fit her brother. They must be a couple of sizes too large in order to allow him to 'grow into' them, yet in a good enough condition to be passed on to his younger sister when she started school in a year's time. She passed over pair after pair, never taking her left hand from Jamie's shirt collar.

Zoe overcame her aversion to the horse and wandered across the cracked flagstones to watch as her sister lifted Jamie onto the edge of the cart, forcing a pair of ugly black boots on to his filthy feet. She seemed satisfied with the fit, or lack of it, as they slipped up and down his scrawny ankles. The boy sat resentfully as she lifted and dropped each foot in turn, treating the performance with disdain and earning the threatened clip. His chin quivered as the blow rocked his head, but he made no sound. The girl turned from him, her peevish expression turning to cunning.

'Ow much?' she demanded of the alert ragman, whose eyes flickered like a snake's tongue from customer to customer, fearful of missing a sale, or a stealthy hand stealing his stock.

'Sixpence, Queen,' he replied genially, eyes never still, the false smile of bonhomie creasing his cheeks.

'Give over,' she said derisively, running a rough hand over the worn toecap of the left boot, 'They're falling apart, worth no more 'an a penny, two at the most.' A feral smile lifted her lip.

It was wasted on the ragman.

'Go on, I'll give yer tuppence,' she continued, with an air of making a great concession.

The ragman, an old hand at this game, shook his head, the jovial smile still intact.

'Cost me fourpence to buy 'em, luv. What d'yer want me to do, sell 'em for less than I give? I gotta make a livin', same as anyone.'

'Come off it, y'old skinflint, you've got 'ouses in the bank, you 'ave. Tell yer what, tuppence farthin' an' that's me last offer.'

The customary haggling continued, until they agreed on threepence farthing. The girl jerked her sullen brother to the ground, first removing the boots from his feet, (for they were to be worn only to school) and leaving him in the gutter stalked back to her door, slamming it behind her.

Soon the ragman flogged on his jaded animal to the next street. Children kicking a bundle of rags scattered before him, and as he turned the corner, the child on the doorstep sighed at the ending of the small drama in her day, and her arms tightened about her 'baby'.

She resumed her position on the kerb, her face soft and gentle, as she whispered to the unpainted lump of wood. The words were indistinguishable, a caressing murmur to comfort herself more than the doll for some lack she felt, some unknown longing she could not describe. Her eyes, limpid with frustrated tenderness, followed the movements of the four girls as they continued their interrupted game, and the melody, her own, sang inside her head in time to the stamping feet.

*

Zebediah Taylor was a drunkard. He had not always been so. When he had married Matilda Baker in 1895 his youthful optimism, his robust constitution, his love for Matty and his cheerful nature had combined to carry him through the first five years of marriage despite the soul-destroying poverty into which they were helplessly dragged. He was a dock worker and in the days before the Labour Exchange supply and demand of workers was haphazard. Labour was cheap as a consequence, and most work was carried out by casual labourers. In some weeks Zebediah had only a day, a half-day, or even an hour's work. Sometimes not even that. With the meagre four or five shillings that Matty sweated to earn making matchboxes – the only employment to be had for women forced to remain at home with young children, at twopence farthing a gross – they barely existed. Their fifth child in four years was born in November 1899, and as the new century was rung in, Zeb's striving to make even a living wage on which to raise his ever-increasing family gave way to gradual despair and disillusionment. Even Matty's poor contribution to the wage packet had dwindled as the babies arrived. She needed to make seven thousand matchboxes a week to earn five shillings. It was impossible.

They lived in a tiny, back-to-back, one-up and one-down cottage in Love Lane, an ironic name for the street, built in the late eighteenth century. Hundreds and hundreds of these cottages marched in symmetrical rows; separated from the River Mersey only by the warehouses, and the dockyard itself. For over a century they had housed the families of dock workers and from the day they were first erected not a single improvement or even repair had been done to them.

The majority of the occupants of these hovels were, like Zeb, casual dock labourers, frequently without work and receiving 'out-door' relief from the workhouse or 'union', teetering on the tightrope between life and death. They fought tooth and nail to keep themselves and their families from the workhouse, the ultimate in degradation. But for many of the women, the war was not only with dirt, disease and hunger, but with their husbands' drunkenness. Desperate, degraded men, humiliated by their frustrated inability to work and support their families, found comfort in the only occupations left open to them, copulation and drinking. The Taylors had a slight advantage over the twenty-five neighbouring houses; the privy and the standpipe were next to their cottage. Their noses had long grown accustomed to the stench of the privy, and they did not have far to carry their water.

They had two rooms. The front door opened directly into the scullery, and it was here that the family ate, cooked, washed, fought and worked. On one wall the kitchen range stood in its garb of soot, dirt and grease, the glowing coals emphasising the drabness. To the left of the range, in the corner, a stone shelf supported a tin bucket which was used for all washing purposes, from pans to persons, but not very often for either.

Crowded against the flaky plastered wall was a sagging couch and in the middle of the room, a rickety table, a chair and two orange boxes. A small window allowed a little light in through the grime of the years, and it fell on these meagre possessions, showing up the cracks, the green-stained, mildewed walls, and the bare red brick floor.

Through a doorway from which the door had long since disappeared for firewood, a boarded staircase led to the bedroom. There, on the floor, lay two palliasses, one for the girls, the other for the boys and their father, and both shared by sundry bed bugs, silverfish, the occasional mouse and once even a rat. On the walls of this room were hammered hooks at various heights, from which hung the garments they discarded at night as they crept between their thin, grimy blankets.

In neither room was there one possession which did not have some use.

As the years passed, Matty gave up the struggle to keep a clean and decent home and became as slatternly as her neighbours. One water closet and standpipe served twenty-five houses in the street, the water being switched on for two hours a day, and not at all on Sunday. It needed a great deal of ingenuity, hard work and plain strength of mind, besides many buckets, to keep five children and two adults clean, and as the years passed, with the regular arrival of another child, it was easier to remain dirty.

In 1905 Matty gave birth to her eleventh child. Worn out with the fight against dirt and squalor, malnutrition and childbirth, she died in a wave of her own blood, which the neighbouring women and her ten-year-old daughter were unable to staunch. The baby, another girl, survived. She was hastily bundled into a heap of rags and deposited into the arms of a neighbour, who, having a kindly nature, a baby of three months, and a drop of milk to spare, put her to the breast.

From that moment the child, as if aware that in the world into which she had been so violently forced you took what you could when you could, and made the best of it, drank lustily and survived.

She was named Zoe for her paternal grandmother.

Zeb Taylor knelt at the bedside of his dead wife, decently laid out by the women of the street, and wept, his tears falling more in self-pity than in grief for Matty's death. In the last ten years Matty had aged thirty, and in her struggle to bring forth the new life her haggard features had become as drawn as a woman of sixty. Now, at peace, her skin was smooth, flawless, her long fine eyelashes sweeping the lilac hollows above her high cheekbones. Her silky eyebrows curved sweetly above eyes closed as if in sleep and her wild tangle of sweat-stained curls was brushed and glossy.

Zeb looked upon her gentle face for the last time and rebellion ran through him as his memory took him back to the sweet days of his courtship of the pretty seventeen-year-old who now lay lifeless before him. In eleven years she had known nothing but hardship and hopelessness. Sullen resentment finally overcame his last scrap of optimism, and the pattern of his days was set.

He staggered to his feet, his mind seething with thoughts

13

of the brood of children downstairs – seven now, with Zoe. Of the eleven he had fathered, four had mercifully died, one at birth, two of tuberculosis, and the fourth under the hooves of a massive Shire horse pulling a coal cart, when as a baby he had crawled into its path from the doorstep where he had been put to play.

Who was to care for the motherless family? Zeb's tired brain was incapable of answering, but scuttled here and there in search of some comfort. Finding none, he settled for what was to become the answer to all his problems, the palliative for all his ills, in the years to come.

He put on his cap and made his way to the corner pub.

Sarah Taylor was ten years old when her mother died. Born and brought up in the slums, death, dirt and hunger were familiar companions. The close proximity in which the family was forced to live had made her a part of her brothers and sisters almost from the moment of their conception, an act she frequently overheard and quite often witnessed, for privacy was unknown in her world, and from the age of five, when she was able to understand and obey the orders of her elders, she had not only watched them come into the world, but had ably assisted.

She had never gone to school; by the time she was of an age, she had a brother and two sisters and was indispensable to Matty, feverishly turning out hundreds of matchboxes each day. Together they had successfully evaded the school inspector, when the Schooling Act became law, becoming adept at the hide-and-seek game played by so many mothers and children able to earn. Very often the few pence they brought in meant the difference between life and death, so fine was the precipice of starvation.

Despite her lack of education, Sarah was as sharp as a tack. From an early age she had done all the shopping for her mother, and could count, adding and subtracting the meagre sums which passed through her hands, her sharp eyes never missing a farthing short in change, or her shrewd brain the chance to strike a bargain. She was on

14

familiar terms with all the local pawnbrokers and knew to the blink of an eyelash whom she could seduce with her huge, heartbreaking eyes, and whom the performance would leave unmoved; and she knew, to the last half-penny, how much she was in debt. Gradually, her mother left all money matters in her hands, and as Matty toiled in her poverty-stricken home, striving to rear her children, fighting, always pregnant, to keep her family out of the workhouse, Sarah was the crutch on which she leaned more and more heavily; the one person in her harsh world on whom Matty could wholly rely.

It was this upbringing which trained Sarah to be the guardian of her family as her father, at the age of thirty, gave up the struggle and started on the long road to alcoholism. His despair might have been less acute had he realised the extent to which the girl had managed the household before her mother's death, but he had not, and he wallowed in self-pity, believing himself the family's only support and mainstay.

He was wrong.

Sarah was not a loving child, far from it, but she was independent and fiercely loyal, and her brothers and sisters, though lacking all the warmth and tenderness of parental love, could not have had a more efficient caretaker to guide them through the years until they were able to fend for themselves.

She prised from her father every farthing her cunning mind could contrive, and she kept it from him too, which was even harder to achieve, when in a peevish rage he demanded its return so that he could flee to the Sefton Park Arms. Sarah would stand unmoved as he kicked over the thin sticks of furniture, would watch impassively as the battered cooking pots were flung against the walls. She dodged as he lunged at her, and never once did her eyes move to the loose brick in the corner, carefully prised out one day when she and her mother had been alone. Behind it was a hollow; here Sarah kept her small hoard.

Who was to say Zeb was selfish? Life had made him as he

was and his one comfort, the warmth of his wife's body, had been taken from him. Who was to blame him for looking elsewhere for relief from an existence which gave no hope or comfort? Not Sarah, for she was a realist. And she ignored his words and avoided his heavy hand.

She insisted, though, that all the children attend school, and scrimped and saved together every halfpenny in order to clothe them for this privilege. At home they went barefoot, unwashed and virtually unclothed, fed on whatever she could afford: potatoes; bread and margarine or lard when times were really bad, and scouse when they were not. But at the age of five they were clothed, shod (after a fashion) and, every Sunday night, thoroughly washed for school.

In September 1910 it was Zoe's turn.

Chapter Two

The last child of Zeb and Matty Taylor was the only one not to have known the sweetness of a mother's love. Jamie, twelve months older, had for one short year experienced the comfort of a soft lap and loving arms about him, the murmured endearments, the loving kiss, as had his brothers and sisters, for Matty had been a kind mother. Perhaps for this reason, one would suppose they would miss her more, but it was not so.

From her first drawn breath, in some mysterious way Zoe missed and longed for the mother she had never known. Her baby heart yearned to be loved, her body to be kissed and caressed as she had seen even the sorriest mothers casually fondle their offspring, but when she had first tried to climb on to her father's knee he had pushed her roughly away. She curled up to her sisters, Lucy and Emma, who slept beside her – Rebecca and Sarah sharing the bottom half of the bug-ridden mattress – but they were exhausted after long hours of helping Sarah with the matchboxes. Impatiently, they too rejected her.

It seemed her warm heart would dry up like a sponge in a desert.

Crouched on doorstep or kerb, nursing the lump of wood on which she spent her enormous love, Zoe was a familiar figure in the street. The other children largely ignored her, for she was too young for their games and too 'soft', easily hurt by an unkind word, distressed by their jeering.

When she started school, she at last found someone not only eager to accept but to give, and give again, all the warm affection she craved.

Her name was Joanna Dale.

*

The week before Zoe started school had been a good one. Zeb had worked for three whole days and had earned fourteen and sixpence. Sarah had fashioned matchboxes until her fingers had bled, and she had been forced to give up for fear of staining the materials. She had still managed to earn four-and-elevenpence-three-farthings, and the three girls had been taken on at a local factory, licking adhesive labels for tins until they had vomited and had been sent home. Nevertheless, between them they had managed eight-and-sixpence-halfpenny for the week.

The ragman on his weekly journey down Love Lane was pleased with the business he had done with the sharp-witted Sarah, who had bought a drab merino dress, grey pinafore, a pair of boots and knickers for Zoe, and another pair of boots for Jamie, the previous pair not having survived a year of boisterous games in the school yard.

The night before school started, the tin tub was lifted from its hook on the scullery wall and set before the fire on which a kettle was boiling, and for the second time in her life (the first was at her birth) Zoe was completely immersed in tepid water. The harsh carbolic soap stung her eyes and scalp and scoured her soft flesh, but the vision which emerged from the rough handling surprised even Sarah, and took her father's breath away.

The layered filth was gone, leaving a smooth, satined, rose-flushed skin. Her hair shimmered in the firelight, the colour of polished chestnuts, framing a face so sweetly appealing, so delicately lovely, that Zeb lowered hastily his eyes to hide the sudden tears. He had not seen that innocent face for sixteen years, and his heart ached at the memories of his sweet dead wife.

Naked, Zoe shyly smiled at him, and he remembered with sorrow the many times he had rejected her loving baby advances. Even her meagre diet had not marred her, though she had little flesh on her fine bones. Her smile deepened when she saw his gaze upon her, revealing white, perfect teeth.

'Get sum clos' on 'er, our Sarah,' Zeb barked, the emotion

which he was embarrassed to feel, making his voice harsh, his face stern. He was finished with feeling, with emotion. He asked only for peace, oblivion from daily troubles, and he put his cap on and left the house to find it.

He strode the uneven flags as though a ghost stepped behind him, as indeed it did, and his deadened memory was agony as it came alive. He was almost running as he reached the open door of the Seffie.

With a pint glass in his hand and his shoulder companionably rubbing against that of Ally Briggs, often his partner in the dole queue, or on a temporary job at the dockyard, and therefore understanding his desperation, he soon began to feel like his old self.

In other words he was quickly sozzled.

His youngest daughter stepped from the scum-covered water. Her scrap of a dress was flung at her, for not until tomorrow was she to be allowed to wear the finery which she had folded neatly, lovingly, on the table, the boots – two sizes too large, of course – topping the small pile.

Zoe lay that night between her sleeping sisters, her dolly held in the crook of her arm, the strangeness of her clean hair and skin making her itch. She was too excited to sleep, conscious that she was on the threshold of a new world, a new beginning.

What would it be like, this adventure? Their Rebecca and them seemed to quite like it, and she could say the words when she looked at the fascinating squirls and squiggles on the piece of paper, could their Rebecca. She was right clever. She could say 'One and one is two, two and two is four, four and four is eight' and wonderful things like that, although Zoe wasn't quite sure what they meant. And once she had told Zoe that there was an old man who lived in the sky where their Mam was. He had a little boy and some cruel men had nailed the little boy to some wood with great big nails. It must have been awful, but she supposed it was true 'cos they said so at school. Just fancy. And tomorrow they would tell it all to her. Mind you, their Jamie hated it,

19

and played hookey as often as not. Bluddy waste of time, he said.

She put out her hand in the darkness and gently touched the neat pile of clothes on the floor beside her and her last thought as she finally drifted into slumber was the joyful anticipation of wearing her new knickers.

The child sat at the double desk, her fellow on the seat bench a rickety boy with a squint.

Joanna Dale noticed her at once, for who could not, so appealing was she to the eye, her alert vivid face showing her eagerness to begin whatever one did in this magical place. Her head turned constantly so that she might not miss one word or movement from the rest of the class. She had absorbed the classroom, the like of which she had never seen or imagined. The walls were a beautiful glossy brown, painted to shoulder level, with windows above to allow teachers to oversee each other's classes when colleagues were forced to be absent. She had admired the brightly-coloured paintings, perfect in her eyes, done by children of last year's class and pinned to every available square inch of wall, for her senses were starved for colour. She had looked with luminous interest at the blackboard and chalk, at the teacher's high desk, and waited patiently for the proceedings to begin.

'Class, stand up.'

Zoe fixed her eyes on the vision who stood two paces from her and wondered that such an exquisite creature, surely an angel from the sky in which her own mother lived, could be a teacher. She had never seen a woman dressed like that, so clean, sweet-smelling, sweetly smiling.

A feeling of joy, never before experienced, filled her small body.

They stood, some slowly, some clumsily, some quickly and noisily, but the child rose neatly, gracefully, her hideous boots making hardly a sound on the wooden floor as the others thumped and banged.

'Now, children, my name is Miss Dale. Will you remember that, please?'

There was silence.

'Say, "Yes, Miss Dale."'

'Yes Miss Dale,' said thirty-one five-year-old voices in varying degrees of enthusiasm.

'You may sit down and I will call the register,' said this being, and they sat, awed and silent.

'I will call your name and when you hear it I want you to answer, "Here, Miss Dale." We shall do this each morning so that I may know who is here and who is absent. Do you understand?'

There was not one who did but a voice replied, 'Yes Miss Dale.'

It was the beautiful child. She stood up and smiled winningly.

It was a mistake to single out one pupil. Joanna Dale knew it. For the sake of the child if for no other: it made for bad feeling among the other children and trouble for the favoured one, but who could resist the clear intelligent eyes, the interest, the eagerness to please and to become a part of this new world in which she found herself?

Not Joanna Dale.

All her adult life had been spent with children and most of them had been born and brought up within sight of the dirty river which gave their fathers their livelihood. Families of ten and twelve lived on nineteen shillings a week, the average wage for a casual dock worker. An extra shilling or two could be made by women and children, buttonholing, matchbox-making, trouser-finishing at a penny-three-farthings a pair. Their mothers might be lucky and get a bit of 'charring', but they lived from hand to mouth at the best of times. When employment could not be found or illness struck there were hungry stomachs. They would be forced to part with some treasured possession, perhaps only an old framed picture which had belonged to a grandmother in better days, or perhaps the boots off their feet. They got into debt with tradesmen and lived for weeks on bread and tea.

Joanna Dale had seen it all. The thin peaked faces and wasted frames, the long absences – for how could a child come to school with bare feet? Children who all looked curiously alike, in build, in size, even in colouring, for poverty seemed to drain pigmentation from skin and hair. But among them there would be one, perhaps two, who seemed able to rise above their environment, who stood out like stars in a dark sky. The others were apathetic, uncaring, the drabness and hardship of their lives deadening their brains, glad only of the warmth of the classroom in winter, and the small treats in the shape of a 'sweetie' from the teacher. Then there were the triers, the strugglers, the gamecocks. The ones who defied their surroundings and conditions and the bitter life they had known from birth. Despite empty bellies they would be hungry for knowledge, thirsting for new experiences, vivid, their eyes alive. Their grasp of the first simple sums was immediate. Their mastery of the written word was a delight to the woman who, day in and out, struggled to impart some practical skill – perhaps only to count to ten and recognise their own name – to their fellows.

And here was one before her, one of the special ones. She could see it in the child's eyes, in her stance; tenacious, resolute. These characteristics were written on a face at the same time gentle and lovely, loving. The baby lips were soft and parting now, but the strong inward quality was there, the hint of waywardness to come as she grew. It was written in her face, in the strong jawline still moulded childishly, but the teacher was blinded by tenderness, even on this, their first time of meeting, and refused to see beyond the soft curving lips and shining eyes.

Something in the child cried out silently, and Joanna could not help herself. She felt her heart move like a small imprisoned bird she had once held in her cupped hands, and before thought could intervene, she smiled and heard herself say softly, 'What is your name, child?'

'Zoe, Miss Dale.'

'Sit down, Zoe, and we will mark the register.'

That day the bond of love was forged between them: a five-year-old motherless child crying out for someone to take the love she had in abundance, and the thirty-year-old woman, long-resigned to her childlessness, taking that love and returning it a thousandfold.

'Mary Adams.'

'Here, Miss Dale.'

'John Andrews.'

'Here . . .'

'Albert Ayrton.'

'Here, Miss er . . .'

And so on, until:

'Zoe Taylor?' A glance shining over the register, an answering look of recognition.

'Here, Miss Dale.'

Chapter Three

Once having known the simple comfort and pleasure of being clean, Zoe fought to stay clean, and in the crowded confines of the house in Love Lane, it was not easy. Even bringing the water from the standpipe was made complicated by the lack of vessels: by morning the only bucket was full of urine and until someone emptied it in the privy or down the gutter, it could not be used for washing. The bucket was heavy and Zoe was slight, but she managed it every morning, and it became her job, emptying the slops, scrubbing out the bucket under the standpipe, and bringing the water back to the house.

She washed herself each day before she went to school, and each evening she changed from her school clothes into the old garment she had worn for so long. Her things were folded neatly and hidden away with her boots, except for her knickers, for she could not bring herself to go without them, and each weekend, with a thoroughness which belied her years and upbringing she somehow managed to wash and dry these treasured garments, presenting herself each Monday as crisp and as clean as her beloved 'Miss' herself.

The teachers at Milbank Road School were aware that there were two kinds of poverty in the area in which they worked. There was the so-called 'clean poverty' which, to the ones who fell into the second category, was no poverty at all; the children had enough to eat and were clean; their fathers were probably in work more than they were out, and although there was never money to spare for anything but the necessities of life, at least they had the necessities. The poverty into which most of their pupils were trapped

25

was not of this kind, however. Theirs was sordid, cruel, heart-rending.

Joanna Dale could not be blamed for believing that Zoe fell into the first; for thinking that a caring mother sent out the child each morning with the pride in her appearance which only the very poor have left to them.

Zoe never spoke of her home life.

Day after day she arrived at school, her face scrubbed and shining, her riotous curls carefully dampened, combed and tied back with string. Joanna was not to know of the early struggle Zoe endured, rising before the rest of the family so that she might wash and dress before the scullery became a scene of chaos as everyone scrabbled and pushed for something to eat. She was not to know that the neatness of her hair was achieved with nothing more than fingers and a damp cloth – the child had never seen, let alone owned a comb – and that the gloss on her boots came literally from spit and elbow grease.

As the months drifted from the calendar, and the child became more dear to her, Joanna noticed that her clothes, though perfectly clean, were becoming frayed, torn in places, for Zoe knew nothing of sewing. As she grew and the clothes shrank with constant washing, more and more of the thin stems of her legs and fragile wrists were revealed until the teacher's compassionate heart could stand it no longer. Perhaps the child's mother was ill, or so overworked she had not the time for mending.

She spoke to the Headmistress, who always insisted that 'interference' in the home life of her pupils was reported to her. As a consequence, the following Saturday found Miss Dale knocking on the door of the Taylors' house in Love Lane.

She left several minutes later in a state of shock, appalled at the sights she had witnessed, at the life the child knew away from the schoolroom, at the realisation that there was no mother in the squalid home, and that this miraculous five-year-old kept herself and her clothes clean with help from no one. She had seen her in her weekend garb, the short flimsy garment she had always worn barely covering her naked buttocks; her schoolwear, including the beloved knickers, drying in front of the flickering, smokey fire. Her heart was aching as she hurried away from the curious stares of Zoe's sisters, and the memory of Zoe's downcast eyes.

How did the child manage to present herself so neatly each day; Joanna had seen no sign of a tap – she missed the standpipe – or of soap. Her eyes were clouded and unseeing as she ran like a rabbit across the pavement which only minutes before she had trodden with such confidence. How satisfied with herself she had been. How smug. She had thought that all she had to do to help the child was to go along and have a few condescending words with the mother. Tell her of the charities that only needed application to the School Board to bring untold wonders in the way of secondhand clothing to the impoverished family. If she were completely honest, she didn't care about the family: she saw that now, understood and was ashamed. It was Zoe, only Zoe. She must be warm and fed.

She tripped on an uneven flagstone, almost blind with unshed tears and would have fallen but for a convenient lamp post. She gripped it fiercely and stood for a moment trying to regain her composure.

Someone laughed derisively. It was not often a 'swell' walked down Love Lane and to see one nearly go arse over tip had evidently made someone's day. The laughter faded and a door banged shut.

Joanna walked on and the tears disappeared as she became determined to help the small girl she had just seen crouching like an animal in its lair.

She straightened her back and spoke the words out loud, careless of who heard her.

'I'll do it. By God I'll do it.'

She'd get her some decent clothes, and if she had to lie and deceive those about her, she'd see that the child had enough to eat.

27

The rational belief that education was the only way to better the lives of 'the poor', was jettisoned, and taking its place was the unthinking love of a woman for a child.

The following Monday Zoe was led into a small room adjoining the teachers' sitting room, and with several other needy children was given a selection of clothes supplied from a charity approved by the School Board. Against all the rules about favouritism, Joanna Dale had put to one side a warm woollen dress the colour of wild strawberries. It had been given by some kindly woman whose own daughter had outgrown it, and strictly speaking was not the sort to be approved by the Board, who favoured sensible colours like brown or grey, but it was too good to be rejected. With an ankle-length pinafore, frilled across the shoulders, soft black boots and stockings and, joy of joys, a complete set of warm underclothes, including two sets of woolly bloomers, it might have been Christmas.

Zoe was enchanted. Seeing her happiness, Joanna drew her into the teachers' room, empty at that time of the day. A small, comforting fire flickered in the grate. The rug before the fireplace had been made by some long-gone teacher from the snippets of much-loved materials: greens, blues, yellow and red, soft pinks. Gently, Joanna undressed the child, and Zoe stood for an instant in the warmth, naked, her skin, scrubbed that morning as usual, rosy in the firelight. Joanna knelt before her, longing to clasp the smiling child in her arms. And the little girl longed to throw her arms around the teacher.

Before they left the room, Joanna felt in the large pocket of her plain dress, where she kept the dozens of small things which might be needed in a class of thirty-odd children. Handkerchiefs, safety-pins, sweets, a comb . . . with a flourish she produced a beautiful bright red satin ribbon. She took the string from Zoe's hair, carefully rolling it into a neat ball and tucking it into the child's pinafore pocket. She combed the warm, springy curls, and at last tied the ribbon into a huge bow at the back of the neat head.

She stood back to admire the effect. Zoe watched her

anxiously. The teacher smiled, and Zoe smiled back, her face sweet with love and understanding. She knew that the ribbon was to be removed at the end of the day and the string replaced. For a second they continued to smile at each other and with a quick gesture Joanna touched the child's soft cheek with her finger. Then they left the room, the bundle of old clothes tucked neatly under Zoe's arm – they would do for home, she thought – and went back to the classroom.

The hours Zoe spent at school were the happiest she had ever known, the holidays an eternity to be got through as quickly as possible.

She was always the first child to arrive in the playground each morning, impatiently awaiting the nine o'clock bell, jiggetting about from foot to foot, not joining any of the interminable games that were played, afraid that she might lose her place in the front of her class line. Not for her 'the good ship sails through the alley alley-O' or 'the wind, the wind'; no skipping, or hopscotch or marbles, no whip and top, even if she had possessed any of these things. She was the first in the classroom, her loving eyes hardly able to wait to look upon her beloved Miss Dale, and to receive the warm glance which fell on her like a caress. The routine of the register, the Lord's Prayer, the Scripture lesson, all soothed her mind. The bright eyes never wavered from the teacher's face, her ears missed not a word and she absorbed arithmetic, reading and writing – even real writing – with ease. Her handwriting became neat, legible and roundly pretty, and gradually, without conscious thought, she began to imitate her teacher's manner of speech.

This ritual each day filled Zoe's heart with content, fulfilling some part of her nature that rebelled against the slovenly disorder of her home. And the very centre of her existence was the woman from whom she received the only affection she had ever known. She grew stronger and more confident, basking in the sunshine that shone from Joanna's eyes.

When the class was dismissed, she lingered, waiting

hopefully for some small task, and if there was none, one was created by Joanna. Zoe would have polished the desk lids, scrubbed the floors, or cleaned out the ashes from the pot-bellied stove if she had been asked, but instead she collected books and rulers purposely left on the desks by Joanna, who should have insisted on each pupil returning their individual equipment to her themselves; she wiped the blackboard clean standing on a chair to do so and waiting, tip of nose pressed against Joanna's high desk, eyes enormous, eager, loving, for further instructions.

They would look at each other and smile, then gaze about the room as if to say 'What more can be done to keep us together?' Their eyes would meet again, and reluctantly they would silently agree that the time for parting had come.

'Goodnight, Zoe,' Joanna would say.

'Goodnight, Miss.' A tremulous smile, a sigh, and the small girl would move towards the door.

Very often Joanna would find her still in the playground ten minutes later.

'Go home, Zoe. Your family will worry,' she would say, knowing, as the child knew, that no one would even notice that she was not there.

The long dark days of January set in. The bitter winds blew off the river, seeking the cracks in the ill-fitting doors and windows of the classroom. The snow clouds raced and settled over the 'Liver Building', then rushed on towards the Pennines, leaving small mounds of dirty white flakes heaped on doorsteps and against chimneys. The big pot-bellied stove in the corner of the classroom devoured coal; the children were allowed to wear such outdoor clothes as they had at their desks and Joanna's heart was heavy with compassion at the motley collection of moth-eaten shawls and sugar sacks which passed for coats.

It was during this spell of bitter weather that her sharp, watchful eye began to notice the decline in Zoe's sparkling appearance, a dragging of the black boots which usually danced into the classroom. Her eyes were not so bright, though her smile was always the same, loving, almost maternal in its gentleness.

Joanna was alarmed one afternoon as the day was drawing to a close to see the child wearily put her head upon the desk and, amid all the commotion of banging lids and chattering children, fall asleep.

It was Friday. The stove had been allowed to die down and the room was chilling rapidly. The last boy left the room, the door closing with a crash behind him, and still Zoe slept, her tangle of glowing curls falling over her face, a fine tendril lifted by her light breath. Joanna felt the familiar flutter in her chest and her arms longed to hold the lovely sleeping child, to smooth the mass of hair.

She left her desk and sat down on the bench next to her; instinctively her hand tenderly brushed aside the vagrant curl. The thought that she must let her go, back to the dirt, the paralysing cold, the smells, the uncaring family, back to that foul slum, filled her with despair.

As she watched, Zoe stirred. Slowly, drowsily, she opened her eyes. She looked directly into Joanna's face and as naturally as the sun touching a flower, leaned forward and pressed her soft lips to Joanna's cheek.

It was that moment that Joanna Dale came to a decision which was to alter the course of both their lives.

Lifting the slight frame from the bench, she sat her on her lap, holding her with arms which had longed for this moment from the child's first day at school. They sat for several minutes, at peace, gaining warmth and strength from each other, whilst Joanna turned over words in her mind, words with which to coax from Zoe the reason for her obvious weariness.

'Tell me Zoe,' she said at last, 'have you been busy at home?'

'Oh yes, Miss,' she replied innocently, 'it's the matchboxes, you see.' She settled herself more comfortably in the arms which felt as she had always known they would.

'The matchboxes, Zoe?'

'Yes, Miss. We have an awful lot to do. Me . . . my Da's

31

been out of work for . . . er . . . three weeks, I think it is, and our Jamie 'as . . . has to have some new boots. He wore 'em out playing footie and our Sarah was mad as anyfink wiv 'im.' She laughed at the remembered storm, making Joanna smile, but she drew her back to the conversation.

'You say your father has . . . not worked?'

'Yes, and he's got the drink on 'im, too,' she said confidingly, 'so we have to do a lot more, me an' Rebecca an' Lucy . . . and Emma.'

Joanna felt her eyes mist, and her heart ached with emotions she had never felt before. Rage that this small bundle of humanity should be exploited. Protectiveness, fierce and anguished, and a rigid determination to put a stop to . . . Her mind stilled as she saw a blank wall on which was written: 'This child is not yours. It is not for you to say what should or should not be done with her. She belongs to another and, within reason, he may do as he pleases.'

Her shoulders sagged and she rested her cheek on the child's bright curls. If only . . . if only . . . Her thoughts raced again. He didn't want her. He had six other children. Like a bee buzzing from flower to flower, her mind skittered from one thought to the next, discarding, considering, retaining, until, as the child drowsed against her breast, she finally allowed in the idea which she knew had been trying to enter for many weeks.

She would adopt her.

The darting, ecstatic thought sent a charge of excitement through her veins and she trembled with joy. Then suddenly as it had come, her elation left her, and her arms slackened around the child.

They would not allow it. To take a child, one of her own pupils, a child of the slums, and bring her up as her own: it was not possible. She almost groaned aloud. The child, sensing her pain, moved in her arms, gazing up at her.

Joanna looked down into her troubled face, and flinched, realising that her dreams were only dreams. She could do nothing so dramatic as rescuing Zoe from her existence –

but she could perhaps help to ease it. The family needed money, and the children were providing it with their matchbox making.

But there was other employment open to children today. Domestic work, for instance.

Her eyes were sharp as her mind raced. If the Headmistress knew of it, Joanna would lose her job. Employing one of her own pupils, and one only five years old at that. She wanted to giggle hysterically. It was all so ridiculous. The job would only be a blind to satisfy the father, but if it worked, and she could see no reason why it shouldn't, she would have Zoe every weekend. Perhaps she would spend the night on a Saturday, Friday as well if the father had no objections.

With an effort she calmed herself. She would go and see Mr Taylor the very next day. Oh, how her heart sang, now that she had a plan.

Joanna rested her cheek once more on Zoe's soft curls and her arms tightened possessively about her. Zoe moved, like a baby chick settling more comfortably under the warmth of the mother hen, her cheek resting delicately against the swell of Joanna's breast.

The room became colder as the winter wind forced its way through the chinks of the old windows, nipping the ankles of the quiet woman at the desk.

A bodiless head floated along the corridor, glancing with surprise through the shoulder-high windows at the still tableau in Form One, wondering with half a mind why Miss Dale should be still in her classroom at half-past four and nursing a small girl. The vague thoughts flitted down the hall with the hurrying footsteps, dying away as the quiet seeped through the now empty school, and a great peace filled the gentle hearts of the woman and child.

33

Chapter Four

Joanna's nostrils were filled with a stench so noxious that she felt her throat close in self-protection. She was unaware that it came from the overflowing ash-pit and midden at the back of the mouldering row of houses. It was three weeks since the impoverished inhabitants had been able to scrape together the shilling the corporation charged to cart the rotting mound away. It was January and most of the men in the street, casual dock workers, were unemployed. Bellies were empty, the smell was the same as at any other time of the year, and the heap stayed, scavenged by rats.

Joanna retched. 'My God, if it's like this now;' she said out loud to a tabby cat which eyed her cynically, 'what must it be like in the summer?'

Joanna pressed gloved fingers to her lips.

Love Lane in winter was deserted, even on a Saturday morning. As she had turned the corner into the street's awful familiarity, her light footsteps had echoed against the walls. She approached the Taylor house, and the sounds had slowed as her heartbeat quickened.

Annoyed by her own nervousness, she knocked timidly, almost wishing that her gentle tapping would be unheard and she might leave unobserved. Her horror of Zebediah Taylor's refusal made her afraid to ask. She made herself knock again, harder this time, and then again, but still no one came.

Her body trembled and she turned away with relief, ready to run. She'd leave it until another day – the man was probably at the pub, and might not take kindly to a stranger disturbing his weekend relaxation. Imagine how it might feel to have some busybody person coming to his front door and boldly asking if she might remove his daughter from

35

his care. After all, she was his child, and he must certainly have some affection for her. What a cheek she had. He would be suspicious, obviously; shocked, probably abusive. He might even become violent . . .

She knew it was common practice to exploit indigent children by taking them from their homes and putting them to work, under the guise of 'giving them a decent home'. Perhaps Zeb Taylor would think that this was her intention. She backed away.

Suddenly, the chaos in her mind was stilled. What an idiot she was. What did Zeb Taylor care about the child's wellbeing? She, Joanna Dale loved and wanted her, and she was going to have her.

She resumed her fierce knocking on the frail door. Still no answer. She stepped backwards to peer up at the bedroom window. It was as blank as though it had been painted in. Where was everyone? It was so cold she could imagine no outing which might lure them from their fireside.

The water which dripped unceasingly after each downpour, had turned into thin, twisting icicles, hanging in varying lengths and shapes from each unmended gutter. It had collected on the uneven pavements and frozen into a thin sheet of polished glass on which Joanna's feet could find no purchase, and she slipped and slid, clinging for support to the rough brickwork around the doorway.

A door banged further up the street, and a boy emerged carrying a bucket. He turned in her direction, the boots on his feet so large that he was in danger of stepping out of them with each stride. His hands clutched a man's jacket about him in an effort to keep the garment more warmly to his shivering body, the bucket on his arm clanging against him with each step he took. As he passed, he turned his thin pale face towards her, staring at her curiously with his black and sunken eyes, and a saying she heard somewhere came to her mind. 'Like pissholes in snow.'

She shivered suddenly, the boy's waxen pallor making her conscious of her hands in warm woollen gloves tucked into a fur muff, of the cosiness of the fleecy scarf about her neck, and of her feet, deathly chilled, even though they were shod in lined boots.

Impatiently she turned again to the door, then back to the kerb, stamping her feet on the ice-coated pavement. She looked up at the frozen roof, but no smoke drifted from the chimney and the curtainless windows stared unseeingly.

Her glance was caught by a slight movement at the upstairs window.

Was it Zoe? Had she seen a pale face float for an instant at the greasy glass? She waited, listening to the crack and snap of the ice crusted on the brickwork and pavement.

Was that a sound behind the door?

Her anger began to mount. She had only come to speak to the father, not to arrest him. Did they think she was the bailiff, or perhaps the rent collector?

Her irresolute thoughts of a moment ago were forgotten: she wanted to confront the stranger who held her future in his hands. She was ready to do battle now.

She was conscious of a dozen eyes watching her frenzied efforts to gain admittance, eyes peering from grimy windows up and down the street.

At that moment the door opened a crack, and she saw a face pressed to the opening, but whether male or female, she could not determine in the dim light inside. All she could see was a pale oval in which dark, circled eyes floated, framed by a tangle of hair, and all seemed to waver at waist level, staring and mouthing something incomprehensible.

Joanna took a step backwards.

'I've come to speak to Mr Taylor. Is he at home?'

The face bobbed and dipped, still addressing her hoarsely. A hand stretched towards her, thin and dirty.

Then the door was flung wide and a voice grated from the dimness of the room.

''urry up an' gerrin, fer God's sake. It's col' enough wi'out bloody door bein' open.'

Her face aflame at being spoken to in such a manner, Joanna stepped nervously over the threshold and was immediately aware of the dank, bone-chilling cold within, where she had expected warmth. The door was slammed violently behind her, making her jump.

For several seconds she was blind in the murk. She stared about her, trying to pierce the greyness, to identify the objects which would be found in the living room of a home, but after the diamond-sharp light of the day, she could see nothing. She was aware only of a slight lessening of the dreadful smell and of the intense, stupefying cold. Then, her eyes becoming accustomed to the gloom, she realised that the room was empty except for the two figures who had admitted her, both swathed in an assortment of threadbare jumpers, cardigans, skirts and scraps of rotten blanket, beneath which matchstick legs dangled, ending in bare, chilblained feet.

The tallest figure spoke:

'Oh, it's you again is i'? Wha' d'yer wan' this time?'

Joanna became aware that the speaker was Zoe's eldest sister – what was her name? Sarah.

'Ge' back to bed, our Lucy,' she said to a cowering figure on the stairs, 'an' I'll try an' get a bit a summat to ea' in a bi'. I reckon we migh' be lucky in a manner o' speakin'.' She gave Joanna a sly, half-wink.

As the pale milky light from the window fell across the child's face, Joanna saw that Lucy had a hare lip and – obvious from her speech – a cleft palate. She sidled to the doorway in the corner of the room, and tripping and stumbling on her clothing, disappeared upstairs.

Joanna turned back to Sarah, who was watching her with a mocking smile. 'You've seen nothing yet,' it seemed to say.

With an effort she calmed her shivering body.

'I would like to speak to your father if I may?'

'You can't. He's . . . not well. He's still in bed. What d'yer want, anyway?' The girl's eyes were wary, but without fear.

Joanna looked around the stark, freezing room. Why was there no one about at this time of the day? Why was the fire

38

unlit? Where was Zoe? Later she was to shake her head wryly at her own naïvety.

Sarah's steady eyes regarded this creature from another world. At fifteen she was wise in ways that Joanna would never be wise: in the ways of the poor, of those whose wits were sharp-honed in the fight for survival; and in some strange manner, surprising even to herself, she pitied the woman's ignorance. She eyed the ankle-length woollen coat edged with a soft fur, the matching hat snugly protecting pink ears, the sturdy leather boots, the gloves, the scarf and the warm muff which hung from Joanna's neck on a cord. She could see the questions trembling on the teacher's lips and felt a small surge of contempt replace the pity. This woman had no notion of the life she and her family were forced to live. Her lip curled.

'I suppose yer wundrin' wha' we're all doin', still in our beds a' this time a day, aren't yer, Queen? Well yer see it's like this 'ere. We 'ad a do last night. Nutten special, like, bu' a righ' goodun it were, an' we all decided to 'ave a lie in, like. We've not much on today, no engagements or nutten like tha', so we're 'avin a lie-in.' She was grinning now, the discomfiture written on Joanna's shocked face delighting her. Then her grin was gone, and the middle-aged child that she was took over. Her head rose and she sneered as though their roles were reversed, as if she were proud of her poverty.

'The truth is, madam, we ain't got no coal,' she declared loudly, 'so we're 'avin' to stop in our beds. We 'ave to keep warm, somehow. Me Dad's drunk, 'ungover an' spent all 'is wages.' She took a step forward and for a minute Joanna thought she was about to strike her. 'So if yer've owt to say,' she continued, 'say it ter me, cos me Dad's no use ter man nor beast.' She paused. 'I suppose it's about our Zoe. Nutten else'd bring yer 'ere.'

Her face revealed a spiteful pleasure at the distress she caused. 'She's in bed an' all.' She grinned maliciously again. 'Yer can come up an' see 'er if yer like.'

Her face creased into a mask of unholy joy at the thought

39

of this dainty creature reviewing her drunken, snoring father, the huddled forms of her brothers and sisters in their verminous blankets.

As she stood, smirking in caricature of some hostess exchanging pleasantries with a guest, a small bundle of rags eased itself cautiously down the last few steps of the staircase. The pallid light revealed a pinched white face, the enormous, unnaturally bright eyes of the child.

Zoe.

Joanna's instinct to run and gather the pathetic figure into her arms was swiftly checked. She must be cool, restrained. And she must provide for the whole family if she was to help the child.

She lifted her head, her clear eyes flashing across Sarah's face.

'Call one of your brothers, if you please. You must have heat or you will not survive, and food. Will you go to the shop?' She fumbled in her purse, withdrawing the first pound note Sarah had ever seen in her life, and held it out.

'Please take it. I know it must be hard to accept . . .' She was interrupted by Sarah's snort of laughter. 'Gawd, if that don't take the bloody cake! Best I've 'eard today, that is. 'Ard, you say? 'Ard? We've no pride 'ere, missus. Pride don't fill yer belly.'

Snatching the money from Joanna's outstretched hand, and almost before her fingers had closed over it, the girl was at the bottom of the stairs.

'Jackie, Jamie, get yerselves down 'ere, quick. I want yer to go t't Dolly shop for me.'

She grinned over her shoulder as she stood at the bottom of the stairs listening to the sounds of her brothers getting into their boots.

'Come on, lads, I want a bucket of nutty slack, 'taters, a loaf, a big 'un, maggy-ann, some meat scraps, we'll 'ave scouse . . .' She ticked off the list on her fingers. Joanna looked at Zoe, hard put still to remain calm. The little girl seemed to have shrunk since yesterday and her determination to take her from this hell-hole grew. She met the child's gaze, not seeing the confusion, the nervous dread that Zoe quickly hid behind lowered eyelashes. How could she know the fear that had crept into the heart of the small girl when she had seen her teacher standing in the scullery. Was she to be prevented from going to school? Had she done some wrong? It must be something bad for Miss to come to the house.

Her fear grew and she clutched the familiar carving of her beloved doll beneath her rags.

The boys clattered down the stairs and taking their cue from their sister, ignored Joanna, staring with astonished disbelief at the pound note Sarah held out to them. With a stream of instructions, she hurried them out of the door and up the street.

At last Joanna had her attention.

'If your father is too . . . ill to be consulted, perhaps I may speak to you about my reason for coming.'

Sarah regarded her impassively.

'I wanted to engage one of your sisters for light domestic duties at the weekends. It would not be arduous work . . .' She stopped at the girl's look of confusion. 'The work will not be hard,' she amended, and went on in a rush; 'and I think Zoe will suit me ideally. She would only be required to do a little light dusting, clean the silver, that sort of thing, nothing heavy or beyond her capabilities . . .'

She was interrupted by Sarah's snort of derision.

The child, ignored, uttered a small plaintive sound.

'Dust and polish? A five-year-old?'

'It will be no more difficult than making matchboxes,' Joanna retorted. 'I am willing to pay your father, or you if you are the housekeeper, the sum of five shillings a week. I shall require her to come to my house on Saturday and Sunday. Will that suit?'

Sarah's eyes gleamed, and Joanna could almost hear the clicks and whirrs as she added up the pennies, deducting the meagre sum she would save on food for the girl at the weekend. The profit was obvious.

41

Joanna continued. 'I would, of course, have sole option on Zoe.'

The girl was out of her depth again.

'She would not work for anyone else, including you. If I hear that Zoe has been used during the week to make matchboxes, or anything of a similar nature, I shall take action.'

What action she would take she had no idea, and prayed that the girl was similarly mystified. It was not unknown for children of this age and from this background to be employed and very little was done about it by the authorities. But Sarah, Joanna hoped, was ignorant of the law, would be impressed by the threat, and dissuaded from working her youngest sister, if not the others. Perhaps the steady income would keep her mouth shut.

Zoe stood looking from one to the other, not understanding, only aware that the one person in her young life to have shown her kindness, was standing in their scullery talking to their Sarah about her, using big words which she did not understand. She did know that it was important. She could tell by the stern look on Miss Dale's face though their Sarah laughed a lot. A funny laugh. She did not like it.

Sarah stared at Joanna calculatingly. She was not a bad girl, only what life had made her, and it had made her grasping. Zebediah had not worked for three weeks, and the pittance which the children had earned had barely fed them. She was in desperate straits. The coal had run out during the week and there was not a farthing in the house: Zeb had seen to that in the pub last night, spending the shilling he had earned carting away some rubbish for the publican during the afternoon. She would have sold herself for five shillings, had she known how to go about it, and now here was this fastidious being from another planet, offering her five shillings a week.

'Six shillings,' she said matter-of-factly.

'What?' Joanna was bewildered.

'Six shillings for the weekend. She can come Friday till Sunday night.'

Joanna felt a surge of anger so powerful it threatened to engulf her, to throw away the restraint to which she was clinging. For a moment she almost gave way to her fury, but some instinct stayed her tongue. What did she, Joanna, know of the circumstances which had brought the girl to this? She pictured herself as she had been at fifteen, cosseted, warm and happy in the cocoon of her parents' love.

Her anger drained away and was replaced by pity and joy.

She reached once more into a purse and counted six shillings into Sarah's eager hand.

'Just one thing more,' she said, keeping a hold on the girl's wrist. Sarah turned impatiently towards her, her mind obviously finished with the teacher, racing forward into the days ahead, days when they would eat, and be warm. She must think of some tale to explain Zoe's absence each weekend to her father, supposing he even noticed it. She must keep from him not only the few pitiful shillings, but where they came from. He must not know of this windfall or he would drink it away.

She became aware that Joanna was still holding her wrist.

'What?' she said truculently.

Joanna took a deep breath. 'I'm taking her now,' and she paused, knowing she was putting her teaching career in this girl's hands, 'this is just between you and I.'

'Look, Miss,' Sarah breathed, 'You're 'appy, our kid's 'appy, or she will be when she's sorted out wot the 'ell's goin' on. I'm 'appy and the rest of the kids are goin' to be fed. That's all I care about. Don't worry – I'll keep my trap shut.'

For a moment the girl looked piteously at Joanna, the load she carried nearly too much for her, then remembering Zoe, still standing to attention against the wall, she threw off the restraining hand and gaily called to her.

'Come on our Zoe, get yer duds on. Miss is takin' you out.'

Chapter Five

Joanna Dale was the only child of John and Amelia Dale. John Dale, a doctor, had held liberal views on the education of women and had dearly wanted his daughter to follow him into the medical profession. Though an intelligent girl, and quite able to do so, she was not attracted to the idea and from an early age had wanted to be a teacher.

She was a serious little girl, loved devotedly by the elderly couple who had long given up hopes of a child. She was the result of a gentle coupling, lukewarm on John's side, dutiful on Amelia's, and was often to wonder, as children do, at the improbable picture of her parents performing the act which had produced her . . . Not that her own experience was great in the matter – biology classes, and that with animals – was the extent of her knowledge, and a passing acquaintance with her father's books.

Being an only child, Joanna never learned to play. From an early age she read. Shelves of books lined her room, and possibly the nature of her father's profession and his compassion for the needy, the destitute, the underprivileged, firmed her resolve that only by teaching those unfortunates how to lift themselves from poverty could she help humanity.

She knew that if only they could be taught, these have-nots, to reason, to plan, to be organised, to be clean and careful; taught a skill, a trade, a profession; to restrict their families, they could rise from the ignorance which surrounded them.

This she knew from reasoning, from her reading, from her own education.

She knew nothing of the real life, the day-to-day fight to survive, of the people she cared about.

At eighteen she had enrolled at a Teachers' Training College, and at the end of two years had gained her teaching certificate. She had spent a further year probationary teaching and at twenty-one had gained a post at Milbank Road Infant School, Dingle.

Her mother and father had died within a few days of one another in an influenza epidemic when she was twenty-three and for seven years she had lived alone in the comfortable semi-detached villa in Princes Park which they had left her, along with a hundred pounds a year.

Joanna was a plain woman, with one redeeming feature which lifted her face out of the ordinary. Her eyes were large, brilliant, intelligent, a startling aquamarine mixture of blue and green, and so full of friendly kindness, that people seldom looked further. She was completely lacking in sex-appeal, though men liked and trusted her. She had longed for a child for many years, though marriage and all it entailed did not appeal to her. She was a modern woman, ahead of her time, and had even considered the shocking idea of conceiving and bearing a child without the benefit of wedlock, so desperate was her longing, but she had not done so, simply because she did not know how to achieve this happy state. Her tiny circle of friends included few men and they were already married.

She was fond of, and kind to, every child in her class, but until Zoe Taylor came into her life, she had done nothing but dream and ponder vaguely on the idea of adoption. She would probably have continued in this vein until it was too late, but from that first meeting last September, her passionate love for the slum-child had grown and swamped her, filling her life with un-named longings and causing her usual good sense to desert her.

Joanna and Zoe turned into Pinehurst Place, a region so different from the street they had left just a short time ago, that it might have been another world.

It was another world.

The double row of solid, well-cared for houses sat in complacent pride, fenced by naked trees, stripped of their summer beauty. A small garden, white with frost, silvered by ice, crouched in front of each Victorian villa. An atmosphere of comfort, of pleasing wealth, not great but sufficient for gracious living; of good, middle-class prosperity, shone from every gleaming window and drifted from each chimney, with the smoke from a hundred glowing fireplaces.

A small hand, none too clean, grasped the larger, an invisible cord drawn tight between them. The fur muff hung almost to Zoe's knees, but no coaxing could persuade her to put her hands within its cosy warmth. Its glossy perfection was too much for her bewildered senses: a small animal, hanging from around her neck, it frightened her.

She had not spoken since Sarah had tumbled her into her 'best' clothes, and then it had only been a whispered request for the privy. Sarah had smiled and glanced at Joanna, the thought in her mind to send the teacher with her pupil. She would have given a bob or two to have seen the expression on the face of the daintily-clad woman when she saw the condition of the frozen, stinking outhouse.

The tram ride from the Pier Head had left Zoe trembling. Now, bent against the keen wind, Joanna slowed to keep in step with her timid steps. Zoe's eyes were never still, darting from one wonder to the next, her tongue flickering in and out between her moist lips in nervous excitement. Her small feet arched until she tip-toed across the frosty flagstones, as if afraid she might disturb this magical dream, and wake between the thin, rough blankets of home.

At last they stood before the house which had been Joanna's home since the day she was born. It was handsome, strong, protective: all the characteristics of the perfect lover, and Joanna loved the four walls as she might have loved a husband.

47

Zoe paused in the gateway, hanging back shyly, for who knew what this magnificent building might contain? The King of England, perhaps – it was certainly grand enough.

'Come on, Zoe,' Joanna said softly. 'There is nothing here to frighten you. This is where I live.'

She urged the small comical figure up the short path to the glossily painted front door. The knocker, the head of a laughing dog, was highly polished, gleaming brass, the wink in its eye seeming to welcome the hesitant visitor. Zoe loved it at that moment and always would.

Joanna inserted her key in the lock, slowly opening wide the vivid, red-painted door, revealing a world of luxurious comfort. The gentle warmth from the fires in all the main rooms enveloped them as they stepped over the threshold. They trod the pile of the leaf-green carpet, and the soft light of an electric lamp, which Joanna had recently installed to replace the gas mantles of her parents' day, glimmered on polished mahogany, copper and brass. China ornaments marched proudly along a shelf, and directed the eye to the wide sweep of the staircase floating to the upper floor. The hall was broad and uncluttered. Joanna had cleared out the mass of Victoriana beloved of her mother, keeping the plain and simple pieces to enhance the individuality of her home. Her taste was good and she had achieved a perfect setting for her own quiet personality.

She led the bemused child into the drawing room which contained the style of furnishing she admired, far ahead of her time. The walls were white, the velvet curtains a deep, crushed strawberry and the plain carpet a dark, mossy green, almost black in the mid-afternoon gloom, a gloom dispersed to the four corners of the large, square room, as Joanna lit the lamps and stirred the glowing fire.

Overcome by the simple beauty shining before her, Zoe stepped reverently across the smooth carpet, her eyes in her pale face enormous. On the far wall hung a water-colour, a field of crimson poppies: slowly, she walked towards it and stood as if entranced. The room dimmed, the present moment blurred, and she floated amongst the massed heads of colour, smelling the fragrance of the bright field, hearing the music of the wind.

'What is it, sweetheart?' The kind voice brought her back and she turned, her eyes brimming with starry tears.

Joanna looked at her, astonished at the joy on the little face of this child of the slum, so moved by the painting's loveliness. This was no ordinary child.

Zoe drank it all in: the deep, comfortable sofa, upholstered in a velvet mixture of greens and reds to match the curtains and carpet; two large armchairs; two or three small tables, a delicate piece of porcelain on each, and; standing in elegant splendour, its rich ebony glowing against the whiteness of the wall, a grand piano. But the heart of the room was the simple perfection of the reproduction Adam fireplace, above which hung a beautifully framed mirror.

It was a comfortable room, the years giving it a lived-in, homely atmosphere. A clock on the mantelpiece ticked in a ponderous and dignified manner; the newly tended fire crackled and hissed. A brass fireguard stood before the grate, the flames reflected cheerfully in its polished surface, and standing sentinel to one side, a large brown and white pot dog, a jovial expression caught for ever on the glazed face, watched the timorous steps of the child as she walked towards the warmth.

Joanna smiled, and beckoning Zoe to her, sat down in the armchair, the firelight gilding her face, enhancing the brilliance of her eyes. She took off the child's ragged coat, her fingers savouring the task. She bent her head to kiss the rounded cheek and asked gently, 'Do you know what is happening to you, Zoe? Do you know why I have brought you here?'

'No, Miss.' But her eyes said it didn't matter; she would trust Miss to the ends of the earth. Joanna looked into that face of hopeful innocence, her heart aching with tenderness. She has come with me today, she thought, to a place so alien to anything she has ever known, it would terrify the most valiant. Though her own home might be a festering hovel, it was at least familiar.

She spoke slowly. 'Do you like it here, Zoe?'

Zoe looked at her, confused by the question, for what was there to dislike? It was paradise, heaven on earth. It was softness, security, warmth, gentleness, fragrance of flowers.

'Oh, yes, Miss,' she breathed.

'And would you like to come here . . . quite often?'

'Oh, yes, Miss.' Her eyes shone like twin candles.

'Perhaps each Friday . . . after school.'

The small face was a picture of mixed emotions. Delight struggled with disbelief, awe and hope contested with doubt.

'Oh, Miss.' The words were a prayer.

For a moment they looked into each other's eyes and the child saw the truth shining from the woman's: she would come here again, many times. She put her hand in Joanna's and, crossing one foot over the other, the tension draining from her, she leaned comfortably against the teacher's arm, her gaze directed into the heart of the fire, her eyes unblinking, hypnotised by the love and comfort.

They stayed like that for several minutes. Then, breaking the spell, Joanna gently turned the thin figure to face her. Her mood had changed and merriment twinkled in her eye.

'Now we're going to have some fun,' she said, smiling. 'What do you say to a nice warm bath, some cocoa and biscuits, and then a game of Ludo.'

Zoe's face twinkled back. She had no idea what Ludo might be, but she was willing to do anything to please this woman who had become the very core of her world. She didn't care too much for the idea of a bath: tepid water floating with grey scum, rough zinc bath, sharp-edged, hard sacking on soft skin, but if it would make Miss Dale happy, she would brave the oceans of the world.

She smiled her acquiescence.

Joanna led her up the stairs to a wide landing, off which were several doors, all open to reveal further marvels:

shadowy bedrooms, with vague shapes of furniture, all mysteries to the shy peeping eyes of the child. At the end of the landing Joanna entered another room, clicking on the bright electric light. Zoe followed slowly, and stopped at the door in amazement.

Gleaming white tiled walls; a large smooth porcelain bathtub, standing on clawed feet; a washbowl as high as her head, shining taps and mirrors, and a . . . a . . . it was a . . . lavvy . . . like none she had ever seen. A lavvy inside the house, right inside the house. It bore no resemblance to the filth-encrusted horror which was the lavvy at home, nor to the grubby bowls at school. This was bright, gleaming, the seat lid patterned with roses. And what were those soft hangings draped on the rail on the wall – one, two, three, and in such bright and beautifully coloured profusion? She smoothed the gay towelling rug beneath her booted foot, and stepped carefully across the black and white tiled floor to stand nervously next to Joanna. The woman turned from the bath which she was filling with warm steaming water, the sweet aroma from the bath salts which she had thrown in filling the air. She looked at the bewildered child and her heart filled with compassion.

She was going too fast.

What she took for granted, was confusing, even frightening to Zoe. She knelt down and put her arms about her, held her gently, feeling the tension in the small frame.

'Come, I'll show you how everything works, Zoe.' She smiled. 'There's nothing to be afraid of.'

She led the cautious child through the simple ritual of turning on and off the taps, flushing the toilet, feeling the thick, fleecy towels, sniffing the bath salts; showing her the magnificence of the warm airing cupboard with its overflowing abundance of clean linen and the cupboard stocked with toilet rolls, deliciously scented soap and tangy toothpowder.

Zoe was enchanted.

The delight of the next hour was to set the pattern of their days and years together. Joanna had never before seen the sheer joyous exuberance shown by the child; even Zoe had not known she had possessed such a noisy, natural, fun-loving capacity for enjoyment.

They splashed and shrieked, the sparkling drops showering Joanna as she knelt beside the bath. She found a floating duck and a small battered boat on the top shelf of the cupboard, left from her own childhood. Leaving the happy child for a moment to find some nightdress which might be cut down for her, she re-entered the bathroom to find her, pink and perfect, the flawlessness of her baby skin enhanced by the moisture which clung to it, her damp profusion of curls, which had been scooped into a tawny mass on top of her small head, drifting in soft tendrils around her face and neck, peacefully sailing her small flotilla on the warm, sudsy water.

She looked up, her flower-like face tranquil, and in perfect understanding they smiled, content.

In the soft glow from a nightlight, her face drowsy, her eyes half closed as sleep laid its loving hand across her, Zoe heard for the first time the lullaby she had longed unconsciously to hear all her life:

Go to sleep,
Mommy's little baby,
Mommy's going to smack you, if you don't.
Rock-a-bye, hush-a-bye,
Mommy's little baby,
Mommy's little alla calla coo.

Chapter Six

Summer 1911

Many times during the next six months Joanna Dale was to wonder whether, in gratifying her own desires, she had given more grief to the child than was balanced by the happiness they shared.

As each weekend drew to a close and the time came for the tram ride back to Love Lane, the tears became more and more anguished, the passionate 'Please let me stay with you, Daly,' more and more insistent.

Zoe's despair at these times almost broke her heart.

Should she have left her with her own kind to struggle for existence? Somehow most survived. Or did the way of life which she had revealed to Zoe, the sustenance which she had provided for her mind and body, make it worthwhile?

The contrast between the child's weekday life, and the hours which she spent with Joanna was cruel, and the adjustment which was needed – for them both – was appalling. The joy which they experienced as each Friday dawned was made more poignant by the knowledge that on Sunday evening they would be torn apart, quite literally, for Zoe, screaming, had to be forcibly removed from Joanna's arms, at the door of the dilapidated cottage.

At school she became sullen, her wretchedness making itself clear in tantrums and fits of naughtiness, alternating with loving contrition and constant demands to be nursed like the baby she still was. Her infant mind was not able to adjust to the ebb and flow of her unnatural way of life and her school work began to suffer.

Joanna was in torment as she watched Zoe's misery increase. She knew that something further had to be done and at once her sharp mind began to look for an answer.

Back to the beginning she went – to her first dreams of adoption.

Joanna was ignorant of how to take such a step – but if only she could persuade Zeb Taylor to let go this unwanted child of his, surely he could be made to see the opportunities being offered to his daughter, and the harm inflicted upon her by her double life?

Late one Sunday night, hours after Zoe had been returned to Love Lane, Joanna sat before the last flames of the fire, her head in her hands. Her heart was heavy. She knew she was to blame, but she had only meant good for the child. And for yourself, said a small voice. It was true, she had thought of herself, but the child came first. Her mind worked like a small animal trapped on a treadmill, round and round, searching for an answer. She knew what she wanted and she knew what Zoe needed, but what was the solution? Always one came back to the same answer.

But even if Zeb could be convinced, bribed – she admitted the word – what of the school authorities? Would they look kindly on a teacher, a spinster, attempting to adopt and bring up as her own daughter one of the slum children from her own class?

Joanna got up from her armchair and crossed the room in the darkness, to stare into the quiet street, deserted now.

The lamps made small, wavering circles along the pavement as a gust of wind blew the trees, the leaves dancing across the yellow spheres of light. The summer night was almost gone and the sound of horses' hooves as the milkman entered the street, came faintly to her. She could see the muted pearl of sunrise tint the sky above the roof tops. Her head drooped until her forehead touched the cool window pane.

She knew that she must act soon, before any further harm was done to Zoe's health, to her bright charm. Before she was turned from a loving and lovable child into a tormented, resentful young girl.

With a positive shake of her rounded shoulders, like a

soldier squaring up before battle, Joanna turned and left the room.

It was a day of perfection. A day to remain in the memory for ever, like a bright gem glowing down the years, a day which shines from the past and is brought forth at family gatherings. 'Do you remember . . . ?' and all present do so, for was not the weather more glorious, the company more convivial, the setting more agreeable, then – it always was in one's childhood.

Joanna and Zoe boarded a bus at Seacombe, riding along the winding route, through the sweltering dusty streets of Birkenhead, to Bebbington and Ellesmere Port. Their pitying glances fell on the inhabitants of the poor houses they passed, the heat reducing the few who were about to a somnolent crawl on the shaded side of each street. Doors were opened wide in an effort to catch any stray breeze, and fretful children lolled on doorsteps and kerbstones.

The character of the houses altered as they drew near the limits of the city: they were small, semi-detached, with tiny square gardens, the shade of trees along each pavement to cool the stifling roadway, and the pleasing oasis of parks, though the green lawns were now brown and dry. Further on they changed yet again, to substantial detached villas, each set in half an acre of sparkling, flower-filled lawn, the veil of water which fell from watering cans held in the hands of slow-moving gardeners blurring the colours and shades beneath magnificent oaks.

Even these were left behind as they roared on to the empty, powder-coated road across the moor. With no particular destination in mind, the tall, pleasant-faced woman and the chattering child left the bus in the middle of a vast, open space filled with rolling hillocks and gently rising outcrops of rocky plateau, stretching onwards as far as the eye could see. The perspiring bus driver had told them he would be passing the same spot at five-thirty, on his return journey, and after arranging to be picked up there they set off across the springy turf, Zoe running and skipping, darting off the rough path trodden only by sheep and the occasional hiker, investigating everything on which her quick eye fell.

For a moment her troubles were forgotten.

She was dressed as Joanna had always imagined her: in cool white muslin, sprigged in mint green; white stockings and soft leather shoes; a flat boater hanging from a green ribbon bumping against her narrow shoulders as she ran. The change in her since that cold, January day seven months ago, when she had first entered Joanna's home, was incredible. Her face had filled out; the eyes were bright, shining with health and intelligence. The legs which had hardly seemed able to support her weight seven months ago were covered by firm childish flesh. Her shining hair was tied back from her flushed forehead in springing curls. She kept up a continuous flow of chatter, her bright expression and brilliant glance for ever returning to Joanna.

The inevitable journey back to the slum was for once forgotten.

'Look Daly, see that flower, what is it called? Clover, pretty pink clover . . . and see the bird, a thrush, that's what it is, Daly, a thrush . . .'

They tramped on, alone but for the black-faced sheep. Suddenly they came upon a hidden stream, set in a steep hollow, the grey, lichen-covered rocks tumbling and scattered down the slopes until they fell into the clear, rushing water. Its song filled the air, the gentle melody an orchestral background to the ecstatic song of the lark.

There was no living thing in sight except the curious sheep, chewing and roaming, raising their heads for an instant at the sound of the excited cries of the child.

'This is a good spot, Daly! Can we sit here for a while? And may I take off my shoes and socks, please? I'd love to paddle, wouldn't you? Will the water be cold.'

Laughing, shedding her years along with her shoes and stockings, Joanna held the small hand in hers and together they shivered with delight as they stepped into the icy, tumbling water, slipping on the smooth stones, screaming in mock alarm, uncaring of their wet skirts.

The sun was hot on their backs, the hollow in which they played protected from the cooling breeze which skittered across the flower-sprinkled turf.

Tired, hot and hungry, they spread a cloth on a flat-topped rock and opened the wicker basket. They had prepared the picnic together, as they did everything, and now the two companions in the neat and precise manner which Zoe had learnt from Joanna, set out the salad, the cheese, fruit and biscuits and the milk which Joanna coaxed Zoe to drink at every opportunity.

Joanna did not remember when last she had experienced a day of such radiance. Her heart was at peace, for she knew she was committed to the course begun almost a year ago when she had first looked into the loving eyes of the child drowsing against her. She touched the warm cheek, watching the flutter of the fine lashes, the small indent at the corner of the pink mouth. Her promise had been made silently to Zoe – even if it meant the loss of her teaching career.

She could not live without her now.

She would call on Zeb Taylor at the very first opportunity. She would continue to pay him for the loss of the income which might result from the removal of his youngest daughter from his home, for one must expect that Zoe would have been put to work like her sisters, but she was confident that she would have no difficulty in persuading him to part with her permanently. Methodically she disposed of Zeb's possible objections. She supposed the extra money might disappear straight into the publican's till, but she could do nothing about that; her concern was for Zoe.

Her heart soared. Smiling into the endless blue void, she lay back on the sweet-smelling turf, and closed her eyes. Ahead stretched endless years with Zoe for ever by her side.

*

Joanna stood with her back to the closed door of the scullery facing Zeb Taylor and his eldest daughter, the words she had just spoken hanging in the frowsty air. Sarah had been doing a wash and the grey water which collected and seeped through the red brick floor to the damp and unsavoury soil beneath, gave off more than the usual offensive stench.

Joanna looked from one blank face to the other, trying to gauge their reaction. Zeb, in a drunken stupor, seemed unaware she had asked a question. Cunning, poker-faced Sarah, on the other hand, was, as they said in that part of Merseyside, 'all there with her acid-drops'.

Adoption.

The word had fallen like a stone between the three, but already the girl was inwardly weighing the advantages she might gain for the rest of her family, against the loss of one small child. The softening influence of Joanna's home made Zoe little more than useless for matchbox making, and Sarah would not be sorry to see her go. But the higher standard of living which the teacher's weekly payment provided had been a godsend and one which she would plot and scheme to hold on to.

All her bargaining instincts were aroused. She would keep the woman on tenterhooks, make her all the more anxious to buy, and who knew what the end of the week might bring.

She spoke abruptly. 'Me an' me Dad 'll 'ave to 'ave a talk about this. It's not summat you can decide right away, like. It wants a bit of thinkin' about, you know what I mean.'

Zeb stared blankly from his chair.

Joanna swallowed, her heart pounding. 'Of course, I quite understand you will wish to discuss . . . When may I . . .'

'Friday,' Sarah interrupted rudely.

Joanna knew the decision was Sarah's and the possibility that she might refuse filled her with dread. She glanced from the girl to Zeb and back again, looking for reassurance, but none was given. She felt a wave of nausea wash over her and prayed that her calm would not desert her now.

'I'll call again on Friday then,' she ventured, reaching behind her for the latch on the door, fumbling, angry at her own response to this young girl, who made her feel inarticulate and gauche. She knew it was caused by her own humble pleading on Zoe's behalf, behaviour which was foreign to her nature and which she found galling.

Somehow she managed to leave, her composure almost gone, and apprehension stalked her along the street which was becoming as familiar as her own.

Dear God, that girl was a bitch. She seemed to revel in the game of cat and mouse, and for what purpose? Why could she not give an answer now? The pose that she must discuss it with her idiot father was nonsense, but there was nothing that could be done about it. Lord, it made her blood boil, to be in the grasp of an uneducated snip of a girl. She has me, she thought, over a barrel.

In the tram, Joanna rested her aching head against the vibrating window, staring unseeingly at the dusty streets. She reached home thankfully, closing the brightly painted door behind her and as if drawn by a beloved baby hand, soft and familiar, she climbed the wide staircase, gently smoothing the glossy surface of the bannister, smelling the sweetly mixed aromas of her home, as if she had only just now become aware of them. Furniture polish, freshly-ironed clothes airing on the clothes horse, her own faint scent of lavender, and, from Zoe's room, an unmistakable breath of roses. Tiny, unopened rosebuds which she had gathered the day before, and put there to bloom for the child's next visit.

If Sarah's answer was 'no', then Joanna would have no purpose in her life. It was as simple as that.

She entered the pretty little room and sank on to the bed, her fingers trembling across the counterpane, and gazed unseeingly at the flower-sprigged white wallpaper, the deep rose curtains, the hundred and one reminders of Zoe. There was a dreamlike feeling in the atmosphere, as if the child had just left the room and would reappear at any moment.

Joanna sat motionless for several minutes, her mind in torment. Then she sank trembling to her knees. Her head bowed until her face rested on the dainty bedspread, and with muffled words she prayed to a God in whom she did not believe. The jumble of soft sound came senselessly from her lips as she begged him to intercede for her, to sway the hard heart of Zoe's sister. Though there was no one to hear her, the litany of supplication soothed her and she rose from her knees refreshed.

They faced each other like combatants in an arena, ready to do battle for what each held most dear.

Sarah's cause was basic. To keep at bay the enemies she had fought all her life, which women in endless squalid hovels in endless streets all over the country fought all their lives: hopelessness, dirt, disease, fear, hunger.

Joanna searched the young girl's face for some expression which might reveal her thoughts, but there was nothing but the brief flicker of a scornful smile, and her heart sank. For five days she had swung between hope and despair; now tightly holding Zoe's hand, she said abruptly: 'Have you come to a decision?'

Sarah's smile deepened. 'Yer eager, ain't yer?'

'I am anxious, yes. I'm extremely fond of Zoe and I feel I can give her a good life, and I am not averse to helping the rest of the family in any way I can. I am willing to give consideration . . .'

Sarah cut her short. 'Me an' me Dad, we think . . . that is, we've 'ad a good talk an' we reckon our Zoe'd be a good little 'elp 'ere at 'ome . . .'

Joanna interrupted her, dread gripping her like a vice. 'Does that mean you withhold your consent . . . ?'

'You use big words, Miss, but you can't . . .'

Joanna could endure no more. Her voice rose.

'Look, will you please stop fencing with me. Will you allow me to adopt Zoe? Yes or no?'

'No.' The word shattered the still, warm air of the room.

Joanna thought she would faint. Her face ashen, she stepped backwards, her free hand feeling for the door frame.

A small, hot hand grasped hers, fiercely, protectively.

They had both forgotten the child pressed against Joanna's skirt, her fearful eye moving from one to the other as they spoke. Now, as Joanna, stricken, speechless, looked blindly down, the loving face searching hers for understanding gave her strength. She was able to stiffen her spine and regain her shattered composure.

Sarah was speaking again.

'You can't adopt 'er – me Dad won't 'ave it. But yer can foster 'er if yer like.'

Joanna almost laughed in Sarah's face at the absurdity of the idea, and might have done so if the situation had been less desperate, but only one word winged its way like a bird of hope straight to Joanna's bruised heart. Foster her . . . foster. Not as satisfying as adoption – Sarah would always have a hold on her – but better than nothing, oh, dear God, better than nothing. And if she made the payments attractive enough, Sarah would never claim Zoe back.

She cleared her throat. 'What would that mean . . . ?'

'We want ten bob a week for 'er, an' a course she'll allus be our kid. Me Dad won't 'ave no daughter of 'is adopted.' Sarah lifted an eyebrow, mocking, 'Ony basterds is adopted, an' our Zoe's no basterd. We wouldn't want neighbours to think there were 'owt funny in our family, so we're only lendin' her like. If she don't like it, she comes back, an' if we fink she's berrer of wi' 'er own kind, she comes back. That's what me Dad says, so take i' or leave i'.'

She turned away as if indifferent. As if ten shillings a week were nothing to her. But she lowered her eyes, fearful that she might have overreached herself.

The silence which settled about the three figures was almost palpable.

'Ten shillings,' Joanna said at last.

'Yeah, she's werf it, aint she, an' that's abou' what we'd lose if she came to you, like. Be a good little earner in a year or two.'

Still Joanna stood, rooted like a tree in a storm. So that was it. Blackmail. She was to be always in the clutches of a fifteen-year-old girl. Backwards and forwards the child would be shuttled; more and more money would be demanded.

Unaware that Sarah was studying her uneasily, she looked round the room. It was like a furnace, with all the doors and windows tightly shut, for Sarah wanted none of her neighbours to spy on her new business venture. There was no sound from above, or from the street. Where was Zeb?

Joanna could feel anger building up, threatening to burst from her like steam lifting the lid of a kettle, but a tiny voice within her spoke softly.

Keep calm, girl, keep calm. There is a lot at stake here. And think of the child. She is worth it. What does it matter what is said, or done. Ten shillings. What is to you? Say nothing. Bite your tongue. Somehow you will get the better of this . . . this monster.

You'll outwit her. Go to the authorities, convince them that Zoe is better off away from all this.

She glanced again about the dingy, stifling room, nodding as though she was already in conversation with the school board and its members. As she did so her confidence returned and her eyes slitted like a cat. She'd do it.

The battle she fought with herself was very evident, and the defiant girl saw it, and despite herself, felt a spark of admiration for the proud woman.

'I will pay it, but I want one thing clearly understood. She is mine.' Joanna's voice was soft, but threatening. 'All mine. Do you understand? I will not have her shifted from one place to another like a parcel. She will be well treated and unless she wishes it, will not come back here. I will arrange for the money to be paid to you weekly, but you are not to approach Zoe again, any of you. I will leave an address where I may be contacted, should you need to do so.'

Sarah shrugged. She had won: no matter what was said here, she had the upper hand, and a meal ticket for many years to come. She smiled sweetly.

'Righ', Queen, yer gorra deal.'

As Sarah spoke, Joanna's anger drained from her. She could afford the money: that had not been the reason for her sudden bitterness. The reason was standing beside her, afraid, insecure, clinging like a small vine to her arm, and she was to be sold for ten shillings a week.

Her heart was sad as she gazed down at the trusting face, and it softened imperceptibly towards Sarah. If she could keep those few shillings a week from her drunken father it would mean the difference between empty bellies or full, between hope and despair.

She smiled down at Zoe. 'Come on, sweetheart,' she said softly. 'We will go home now.'

Chapter Seven

The class was quiet. Heads were bent over desks, tongues protruded from between parted lips, and faces screwed themselves into moulds of confidence or dismay as thirty pairs of eyes darted back and forth from paper to blackboard. Thirty throats sighed, and in the back row a girl giggled as the boy on her right tugged her plait towards the inkwell.

The teacher at the front of the class looked up in disapproval and the room was quiet again, but for the scrape of pencil on paper, and the harsh squeak of chalk on boards. The faint cloud from the chalk lifted and hung about the ceiling.

A thickset boy in the front row lifted his head and cursed under his breath: a close observer might have seen a minute, lively creature jump cheerfully from his lank hair on to his torn shirt. Scratching his head, the boy looked round the classroom. His gaze fell on the daintily clad girl in the row behind him; and a look of venom crossed his peaked face. He darted a swift look at the teacher, and worked his filthy finger up his stubby nose. He pushed and pried for several seconds, then with unerring aim flicked the mass he had dislodged at the object of his hatred.

It landed on her hand.

Before she had time to react, the boy's head was down and his face devoid of all expression.

Zoe screamed and jumped to her feet. She rubbed at the horrible mass on her hand, but as harshly as she rubbed it just transferred itself from one hand to the other.

The class, mouths agape, watched with fascination.

Joanna leapt to her feet, and ran to Zoe's desk.

'What is it, what is it, sweetheart?' she cried, alarmed and mystified.

'Look, Daly, look,' howled Zoe.

Joanna looked down at the offending 'bogey' and shuddered. Glaring with mounting anger at the stunned children, she felt in the pocket of her skirt, produced a clean handkerchief and tenderly wiped the child's hand. She kissed her wet cheek and pulled her into her arms, holding her close and crooning softly to quieten her.

'Don't cry, sweetheart. Daly make it better. See, it's gone now, all gone.'

But Zoe would not be comforted.

'Look, darling, it's gone,' Joanna entreated. She blinked in anguish into the broken-hearted face. It seemed that these days the slightest upset tore the child to ribbons. Her aversion to any sort of dirt was becoming obsessive. She would insist on two baths a day and would wear no article of clothing more than once without laundering. Her hair was washed each night and her passion was cleaning, polishing, 'bottoming' her room – a word she had picked up from Joanna.

'I know,' Joanna said brightly, 'we'll go and wash your hands. Will that do? I'll take you into the teacher's bathroom, and wash your hands. There's some of that lovely flower soap, just like the one we have at home. Will that make it better, darling?'

The silence in the classroom was so great you would almost have heard a spider as it stepped across the wooden floor.

Zoe hiccoughed and allowed herself to be taken by the hand as Joanna stood up. The world, the school, the classroom and all in it, existed for neither of them, and the utter stillness went unnoticed. They were intent only on each other.

They both looked up together.

For the first time they saw the familiar figure of Miss Briggs standing in the doorway of the classroom, her hand on the doorknob, her face like a lump of dough ready to be placed in the oven. It was colourless, shapeless with shock and outrage.

Miss Briggs was the Headmistress of Milbank Road Infant School. As last she spoke. 'I'll see you in my study, Miss Dale. Immediately, if you please.' She beckoned with an imperious finger to a cowering girl in the front row. 'Go and tell Miss Atkinson that Miss Dale is to be absent for a while and that she is to oversee this class as well as her own. Go along, child, quickly.'

The girl slipped like a whipped dog past the terrifying figure, not even sure what her erand was, and ran into the next classroom.

Joanna and Zoe stood like two figures in a game of Statues. Then Joanna spoke. 'Yes, Headmistress, of course. I'll just take . . . this . . . Zoe Taylor to wash her hands. You see, some loathsome . . .'

'At once, Miss Dale, if you please.' Miss Briggs cast a withering look at Zoe. 'I'm sure that this child is quite capable of washing her own hands, and in the children's toilets.'

She stepped back a pace to allow the woman and the child to pass her.

Joanna turned to Zoe and gently, sadly, she placed her at the desk from which she had leaped only minutes before, sitting her down as though she were made of delicate porcelain. Turning to the class she looked around her. She drew back her shoulders and was 'Miss' again.

'I will be gone for a few minutes,' she said quietly. 'If there is any noise, or if one child leaves his or her desk, I shall know of it and the offender will be punished. Is that understood?'

The scene, awesome as it had been, was over, and the wide-eyed children settled back to their writing.

'Yes Miss,' they said in unison.

Only one voice did not answer.

'Now then, Miss Dale, an explanation, if you please.'

'If you please' was a favourite expression of Miss Briggs.

67

Joanna sat in the hard-backed chair which was placed squarely in front of the Headmistress's desk. They looked at each other, the two childless women, and Joanna prayed that she might be able to reach the heart and understanding of the other. Where to begin? How to explain that scene?

The room was austere, tidy to a point of emptiness, chilly on the warmest day. A row of forbidding, sepia-coloured photographs looked down from the walls reprovingly, past guardians of the school, not only of the education of its pupils, but of their morals too.

'I am waiting, Miss Dale.'

Joanna's heart foundered. She took a deep breath and began to speak. For ten minutes her quiet voice filled the room. She said nothing of the love and need which bound the child and her together. Miss Briggs would not understand. She told of the conditions of Zoe's home – her mother's death, her father's drunkenness, the destitution of the family. She did not speak of the financial arrangement between herself and Sarah which seemed to be working so well. She lingered on the helplessness, and hopelessness of the environment from which Zoe had come, and pointed out several times the Christian duty which one felt towards those less fortunate than oneself. She had never spoken so eloquently, or so impressively, for desperation gave a fluency to her tongue, but she knew without a shadow of a doubt that Miss Briggs believed not a word.

There was a deep silence in the dismal room as she finished speaking. Miss Briggs looked across the desk at the woman before her and for an instant she was herself a young teacher again, enthusiastic, confident, eager. The face of a child rose before her, a little girl not unlike Zoe Taylor: she remembered, and understood. But did not condone. Oh, no. This must be brought before the Board.

Taking in of children by anyone, let alone a teacher, must not be encouraged on any account. It would be seen as an incentive to the irresponsible poor to abandon their children. It would encourage the immoral to become more so, if the degraded and degrading women thought that the bastard offspring of their illicit relationships would be taken care of. Homeless children must be dealt with as they had always been: sent to the orphanage or fostered with other poor families already on 'relief'; kept in their own class. Besides, the child already had a home, albeit a poor one. No, the whole idea was ridiculous and Miss Dale must be made to see the whole matter in its proper perspective.

Miss Briggs picked up a pencil from the neat row on the desk and pulled her blotting pad a little nearer to her. She placed a clean sheet of notepaper in the exact centre of the pad. Without speaking she began to write, line after line of precision in the tidy, well-formed penmanship which she had been taught as a child.

Joanna watched. Her heart beat erratically, her mouth was dry, and she could feel the trembling in her legs travel up her body. She tried to press her feet more firmly on the floor.

At last Miss Briggs put down her pencil and looked up. Her words were slow, considering. 'It is quite out of the question, Miss Dale, for you to keep this child. Apart from the difficulties which would ensue in the classroom, you must consider the effect on the child when the time came for her to be returned to her own environment. And return she would, Miss Dale, make no mistake about that. Her family will demand it when she is of an age to be put to work.'

Joanna's pulse beat faster. She was about to tell Miss Briggs of the bargain which had been struck with Sarah, but something held her back.

Miss Briggs continued. 'We have our position here at the school to consider, Miss Dale. It would not do for the parents of the . . . er . . . unfortunate children in our care, to imagine that they might shrug off the responsibility of one or two of their offspring on any unsuspecting teacher with a modicum of compassion. If you were married, perhaps – but even so I am sure that the Board would not look kindly upon your actions, philanthropic though they undoubtedly are.'

She leaned back in her chair. 'And then there is the legal implication. Should you . . . pass on, your estate might be in . . . well, any relatives you might have would be . . .'

Joanna stood up so abruptly that her chair crashed to the floor. 'I know that you mean well, Miss Briggs,' she said, her voice strident with emotion, 'but we are talking about a child. Not a puppy which one has bought, and finds that it does not quite suit. A human being, Miss Briggs. Zoe . . .' her voice cracked on the name and Miss Briggs' face hardened as Joanna's eyes starred with tears, 'Zoe and I have become very close. She has been with me for several months now.'

The Headmistress set her mouth at its most severe.

'We cannot be parted now. I look upon her as my own child you see,' Joanna said simply. 'You must, of course, do as you think fit. I am quite willing to go before the Board, in fact I am eager to do so. It will relieve my mind considerably to put my relationship with Zoe on a proper footing. I am sure that the Board will look more kindly on the . . . advantage Zoe will receive than you appear to do.'

Miss Briggs' mouth opened, ready with words of retaliation, but Joanna was too quick for her.

'I should just like to add that I will never give up the child, despite what you, or the Board, might say. Now, if there is nothing further, I will return to my class.'

She turned, picked up the chair, placed it carefully in front of the tidy desk and left the room.

The next few days passed as though nothing had happened. Miss Briggs bowed her head in Joanna's direction each time they met, but she did not speak. Meanwhile, Joanna and Zoe continued with the routine which they had built up over the past months.

It was November. At the end of each afternoon, Zoe would wait for Joanna at the end of Milbank Road and together they would board the tram to Princes Park. The grinning dog would greet them at their front door. There would be much bustle and soft laughter, as fires were lit and the little girl would set the table as Joanna prepared their evening meal. Afterwards, Joanna did the washing up and Zoe would carefully wipe each plate, or cup as it was handed to her. It was her joy to be allowed to put away each piece of crockery, plates upon plates, saucers in a neat, symmetrical pile, cups all facing the same way on their hooks, and when she had finished, she would stand for a moment in the doorway of the bright kitchen, drinking in its perfection. She could not seem to get enough of order, of shining and polishing, of neatness, and even after Joanna had settled herself in the comfortable armchair in which they both sat for a 'good read' or a game of Ludo, Zoe would return to the kitchen for one last check, as if anxious that some small untidiness might occur the moment her back was turned.

Then she relaxed, with the warmth of the fire, the loving arms, the giggles as the game progressed, or the spine-tingling charm of *Treasure Island* as Joanna read aloud. The steady ticking of the clock, the street noises shut out by the velvet curtains, half-heard but deliciously not of their world, the crackle of the flames, were all a prelude to the part of the day Zoe loved most.

The bathroom would be warm, the bath water soft and slippery, and the air full of sweet-smelling steam. She would play and splash and Joanna would watch, waiting with a huge bath towel to cuddle her dry.

It was Monday of the following week when the letter came. The School Board of Governors would be grateful if Miss Joanna Dale would appear before them on the sixteenth of November.

Chapter Eight

November 1911.

There were eight of them. All men and all looking exactly like the photographs on the wall of Miss Briggs' room.

It started out quite reasonably. Alfred King, who was the Chairman, asked her to sit in the chair placed before a long table. She was at one side, the eight men on the other. No one smiled, with the exception of one gentleman. He was a minister, but of which church or denomination she did not know, nor care. He had smiled and it helped to steady her.

The room was icy cold. No one had removed their coats, and Joanna was glad. Perhaps it would hurry up the proceedings, she thought, if the gentlemen were eager to be away to their warm firesides.

Mr King politely introduced her to each member of the Board and she nodded at each in turn. No emotion. Please God, or whoever is up there looking out for mothers and small children, let me not be emotional, or just enough to move their hearts, and not turn their minds away from me. Let me be concise, lucid, articulate. Let me put into words my caring, but in a matter of fact and unsensational manner. Please, help me, help me.

Mr King was speaking. 'Now, Miss Dale, I am sure you are aware of why we have brought you here?' He looked enquiringly over the top of his pince-nez, which had slipped to the end of his pulpy nose, and his eyes regarded her gravely.

She nodded.

He looked down at a sheaf of notes which lay before him, and, as though on command, the other seven heads looked down also. They all studied their individual papers, and, on command again, each looked up at her.

Mr King continued. 'The child who is concerned in this matter – she is no relation to yourself?'

'No sir, she is not, but . . .'

'Just one moment, Miss Dale. Please answer the questions put to you and then you will be given the opportunity to speak.'

Joanna bowed her head humbly.

'She is . . .' He consulted his notes again, '. . . just six years old.'

'Yes, sir.'

'She comes from a poorer district of Liverpool, I believe.'

'She comes from an overcrowded slum, where they are . . .'

Mr King held up his hand and his face firmed into lines of deep disapproval.

'Miss Dale, will you answer my question without any embellishment, please.'

Joanna opened her mouth to protest. As she did so her eye caught that of the Minister. He shook his head slightly. She shut it again.

Mr King resumed his interrogation.

'Now then, I believe she is one of seven children.'

'Yes, sir,' Joanna answered. She had learnt her lesson and was beginning to feel she had at least one supporter. With a little luck, and a chance to speak as she had been promised, and with the help of the Minister, she might just be able to persuade these stern-faced men that she was the right and proper person to continue the upbringing of her darling girl.

She began to feel more confident.

'Her mother is dead and her father is employed as a casual labourer on the docks.'

'Yes, sir.'

'And I am led to believe that he has a . . .' said delicately '. . . a problem with drink.'

Better and better.

'Yes, sir.'

'Is the child ill-treated?'

Joanna hesitated. As far as she knew Zoe had never been subjected to beatings or any kind of abuse. Would neglect constitute ill-treatment? In her opinion, yes, but she was afraid to elaborate.

'No, sir,' she said.

There was a pause and Mr King looked from right to left along the line of his fellows as if inviting them to speak.

One did. It was the Minister.

'Why do you wish to adopt this child, Miss Dale?' he said innocently.

She almost fell into that one. She almost said it out loud. 'Because I love her, you old fool,' she was about to say, 'and because she needs me. Because she is the only human being I have ever loved purely, without thought or care for myself. You, a Minister, should understand.'

She said as placidly as though he had asked her about the weather: 'She is a bright child, sir, and I felt that I had something to offer her. She lived in a slum with a drunken father who is not capable of supporting her, and her brothers and sisters. Though I would ideally like to help the whole family financially, it is not possible. In view of this I took Zoe. She is intelligent, and I am sure that with help from me and the education I shall be able to give her, she can make something of her life. Her health has improved, and for the first time in her life she is receiving the care which surely all children are entitled to.'

She hopefully looked from one face to another. 'I wish that you could see her, gentlemen.' There was no sign that she was making the smallest impression on them. 'Another factor to be taken into consideration,' she went on, 'is that by giving Zoe a home I am relieving the family of feeding and clothing her, and also, in the long run, the authorities, because I am sure that the time will come when the whole family will be forced to go on relief.'

She smiled at the Minister. 'I am trying to help a family in need, sir. Surely that is what we as Christians are taught to do.'

The Minister smiled and leaned back. He turned to the

rest of the Board and nodded, but a look from Mr King that said 'We're not finished here yet, Vicar, so wipe that smile off your face,' made him sit up once more with an apologetic glance at Joanna.

The attack, when it came, was fierce and was flung at her by James Bowker – or was it John McCauley? Their faces were beginning to take on a pattern of identical severity.

'You intend to keep this child as your own, Miss Dale? Bring her up as your own daughter?'

Joanna's eyes shifted uneasily, looking for a trap.

She answered hesitantly, suddenly afraid. 'Yes, sir.'

'Do you have any servants, Miss Dale?'

'No, sir.'

'And the child is . . . six years old, you say?'

'Yes, sir.'

'After living with you for several months, she is by now, one would suppose, growing into quite a strong and healthy girl.'

'Oh, yes, sir.'

'And a help to you in your household duties?'

So that was it. That was where he was leading, the insufferable hypocrite. Insinuating that she was only interested in an unpaid servant. Joanna's face washed over with colour, and her eyes flashed. If only she could tell them the truth, that she was making payment in order that she might be allowed to keep the child. But for some reason, unexplained even to herself, she knew she must not. They would believe her unhinged, and not a fit person to have the care of a young child. She must be careful, and clever.

'No, sir,' she said calmly, though her heart beat like a hammer. 'I have no intention of exploiting a six-year-old girl, and if you could see her you would know that I speak the truth. You may find it difficult to believe that I could take in a child for no other reason than the one of charity; that I would give her a home without money being paid to me for her keep, but that is the truth. I wish to adopt the child. I know that this is not possible in the present state of

76

the law, but de facto adoption has existed for hundreds of years. This is what I intend and, I hope with your help, I shall achieve. Surely it is not a sin to wish to help a fellow creature, particularly a motherless child.'

She turned to the Minister, passionately.

'Even Jesus said "Suffer the little children . . ."'

But Mr King was having none of Jesus.

'Yes, yes, Miss Dale,' he said impatiently, 'we are all aware of the tenets of Christianity, but that is not the issue here. We are concerned with the welfare of the child and the obvious difficulties which might be caused by . . .'

It went on and on. Her background and her father's. Her financial position. Her own health – she thought that they might ask to examine her teeth – her interests and hobbies. Did she have relatives living? Was she not able to take in some child of her own class? Did she wish to continue teaching? (Was that a veiled threat?)

On and on, until she thought she would fall from her chair in a faint. They were trying to trap her, she knew. To find a hole in her story. To discover . . . what? She did not know, she only knew that if they did not stop soon, she would no longer be able to keep her wits about her.

Suddenly it was over. There was silence broken only by the sound of shuffling feet beneath the table and the tap, tap of paper being placed in neat bundles.

Joanna felt the perspiration run down her and her body was on fire. The cold bit into her feet but she was not aware of it.

Alfred King cleared his throat.

'Hmmm . . . Now, Miss Dale,' he said, brooding over the notes in front of him. 'We have listened carefully to your motives for wishing to adopt this young person, and from your remarks it appears that you are acting for the best of reasons.'

Joanna's hands tightened again about her bag.

'However, my colleagues and I must, of course, confer on this matter. We will let you know of our decision as soon as we are able.'

77

He peered once more over his pince-nez.

'Thank you, Miss Dale, that will be all.'

She sat for what seemed an eternity, looking from one face to another, trying to find some indication of what each man was thinking, but there was nothing. They were well versed in keeping their thoughts to themselves.

At last she rose, putting her hand on the back of her chair for support.

'Thank you, gentlemen.'

There was nothing more to be said. Nothing she could do but wait.

Christmas came and went and there was no word. It had been a time of enchantment for the woman and the child, made more so by being the first that they had spent together, and, although only Joanna was aware of it, perhaps the only one they would ever share.

There was no school for a fortnight, and during those two weeks they saw no one except the tradesmen and shopkeepers.

They decorated the green, sweet-smelling tree with the golden balls and dainty, glittering objects which had been a part of Joanna's life since she had been a child herself. Zoe had never seen such lovely things and handled each piece reverently, placing it with gentle care on the branches of the tree.

There were presents to be wrapped, Zoe's to Joanna and Joanna's to Zoe. For weeks they had discussed this magical event, Joanna explaining the meaning of Christmas and the giving and receiving of presents. Zoe was alloted a small amount of spending money each week – her 'Saturday penny' as she called it and with a bit of extra help from Joanna, had bought a dozen small items, which in the privacy of her bedroom, and with a great deal of self-important giggling, she encased in the bright wrapping paper with which Joanna kept her constantly supplied. In half an hour she would be down again, sidling into the room, imploring Daly 'not to peep' as she placed yet another neatly wrapped and prettily decorated parcel beneath the tree.

On Christmas Eve, when Zoe was at last asleep, flushed excitement giving way to smiling peace, Joanna returned to the warm living room, and sank with a sigh into the chair before the fire. She rested her head wearily on the back and closed her eyes. Would they never come to a decision, those grim men who held her happiness in their hands? Her mind went over and over the questions they had asked her: had she given the right answers? Should she perhaps have been more business-like? No, that was not the word – more detached, less . . . committed. She smiled wryly. Fond and foolish were the words she would use, if she were honest.

Restlessly she stood up and moved to the Christmas tree, smiling despite her heartache at the carefully wrapped presents which Zoe had placed beneath. So many, she thought, and all for me. Not once did it dawn upon her that she was not to be the only recipient of Zoe's generous spirit.

What has she bought me? she thought fondly, and with so little money. She picked up the first small present and looked at the pretty tag.

In childish hand was written:

'To ar Serra. Hapy Krismas and wiv luf from Zoe.'

The next one read:

'To ar Dad, Hapy Krismas wiv luf, Zoe.'

One to Lucy, another for Rebecca, Emma and Jackie and Jamie. Each one had a present. There were four parcels left. Addressed to Joanna. Twelve in all.

She stared in stunned disbelief. Oh that child. She had listened whilst Joanna had carelessly told her the story of Christmas, and its meaning, and she had taken it to her heart. This was the Christmas spirit in the true meaning of the words.

Joanna hung her head and the tears came. The strain of the past weeks was tearing her apart, and now this. She grieved for the small girl who had spent so much time and loving attention on the giving of a present to her uncaring brothers and sisters. It was Christmas and the time for giving, and she gave. And those . . . machines, who called themselves the guardians of those who spent their lives in misery, were 'considering' the future of a child who could do this. They would return her to squalor, to degradation, to poverty and a mindless, hopeless future.

She sank to her knees and the room echoed softly with the sounds of her grief.

Chapter Nine

January 1912

The doorbell needed a touch of oil, and it screeched pain-
fully as the caller made another vigorous attack.

Joanna tutted in annoyance and, lifting her hands,
covered with blobs of pastry, from the baking bowl, she
wiped them on her apron. Zoe, on the other side of the
table, was absorbed in cutting out serrated circles: on this
wet January morning, a Saturday, they were making a few
mince pies for tea.

'Now who's that?' Joanna enquired of the bent head of
the child. 'Just when we're about to get these in the oven.
You carry on, sweetheart. I won't be long.'

She took off her apron. Perhaps it was news from the
Board. She hurried nervously down the wide hall and
opened the door.

Standing on the doorstep in a shuffling, giggling group,
were six young people, ranging from a teenage girl to a boy
of about seven. All wore cast-off clothes – odds and ends of
jumpers, torn trousers, filthy boots, skirts with patches.
One had a scarf around its head. The rest wore men's caps.
All were incredibly dirty.

The tallest one spoke.

''ello, Queen.'

It was Sarah.

Joanna looked at the party in horror, distantly observing
with one part of her mind that none of the money she gave
to Sarah was finding its way on to the children's backs.

Sarah grinned, and Joanna noted that since they had last
met, she had lost a front tooth. The cap and the missing
tooth gave her a comical, cheeky appearance, that was at
one and the same time, endearing and frightening. The

look in her eye was enigmatic, and Joanna knew without a shadow of a doubt that trouble brewed. She lifted her chin resolutely, ready to carry on the war she had declared so many months ago. The group pushed past her, their muddy boots tramping dirt into the plushy green of her carpet. They stood in the hall, some of their bravado draining away as the magnificence of the house surrounded them.

'What can I do for you?' Joanna asked politely, for all the world as if they called regularly once a week, and were quite welcome.

The children looked at each other and sniggered.

'We come to say Ta to our Zoe, for't presents, like,' Sarah smirked.

Joanna's heart sank. Zoe had insisted on sending the presents by messenger to Love Lane on Boxing Day. How could she have deprived her of that joy?

'Well that is very thoughtful of you, and I will certainly pass on your thanks to Zoe. Just now she is away with . . .'

At that precise moment the kitchen door opened and a small, flushed, smiling face, crowned by a tangle of pastry flecked chestnut curls, popped comically round the door.

No one spoke.

Zoe stared at Sarah, the smile slowly fading. Her eyes travelled warily from her eldest sister to the gibbering Lucy, to Emma, to Rebecca, Jamie and then to Jackie. And she was afraid.

As though to ward off the badness which had come in at the front door with their Sarah, she began to babble, saying the first thing that came into her head.

'You are all very naughty to come into the house in your dirty boots. Daly will be very cross.'

Sarah laughed mockingly.

'Eh, our Zoe, y'are a one. "Daly will be cross,"' she mimicked, and the rest of the children joined in the fun.

Zoe's piteous eyes looked at them, and a wan smile flickered. Then, with a cry, she rushed across the hall and flung herself at Joanna.

'I wont go with them, Daly, I won't. Make them go . . . I want to stay wiv you, Daly. They're dirty, horrid . . .'

The words rose shrilly, as hysteria caught her in its grip, and the other children grouped warily around Sarah, uncertain, now that they were here, that they should have come at all. It was their Sarah who had insisted, and at the time it had seemed a bit of a lark. They had walked the three or four miles quite easily. Sarah might not be too concerned with their appearance, but their diet had certainly improved since she had become ten bob a week better off, they were not the starvelings of a year ago. But now, what with their Zoe yelling her bloody head off, and the look on the woman's face, it seemed the best thing to do would be to scarper.

But they reckoned without their Sarah. She was not finished yet, not by a long chalk.

'Give over, our Zoe!' she bellowed.

Joanna flinched and the child, with her old reactions of fear and instant obedience to their Sarah aroused, stopped her wailing immediately. Her shoulders still shook, and she kept her face buried defensively in Joanna's skirt, but only soft whimperings emerged.

'Yer sof' sod,' Sarah continued amiably. 'We ony come to say Ta for't presents. They were real nice. Me Da' would a come an' all but 'e were'nt so well.' She winked a⁺ Joanna as if they shared a joke, and nudged Rebecca. ''E wern't so good, were 'e, our kid?'

Rebecca shook her head.

It seemed there was little else to be said, and Joanna was just about to reach out a tentative hand to the door knob when Sarah spoke again.

'We wudden mind a cuppa, would we, kids? We cum a long way, like, didden we?' She looked around brightly at her brothers and sisters, who were by now longing to leave, but their Sarah was just getting into her stride. She loved this kind of situation. To pit her wits against another, especially when she knew she had the whip hand, and particularly against one who would, in other circumstances, have the advantage of her, filled her with glee, and she was going to spin it out for as long as it pleased her.

The next hour was a nightmare. The group of children sat around the kitchen table, and drank tea, and ate chocolate biscuits for the first time in their lives. Zoe clung to Joanna like a leech.

Sarah acted as though she and Joanna were old friends, and even in her distress Joanna was forced to admire the girl's spirit as she asked for more tea, and passed round the plate of biscuits to her silent family. She even asked to use the 'lavvy', jumping cheerfully from her chair with directions to Joanna to 'Stay where you are, chuck, I'll find it,' before disappearing through the kitchen door and thumping up the carpeted stairs two at a time. She was gone for ten minutes and returned without flushing the toilet.

At last it was over.

They left as they had come, dirty, smelly, verminous. Sarah waved cheerily from the gate and winked again.

When the last teacup was washed and dried, and returned to its proper place, when the table had been scrubbed, and the carpet brushed, when the toilet had been scoured, and every vestige of the presence of her family had been removed, Zoe kicked and screamed, berating Joanna for allowing 'their Sarah an' them' into 'our' house.

'Dirty, dirty, dirty!' she repeated over and over again. 'Yer shudden 'ave lerrem in.' Joanna was deeply saddened to hear the speech of the slum-dweller return, a sign of sure disquiet. Zoe was torn in two. Her generous nature had given her the idea of traditional Christmas presents for her family, with no thought of the possible consequences. She had wanted to share her good fortune with them, but not herself, nor her life with Joanna. Her confusion was a weight she would carry for ever.

It was days before she returned to a semblance of her usual sunny self, and even then a shadow lurked in her eyes. She jumped at each knock on the door, and would not allow Joanna to open it until she had first checked from behind the velvet curtain, to make sure that Sarah had not returned. When they ventured outside the house she clung to Joanna's hand, looking nervously over her shoulder.

If only I could hear from the School Board, Joanna agonised.

They returned to school just after the New Year.

On the first day of the second week of term she received a letter.

It was worded exactly as the first, only the date was different.

The setting was the same, as were the men. But this time the sun shone, and though it was still only early February, its warmth was benign. She noticed the crocuses in splattered patterns of purple, yellow and white as she walked up the path towards the council building. Daffodils stretched their beautiful heads in the direction of the bare branches of the trees, under which they clustered. Already tiny buds of spring green showed against the winter wood of the sycamores. She allowed herself a faint prick of hope.

They must say 'Yes.' They must.

They said 'Perhaps.'

They must speak to the child's father, to the school medical officer, to the local welfare officer, to Zoe. Enquiries must be made of innumerable august bodies, including the church, to ascertain Joanna's fitness to care for a child. She would be allowed twelve months in which all the concerned parties might have a time to consider.

But they did not say 'No.'

Joanna almost danced her way back amongst the spring flowers. A year. A whole year of loving care, of security, of learning, of becoming the daughter of a well-mannered, civilised lady. Zoe would be a different child from the uneasy changeling who haunted the drawing room window. When their small world was secure again, when she herself was at last free from doubt and uncertainty, the child would know peace.

As she latched the gate cheerfully behind her, stepping out with a spring in her heels and her head thrown back to stare joyfully into the pale blue sky, she failed to notice the shabby figure who lolled against the stone wall on the other side of the road. If she had done so her confidence in the future might not have been so positive.

It was Sarah.

Chapter Ten

Summer 1912

It seemed that just as she was about to relax her vigilant watchfulness, to let down her guard with bright hopes that at long last the child was in safe harbour again, some small incident, perhaps only a word, would send Zoe back into a world of uncertainty.

She would cry broken-heartedly, her small reserve of composure shattered, would climb onto Joanna's lap and shiver, whimpering, seeking comfort like some small whipped animal. She had thought her new home was safe, a castle to which she and Joanna might retire each day, pulling up the drawbridge against intruders. Her shock at the sight of the nit-picking gang who were her own family, actually sitting around her kitchen table and calmly eating her chocolate biscuits, had been overwhelming, and it seemed that nothing Joanna could say or do would give back her sense of security. The terror that haunted her, that Sarah would come for her, grew as spring blossomed into summer.

Joanna decided that they must have a holiday. In July, as soon as school was finished for the summer, she shut up the house, and with a mountain of luggage stowed away at their feet and stacked on the rack at the rear, they took a cab to Exchange station and a train to Blackpool.

From the moment they stepped, hand in hand, elegant lady and becomingly dressed child, into the dim, high arched bustle of the railway station, the rise in their spirits was dramatic.

At first Zoe had been fearful of the noisy monster on the track, the first she had ever seen. But once aboard she sat on the sun-warmed plush seat next to the window and looked about her with interest. The gentleman opposite beamed at her, and she bobbed her head shyly, before giving him the benefit of her own radiant smile. He was enchanted and politely asked Joanna if he might give her lovely daughter a piece of Cadbury's milk chocolate.

The train started and Zoe gasped in growing delight as the train inched forward. She watched the marching rows of identical, back-to-back houses with copycat chimneys reaching fingers to the sky; then tiny cottages set in patches of multicoloured garden; then mile after mile of fields, laced with buttercups in which placid cows chewed. She adored the heart-stopping swoosh of their arrival into the echoing steam-filled stations along the way.

But it was nothing to the emotion which she had experienced at her first sight of the sea.

Zoe felt herself quite a seasoned traveller by the time they had arrived in Blackpool, and on the cab journey down to the Promenade, and the quiet splendour of the Royal Hotel sat happily looking around her.

The streets were filled with a milling throng of holiday-makers. Candy floss flowered from grubby fists, and toffee apples bulged young cheeks, pink with sunburn. They streamed from one end of the promenade to the other, on to the flat, wrinkled sands, perched precariously on the placid donkeys, screaming their joy, showing their knickers, clutching their hats, eating shrimps and cockles with dripping, vinegar-soaked fingers. They sat on deckchairs in their braces and shirt sleeves, and the good humour enfolded every soul in a benevolence which would last them into next year.

Zoe was captivated. Then the taxi turned the corner as it came to the North Pier and there it was.

The sea.

The tide was in and the water lapped gently against the grey stones of the Promenade. The sun turned the brown water of the Ribble estuary into a sparkling rippling surface of polished metal. Zoe caught her breath and she stared at the beauty before her. She did not see the thick mud which lurked beneath the shining waves, nor the great clots of seaweed which heaved along the water's edge. The flotsam thrown carelessly from passing cargo boats, far out on the horizon, was not yet washed ashore, and on today's currents would drift further along the coast, landing in the marshes near Freckleton.

'Oh, Daly, look,' she breathed reverently, and Joanna clasped her hand, smiling.

They had time only to be shown to a large double room on the first floor of the hotel – on the front, of course; to unpack a thing or two; to have a quick wash, and an even quicker cup of tea, before Zoe was pulling Joanna by the hand across the tram track, and down to the rail of the promenade.

The tide had turned and a thin, ever-widening strip of wet and shining sand was visible. The retreating water sighed and whispered in welcome to the delighted child, running delicately along the hard ridges left by the water in the sand.

Zoe stood entranced at the water's edge, watching the play of light across the waves as they broke on the wet ribs, and with her fingers tried to catch the flashing crystals that radiated in the cool depths.

She begged to be allowed to remove her shoes and stockings as other, more ebullient youngsters were doing, and her bare feet splashed in the sun-warmed pools left behind by the ocean as it retreated from her. She was careless of her dress as she knelt, her searching hands and eyes fascinated by the life the water had deposited in its rush to the land; tiny crabs burrowing deeper as she probed, shells, starfish and long, soft tendrils of seaweed.

It was another world to the child and Sarah was forgotten.

They spent four weeks in Blackpool, in the best summer the cautious weather forecasters had known for twenty years. Day after day, Zoe and Joanna took their swimming dresses and towels, changing in the beach huts which lined the edge of the sea. These were brought down by horses each day, only pulling back when the tide came up. The two happy and carefree adventurers were loaded with buckets and spades, picnics and calamine lotion, a coloured ball and deckchairs hired from a white-coated attendant for two-pence each for the day, Joanna's camera, sunhats and a big parasol.

Sometimes they took the tram to South Shore to sit on another part of the beach. They would loll for hours, interrupted only by hunger. Then, hand in hand, they ran apprehensively across the tram track, keeping a sharp look out for the rattlers which hurtled from Fleetwood or Starr Gate. They brought back a tray of tea from the cafe on the corner of Waterloo Road, to be drunk with the sandwiches which always seemed to be peppered with sand, though still delicious, tasting as no other food was ever to taste.

Their faces and arms became honey brown; their mouths were creased in endless smiles of contentment.

On the Thursday of their last week, they took a charabanc from the promenade, following the roads to the outskirts of the town, along the meandering lanes eastwards, out to Garstang, and the gentle hills of the Trough of Bowland.

The company aboard the omnibus alighted and looked about them nervously. It was so quiet. They assured the driver, unnecessarily, that they would all be back for four o'clock, whereupon he settled himself on the back seat, with a newspaper over his face and forgot them all as he had a quiet zizz.

Zoe and Joanna soon left the noisy crowd behind and made their way along the rough track which ran beside a small stream. Sheep followed them curiously.

They sat by the stream, ate their sandwiches and drank from a bottle of lemonade. It was warm and delicious, and Zoe fell asleep.

Joanna watched her, her heart overflowing with love. Just a few short weeks had transformed her into the sweet and gentle girl she had once been, before fear had sharpened her. Sarah, and the trouble she brought with her, were a million miles away.

Joanna drowsed a little, letting the warmth and stillness seep into her mind. It acted like a drug, and she could feel her limbs grow heavy against the springiness of the bracken on which they lay. Midges danced in a graceful cloud above; clear in the distance, from more than a mile away, came the high laughter of one of their travelling companions.

A tangled sheep, trailing two grown lambs at her heels, crept confidently nearer to the sleeping forms sprawled by the stream. She lifted her head at the sudden noise, listening; then, reassured that no danger threatened, resumed her quiet cropping almost at Joanna's feet.

Soft breath mingled with wine-clear air. A bee hummed its song as it drifted to a stand of clover inches from Zoe's nose.

Cradled in nature, the two slept on.

It did not take long in coming. Just a week.

It was as though she had been watching the house, waiting for them to settle in, to feel a sense of wellbeing, of false security, before she came back to torment them.

The long, lovely summer was dying a little, and Joanna and the child were in the garden at the back of the house. The sun was sliding gently towards the roof top of the house behind them, and the shadows were long and soft. Someone mowed a lawn several houses down, and the fresh scent of the grass, perhaps the sweetest summer smell of all, drifted over the high brick walls.

Zoe played with two tiny kittens, one ginger and one coal black, given to her only the day before by the red-faced, harrassed wife of the milkman. A basket was lined with a soft blanket and they were named Polly and Amber and must sleep in her room with her, for they would be lonely without their mother.

Joanna agreed to this, exasperated, but only a little, for the child could do no wrong. She had no wish to disturb the almost idyllic happiness which lay about the house. All the doubts and unease which had troubled the little girl had been blown away in the bracing air, and cheerful, down-to-earth humour of Blackpool.

The kittens skittered on the lawn, and she and Zoe laughed, and did not hear the doorbell.

'Naughty Polly,' said Zoe lovingly, watching the pursuit of a butterfly.

The doorbell rang again.

This time they heard it, and the bright summer laughter left their faces. 'Bring the kittens indoors, sweetheart,' Joanna said brightly.

She walked slowly along the path to the house, and Zoe lifted the two kittens into the big basket and fastened the lid. She turned in time to see Joanna come to the kitchen door. There was someone with her.

The sun had almost gone; only a half orb of amber glowed above the high peaked roof, but the child's head and shoulders were still bathed in the rosy light. She stared, lifting her hand to shade her eyes, trying to pierce the shadows which clung about the kitchen door.

Who was it who stood so quietly behind Daly? It was a woman, that much she could see, but who was the third figure who lurked in the half light of the doorway? Her heart thudded painfully in her chest, and her mouth dried, leaving the bitter taste of fear upon it.

Joanna walked slowly down the steps from the kitchen door followed by a young woman and . . . ? Zoe's heart tripped and hammered.

It was Sarah, as she had known it would be.

Behind her was their father.

Joanna spoke falteringly. 'Sweetheart . . . we have visitors.'

Sarah and Zeb stepped onto the smooth grass. They were neatly dressed, and clean, and it was evident from the tiny squares of blood-soaked paper sticking to his skin, that Zeb had shaved that day. His eyes were bloodshot, but perfectly sober, and the expression on his face was unreadable.

Zoe stared at them in horror. She took a step backwards,

kicking the kittens' basket, and set off a frantic miaowing and clawing.

'Oh, the poor little cats. They want to be out, Daly. Shall I let them out?'

But Sarah answered harshly: 'Never mind bluddy cats, our Zoe. Me Da' an' me 'ave come for yer.' Her voice was bitter, and she turned to look at her father. 'Come on, Da'. Tell 'em wot yer said ter me the other day.' She glanced at Joanna mockingly.

"'E's go' summat to say. After all this bluddy time, buggers go' sommat to say.'

She turned her ridiculing glance on her father, but it was as though he was struck dumb as he looked at Zoe. At last he spoke.

'I only just found ou', Queen,' he said to Joanna apologetically, and his face worked with emotion. 'I bin . . . hittin' the bottle, like, an' I never knew. Our Sarah . . . ,' he turned to her for confirmation, '. . . she said, like, tha' our Zoe were stoppin' wiv a lady . . . She never said it were fer good, like.' His face seemed to shrivel and his eyes were moist. 'Matty . . . the missus . . . she wudden like i', Queen, not to lerrour Zoe stop wiv someone fer good, like. She wudden like the family ter be splirrup, like.'

His gaze fell on the terrified child. As the full horror of the situation reached her, she began to cry in a high, wobbling scream.

Joanna held her tightly, 'Don't cry, sweetheart, don't cry. Daly has you. Don't be frightened now. Daly won't let you go. I'll get the police. They won't let them take you.'

The sun was gone now, and the long summer evening began to dim. The lawn mower was silent, and the sounds of nature settling to sleep hung sweetly on the air.

Sarah turned away in exasperation, moving a few steps towards the house.

She was a plain girl, sharing only one glory with her sister; the colour and abundance of her hair. It stood out about her head in a cloud of chestnut confusion, curly, unruly, but brushed now, and shiny. A tiny knitted beret, in a vivid shade of emerald green, perched cheekily on top of the puff-ball of tight ringlets, threatening to fly off with each turn of the tossing head. The tooth she had lost had been replaced by a brilliantly white creation, and stood out like a new tombstone amongst the discoloured ones she called her own. She was thin to the point of ugliness, the extra money which she had gulled from Joanna coming too late to put flesh on her bones.

She turned back to the two trembling figures who stood like condemned men waiting for the noose. She looked at them for a second, then her gaze passed to her father, who still appeared hardly to know why he was here. Some long ago memory had him in its grip. A soft voice had spoken to him as he lay in drunken torpor, a voice which told of love, of children, of hopes and bygone happiness. His conscience, dead so long, had come painfully back. He had looked at his children. He had seen them properly for the first time in years, and he had been pleased with what he saw. And so would Matty have been, he said in self congratulation. Not too clean, certainly, but that did not matter, for which kids didn't get a bit of muck about them when they played out? But what did delight him was their sturdy limbs and the look of properly fed young animals that contrasted sharply with the children of his neighbours.

He did not stop to question why? After all, if they appeared well fed and healthy, why should he bother his befuddled brain as to the how of it. It was enough for him. He'd done right well with them, he thought smugly. Nothing to be ashamed of here, Matty, he said to the face of his dead wife, as she stared out from the only photograph they had ever had taken. A wedding photograph. Bye, she was lovely, he said to the picture. His Matty had been lovely. Just like their Zoe.

It was at this point that he had noticed that his youngest daughter was missing.

Zeb moved towards the clasped figures.

'Come on, chuck,' he said encouragingly to the cowering figure of his daughter. 'Ge' yer little duds an' we'll be off.

You've no rights to be 'ere, away from yer fambly. Come on then, let's be 'avin' yer.'

He put out his hand placatingly, and smiled, showing the wreck of his teeth. His eyes were pleading, for in his own befuddled mind he was doing the right thing by his child. She was Matty's daughter, and Matty would turn over in her grave if she knew he had allowed one of her children to be fostered out.

Joanna took a step backwards, then another, dragging the wailing child with her. 'Get away,' she screamed as Zeb moved towards them. 'Don't touch her with your filthy hands. She's mine! The School Board said I might keep her for twelve months. A trial, they said.'

The man looked bewildered, turning to Sarah, but she avoided his glance.

'. . . and then if she wants to go back . . .' She looked down imploringly into Zoe's streaming, vacant face. 'You don't want to go, do you, darling?'

Zoe's voice was high, filled with terror. 'Daly, please, please, don't let them take me. Please let me stay here with you. Don't let them take me, Daly. I don't want to go with them.'

Sarah strode forward, took hold of Zoe's arm, and tore her away.

'No, no, no!' screamed the child and the woman simultaneously, struggling to get to each other.

But Zeb grabbed Joanna and threw her to the grass.

'Shirrup, yer stupid cow!' he shouted, 'she's my kid, mine an' Matty's, an' she don't belong 'ere. Leave off,' he roared as Joanna tried to get to her feet to reach the struggling, shrieking child. 'Leave off or I'll fetch ya a good 'un.'

He half carried, half dragged the hysterical little girl towards the steps which led up into the kitchen. As they reached the bottom, Zoe fell, cracking her forehead sharply on the brickwork. Zeb hauled her to her feet. A welt as red as fire raised itself against her white skin and a dazed look filmed her eyes.

She stepped docilely now past her father, and disappeared into the darkness of the kitchen.

'Zoe!'

One scream split the air, and then the woman was silent, falling back on to the grass in despair.

Sarah stood for a moment. She took a step towards Joanna, then stopped and looked towards the doorway through which her father and Zoe had gone. With a shrug, she followed them.

The kittens cried piteously and it grew dark but still Joanna lay.

Long afterwards she got up from the grass and walked like an old woman into her empty house.

Chapter Eleven

Summer 1912

Zoe shifted restlessly between the sleeping forms of her sisters. Her eyes were bright and wild, her face flushed with fever, and the 'egg' on her forehead stood out, hot and throbbing, though it was almost a week since it had been inflicted.

The room reverberated with the noises made by eight people; from the far corner, her father's snores rose and fell rhythmically. Lucy muttered in a dream. Zoe listened to the song of the river, a tug's hooter; a boat's siren in the silence and dark; the wind wailing gently over the murky water and rising with a whine into a ship's rigging. Tears sprang hotly to her eyes.

She scratched miserably at her flea bites. Beside her Rebecca was scratching too, but still deep in sleep.

Zoe could feel her head swell and throb and she lifted her hand to her forehead, trying to ease the pain. Since her return 'home' six days ago, she had not moved from the mattress except, with a shudder, to use the bucket left by Sarah for her needs. It had been emptied once.

Since the night when she had been dragged carelessly through the front door and delivered into the indifferent hands of her sisters, she had not seen her father except as a vague form as he stumbled into his bed.

He had been triumphant as he swaggered to the Seffie, satisfied that his Matty could now lie at peace, in the knowledge that her baby was home with her family. He had done what his half-baked mind had told him to do, and could once more relax into his twilight world. The damage he had done, the tearing apart of two people's lives and hearts, did not enter his head.

Zoe moaned softly in the darkness.

'Daly, Daly.' Her whisper joined the other noises in the room, and was lost.

She tried to ease herself away from contact with Sarah, but the movement only served to make her more uncomfortable. Oh, why did her head not stop aching, and why was she so hot? Her body was slick with sweat, and felt incredibly dirty inside the coarse nightie which Sarah had put on her, and oh, she did want to go home. She thought longingly of the comfort of the big, white bath in Daly's house, of the fluffy yellow towel which was her favourite, and the smooth, clean bed which had been hers. She imagined the gentle hands of the woman she loved and missed so desperately, soothing her wounds, bathing her hot face, giving her medicine, and she cried out loud.

Sarah groaned in her sleep, and tossed fretfully.

Zoe twisted and stretched. She wanted to be with Daly, and the kittens would miss her so.

She began to cry, but it hurt her head too much, and she tried to stop. For a moment she held her breath, but the longing for warm arms, and the tender care she had known for a year or more overcame her, and she wept again. I want to go home, I want to go home, she wailed silently, knowing that if she woke their Sarah she would probably get a back-hander.

She had to use the bucket. Reluctantly she crept from beneath the stale blankets and softly trod the splintered floor to relieve herself. From sheer force of habit she looked for the soft sheets of toilet paper she had grown used to. Finding none she wept again.

As she fumbled her way back to bed, she almost fell over clothes thrown carelessly to the floor as the owner had leaped into bed.

It was their Jamie's trousers.

It seemed that the idea, never far away, came to her as she picked them up, ready to throw them in disgust as far away as possible.

She would go home. She wouldn't wait another moment for Joanna to come and fetch her, as she had never doubted for one second that she would. The thought of the dark terrified her, but she would do it.

She held her breath. No one stirred.

She stepped into the trousers, and pulled them up round her chest. They were too big, and the braces kept slipping off her shoulders. Never mind; when she got downstairs she would look for a bit of string to tie them with.

Carefully she stepped across the tiny room, past the sleeping forms of her brothers, who were nearer to the head of the stairs. She placed one foot delicately on the top step, holding her breath for the expected creak. It did not come. Down she went, inch by inch, and her head thudded so fearfully she thought she would fall. Her eyes seemed to have blurred, so that she could hardly see, but she crept on down.

She could make out shapes now, for the summer night seemed to seep through the filthy windows. Crossing the room she opened the front door a crack, and peered cautiously through into the deserted street. Afraid to close the door in case she woke them upstairs, she stepped across the threshold and on to the cool flagstones of the pavement. They felt good on the soles of her hot, bare feet.

She began to run towards the corner, holding desperately to the slipping braces. In her eagerness to be away, she had forgotten about the string, but never mind, she'd hold onto them, though it was a bit awkward. Her head seemed as though it were between hammer and anvil, and she could feel the nausea begin to rise and fill her throat. Her limbs felt floaty as she tried to run; she sweated copiously, and her breath rasped in her chest as she floundered on.

Along Pall Mall and into Tithebarn Street. Left into Moorfields and right into Dale Street.

As she turned the corner she shrank back suddenly, squeezing herself into the corner of a darkened shop doorway. It was as bright as day here, and there were people about – the night people, who came from clubs, and passed easily from one hotel to another. A couple passed, laughing hysterically, and holding on to one another. The man stumbled into the roadway to hail a passing taxi-cab, and they fell into it, the woman on top of her companion, in a welter of arms and legs. They did not see her.

A tram clanged and rattled as it made its way to the Pier Head. A dray passed her loaded with vegetables for the market and pulled by a massive horse, his hooves striking sparks from the roadway, and as she peeped cautiously from her hiding place, she saw the slow-moving figure of a police constable. He was trying door handles at each shop as he passed. In a minute he would be inspecting her dark hidy-hole.

Quick as a squirrel she was across the road and into North John Street. She nearly lost her trousers and her toe caught agonisingly against the kerb, but she made it, waiting for the constable to shout, expecting the thud of feet behind her and his hand on her shoulder.

But oh, she did feel poorly, now.

On she went, mile after mile, keeping to the shadows, though they scared her so. Park Lane. St James Street. Great George Place. She made a wrong turn once, finding herself facing the river on Grafton Street, when she should have been walking away from it, but at last she came to Princes Park.

It was almost light now, and she was fearful that someone would pass her on the way to his work and wonder. Perhaps stop her with questions. If she could have seen herself she might have worried more.

Her face was ashen and moist with sweat. Her hair hung in rats' tails, lank and wet with perspiration. Already lice were living there. She was dirty, and her eyes, which had sunk into hollows of purple, were dazed. The swelling on her forehead was raw and angry.

She moaned a little with each step, instinct more than reason carrying her onwards.

She turned into Parkfield Road.

Not far now, her dazed mind recorded. But I'm so tired, her weary limbs answered. Not far. Not far.

A milk float rattled merrily round the corner; the horse lifted its head sharply at the sight of the child, and rolled its eye, but the dairy man, who walked on the far side of the wagon, reins over his shoulder, was occupied with his order book, and did not look in her direction. Zoe sagged painfully inside a gateway, waiting until he had disappeared behind a thick hedge, before stumbling on.

Daly. Daly. Daly. Her footsteps sounded in a rhythm as she staggered into Livingstone Drive. Day on the left foot. Lee on the right foot. Day – left. Lee – right.

She fell heavily over something which she did not see. She did not know it was her own faltering feet. She lay for a while, nestling against the flagstones. Oh, how sweet it was to lie here. Thank goodness she had arrived home. It was so good to be here, in her own bed and in a minute Daly would come in with a . . .

She lifted her head which rang and shattered with pain. What had awakened her, she wondered. She stared blindly at the neatly painted road sign, which was only a foot or so from her raised head.

Croxteth Road. That was . . . that was only . . .

In a lurching gait which threatened to throw her into the gutter, she managed to reach the corner.

There it was. Pinehurst Place. She was home.

On and on and on. Past gardens, sweetly smelling of roses and phlox and freshly-cut grass. Birds trilled their joy at the new day, and the sun etched itself behind the beloved house, as she reached the gate.

'Daly,' she croaked, 'I'm home.' She crawled up the path, and her friend the grinning dog greeted her with pleasure. It was a long, long way and the bell was so high, but at last her finger reached it and she heard it peal inside the house.

Then, like heaven's gates, the door opened and a great cry lifted her upwards. She was there. Daly was there.

Those arms were about her, cradling her tenderly; she was lifted up, felt the warmth and wetness of tears and knew no more.

Chapter Twelve

She grew sweetly now, for Sarah and Zeb left her alone. Her scars faded and in the gentle atmosphere of protective love with which Joanna surrounded her, nothing could harm her.

It had taken many months to heal her.

Joanna would remember to her dying day that moment when, sleepless, she had heard the bell ring and opened her door. Many hours later, when the doctor had gone and the child lay, clean and sleeping under the influence of a sedative, she sat in the darkened room rocking gently in the chair by Zoe's bed. She watched the little girl's face, a wreck of its former loveliness, flushed with fever, and listened to the light breathing.

A concussion, the doctor had said, as he bathed the infected rawness of her brow. She must rest and eat lightly off eggs and milk. 'A drop of sherry in the mixture won't hurt either, and when she feels like it, bread and milk, warm, of course. Put a lining on her stomach, that will.'

As she rocked Joanna thought over the last few days. The police could do nothing to get Zoe back that night, no matter how much she screamed and pleaded. Nor could Hadfield and Fleming, Solicitors, when she called on them the next morning. Zoe Taylor belonged to her father, and as long as he wanted her to she must stay with him.

Unless he abused her.

Joanna leaned over the small bed, tenderly touching Zoe's feverish cheek. She murmured in her sleep, and a tiny smile lifted the corner of her cracked lips. The doctor had said he had hardly seen anything like the poor bleeding feet which had carried the child for over five miles, and that if she did not have complete quiet and freedom from fear he would not answer for the consequences.

'She is vastly underweight, Miss Dale, for her age. Yes, yes, I know she was healthy the last time I saw her, and it is beyond my comprehension how any child could get into such a pitiable condition in such a short time. The father must be . . . well. I can only say that you will have my full support in any action you may wish to take.'

Joanna smiled for the first time since Zoe had gone from her. Her face was grey and sunken. But now, at last, she had the trump card.

She leaned over the bed once more and placed her lips lovingly on Zoe's forehead. Then she crept from the room, leaving the door ajar. The hall was bright with sunshine, and the copper jugs ranged on the shelf above the picture rail winked brightly. Halfway down the stairs, Polly clung to the carpet, mewing forlornly. Joanna picked her up, and carried her down to her basket in the kitchen.

Then she lifted the telephone receiver. She gave the operator a number, waited for a voice to answer, and spoke for several minutes, before returning the receiver to its hook.

She smiled in satisfaction as she climbed the stairs. 'Miss Dale, if I hadn't seen it for myself, I must admit I would have sworn that you were exaggerating. That poor child. And she was settling so well, and doing good work at school. Why, only last week I had her books before me, preparatory to sending a report to the School Board. I can hardly . . . that poor child. Did he strike her, d'you think? What a dreadful injury, and what she must have suffered to walk all that distance . . .'

Miss Briggs cleared her throat and blinked rapidly. Rooting furiously in the depth of her tapestry bag, she produced a large handkerchief, and blew her nose soundly.

Joanna smiled sadly and blinked a time or two herself.

What a windfall this was.

First the doctor, now the Headmistress. She only needed the Chairman of the School Board and her plan, which had hatched itself in her mind as she had sat by the child's bedside, and gazed upon that poor battered face, would be completed. She certainly wasn't going to tell anyone that Zoe had hurt her head by falling on the step. And if Sarah spoke up – well, who was going to believe the daughter of a no-good drunkard, against the word of a respectable, hard-working teacher? But Sarah wanted the money, nothing else, and she should have it, providing she said nothing.

Miss Briggs was speaking again.

'What do you intend to do now, Miss Dale? The child can hardly be returned to her family.' She sniffed delicately, quite taken out of her usual stoicism by the sight of the sleeping, lacerated face which she had just seen.

Joanna put out her hand.

'Thank you, Headmistress, and that brings me to the reason why I have asked you to call. I feel that Mr King should be here when the doctor calls. He must be present when Doctor Blair dresses the wounds on her feet, and of course, to see the scars on her face. I fear that they may be permanent.'

Miss Briggs moaned sympathetically and Joanna hung her head.

God forgive me, she thought, but I would go to any lengths.

'You see, I want to protect Zoe against this happening again. As things stand, her father might come and remove her whenever the fancy takes him. I wish to be protected legally, and I can only obtain that legal protection through you, and Doctor Blair, and of course, Mr King. Doctor Blair will be here in about an hour, so I thought . . .'

Miss Briggs sprang to her feet.

'Say no more, Miss Dale. I shall be only too pleased . . .'

It worked. It worked so splendidly that but for Joanna's insistence that she wanted no further trouble, Zeb Taylor would have been hauled off to jail charged with the ill-treatment of his daughter.

And so began a period of tranquillity and quiet happiness for Joanna and Zoe. Zoe was away from school for almost a term. Joanna was given leave of absence – unpaid of course – to nurse her and as Christmas approached again, Sarah called for the last time.

She was almost penitent.

'Me Da's gone round 't bend,' she said stiffly, 'an' can't work. I'm askin' for nowt for mesel'. I gorrer job. But it's the kids. It's into an 'ome for 'em if I don't find summat to keep 'em wi' me.'

The strong independence and loyalty which she had clung to ever since the death of her mother, showed fiercely in her eyes, before a softer, almost frightened expression washed over her face.

'I won' bovver yer again, nor our Zoe, bu' . . . if yer could jus' . . .'

Joanna crossed the room to stare out of the window into the cold November day. The clouds were low and dark, and the last wet leaves spun to the ground. She shivered, imagining the bleakness of the house in Love Lane. An early robin hopped hopefully on to the fence.

Sarah moved restlessly in her chair, and looked about her at the lovely room. The fire glowed off the polished surface of the piano where her sister had sat only half an hour ago. The colours of the curtains were soft and warm, and the lamps which Joanna had just switched on, made pools of gentle light on table and carpet. She had never in her life been in such a room and never would again, she thought, but she was not envious. This was not her world, and she did not want it. In her own way she was content with her life. She asked nothing, at the moment, but that the kids were fed. Her sharp mind told her that one day, if she could just get the kids to a decent age, she might make something of her life, but at the moment she could not escape the trust which she had taken on when her mother died.

This woman could help her. No one else. And if she sat quiet as a mouse and played the soft fool, she would get what she wanted. She still had a hold on Joanna. The School Board had seen to that, when they had investigated the circumstances of Zoe's 'accident'. She had watched

Joanna's face that day, and seen her expression, and she had known that if she kept her trap shut, the way would always be there to 'touch her up for a bit'.

Joanna turned and looked at Sarah. There was perfect understanding between them.

'You will never come again, Sarah. I will help you only on that understanding. I will give you the ten shillings a week, until your youngest brother is working, but then it will stop. And if I once see any of you within a mile of my house, or near the school, it will stop immediately.'

Sarah nodded and rose from her chair. They walked silently, one behind the other, out of the drawing-room and across the hall. Joanna opened the front door and a great gust of wind blew inwards, carrying soggy leaves onto the carpet.

Sarah turned, not looking at Joanna, but up the staircase towards the room where her little sister played with her kittens, and her face was inscrutable as she said quietly, 'Poor little sod.' Without another word, or look in Joanna's direction, she ran down the steps.

Joanna watched for a moment. Then, with a sigh and a sense of foreboding which she did not understand, she shut the door.

Chapter Thirteen

It was the crash of glass, as it shattered and fell in a thousand pieces to the pavement, that first attracted their attention. People turned, hesitated, stopped and for a moment, the Saturday afternoon crowd milled about in confusion. Questions were asked, and went unanswered, and women drew children anxiously closer to them, for there was, suddenly, a feeling of unease in the air.

A shout rang out, mindless, incoherent, and more voices joined the first. Another loud report, unidentifiable this time, lifted above the noise of the traffic, and a murmur began, growing louder, angry.

Joanna held tightly to Zoe's hand and edged her way across the pavement, trying to avoid the throng who were beginning to jostle their way in the direction of the tumult. A long drawn-out wail of fear and outrage rose above the crowd and was cut off, as though some hand had gripped a throat.

'What is it Daly?' Zoe asked fearfully, for even though her life was serene now, freed from the dread of Sarah and Zeb, any untoward occurrence touched a raw nerve.

'I don't know, darling, but I think we'll try and get across the road to Bunny's. Perhaps someone had an accident.'

Joanna pressed Zoe's hand. The crowd was thicker now, people coming from doorways of shops like flies drawn to a carcass. A whistle shrilled, and another, and Joanna felt the first prickle of fear touch the back of her neck.

The air seemed to smell of evil. The fear grew and her grip on Zoe's hand tightened.

'Oh Daly, let's go, please. I don't like it. What's happening?' Zoe's face was ashen.

'I don't know, love, but we'll get out of this —' She was

109

about to say 'mob', but stopped herself suddenly, realising that the very word spelled danger, fear: she did not want to alarm the child more.

But no matter how she pushed or shoved, she and Zoe were carried along like leaves before a sweeper's broom. The noise was appalling. Screams came from up ahead, and shouts which surely could not come from human throats.

Tears streamed down Zoe's face. Her boater was gone, her hair flew about her head, and hung in dishevelled curls down to her waist. Her dress was torn at the hem.

'Daly, Daly, please . . . please . . .' But her words were lost.

'Dear God, let me only hold on to her,' prayed Joanna, the sleeve of her own dress nearly ripped from her shoulder.

Suddenly they were there, and as they emerged from the crowd pushing towards the corner of the street, the scene in all its horror lay before them. Although the din still raged at the back of the crowd it was curiously silent here. Men stood like waxen figures in a tableau.

It was a jeweller's shop. Once it had been fine, splendid even, with fresh paint, and gleaming glass, double-fronted, with bow windows which displayed sparkling pieces on black velvet. Joanna remembered stopping to admire the rings and bracelets. Elegantly and expensively dressed women had come and gone, attended by chauffeurs who opened car doors, and fussed with rugs, and umbrellas.

Now it was as though some enormous hand had made a fist and thrust it through the window. Glass lay everywhere; bricks and broken wood littered the pavement.

Their cue given, half a dozen men came suddenly from the shattered doorway. Between them they half carried, half dragged a small elderly gentleman, dressed in a black frocked coat and striped trousers. One of the men gripped his neck in a stranglehold, and he was choking, his face a brilliant purplish red.

The crowd which circled the shop was silent now,

except for a wail of a small boy, who clung to his mother's skirt.

Zoe stared, unable to look away, and Joanna could feel her fear.

'Bloody Germans! You scum – give you some of what you've been giving our – All those poor bloody little kids!'

The yelling man held his prisoner in a cruel grip, sobbing in grief and anger. His cap fell to the ground, revealing a short crop of grey hair.

'You killed 'em, yer sod, yer – Kraut,' he sobbed, and the men with him, faces set, forced the elderly man to his knees. The sound of breaking, crashing objects could be heard from within the shop, and a girl's cry rang out, followed by loud weeping.

As his tormentors released the hold on his neck, the old man tried to speak, pleading, looking up into their implacable faces, but his cries were spoken in a language they did not understand, for in his terror he mouthed the words of his youth.

'I seen the papers this mornin',' the incensed man continued. 'All them wimmen and kids – an' warra 'bout them what was done in by Zeppelins, in Dover and Southend? My boy, my boy . . . Flanders . . . an me sister's boy at Mons.'

The words were punctuated by kicks and blows and the little old man fell slowly and silently, until his bloody face rested on the pavement.

The mob swayed. Joanna could feel the hysteria and hatred rise like a wave, and was appalled to see the righteous exaltation on the faces around her. Then the sound of the whistle came again, shrilly, nearer now. Again and again it pierced, and suddenly, pushing roughly through the crowd, the police were there, truncheons ready.

The crowd roared, but in moments it was over. A van arrived and two of the men were hustled into the back, one arguing, one weeping. The rest had slipped away in the mêlée.

111

The old man was put on a stretcher, and taken away by ambulance, and slowly the crowd dispersed. Zoe and Joanna stumbled along Dale Street, unseeing, almost paralysed by the horror of what they had seen. They did not speak, for what was there to say? Joanna patted the child's hand automatically but her mind was hardly aware of what she did. She could still see the name above the shop etched clear and bright, in letters of gold.

JACOB MEYER & SON, JEWELLERS

It was April and three days ago a German torpedo had sunk the Cunard liner *Lusitania* off the West Coast of Ireland. Two thousand passengers had drowned.

The elderly man had paid the price of having a German name.

It was many weeks before Zoe could be persuaded to go into town again. Her dread of a repetition of the ghastly scene she had witnessed that afternoon brought back the jittery child of three years ago, and it was all Joanna could do to calm her fears so that she might get her to school. Even there she was afraid that some disturbance might upset the fine balance of the child's mind, for her classmates wept for lost fathers and brothers, and emotions ran high.

The talk was all of war, and the papers drummed up anti-German feelings with lurid tales of atrocities.

Headlines such as:

REFUSE TO BE SERVED BY AN AUSTRIAN.
ASK TO SEE THE PASSPORT IF YOUR WAITER
SAYS HE IS SWISS,

were commonplace, and in the Spring of 1915, to the outrage of all its fans, the football managers, forced by pressures they could not withstand, declared that this would be the last season, until hostilities had ceased. Players should be in the trenches, and those who watched, at the factory benches.

Zeppelin raids continued: on Dover and Southend, on London and the south-east counties.

The Battle of the Somme. On the first day twenty thousand men died.

The Marne. Dardanelles. Gallipoli. Names and places which became commonplace and the young men of Britain continued to die in their thousands.

Khaki was a common sight now on the streets of Liverpool, for the Royal Engineers were stationed at the Seaforth Battery, and everywhere young girls could be seen hanging on to soldiers' arms.

Troop ships left Gladstone Dock for Belgium, bursting at the seams with cheering, fresh-faced volunteers, and later, in 1916, conscripts sailed: not so eager, not so young.

The ferry service to the other side of the river was cut, as the ferries were drawn into the war, taking troops to Belgium and France, and bringing back the wounded. On one occasion when Joanna and Zoe were at the Pier Head, having decided on a trip to New Brighton, one bright Sunday, they were appalled to see the *Iris*, battered and wounded, tied up for repairs. Blood stained her sides, where it had run from the decks, and people stared with dread curiosity, and women wept. One woman in black fell to the dock in a faint.

Feelings, dulled by two years of war, flared at the execution of Nurse Edith Cavell, and there was a fresh wave of attacks on shops with German-sounding names. One shop in Brunswick Street, with the English name of Emmett, had a brick thrown through its window because it sold German sausage. Saxe-Coburg Street became Saxby Street; a German Dachshund was kicked to death before its distraught owner's eyes.

Lord Kitchener drowned on a mission to Russia. Far worse to Joanna were the columns after columns of small black print in the newspapers listing the dead and wounded. Fifteen hundred each day.

Joanna became proficient at making haricot bean

113

fritters, savoury oatmeal puddings and barley rissoles. They ate Government bread and margarine, and Government-control tea.

Tipperary was sung and whistled.

Ypres, or as the British 'tommy' called it, 'Wipers'. Passchendæle. Cambrai.

The United States became an ally. But in the summer of 1917, the war and all its 'glory' faded into obscurity for Zoe.

Chapter Fourteen

Summer 1917
'Daly, Daly, give me your answer, do . . .'

The young girl in the cream shantung dress sang as she grouped the armful of flowers in the crystal vase. She was almost twelve now, and her beauty was breathtaking. The sun had coloured her skin to a pale honey; her chestnut hair shone and her eyebrows, silky and fine, matched the long lashes which framed the deep green eyes, filled with intelligence and sweet humour.

Zoe stepped back from the kitchen table, eyeing her efforts critically. Giving a last exasperated flick to a tumbling rosebud – always her special favourite – she picked up the vase and carried it carefully into the dining room. She set it gently on the lace mat in the centre of the polished, oval table. She cast an admiring eye over the arrangement of silver, crystal and china, and delicately-tinted, still unlit candles in their gleaming holders, the snowy damask napkins edged with lacy crochet, lovingly worked so long ago by Amelia Dale. She was satisfied.

Returning to the kitchen, she smiled complacently at the sponge cake which she had just removed from the oven. Testing it gently with her knuckle, as Joanna had taught her, and finding that it had lost much of its heat, she eased it gently from the baking tin on to a wire-mesh mat, and put it on the marble cold slab in the larder, to cool completely before she iced it.

She scrutinised the neat and shining kitchen. Everything was in its place, and with a last loving touch of the scrubbed table she wandered out through the kitchen door, down the five steps into the garden, and into the warm, July sunshine.

115

The walled garden had been created by Joanna's father, whose skilful touch showed plainly here. The walls were brick, in many shades, from soft pink, to burgundy, almost covered now, by climbing clematis, and honeysuckle. The huge oak tree shaded the bottom half of the garden. A garden seat had been built around its trunk; it was old and weatherbeaten, but a favourite spot on a hot day such as this. Zoe idled along the brick path, made from the leftovers when the house was built, the colours matching the six-foot-high surrounding walls.

The air was fragrant with the scent of roses, and the sharp aroma of cut grass, heaped in the shady corner behind the tree. A deckchair, the striped canvas lifting gently in the warm breeze, was placed on the gradual slope of the lawn.

Zoe sat down gracefully, and she settled back to dream.

It was Joanna's birthday, and the memories of six years, some dim, others as clear as a moorland stream, came to glide across her mind. She often daydreamed. 'To keep me company when you are away,' she would laugh when Joanna called her 'head-in-the-clouds'.

Her head nodded peacefully.

Suddenly, the thought of the cake brought her back to the present. Joanna would be so pleased.

An ebony shape flashed in a streak across the grass, followed by another, this time the colour of marmalade. With a triumphant miaow Amber landed lightly on to the sprawled lap of the reclining girl. Polly trailed behind as if to say that she didn't want to be first anyway, and Zoe laughed and yawned at the same time.

'Come on, Zoe, my girl. Get up off your bum . . .'

She had spoken out loud, but as the sound of the last word fell on the warm air, her hand rose apologetically to cover her mouth, as if to press the rudeness back. She grimaced comically, her eyes bright with laughter. Sometimes a word from her old life popped into her head and out between her lips before she could stop it, and she knew that Daly didn't like her to use words . . . well . . . like . . . bum.

She smiled gently with love, as Joanna's face rose before her, disapproving, doting.

Leaping up and spilling the protesting Amber on to the grass, she fox-trotted across the lawn, an imaginary partner held in her arms, her clear voice bidding farewell to 'Dolly Grey'. Polly patted her lightly as she passed, just to show that there were no hard feelings, and Zoe sang as she skipped lightly up the steps, into the kitchen and across the gleaming floor to the larder, taking the now cold sponge cake from the slab where she had placed it an hour ago.

It was warm in the kitchen, despite the open window and the light breath of air which moved the gingham curtain fractionally. The icing which she had mixed whilst the cake was in the oven had not set properly and now slid slowly down the side of the cake and collected in a circle at the bottom.

'Oh damn and blast,' Zoe groaned, looking guiltily over her shoulder for these were also words which were frowned upon by Joanna. She ran her finger round the plate in an attempt to remove the offending surplus, sucking it off her fingertip with pursed lips.

Polly and Amber sat in a friendly fashion on the table, surveying her efforts with what seemed very like amusement. Zoe glared at them, pulling a face and sighing dramatically.

'I don't know what you two are grinning at,' she said, 'if you can do any better I'm sure you're very welcome to try.'

'Now what shall I do with the dratted thing?' Zoe knew that Joanna would be home soon; she had only gone into town to pick up a new dress which she was having altered.

A harrassed expression crossed her face and she scowled as she smoothed the wayward icing. One of the candles which she had just placed precariously in position slid gracefully over the cake and settled, tip first, into the pink overflow.

Her harrassed expression changed to one of desperation; she would never finish it before Daly came home.

'Damn, damn, damn,' she moaned

At that moment the doorbell rang.

*

Joanna was smiling as she ran across Dale Street, her new dress in a smart carrier bag on her arm. Her thoughts were on the child and the surprise which she knew awaited her when she arrived home.

The tram, which she never saw, dragged her for fifty yards before the ashen-faced driver could bring it to a halt and the screams of the horrified onlookers could be heard above the usual Saturday afternoon hubbub of the street.

She was dead on arrival at the infirmary.

Police Constable Albert Brown, who had escorted her on her last journey, began the task of searching her handbag, which was still on her arm, although the carrier bag containing her new dress had disappeared. He found a letter addressed to Miss Joanna Dale and after checking in with his Sergeant, caught the tram to Princes Park.

It was at times like these that the constable detested the career that he had chosen for himself thirty-six years ago. He walked along Pinehurst Place, his step slowing as he neared the house.

Number forty-two.

He rang the bell and waited.

Zoe jumped when the peal of the doorbell shrilled through the quiet house. The palette knife in her hand stilled on its feverish smoothing.

'Oh, it's Daly,' she groaned. In a flurry, she carried the cake in to the larder and closed the door. Looking breathlessly round the kitchen for any telltale signs that might give away her secret, she turned to leave the room.

The doorbell rang again.

'I'm coming, I'm coming,' she called as she sped up the hall. Her eyes were sparkling with animation, her cheeks were flushed, and a morsel of icing clung to her chin. She flung open the door, her smile a sunburst falling in bright waves on the blue-uniformed figure standing on the doorstep.

For a few brief moments Constable Brown's reason for being there was forgotten, as the oldest feeling in the world, the appreciation of a man for a beautiful woman, overcame him. He cleared his throat and blinked rapidly.

Deep within Zoe's mind an alarm bell sounded faintly, and her smile slid slowly away.

'Good afternoon, Miss. May I speak to your father?' The policeman's glance was embarrassed, his voice gentle.

Zoe's heart beat faster and her mouth dried with apprehension.

'My father?' she faltered.

'If you please, miss.'

Zoe stared at him in confusion. What did this man want with her father? Oh, where was Daly? She didn't know what this policeman wanted of her. Why didn't Daly come home and deal with him?

She tore her anxious gaze from him, and looked beseechingly along the avenue of leafy trees.

The constable took a step forward, wiping his boots unnecessarily on the doormat, and stood just inside the doorway. Automatically, Zoe closed the door behind him, the warning sound inside her growing louder and louder. She walked across the wide hall and into the cool, simple beauty of the drawing room. The constable followed. Sitting carefully on the extreme edge of the settee, she gestured to him to take a seat.

'Have you no one to be with you, child?'

She shook her head. 'It's Daly, isn't it? Something's happened to her.'

Her eyes beseeched him to tell her it wasn't so, but all she saw was compassion.

The shock was still on her face when Sarah walked into the police station. She was sitting on a chair with a dark blue jacket, silver buttons twinkling, draped across her shoulders. Her face was devoid of any expression, and the chestnut wings of her eyebrows made two arched slashes in the waxen pallor. Her eyes were wide open, staring into the horror of a world without Daly. They had tried to be kind to her, the uncomfortable 'bobbies', but after a while they had left her alone, for she did not even seem to know that they were there.

An address had been found in Joanna's desk, after one or two enquiries had been made amongst the avidly interested neighbours, titillated by the sight of the child from Miss Dale's being led down the street by a police constable.

The address was of a slum cottage in Love Lane, and the constable could not believe that the beautiful young girl, sitting like a lost soul in the sergeant's room in the station, could have anything to do with a place like this. He knocked tentatively on the door Joanna had beaten on years before.

There was no reply, but a neighbour told him that Sarah Taylor was at work.

'She's at the munitions factory, chuck. The one in Elacot Road.'

And here she was, still in her long overall, for they had brought her from her machine. Her eager hair was stuffed into a mob cap, and her face was set in lines of exasperated disapproval. Surely they could have brought the kid straight to the house, instead of all this muckin' about? She would be round her neck again, whining for the woman who had been killed, and cringing disgustedly at every bloody thing, whether it crawled or had to be eaten. And the bottomless purse was gone for ever.

'Come on, our kid,' she said. Zoe stood up obediently, the heavy coat falling unnoticed to the floor.

The constable who had put it there picked it up, watching her pityingly as she walked with her sister through the swing doors and out into the warm, early evening sunshine. They caught the tram at the corner, and he stared after it until it disappeared with a crash and a whine down the hill, taking its burden of sorrow.

The difficulty came when Sarah tried to get Zoe across the front doorstep of the house in Love Lane. In her own private desolation, she had gazed sightlessly out of the window, as the tram carried them further and further into the docklands, past row upon row of narrow houses, until they reached the end of Love Lane.

Once again the neighbours were to be entertained by the goings-on of the Taylor family.

Sarah and Zoe had almost reached the cottage, passing the dozens of open doorways, the bands of hopping, skipping children; the would-be footballers; the hopscotch players; the rope-whirling, lamp-post-clinging trapezists, before they were noticed.

Zoe moved like a sleepwalker. Though her face was bleached of colour, tracks of her tears could be seen on her face, like railway lines in snow. Her hair was wild, and tangled, where she had at first run frantic fingers through it, and her green ribbon hung like a dead butterfly, just below her left ear. Her cream dress was stained, the silky shantung creased and marked, where those same fingers had clutched in terror.

At the Taylor front door, without being told, she stopped and turned to face it. Women were slowly coming to their doorsteps now, wiping hands on pinnies, sensing that something out of the ordinary was about to happen. Sarah unlocked the shabby door and stepped over the threshold, beckoning Zoe inside with an impatient finger.

'Come on, our kid,' she said irritably. She was still stunned and resentful at what she considered her misfortune, and was still trying to get her thoughts together. What the 'ell was she gonner do wi't damned kid? Get 'er a bit o work from Arnie Levy's, praps, trouser finishin' or button'olin'. Pity she weren't fourteen, she could 'a gone int' factory, fillin' shells. She eyed the slender figure speculatively. No, she'd never pass for fourteen. She weren't even twelve yet.

'Come on, for Chrissake,' Sarah repeated testily. "Alf bluddy street's out – gerr inside. You'd think they never saw owt, the way they gawp.'

But Zoe stood like stone, only her eyes suddenly alive, as she looked into the dark, open doorway. She remembered the last time she was here: the agony of her longing for

121

Daly, the days she had spent in the filthy bed, bewildered and afraid, her head throbbing. She remembered the fear as she had walked through the night, back to the safety of the beloved woman who . . . who was gone.

Daly was dead and she had no one. This was to be her place now.

For a moment she stood in agony. Then she began to back towards the street.

'No,' she screamed, 'No, no, no! Please, Daly . . .'

The crowd were enchanted.

Zoe's cries echoed along the dusty street.

'Daly, Daly, please come and get me. Don't let them put me in there again. I want to be with you, Daly. I want to go home. You're not dead. You're not, you're not . . .' She sobbed uncontrollably.

Suddenly, with a cry of exasperation, Sarah, who had been staring in amazement at the deranged girl, strode forward, and grasped Zoe's arm.

Zoe wrenched herself away and began to run, cheered by the crowds.

Like a hare Sarah was after her. Zoe tripped, fell, picked herself up again, tried to evade her grasp, but it was useless. In an instant Sarah had grasped Zoe's arm again and was pulling her towards the doorway.

At last she was in and the door banged shut behind her. From within the beseeching cries continued, 'Daly, Daly, Daly!' The crowd began to disperse, stopped for a moment by the sharp crack of flesh on flesh. They smiled at each other as the cries ceased abruptly. That's what she needed, the little hellion.

Later, as the summer night fell, a still form lay staring stony-eyed into the fading, dusty light which hung like a mist in the slanting space under the roof. The torment was dull now, but she knew it would become sharp again, sharp as a knife.

She stared into the night.

Chapter Fifteen

Jamie Taylor was nearly thirteen when he came home from school in the summer of 1917 to find a young girl there whom he dimly recognised. She was sitting on a stool in the corner of the room, staring like summat not right, at absolutely nowt. She looked elevenpence halfpenny in the shilling to him, but he couldn't take his eyes off her.

She was very pretty.

His freckled, good-natured face turned to their Sarah who was sipping a thick mixture of condensed milk and weak tea.

'Who's that?' he whispered.

Sarah laughed shrilly. 'Bluddy 'ell, our Jamie, don' yer know yer own sister? Come ter pay 'er respects she 'as. Come ter see 'ow we're gerrin' on.'

She glared at him, then resumed her noisy sipping, staring pensively into the dead heart of the month-old ashes, still not cleared out from their last fire in March.

'The woman died. Yer know, the one wot took 'er in. Tram gorrer this after.'

There was a moan from the girl in the corner.

Jamie looked from one sister to the other, and despite himself, his sympathy went out to the suffering child in the corner. Their Sarah could be a sod at times.

He crossed the cluttered room. ''Ow do, our kid,' he said awkwardly.

As Zoe lifted her eyes and gazed blindly into his, he remembered the first time he had seen her, at the woman's place, dressed like a princess, glowing with cleanliness and health. She had cried then, her baby face filled with fury and fear, begging the woman to make the dirty children go away. He had despised her.

And the last time, when she had been brought back by their Da'. She had hurt her face, and been poorly, and had seemed not to know what had happened to her. He had been sorry for her then, poor kid, for she had been so frightened, but she had been distant, and he had left her alone. She hadn't stayed long, and when she had gone, he had forgotten her.

He turned back to Sarah.

'Is she stoppin', then?' he asked.

'She'll bluddy after. She's nowhere else ter go.'

'What's up wi' 'er? She looks as though she's bin pulled through a hedge backwards.'

'I dunno,' Sarah said impatiently. 'I never seen owt like it. Goin' on like a bluddy loony, she were, this after. Showed me up in't bluddy street. I couldn't gerrer inside bluddy door.'

She shook her head resentfully, staring at Zoe with contempt.

'What the 'ell I'm gonner do wi' 'er, I don' know, an' me Da'll go mad. That's if 'e notices she's back, like.'

Jamie looked at Zoe, this time with indifference. What was another female in the house? What difference would it make to him?

He was a big, good-looking boy, who had been only a year old when his mother died. He had dragged himself up with the rest of his brothers and sisters, taking whatever life offered, whenever it was offered him. When it was not, he generally managed to acquire it somehow. He went to school when he could not avoid it, and lived for the day when he could leave and work on the docks with his mates. He was cheerful, independent, and completely selfish.

'Is there nowt for ar tea, our Sarah?' he said amiably.

'Yer'd berrer go t't chippie,' she said. 'There's a tanner in me purse, but we'll hafta go careful now.' She was still brooding on her loss. 'Ten bob's a lorrer cash.'

Jamie took the money and ran down the street. The delicious smell of fish and chips drifted, making his mouth water. Perhaps she'd like a few chips, he suddenly thought, as he stood in the queue. He'd buy 'er a pennorth, and when they'd had their tea he'd show her his bird book. She'd like to see his birds. It'd cheer her up.

She would never forget the days and months which followed, for they were the worst she would ever experience.

She no longer went to school. Sarah had decided that because she was the only girl beside Lucy and herself left in the family – Rebecca and Emma had, early on in the war, married soldiers – and because she was too young to be employable except in her own home, that was where she must stay. She would do the housework, the cleaning, the washing, the cooking, empty the slops – Sarah did the shopping – and avoid the school inspector. They had a visit from one of the guardians of the school board. He had been a member of it when Joanna had been given permission to foster the child, and he remembered the case. But there was nothing he could do to help the still-faced waif. The family had first claim, and provided they did not actually ill-treat the girl, she must remain there.

At first they spent their evenings, Jamie and Jackie, Lucy and Sarah, searching the streets for her, for she ran away regularly every day. She was always to be found in the same place. Bedraggled and shabby, hair uncombed, face dirty, eyes staring, she would be sitting on the doorstep of her home in Pinehurst Place. She was beaten each time she was brought back, by Sarah, who seethed with rage at the tenacity of the wild and screaming child. It made no difference. The moment she was alone she would be away, back to Daly.

It would have gone on, for the child was out of her mind and even Sarah despaired of keeping her in the house in Love Lane. But one day, as Zoe sat on the doorstep of Pinehurst Place, shivering, wet and chilled to the bone by the November wind, the door spilled open and a stranger looked down upon her.

The hall behind the opened door was warm and bright,

and the child looked yearningly inside, but the familiar carpets and furniture were gone.

The woman who opened the door was angry. She had been told of the gutter child who had lived here, and who came back each day.

'Get off my doorstep at once, and don't come back,' she said. 'You do not belong here, and if you return I shall call the police. Miss Dale is dead, and doesn't live here any more.'

Zoe only heard four words, and it was as though she heard them for the first time.

'Miss Dale is dead, Miss Dale is dead, Miss Dale is dead.'

The phrase beat agonisingly in her mind as she stumbled along the path, and made her shut her eyes against the light, as though she had a migraine.

She stood outside the gate and looked back at the laughing dog. She put her hand to her eyes to stop the pain, and began to shiver as if she were in the grip of some chill disease. Then she cried for the last time as a child, pleading with a child's mind that expects miracles, for Daly to come back for her, but knowing with her woman's brain, that it could not be so.

All the way back to Love Lane, as the rain beat against her unceasingly, so did those four words and at last she knew, and accepted. But she swore, as the cleansing rain ran from her tangled hair to her chin; with her woman's strength which had replaced the child's pathetic yearning, that she would get out of the squalid place where she had been born if she had to kill to do it.

She never went again to Pinehurst Place. But in the night, as she lay awake in the double bed which she shared with Lucy and Sarah, as she listened to the snores of her father, who was never sober now, and who appeared not to have noted her return, thinking she was either Rebecca or Emma whose departure his sozzled mind had also missed, she would wet her pillow with her silent tears. They slid from under her closed eyelids and into her hair as she lay on her back. Scenes flickered like the new moving pictures of which she had heard, but never seen, and as she wept for the friend she had lost, she re-lived every moment that her memory would allow, of her life with Joanna Dale.

She swept the floors and scrubbed them with strong lye soap. She washed every rag and article of clothing and bedding in the house, drying them round the fire in the kitchen. Every crock and pan and bucket was scoured and even the grimy walls were coated with a thick mixture of whitewash. She cooked for the family on the newly black-leaded oven and each day they came home to the first comfort they had ever known.

Both Sarah and Lucy worked at the munitions factory, and Jackie had found himself a job with the local butcher. Besides his wages he usually brought home a bit of scrag, or some bacon bones for soup, and Zeb somehow, though nobody knew how, managed, even in his constant state of semi-inebriation to go to the dockyard each day.

Zoe's heart accepted at last, though her spirit never did. She mourned Joanna alone in the long days, as she made clean the foul nest in which she must now live. She mourned her and the life they lived together, and she fought Sarah every hour of every day to be the Zoe that Joanna had created. Hers and Sarah's voices could be heard in the dark of the evening, yelling, rising, as the storm that lay within each of them fought to gain dominance over the other. Sarah's voice was derisive, scornful, for she seemed to hate the child who was making the first home they had ever known.

The others would watch indifferently, with the exception of Jamie, but he had learned to keep his trap shut, for it only made it worse for Zoe, when he leaped in to defend her.

Sarah would make some jeering remark, usually about the improved condition of their home, or on Zoe's obsession with cleanliness.

'Eeh, chick, you bin at it again,' she would snide, running a finger across the glossy black shine of the oven. 'Don't know why yer bother. It only gets mucky again, see,' and she would scream with laughter as a splatter of scouse, thick with minced meat, and vegetables, dripped from the end of her spoon onto the clean surface.

Zoe would fly at her, with feet jabbing and kicking in the way of the street fighter. She was fast learning, improving in the art of self-defence, and of attack too. Each time, though she seldom won at first, a little ground was gained in her struggle for self-expression.

Neither girl ever stopped to think about why Sarah should taunt her as she did. It was as though she derived some twisted pleasure in seeing her sister brought down to the level of her own kind again. Their lives had improved beyond measure since the days of seven years ago, but perversely, Sarah seemed to despise that which had helped to drag her family from the pit of poverty in which they had existed, and she knew that the surest way to enrage Zoe was to speak against the woman Zoe loved still.

In her heart lay jealousy, and greed and envy, and conversely, a secret admiration of her sister's emerging spirit.

Chapter Sixteen

The boy turned on the scarred, weather-worn rock, and the agile figure of a girl scrambled up beside him. Like him, she wore breeches tucked into the top of a pair of bright red, knee-length socks, the colour matching their jumpers. They both wore scarves wound round their necks, and the girl's hair was stuffed carelessly into a red beret, from which wispy, damp curls fell about her rosy face. Her eyes shone with keen enjoyment and the smile she turned on her companion was brilliant.

'Oh, Jamie, isn't it beautiful?'

He looked at her as her glance turned to the panorama which spread before them, and his face was fond.

His sharp eyes had turned upwards and were scanning the clear sky with the skilled glance of a true bird watcher.

Was that a meadow pippit hanging there? Oh, if only he could afford some binoculars.

'Aye, our Zoe,' he answered, preoccupied, 'I've never seen owt like it.'

It was March. Frost still lay thickly on the coarse turf, softening the rocks to a gentler outline, turning the bleak uplands into an almost fairyland loveliness.

'Look Jamie, you can see the sun flash on the River Dee – and isn't that Chester? Yes, look, you can see the spires of the Cathedral. I don't think it's ever been so clear, do you?'

Zoe sighed contentedly, and easing the rucksack from her back took out a small groundsheet and spread it on a flat rock.

'What's the name of this place, Jamie?' she continued idly, as she sat down. 'It really is the nicest we've been to.'

Jamie sat down beside her, and took out a map from his rucksack.

'Let's see.' He traced a path with his finger along the route they had come.

'Black Tor Crag, it's called.' He grinned up at Zoe. 'Sounds a bi' spooky ter me. Wonder wa' it means?'

'I don't know and I don't care. I think it's wonderful up here. It's so peaceful. So far away from all that.' With a sweep of her arm she indicated the vague direction of Liverpool.

They had left Love Lane as the first silver of dawn painted the sky. The streets were empty: it was Sunday, and the men who worked the early shift at the dockyard were already gone. Zoe and Jamie stepped out. In their rucksacks were thick slabs of bread and marge, filled with cheese. 'Doorsteps' Jamie called them, and eaten out of doors washed down with pop they satisfied the fiercest appetite.

Shocked by the cold, they hurried along the quiet streets, almost running as they approached the Pier Head, just in time to catch the first ferry to Birkenhead. A great clanging came from Canning Dock, and in the other direction, far away in the misty distance, a flash of light could be seen from Seaforth Battery. The yards were noisy as ships were loaded and unloaded, for Liverpool was one of the busiest ports as the war drew on.

Over the river, and it was light now.

At Seacombe they boarded the omnibus which would take them through the streets of Birkenhead, and into the wooded, gentle lanes of the Wirral, and on to Chester. By half past eight they were in the lovely, medieval old town, and from there it was Shanks's pony.

Packs on their backs, stout boots on their feet, they walked on, never tiring, to Christleton, trees shading a tiny green; across the canal bridge and past the old milestone. Fording the River Gowy they tramped on, as the sun rose higher and the keen, clear air whipped the roses into their cheeks.

They passed through the village of Weston at eleven-thirty, just as the villagers were coming slowly from the ancient church on a corner of the square. Zoe was fascinated by the sight of an elegant couple who emerged from the lych gate, nodding and smiling at the respectfully silent village folk. They stopped for a moment to speak to the minister, who stamped his feet unobtrusively beneath his cassock, then mounted two handsome horses and trotted away down the lane.

The man had brown eyes, the colour of treacle toffee, and they seemed to deepen and glow as his glance met Zoe's. Then he was gone, gathering his horse into a gallop as he thundered after the woman.

At last they came to the edge of the moor, and for a long moment they just stood and drank in the utter silence and tranquillity. It had become like a drug to Zoe. She was an addict who must have a regular dose of the healing medicine that had first been introduced to her by Jamie, and not a weekend had gone by in the last four months when they had not tramped this open wildness, which they were beginning to know like the streets off Love Lane.

It had been the week before Christmas when it started.

The memories from the past years had ridden Zoe hard now for weeks, and she dreaded the time to be got through, the time of peace and goodwill, and Christmas festivities which had once been a part of her life with Joanna. She threw herself into the chores which had become the most important part of her life, working harder and harder, later and later, cleaning an already spotless kitchen for the sole reason that she must be about something in order to keep herself sane. Beauty had gone from her life, but she would have cleanliness and neatness if it killed her.

She went to bed exhausted, and woke at dawn to see her brother leaving the bed he shared with Jackie. She had followed him down the stairs, intrigued despite herself, and in the faint warmth from the fire, left from the night before, he had told her of his expeditions.

'Bird watchin', our kid. Yer seen me book.'

131

Yes, she had seen his book but had not been much interested, to his disappointment.

'Well, I go to't moors. Up by Delamere. There's not much about now, too cold, but it's great up there, our Zoe, it's . . .'

He could find no words to describe the beauty, wild and unbroken, of the huge open spaces, which he tramped to search for his birds.

'Can I come with you, Jamie?' she pleaded.

He had been reluctant. He was strong, nearly a man, and what did he want with a bit of a judy hanging about his neck, especially his sister? But her look of yearning had touched something within him, and he had given in.

That first day, that Sunday, had been almost mild. They had shed their jackets as they leaped from one tussocky hummock to the next, and Jamie had been surprised at the merriment which teased his sister's face. He had seen her laugh out loud for the first time, as a sheep leapt a foot into the air at their approach. He had watched her delight as the magnificence of the uplands unfolded before her, and had seen the harsh grief replaced by childish enjoyment of the moment.

She had been almost content that night, as she cooked their evening meal, and even the usual jibes from Sarah had gone unnoticed.

Now they tramped together almost every weekend, and thanks to Zoe's industry, and Jamie's new job in the dockyard, they were dressed in warm, comfortable garments, and good thick boots. Zoe was also working: only at home, but she had insisted on keeping a small part of her tiny wage. The two sisters had fought like tom cats, lifting enquiring heads all along the street, but Zoe won. With her few pence, and what Jamie could give her, she had bought wool, and knitted two bright jumpers, with hats and scarves to match.

The rag-and-bone man, the same one who had trundled the streets when she was an infant, was carried away by her enchanting manners and large, sorrow-filled eyes. He had found her two pairs of breeches, God knows from where, and boots for them both, plus two rucksacks, and a small ground-sheet. They were well-equipped now.

'What's that smoke, Jamie?' she asked, 'Just over to the left there? It seems to be coming from those trees.'

He woke from his peaceful reverie.

'Dunno,' he mused. 'Looks like an estate or summat. Them's chimneys I suppose.'

They stared intently until their eyes watered, then, losing interest, devoured their 'doorsteps'.

Again they sat and dreamed.

Suddenly, awkwardly, Jamie spoke.

'D'yer like it 'ere, our kid? Wha' I mean is . . . well . . . are yer . . . D'yer feel berrer, like, after . . . yer know . . . ?'

His mind, unused to thoughts of any depth, stumbled.

Zoe turned her face away from him, and the sadness masked it again, then she shook herself, and sighed.

'Yes, I feel better now, Jamie,' she answered quietly.

There was silence again, broken only by the soft cry of a pigeon from the distant wood.

'I know yer . . . thought a lorrer about 'er,' he continued, his tongue agonising on how to say the words, 'bur I wondered if praps . . . wi' us comin' 'ere an' all . . . well . . . you was 'appier.'

Her brilliant look fell on him. Then she leaned over and touched his hand.

'Yes, Jamie, you have made me . . . better. Since I came up here with you I've been . . .'

She turned away. How to tell him of the healing, the mending of her broken spirit, which the hours on the moor had accomplished?

'I don't know, Jamie. I only know that if it were not for these days we have had up here, I'd be . . .'

They both ducked their heads now, in embarrassment, for they were brother and sister, twelve and fourteen, too young to have ease in words. But they understood each other.

Zoe felt as though the moor had laid a spell on her. From

being just a dream world into which she escaped after Daly's death, it had become the only world in which she felt at home, in which she was herself again, the self which had once been happy with Daly.

March blew itself out in blustery days, which whipped her hair about her head, and swept her across the greening turf, and rough crevassed boulders, like a wisp of grass.

April. May.

In June Jamie saw a golden eagle.

In July, Zoe met the lady.

She had walked briskly across the springy turf of the rise, coming at last to the top of the highest peak of the moor. A tumble of weather-worn rocks, rough-pitted, grey, black-veined, spilled in a half circle and tipped over the edge of the knoll, tumbling to rest down the opposite slope.

A patch of clover, the small perfect flowers brushed by the breeze, made a carpet of flowing colour; as Zoe passed by she hesitated, then knelt and inhaled deeply of the mingled scents of flowers and turf, soil and clear air. Refreshed she got up and walked quickly across the small plateau until she reached the scattered rocks.

Zoe's appearance was vastly different from the dainty little girl Joanna Dale had created. Gone were the muslin and shady hat, gone the white socks and green satin ribbons. Gone was the cascade of curls: her hair now lay in a cap of feathery curls about her finely-shaped skull, turning in soft tendrils around the nape of her neck and over her ears. How could she climb and run with Jamie when her hair was for ever in the way? And so she had cut if off.

She sat down on the sun-warmed surface, her back against a boulder worn by wind, rain and age into a comfortable resting place, and let her dreaming eyes roam the panorama before her. The moors stretched for ever, rolling away to the horizon like a verdant ocean, rising and falling. To the north was the smudged outline of Ellesmere Port, a brown shapeless blur from which the sun reflected pinpoints of gilded light. Further west, almost invisible on the line between earth and sky, was the haze which hung over Runcorn; in the east the silky dark green carpet of the Delamere forest.

Shining like a silver ribbon, the River Chess wound between the folds of green and brown and purple and yellow, the patchwork of colours all that could be seen of grass, heather and gorse. It disappeared into the woods on the edge of Weston Hall Estate, and emerged glinting in the village beyond.

Zoe watched the lark, its fluttering shape hardly more than a blurred speck against the brilliant blue of the summer sky. Its liquid notes fell sweetly on her ear. A spiral of smoke wisped gently in the motionless air; it rose in a thin column from the centre of the distant trees. She knew, now, that it came from one of the many chimneys of the Hall.

She felt in the pocket of her breeches and brought out an apple, and a piece of cheese roughly wrapped in a handkerchief, and taking a bite from each in turn, munched appreciatively.

Her attention was caught by a movement in the still, far-off peace. She watched as the dot grew bigger, moving towards the moor along the beaten path until it was identified as a horse and rider.

Closer and closer, larger and larger, it became, a magnificent black hunter whose rider lay low over his neck, lips close to his ears as he pounded the turf. Zoe's heart beat faster.

Taking ditches, stone walls, boulders, the horse never faltered: with a start, Zoe realised that the pair would be upon her in minutes. Instinctively, overwhelmed by shyness, she cast around for a place to hide.

A shallow crevice between roughly-shaped rocks caught her eye, and without hesitation she slipped into it, scraping her chin on the harsh surface as she ducked her head.

She could hear the chink of the horse's tack as it slowed to a walk, and the 'hummph, hummph' of its breath, as the great heart and lungs quieted. A creak of leather told her the rider had dismounted, and boots trod the grass to the same boulder where Zoe had lain dreaming.

Then all was quiet again, save for the soft sound of bird and insect, and the horse cropping the grass.

Five minutes passed, then ten.

Zoe burrowed deeper into her hiding place, her back and leg muscles cramped, the blood from her scraped chin dripping on to the soft red wool of her jumper. She dare not move: the gap between the rocks was barely deep enough to hide her. But a groan made her beating heart leap into her throat, and she almost jumped up. Then an anguish of weeping filled the air. Zoe heard the horse raise his head and move restlessly. She peered out.

The woman rider turned, the horse backed, and Zoe stood up.

The woman was the first to recover. She rose slowly, her face swollen and wet with tears.

'What are you doing here?' The words were soft, still blurred with the storm of her weeping.

Zoe cleared her throat nervously.

Who was this woman? What should she say to her? Perhaps she was trespassing here, and would be in trouble. She wished Jamie was with her. She took a step forward, conscious of the blood crusting her chin, the grass and earth on her breeches. Her huge eyes stared at the woman imploringly.

For an instant the sorrow the woman and girl both knew became a link between them, recognised as it had been so many years ago, by little Zoe and Joanna. Then the woman sank once more to the rocky seat.

'Come and sit with me,' she said. 'This place is made for people who . . . need peace.'

She patted the rock beside her, and Zoe walked slowly across the turf and sat beside her. For several moments they did not speak, and Zoe felt enfolded by a great calm.

Then the woman asked gently, 'What are you doing up here, child?' Zoe's profile almost made her catch her breath: with the plain woman's reverence for another's loveliness,

136

she gazed at her. 'What's your name? Do you come from around here?'

Zoe turned at last, looking shyly into the kind, still damp and swollen eyes of the woman beside her, and suddenly she felt the last of her grief and rage at Joanna's death fall away. Her fear left her and the last step back to normality, begun by Jamie, was taken.

'My name is Zoe Taylor, ma'am,' she said in her well-modulated voice. 'I live in Liverpool and I come up here whenever I can. I love it. I find that the emptiness . . . the . . .'

The woman noticed the hesitation and with an intuition of the girl's heartache bred from her own sorrow, spoke quickly.

'Never mind, my dear. Tell me another time, when you are more able.' She gently patted Zoe's hand. 'I understand what it's like to lose a loved one.' Zoe stirred, for the first time aware of another's pain. The woman smiled. 'So this is a favourite place of yours, Zoe.'

'Oh yes, ma'am. It's so peaceful and . . . empty. I feel close to . . .' She stopped, her eyes clouding a little.

A warm, almost loving expression lit the face of the stranger and once more Zoe was comforted. Then they both stood up, and walked slowly towards the horse, the woman draping the train of her riding habit across her arm. They were silent for a moment, wondering at the peace they had found together, the woman and the child, separated in age by fifteen years.

'Good-bye, ma'am.'

'Good-bye, Zoe.'

With an effortless grace, the figure in black mounted the horse. She looked down at Zoe, the traces of her own sorrow almost gone, and smiled again.

Zoe smiled back, then, shading her eyes against the rays of the sinking sun, watched the horse and rider pick their way down the slope and break into a canter, then a furious gallop, towards the distant chimneys of Weston Hall.

She watched until they dwindled to the tiny speck which

she had first seen only an hour before. Then, turning back to her nest of rocks, she sat once more, her heart lighter than it had been for months.

Chapter Seventeen

Sir Jonathan Weston and Patricia Wentworth had married in June 1913. It was a marriage he had not wanted; indeed had fought against for many months.

The Westons had lived at Weston Hall for nearly four hundred years. The estate and title had been granted to Sir Jonathan's ancestor by Elizabeth I, and the family had prospered. The village had grown around the Hall, cottages for the farm workers, and as the estate grew good husbandry had produced farms which thrived, and a community close-knit and prospering.

Sir Jonathan's father altered all that.

Sir Phillip was a gambler. The estate, rich and prosperous in 1889 when he had inherited it, was ruinously in debt by 1912 when he died, the life he had led for twenty-three years making him a mental and physical wreck.

Sir Jonathan, his heir at twenty-one, knew he had only one course open to him. To sell what was left of his inheritance never occurred to him.

Patricia Wentworth was the only child of Sir Miles Wentworth, the head of an Old Northumbrian family whose estate was so vast, that Jonathan could have placed his own in one corner of it quite comfortably. And for Miles mining ventures brought in a vast income. In 1907 Patricia had been the most sought after debutante of the season. She was, alas, also the plainest. Worse still in many people's view she was more than intelligent, with no illusions as to why she was so popular.

She was twenty-one when she met Sir Jonathan, just after the death of his father, at a party given by mutual friends during the 'little season', where she had been cajoled by her tearful mother to 'try just once more'.

Jonathan was on leave from his regiment, careless and amusing, for he was not yet aware of his father's debts. He was one of the handsomest men she had ever seen, with a whimsical sense of humour which delighted her, and he seemed to enjoy her company. She was not to know that it was his natural good manners which made him incapable of slighting the plain, sensitive girl who made him laugh, nor that the pretty girl he had hoped to see at the party had been laid low with a migraine.

His charm was her undoing, and Patricia loved him from the first moment. He found her pleasant, a good dancer, and with a surprising sense of fun which matched his own, but that was all. He was a hedonistic man, loving good food and wine, a well-bred horse, a pretty woman – but, most of all, the splendid acres of his home.

They met on several occasions during the next few months: he was polite and attentive for five minutes or so, before passing on to the most attractive woman in the room. It did not occur to him how ideally suited she was to be his wife – and his saviour – until the realisation of his financial position was at last brought home to him by the family solicitor.

'You must sell Weston Hall, Sir Jonathan,' he had announced, and the full picture of his father's last downhill race to ruin was made known to him.

To his credit he did not then seek Patricia out deliberately. He was still searching feverishly for some way to save his home, and even when they met again, and the thought was placed in his mind by a friend and brother officer – 'By God, Jonty, she'd get you out of your pickle' – he pushed it from him with repugnance. But the idea of making love to a woman to whom he was not attracted seemed to be the only barrier, and he considered it bleakly.

He had no choice and he knew it.

He courted her with a correctness which drove her wild, for she was of a passionate nature and would have made him an ideal bed partner had he known it, but she bided her time, certain that on their wedding night, when all restraint was gone, the very passion which she felt for him would kindle the same feelings within him. She would have given herself to him at any time during their short courtship, but the bland affection he showed her, and the slight stiffness in their infrequent embraces, kept her at arm's length.

She was under no illusion that he was marrying her for love. She did not care that he was not. Her love for him was as wild and boundless as the moor on which he lived.

Her wedding night and all those that followed were a bitter disappointment to her. He took her considerately, distantly. She was so inexperienced, yet so much in love, she was afraid to give way to the passion she felt for fear of his reaction.

It was from this self-doubt that their marriage foundered on their first night together. He had never, in their years together, been anything but kind to her, but that was the crowning insult, for it implied only indifference.

She had borne him four daughters in four consecutive years, the youngest conceived on the last night of his final leave before he sailed for France, in September 1917.

For over three years he had served with gallantry, as she knew he would, and had been decorated twice. Then, on March 21st 1918, during the last battle òf the Somme, the end of the war came for Jonathan; he was invalided home with a shattered leg to the care of his blessedly thankful wife.

She had carried the hope in her heart that after nearly four years of war, of separation from the life he loved, and from his children, he would perhaps return with joy, not only to his home, but to his wife's longing arms and heart.

Once more she was to be disappointed. He returned to her, to her bed and to her loving arms, but still he eluded her, made love to her mechanically. Afterwards, she would lie by his side while he slept, and wonder if the son he longed for had been conceived that night. But even a son was no guarantee that Jonathan would love her.

One day he would fall in love with another woman. She

knew it, and waited as if she wished it upon herself, living the pain of it before she was wounded, anticipating the suffering like a patient about to lose a limb.

Lady Weston trotted the stallion across the fields which lay to the back of the Hall, leaving behind the path which followed the sheep tracks across the moors, and through the miles of woodland which surrounded the house. Her mind was still on the girl she had met up on Black Tor Crag and her nod was absent-minded, though her smile sweet, as she threw the reins to the waiting groom.

Lady Pat, as she was incorrectly and affectionately known to all her servants, entered the house through the 'back door', an arched porch from the stable yard leading to a passage which in turn led into the main hall.

The hall was large and square with dark, polished panelling, reflecting the dancing flames from the enormous fireplace. The staircase rose from the centre to the high, hammer-beamed roof and was richly carpeted in dark red. A tapestry stirred on the wall as Lady Pat passed by, and she paused, the beauty never failing to move her, even after so many years.

Lady Pat loved her home with an intensity which matched her husband's, and would always be grateful to him for having brought her here, if for the wrong reasons.

She turned the handle of the door opposite the fireplace, and entered her husband's favourite room, where he spent most of his spare time. Three of the walls were lined with handsomely-bound books; almost the whole of the fourth was taken up by an enormous bay window, a deep cushioned seat filling the recess. The view across the park-land to the woods was magnificent, the rolling grassland kept short by the fallow deer which cropped quietly, undisturbed by the sounds of the lawn mower, or by men's voices. Below the window lay terraces; steps and paved walks led down to the lawn.

The leather chairs were deep and comfortable; numerous small tables were strewn with newspapers, opened books and pipes. Sir Jonathan sat close to the fire, two golden retrievers at his feet, his legs stretched to the warmth of the blaze, resting on the crested fire dogs, for even in summer this room was always cold.

The years of war had touched him lightly. The active life he led kept him straight and supple; his hair was darkly vital, and the lines on his face only added to his masculine beauty. His eyes were a deep, glowing brown.

He turned as his wife entered the room and smiled the courteous smile she knew so well.

'Good morning, my dear. Had a good ride? I must say it seems to have done you good – the colour in your cheeks is most attractive.' The friendly smile deepened. 'How about a sherry before lunch?'

He made a movement to rise but she checked him.

'Don't get up Jonty, I can do it.' He only had to pay her some small compliment, and she was a girl again, hopeful and confident in her naïvety. After all these years of disillusionment, she thought, he still has the power, and despair returned.

The dogs rose to greet her, waving their plumy tails, and touched her skirt with their soft noses as she crossed the room, then returned to Jonathan to flop before the fire. She poured them each a glass of sherry and sank into the chair opposite him, her longing concealed as always. They sat sipping peacefully. Though Jonathan did not love his wife, he had come to regard her as a friend, and was at ease with her. She made no demands on him, and the twice-weekly calls he made to her bedroom seemed agreeable to them both. He had always been deeply grateful to her for the lavish amount of money which she had poured into the estate, through her marriage settlement. She had saved his home, and he cared about her and her happiness.

And he wanted a son.

'Well I must say, you seem to have left a part of you behind on the moor,' he laughed now. 'A penny for 'em.'

She smiled, looking at him fully for the first time.

143

'I'm sorry, darling.' She paused, collecting her thoughts. 'I met the most extraordinary child this morning, up on Black Tor Crag.'

'Oh? In what way extraordinary?'

'Well, not the sort of youngster one expects to meet so far in the wilds. To be on her own out there, she must have walked for miles. And amazingly beautiful. Comes from Liverpool, she says. She was dressed in boy's clothes, very slim, with short hair. I suppose that's her protection, the casual passerby would hardly believe that she was female. About twelve or thirteen, I suppose, but absolutely lovely.'

'She certainly seems to have made an impression on you, my dear.' She was staring into the fire. 'You're in a real brown study,' he laughed.

Lady Pat looked up at the handsome face, still drawn from the pain he had suffered, but so beautiful. Oh God, how she loved him. She caught her breath as he looked at her quizzically.

'Yes, she has made an impression on me,' she said seriously at last. 'I don't really know why. I felt . . . as if she was to become something to me . . . does that sound mad? I can't explain it. It is as if we were to be linked in some way. She was so sad . . . so anguished about something. I was drawn to her.'

For a moment her own pain was almost revealed, and Jonathan felt uncomfortable. Then she laughed and stood up. 'I'm being a fool, my dear. Just nosy. Come on, let's have lunch. I'm hungry after my ride.'

She stretched out her hands, her skin prickling as his strong, warm fingers grasped hers, and she pulled him gently from the chair. Linking her arm through his, she slowed to his limping gait as they made their way to the breakfast room where their usual light, buffet meal was laid out.

They took their time over lunch, discussing the affairs of the estate. But standing like a patient ghost at her elbow the warmth of the girl she had met that day haunted Lady

Pat as she and Jonathan played out the charade which was to become more and more familiar to them over the years.

Chapter Eighteen

The second battle of the Marne in July 1918 was the first sign that ascendancy had definitely passed into the hands of the Allies, and as advance followd advance it became clear that the tide of war was turning. By October, the imminent collapse of the German army was expected.

Arnie Levy had provided Zoe with her first job. She worked for six hours a day, finishing trousers at a pennyfarthing a pair. She could have earned more, for as the war progressed, so wages rose, but she would have been required to work in the factory, and even Sarah, with her resourceful ingenuity, could not persuade Arnie that she was fourteen, so she worked at home.

It was still khaki, as the war dragged on into its fourth year. The fabric was heavy and seemed durable, until it got wet, when it collapsed like paper in a rain puddle. The uniforms were churned out as fast as they could be made. Hundreds of dozens a week. They did not last long in the trenches.

From a tiny workroom above a pawn shop, Arnie had enlarged his business into a sweat shop at the back of the munitions factory. He employed a hundred women and girls, besides the dozens of outworkers who sewed in the half-light of their own firesides.

The first indication of something momentous on that November day was the startling boom of maroons, fired from fire brigade and police stations.

Then the bells began to ring, and ships' sirens sent their joyous news across the rooftops of Liverpool. For a brief moment there was utter silence in the dingy room, as machines came to a halt, and the subdued chatter of a hundred women's voices were still. They looked about them questioningly.

Then a woman began to cry, and in a moment, as the realisation washed over them, they were all in tears. They didn't need the confirmation from the wet-faced overlooker who had been having a stealthy fag in the yard, and had been told of the news by a passing,' deliriously waving constable.

It was over. It was over.

They cried and laughed and leaped into the air, hugging each other as they blew their streaming noses on scraps of material.

Their voices rose high into the cobwebbed blackness of the rafters and Arnie Levy's delivery man grunted cynically as he put the small van into gear and set off up Derby Road towards his first pickup of the afternoon in Love Lane.

His name was Arthur. The first time he had seen Zoe he could not tear his eyes from her young, slender beauty as her sister had taken the bundle of work from him. She was slim, her tiny waist would have fitted into the circle made by his two hands; he knew that, if only he had the chance to put it to the test, and her small-breasted body, clad that day in the cream shantung of her 'best dress', shook his big frame with tremors that did not subside until he was a mile away in the van.

Arthur was married to a woman who had borne him four sons and five daughters, and, without complaint, his nightly attentions for twelve years. They were the same age, thirty-three, but she looked twenty years older. An' she does it as if she was twenty years older an' all, he would mutter to himself.

Now, of his five daughters, two were pretty and slim, and when the elder of the two was six years old, he took her into the privvy at the back of the house and raped her.

He never did it again. The sobbing little girl told her mother, and just once, in the long and violent years of their marriage, she stood up to her bull-like husband. She threatened him with the 'bobbies'. He hit her, and the

148

children ran screaming from him. He had liked the flat, tender, young flesh, and he was incensed that it was to be denied him.

Now he wanted the kid in Love Lane.

His mouth would salivate fiercely, whenever he saw her, and his 'thingy' would grow huge, and erect, and hurt like hell. At first he would just suffer it and groan, and when he fell into bed at night beside his flaccid wife, he would pound her flesh with his, until the floor shook and the children who slept beside them and in the room below, would awaken, and sigh resignedly, wishing that Da' would be quick and let them get back to sleep.

For months he had done this, his flesh crawling with longing to be next to that of the flawless child. Each time he called at the house she would be there, eyes averted from his, as she took the bundle and gave him her own finished work, and he would wish her brother, who was always there, a million miles away. If he could just get her alone, he was sure he could persuade her to . . . to let him look . . . at her . . . whatsit. Perhaps just a touch between . . . His breath would come fast, and ragged, and the sweat would stand out on his beefy face, dripping and slipping across his red cheeks into his moustache. His trousers would tighten uncomfortably about him, and he cursed the day he saw her, for since that day, he had known no peace.

His temper, always peevish, became drawn, tight as a fiddle string.

On Armistice day, Jamie was late home from work.

Arthur knocked on the door almost indifferently. He wasn't coming here again. He'd had enough of this torment, he told himself, though he did not use those words. He'd been sniffing after this little bitch for months now, and for what? Nowt. It was enough to drive a man to drink, and he'd be buggered if he were goin' to purrup wi' it any longer.

His expression was petulant. When the door opened a fraction, he had convinced himself that this would be his last pickup here, and he had had enough of this sly piece leading him on, and that he might, just might be able to get their Mildred to go into the privvy with him for sixpence, without splittin' to their Mam.

Zoe was now thirteen. In the two years since she had left Pinehurst Place, she had hardly spoken to anyone in the street. Each day, as the others left, she would begin a conversation with herself and with Joanna, speaking in the clear, cultivated manner which life with Joanna had taught her. She was determined not to let the 'Liverpudlian', 'the scouser', return to her tongue, for she had sworn in the first six months of her return that she would escape again one day. To what?

To something better than this, she thought, looking round the shabby room. As she sewed the coarse khaki trousers, she dreamed of soft, green carpets and pretty rose-strewn curtains, of white towels and yellow soap and talcum powder, and of a kind face which somehow was becoming more and more mixed up with that of the lady on the moor.

She sighed, then smiled a little. One day she would have it all again . . .

Someone knocked aggressively at the door.

He turned towards the opening door and there she was, in all her delicate loveliness. Mildred slipped from his thoughts like water through a sieve. He stood as if poleaxed. She was alone. By God she was alone.

Zoe smiled tentatively at him. 'Just a minute,' she said, and walked gracefully across the room. Reaching for the neat bundle of trousers which she had finished the day before, she leaned over the table. Arthur stared at the slim outline of her buttocks and the fragility of her ankles. Before she could turn round, he was in the room, closing the door quietly behind him. So quietly did he step, and so gently did he shut the door, that only the sudden absence of the shaft of light which fell through it made Zoe aware of what was happening.

Zoe wheeled round and felt the first flutter of fear. She stared at him from huge eyes and her mouth dropped open.

'All alone, are we?' Arthur asked softly.

The fear became terror.

As he spoke it occurred to him that the boy might be upstairs.

Quick as thought, he went to the bottom of the staircase and called hoarsely, 'Are you there, boy?' ready to dart back, ready with some words, some excuse, should there be an answer.

There was none.

Arthur looked at Zoe as a cat watches a mouse in a corner.

'Well, well. And where's the lad, then? Not home yet? Of course, it's the celebrations, I bet. It's 'eld 'im up, I'll be bound. Dancin' in't streets.'

For an instant, Zoe's ashen face showed bewilderment, and he saw that she did not know.

'War's ower, lass,' he said amiably. 'Didn't yer know? Everyone's celebratin', like. Dancin' and drinkin' and kissin'. Ow about you an' me 'avin' our own little celebration, eh? Ow about a kiss?'

He began to move slowly towards her, and she could smell his rancid sweat. The bulge in his trousers grew enormous, and he stopped and stroked it gently with a thick forefinger.

'Thingy wants to come out for a kiss, too,' he said obscenely, and began to unbutton his flies.

She watched as though she lay under a spell, frozen by terror to the spot beside the table. Someone ran past the tiny curtained window and the shadow cast by the moving figure touched the quiet tableau in the room. Someone was whistling, 'Goodbye-ee, Goodbye-ee,' and the fire in the grate moved, shaking up a tiny flame. Zoe could hear bells now, pealing for joy in the distance, and a ship's hooter.

'Listen,' the man said. 'Listen to 'em celebratin'. Our turn now, Chuck.'

His breath hissed as he laughed, and the thing swayed slowly from side to side as he moved towards her.

She began to gibber, her fear so great she could get no

clear word out. As he drew near, the dancing flame shadow was blocked off, and the light in her eyes went out.

Now his hand was on her shoulder and he stroked the fabric of her woollen jumper with a quivering, sweaty palm. His fingers touched the white, defenceless skin of her neck and his other hand fumbled suddenly beneath the hem of her skirt.

He was breathing hoarsely, and his voice took on a chanting rhythm that moved with him as his body began to sway backwards and forwards.

'That's it, that's it . . . lovely . . . good girl . . . lovely. Don't move, pet. Give it to Arthur . . . good girl . . . lovely . . . just a bit more . . . good girl.'

He was gentling her, like a high-bred filly, calming her, hypnotising her with the sighing of his words.

Her scream was wild and piercing as his fingers found the elastic of her knickers, startling him, for he thought she was acquiescent. He took a blundering step backwards, as his hands came off her with a 'No, I didn't touch her, constable,' gesture, she screamed again, high, like a rabbit in a trap, and darted to one side, slipping past him towards the glowing fire. He tried to block her off, but her fear gave her wings, and she was young and slim. His fingers slipped from her arm as she reached the door and panic took him as she wrestled with the catch.

She musn' get out, she musn't get out.

He reached her just as her shaking fingers had obeyed the message from her numbed brain, and had lifted the latch. Silently he pulled her from the door, and as the last vestige of sane thought emptied from his brain, he reached down and slipped the bolt. She tried to run, though by now her mind had gone mercifully into the shadows, but he hit her dispassionately across the mouth, drawing blood. He smiled when he saw it, and leaning forward, licked the bright, red flower with a thick, coated tongue, before fastening his mouth across the girl's soft lips. In the last second before the darkness came over her, she tried to jerk away from the gag across her mouth, but he hit her again, and the red welts rose across her bleached skin.

It took fifteen minutes for Mick Hughes to decide to break down the Taylors' door. He had been their neighbour for ten years, and he and his missus were accustomed to all manner of noises, from the fretful to the violently angry. But Zoe's scream was different. He looked at Nelly and stood up, pushing his chair back from the table.

'That kid on 'er own?'

'Eh, I dunno,' his wife answered anxiously.

They looked at each other indecisively, and Mick scratched his stomach. Then another cry of anguish rang eerily through the cracked bricks of the adjoining wall.

Mick took a step towards the door.

'That scream don' sit right wi' me. Think I'll jus' take a gander . . . he gets more boozed up every day. Not tharr I'm gonner stick me nose, but still . . .'

His voice trailed away as his mind leapt from one possibility to another.

He opened his own front door and walked the few paces to the Taylors' window. Shading his eyes, he tried to peer through the flimsy curtain.

He could see nothing, just an orange glow from the range. He knocked on the door. Silence. Mick stood for a moment, then turned away uncertainly. Had Zeb Taylor gone too far this time, and felled that bonny kid of his with a drunken blow, or had they all gone out after raising the dead with their bloody screaming? His fleshy mouth was pursed, as his brain tried to come to some conclusion. He was not a clever, or an educated man, but he felt uneasy. He fancied something was wrong, but it was quiet and peaceful now, and a doubt grew in him.

Perhaps it wasn't her, perhaps . . .

It was then that he noticed Arnie Levy's van.

At once the hair rose on his scalp. Something was wrong. What was that van doing there all this time? That Arthur only picked up at Taylors', so why was he parked so long?

He stared suspiciously about him, as though to find an

153

answer. At that moment Colly Baldwin, who lived on the other side of the Taylors, poked his head from his front door.

'Hey, Mick,' he said cheerfully, 'what's up? Old Zeb bin at the strap, like? Me an' missus heard summat a while back.'

The bells pealed once more, and a ship's siren shrieked. Both men stared in the direction of the dockyard, then looked at each other and grinned sheepishly.

'Were it the bluddy siren we 'eard, then Mick?' said Colly.

Mick shrugged. 'Could be.' Once more, he turned to the window.

The net moved a fraction. He was about to turn away, fretful with his own nervousness, when a blur of white caught his attention in the corner of the room. It seemed to stand against the dark wood on the stairway. What the hell was it? It did not move, but the white seemed shadowed here and there. For a second he stood, mystified. His breath sighed from between his lips as he stared. He blinked his eyes as the whiteness was covered by something . . .

With a bellow to Colly he was at the door.

Mick and Colly were big men, strong and muscled from years of heavy work on the docks. With a crash, the door burst open at the third blow. The two men fell into the room, and crowding in on their heels came neighbours who not long ago had jeered as Zoe had been forced in here by Sarah.

They did not jeer now. They were brought to a stunned halt by what they saw, and for the space of five seconds the only sound in the room was the pleasing crackle of the fire, and the horrendous grunts which came from the man in the corner. He sounded like a pig at a trough. Clothes were strewn about the room and the smell of fear and lust caught at their throats.

Zoe stood naked in the corner, wicked red welts puffing her face. She was staring blindly above the head of the man who knelt before her, his trousers flung on the floor. He moved rythmically and his penis, huge and throbbing, stood out before him.

There was a shuddering silence. Then, with a great roar of outrage, the two men were on him. Zoe stood alone. She stretched out each arm along the wall, crucified by shame and horror, and a woman at the back of the room began to weep.

Mick's wife pushed her way through the crowd and grabbing the chenille tablecloth wrapped it tenderly around the trembling girl and led her from the house.

Mick and Colly had Arthur between them now. Struggling and cursing. For a moment they looked at each other.

'Who's first?' said Mick softly.

Arthur was found by a passing police constable late that evening, half-dead on a dungheap several streets away. A dozen people had passed him by, but not one had gone near him. He was still naked. His van was parked beside him. He lay on his back, breathing loudly through his mashed and bloody nose though it would have been hard to find it in the mess of his face. His teeth shone in the blood. The skin of his body was black and purple and someone had methodically kicked his genitals until they resembled a red and bursting football.

Jamie had done that in the maddened, guilt ridden, grief which had almost drowned him when he looked into Zoe's dead eyes.

He had kicked and kicked as he wept, and his boots had become bloody before Mick had stopped him. Revenge yes. Murder no.

Arthur's screams had been gagged by Colly's hand and the crowd, men and women had watched dispassionately.

They took care of their own, did Merseysiders.

Chapter Nineteen

She shivered as she walked. The jumper she wore was misted with rain; her feet in their ankle-length boots squished at each step, and the water oozed away to join the puddles which formed in the uneven pattern of the flagstone. Her hair stuck to her head in a dense mat of wet curls, its colour dimmed by the moisture which dripped in a rhythm with her striding footsteps. Her face ran with water, and she blinked constantly to clear the raindrops from her eye-lashes.

She was in Birkenhead now. She had crossed the river by ferry, gripping the rails of the *Iris* with hands that gleamed in the half-light of the rain-drenched day, and her still, upright form drew curious glances as she stared indifferently at the receding bulk of the Liver Building.

She walked on, staring ahead with blank, drowned eyes. The rain beat down mercilessly from a heavy, grey sky on the empty streets.

A red bus came by, the lights inside warm and comforting. It was about to pass her when she suddenly turned and with her arm stretched out stiffly almost flung herself into its path.

The driver cursed and brought the lumbering vehicle to a screeching halt.

The conductor, who had been flung backwards, banging his shoulder against the rail, stared at the dripping young girl as she stepped on to the platform.

'Yer wanner watch that, Queen,' he declared, 'You'll cause a bluddy accident one of these days.' He followed her up the swaying bus. 'Where to, kidder?'

The girl turned towards him, and the look that filled her

eyes, wild and lost, stopped him in his tracks. She told him where she wished to go.

Through the outskirts of Birkenhead, Bebbington, and Ellesmore Port, the bus rolled steadily onwards, parting the curtain of rain. The last few houses disappeared, and they were in the cold, bleak moorland.

It was grey here, where it had once been green. The yellow and purple of the gorse had gone, leaving only drabness, and wet mouldering stalks of bracken. Even the hardy sheep had taken shelter in dips and hollows, and under rocks.

The young girl stood up, and moved along the aisle towards the platform. The conductor automatically rang the bell and the driver brought the bus to a stop. He turned in his seat and peered backwards, as though to confirm that some daft bugger really was getting off here, in the middle of nowhere. He saw the conductor speak to the girl who had stopped his bus so dramatically in Birkenhead. In a moment she had leaped from the platform, and was running wildly on to the short, rain-plastered grass and along the path which led into the heart of the moorland.

The party of men and boys, some from Weston, and others from villages nearby, began the search just before two o'clock, though it was already nearly dark.

It had taken the inspector almost an hour to convince the local constabulary that the conductor on the Liverpool to Chester bus was a steady, reliable chap, and that if he said a young girl was out alone on the bleak moorland in the dead of winter; that she had jumped from his bus in extreme agitation, and disappeared; then it was not a matter to be taken lightly.

Sam Ludlow was in charge of the party. He was a groom up at the Hall, and knew the moors which surrounded the village like the inside of his own stable. He exercised his lordship's fine stallion up there, and took the two little girls on their fat ponies on the gentle slopes at the back of the estate, for her ladyship believed in starting them young.

Besides he was a local man. He had been born and bred in Weston.

They started at the back of the Hall, beating the gorse and shouting. Not that they were likely to find her so close to the estate, but you've got to start somewhere, said Sam, who was a methodical man, an' yer never know.

There were twenty of them to start with, including his lordship, who had insisted that Sam took charge: he was a countryman, and the best for the job.

Walking among them was a stranger. Jamie never told them the missing girl was his sister. He had known from the first frantic realisation that she had gone that this was where she would be. But which part of the vast expanse they had tramped together would she make for?

For an hour they moved across the rough grassland, falling across piles of stones and tumbled walls, tripping in the dusk into pools of rainwater, cursing the weather, shouting in an effort to keep in touch. The dogs they had brought, including his lordship's two retrievers, Candy and Floss, barked excitedly, as they lifted quivering noses to pierce the air for rabbit, and the musky smell of sheep.

Soon the men were only blurred figures to each other in the mist, and by four o'clock they could see only the shimmering torches held above the heads of the tallest. Reluctantly, for the thought of the lass alone in these conditions appalled them, they stopped and made their way back to the Hall, dragging the strange boy with them, for he had wanted to go on alone.

They stood in a semi-circle about the kitchen door. With a furtive look about him, as the others stamped their feet and drank the generous tots which his lordship poured for them, Jamie slipped into the stable and settled himself in the warm straw which lined the loft, listening to the horses' movements, and comforting, snorting breaths. He took the bread and cheese which he had stuffed into his pocket, and ate it, though he had no appetite. He intended to be on the moor at first light and bugger the rest.

He'd find her.

The girl in the crevice between the two rocks, black now with darkening rain, heard the noises made by the men and dogs. She opened her eyes, and the rain fell on them, making her blink.

She smiled and murmured, 'It's all right, Daly, they've gone now.'

It was his lordship who found her, just before noon the next day. It was still raining on to her flower-like face, and he thought she was dead. Her skin was the colour of pearl, and the beautiful symmetry of the bones beneath her flesh, and the parted colourless lips, caught at his breath. He sank to his knees beside her and took her hand. It fluttered like a feather caught in the breeze, and he chafed it gently, overcome suddenly with an urge to lift the lifeless body and hold it against his own, to breathe his warm breath into her slightly open mouth.

The men were still beating the bushes nearby, and he shouted urgently to them.

Jamie was the first to reach him.

'Quick, lad, help me. We must get her warm. Bring the rucksack round. That's right. There are dry blankets in it.'

Without words the man and boy stripped the sodden clothes from the still, white body of the girl and wrapped her like a mummy. Then, followed by the rest of the party, they carried her down from the plateau, across the rock-strewn ground, and along the soggy, squelching path until they reached the meadows behind the Hall.

Swiftly they crossed the sodden grass and passed through the gate into the stable yard. A bright oblong of light spilled from the open kitchen door.

'Bring her in, quickly.'

Lady Pat bent over the slender bundle. For an instant she did not recognise the face which was swathed in grey blankets, hardly seeming larger than that of an infant. Then she gasped.

'Jonty, it's her!'

'Who?' he said, bewildered.

'That child, Zoe, the one I saw on the moor.'

He shifted impatiently. 'Well, never mind that now, Pat. Let's get the poor kid into a warm bed or she'll never make it. She's nearly gone now. Is the Doc here yet?'

'He's on his way, darling. Johnson went for him as soon as the boy told us you had found her.'

Zoe was gently carried up the beautiful staircase, and into a large bedroom on the first floor where a maid was putting coal on to an already crackling fire. The cream curtains, painted with tiny pink rosebuds, were drawn against the dark of the November afternoon, and the soft pink carpet glowed. The bedclothes were drawn back for an instant, and the stone hot water bottles, wrapped in flannel, were moved to the side as the slender, naked body of the unconscious girl was placed within it.

Jonathan drew in his breath as the exquisite form lay exposed for a fraction of a second, then looked away. When he turned back the covers had been warmly tucked about the girl's body. He let out his breath in an inaudible sigh as the doctor walked into the room.

In the yard a quiet figure stood looking at the lights of the house. Jamie was wet to the skin and he shivered a little. For five minutes he stood, the curious looks of the men washing over him, as they made their way out of the yard and vanished into the gloom. When the yard was empty except for a boy who whistled cheerfully as he filled a bucket at the pump, he left, striking away through the meadow and on to the sodden moor.

He walked quickly, almost running, until he reached the road to Chester.

Chapter Twenty

The firelight played a game of touch and run across the polished surface of the rosewood wardrobe, leaping lightly to the window panes, black against the night sky. The warm orange glow was reflected in the oval, cheval glass which stood in the corner of the bedroom, and flickered against the ceiling. The room was bathed in the comfort of the crackling fire, and the delicate scent of the pine logs, burning splendidly.

A uniformed figure rocked rhythmically in the chair before the blaze, bright wool and needles in her hands. Her face was young, rosy, placid and her head nodded a time or two as the calm of the pleasant room, the blazing fire, and the unusual indolence overcame her. The needles slipped a fraction, and a log in the grate fell with a muted crash. In an instant her head jerked, and she looked quickly towards the bed, and the quiet form which lay there.

With a guilty start, she got quickly to her feet and crossed soundlessly on the deep pile of the carpet to the window. Her cheerful face was reflected in the glass and she grinned cheekily at herself before drawing the curtains with a quiet swish. She returned to her position before the fire and picked up her bit of knitting.

Zoe opened her eyes as the soft noise fell pleasantly upon her ear. At home with Daly, the familiar noise was the start of their day. The glide of the curtains would reveal the morning sun, or the sparkling spatter of raindrops, and Daly's loving voice would chide her as she burrowed deeper beneath the warm bedclothes.

She stretched and yawned. The room was so pretty and she was so warm, so warm and comfortable that she didn't want to get up for school. Her clouded eyes closed gently, then opened again, scanning the drift of rose-strewn curtains, the soft cream walls and the pink quilted coverlet which lay so lightly upon her. She studied the enormous copper bowl on the table beside her bed, from which roses spilled; and gypsy grass in a froth of white lace, and frowned.

Something was not quite right.

The figure before the fire moved in her chair, and as she turned her head, Zoe's pulse quickened.

It wasn't Daly. She looked about the room. Where was she? Who was the girl in the chair? And where was Daly?

A soft Yorkshire voice fell on her ear.

'Eeh, lass, yer awake, then. It's gradely to see yer open yer een. Na lay yersen quiet, while I go fetch her ladyship.'

The young girl, crisp and crackling in her immaculate apron and cap, her cheerful face beaming from one red ear to the other, dashed from the room leaving the door open, the excitement of being the bearer of the good news, driving all thoughts of the decorum instilled into her by Mrs Jones, from her young mind. At fourteen, she had been in service for a bare twelve months, and the importance of her job almost overwhelmed her. Her broad country face was creased, and her mouth pursed with satisfaction as she sped along the hallway.

Zoe's heart began to hammer now, and she felt a skim of perspiration film her skin as she tried to sit up. The room tilted alarmingly. Where was she, oh Lord, where was she? How had she come into this lovely room?

She tried to penetrate the fog in her mind. The last thing she remembered . . . remembered was . . . oh no . . . was . . . Her limbs began to thrash, and her eyes opened wide in horror, then closed tightly, to shut out what she saw. Oh no . . . not that . . . please not that . . . not . . . But Arthur's face, swollen and brutal with lust, would not leave her and she began to moan, frantically tossing her head.

The hands . . . oh, the hands . . . the eyes and the foul, foul breath . . . and the . . . oh, please God . . . let me not remember. But she could no more hold the memory away than she could command the sun not to rise. She could feel those coarse, thick-fingered hands crawl like enormous spiders, hairy and obscene across the delicate skin of her breasts, and her flesh puckered and flinched, and the shame and horror cut off her breath. Oh, God . . . oh, Daly . . . Daly . . .

She began to scream.

The sound reached the ears of the young maid as she walked deferentially behind her ladyship. They were not hurrying. She had informed M'Lady, as she had been told to do, immediately the patient awoke, and with a thrilling sense of her own importance, she was smiling happily at Lady Pat's back, as they trod the carpeted hallway.

The scream, when it reached their unprepared ears, raised the hairs on their arms and legs, and young Daisy swore later to Mrs Jones she felt her cap lift as her curls stood on end.

'Dear sweet Lord.' Lady Pat halted for an instant, then ran like a hare along the landing, the panic-stricken maid at her heels. Again the sound came, high and filled with dread. As they ran through the open doorway, Zoe was sitting up in the high double bed, her face a livid red, her open mouth drooling saliva.

Lady Pat put out a tentative hand. Zoe screamed again.

Feet came thundering up the stairs and along the landing, and Sir Jonathan moved into the room. Swiftly he crossed to the bed and bundling Daisy aside knelt down and drew the demented child against his chest.

'There . . . there . . . don't cry . . . you're safe now . . . no one will hurt you . . . ssh . . . ssh . . .'

Zoe struggled desperately. The male smell of him, his male hands . . . It was Arthur. He had come back for her. A hideous cry tore from her throat.

Other footsteps could be heard in the hallway, and figures hovered fearfully by the open door.

Jonathan turned to his wife.

'We'll have to get the Doc back, Pat. Here, take her for a minute . . .'

Lady Pat knelt quickly by the bedside, and took the struggling girl into her arms. She held her firmly, resting her cheek lightly on Zoe's head, whispering gently. At once, even before Jonathan could rise to his feet, Zoe quietened. With a sigh, she relaxed; then with a gesture of utter relief, she put her arms round Lady Pat and buried her face against her.

She murmured something. 'Day . . . oh . . . Dal . . .' Then she was quiet.

Lady Pat laid her gently back beneath the covers. Zoe's eyes flew open, wide and fearful.

'Go to sleep, child. I won't leave you.'

Zoe's eyes closed again. She slept.

Lady Pat turned to her husband her own face wet with tears. 'Oh, Jonty . . .'

Jonathan let out his breath and sagged against the table. He shook his head in disbelief. 'Something has frightened that child to the point of madness, and it doesn't take much to realise it has something to do with a man. The moment you took her, she calmed down. Poor kid, poor little devil.'

In the silence which followed, the still figures in the room and doorway came to life. Daisy hurried across to the bed and bobbed a curtsy.

'Will I bring summat . . . something for you, M'Lady?' she whispered.

Lady Pat looked at the sleeping face of the child she had met not a few months ago. She remembered the sensation which had come over her, the empathy which had seemed to exist between them, and recalled the conversation she had had with Jonty. She had told him then, rather shame-facedly, that she had felt the child would . . . what had she said? She could scarcely remember, but it had been as if a veil had been lifted for an instant, and she had known that their lives were to be linked.

Daisy coughed politely.

Lady Pat looked up at her and smiled.

'Thank you, not at the moment.' She looked down at

Zoe's pale face. 'You and I are going to be busy for a while, Daisy,' she said thoughtfully.

'Oh yes, m'Lady,' breathed the dazzled little maid.

'Yes. You and I are going to take turns, and we shall make her better. I shall arrange for a bed to be brought in here, for she must never be left alone, and between us we will mend her.'

That day was the beginning.

Chapter Twenty-One

For four months she lived in that beautiful room. Even there, safe and cherished, and surrounded by luxury and comfort such as she had not known since Daly's death, she had wanted to die. But Lady Pat would not allow it, nor would Daisy.

They cared for her. They fed her, spoonful by patient spoonful. They loved her and they never left her alone to face the vision which tormented her still.

She had told them the whole, terrible story. Afterwards, the innocent Daisy had slipped away to the bathroom, while Lady Pat rocked the distraught child in her arms, and had retched up every morsel of food she had eaten that day. But she returned, and when Lady Pat had gone downstairs she crept into Zoe's bed, and they had slept with their arms about each other. They did this on many nights in the weeks which followed, and Lady Pat thanked God she had put the severely wounded child with the whole, for the healing process which was slowly taking place was as much Daisy's doing as her own.

Zoe was never alone. The women of the house became her friends, and their visits were greeted with shy pleasure, as a parlour maid, or Mrs Jones, the housekeeper, or Bessy from the nursery brought her a few grapes from the greenhouse, a hot scone from Mrs Hart's oven, or a 'penny dreadful' to while away the hours.

And the little girls were brought to peep inquisitively round the door at the interesting visitor who sat so quietly by the fire in her quilted dressing gown. Their mother held them back, fearful of the impact of their childish energy on the pale ghost of the girl, but their soft, baby faces and bright eyes brought a smile of delight to Zoe's face, and as they advanced curiously towards her she held out her hands and another small victory was won.

Still she would not leave her room, and in all that time she had seen no man.

It was March when Jamie came.

The daffodils had been a living carpet across the parkland and the forsythia waved yellow lace from beyond the clipped hedge to the left of the house. Away in the distance a figure could be seen brushing vigorously the steps which spiralled up the side of the mount, on top of which perched a small garden house, and further away, surrounded on three sides by great trees coming into spring greenery, was the lake. A tiny island seemed to float in the centre and was reflected in the mirror-like surface of the water, and cropping peacefully at the water's edge, as still as a frieze on a Grecian urn, was a small herd of fallow deer.

Zoe and Daisy hung from the window, watching the fallow deer peacefully cropping the turf. As the horse's hooves pounded the grass, the deer raised their heads, and stared timidly, but they were used to the sight of horses and men, and knew they had nothing to fear. They watched for a moment, as though to reassure themselves that the creature would come no nearer, then resumed their quiet meal.

The man on the horse raised his cap gallantly to the two young girls at the window, and Daisy giggled, but Zoe drew back, and the smile of pleasure in the beautiful morning slid from her face. It was Sir Jonathan who had grinned so merrily as he passed, and his dark hair had curled about his head, and tumbled on to his forehead as his cap was lifted into the air. Dark. Dark. His hair was dark and . . .

Lady Pat put her head round the door and smiled at the two girls. Daisy bobbed a respectful curtsy as Zoe moved towards the woman, who had stepped into the room, closing the door behind her. With no thought for ceremony, position, or any of the niceties which hedge our lives about, Zoe put her arms about Lady Pat, and rested

170

her cheek against her shoulder. The woman held her gently for a moment and the shared affection warmed the room. It was as if they drew some secret sustenance from each other, linked as they were by the events in their lives. Daisy stood quietly and waited. She had watched this small scene enacted many times, indeed she was the only one who had. The three of them shared one experience, and it drew them together.

Lady Pat held her hand as she led her to the small sofa which stood in front of the cheerful fire, and they sat down.

'My dear, nothing is going to happen unless you want it. You trust me, don't you?' Zoe nodded. 'Well, then. I shall come right out with it. Your brother is here and wishes to see you.'

For an instant, Zoe's mind was blank. She had lived for so long in the vacuum of safety that the world from which she had come was a misty memory. Even Arthur was fading into the merciful dimness of the past. So successfully had she rid her mind of terror that even the good ghosts had been dismissed.

Then slowly a warm feeling of comfort began to steal about her. The picture of a boy and girl, leaping agilely from rock to rock, racing on the springy turf of the moor, shouting, laughing, filled her mind's eye, and she smiled.

'Jamie,' she breathed.

'Yes, it's Jamie,' Lady Pat beamed. 'You are well, now, child and I think the first person to see you should be your brother. He has asked for you a number of times – he is a very determined young man.'

Zoe laughed excitedly, 'Oh, yes, please. Can he come up here?'

'Of course. I'll go and fetch him.'

Lady Pat waited long enough to see Zoe smile into the stiff face of her brother, and then retired to her own sitting-room to weep with happiness. Daisy brought them tea, then bobbed and retreated. For the first time Zoe was left without either of them.

No one ever knew what was said between Zoe and Jamie.

He was overwhelmed by his surroundings, and inarticulate in the presence of his lovely, prettily dressed sister. The memory of the day he had kicked Arthur's 'balls' in would never leave him, for he would not let it. Unlike Zoe, who had forcibly and consistently made her brain turn away from the atrocity, he dwelt on it, day after day, and but for the fear of God, put into him by Mick and Colly if he should take the matter further, he would have killed Arthur.

Now he was here. At last they had allowed him to see her and she was recovered. If he had any knowledge, or interest in the Almighty, he might have breathed a thankful prayer to him, but he did not, he only listened to her talk, and watched her exquisite face, and drank, awkwardly, the tea which Daisy brought them. Just for an instant, he was taken out of his confused embarrassment, by the appreciative twinkle in Daisy's eye, for he could sense immediately that she was his own kind, as Zoe, though she was his sister, was not. Then she was gone, with a swish of her apron and a backward smile, and he was sorry, for this was not his place, and she had for a moment, relieved his anxiety.

'When yer comin' 'ome, our kid?' Jamie blurted out.

Instantly Zoe's face paled. He saw it, and was filled with regret for he knew at once that she would not come home. Not now, or ever.

The house in Love Lane was back to what it had been before Zoe had returned to them, but it was his home, and he was accustomed to the squalor. But it was not for their Zoe. This was where she belonged now.

Clumsily, he took her hand and she looked down at his. The fingers were straight and firm, slender, with oval, well-shaped nails. The skin was brown from working in the open, and the palm was hard and calloused: the hand of a man who did manual labour. But it was a young hand, hairless and warm, male but holding no terror for her.

She relaxed and looked into her brother's face. Smiling, and with shy affection, she kept his hand in her own as she spoke.

'Jamie, I can't come back. You know that. Lady Pat has said I may stay here, and help with the children . . . But we could meet on the moor sometimes. We would go walking again.'

Jamie gave his cheeky, boyish grin. 'That's right, our kid.' Zoe was going to be all right here; he could feel it. He stood up, winked at her and left.

Later, she sat beside Daisy on the sofa, and answered the maid's eager questions about her brother, laughing at the remembered moments of fun, realising for the first time that she was making humour out of many hardships she and Jamie had suffered together. Those times had been painful, loathsome, but here she was, making light of them. Laughing about slops and cockroaches, bread and marge, sleeping, top and tail, five to a bed, about her father's drunkenness, and her sister's greed.

They giggled like schoolgirls in the spring dusk, the firelight making the room a warm haven of peaceful security.

Lady Pat heard them as she came to the door, and opening it quietly, peeped inside. Her heart was light as she closed it again and went on to her own room.

Chapter Twenty-Two

It began slowly, the second step. Just to open the bedroom door and walk on to the landing, to leave behind the familiar friendly comfort of her room, took all her new found courage. Lady Pat held her hand, and Daisy walked watchfully behind, ready like a mother hen to rush forward and take charge of her chick should there be danger.

Slowly, they went downstairs. A footman stood respectfully at the front door; alarmed Zoe reared back, pulling on Lady Pat's hand. But the man smiled, and his eyes were kindly as he stood back.

Zoe passed him, relaxing a little, and as they emerged through the great door into the gentle spring sunshine she felt a great weight lift from her shoulders, and ran down the wide sweep of steps, leaving Lady Pat and Daisy in the porch.

They turned and smiled at each other, fellow conspirators in their triumph, for the moment no longer mistress and maid, but friends who had worked together for this moment. The children were there, immaculate in their winter coats, fur muffs and bonnets, watched over by Nanny Penny. Baby Rosemary, just a year old, squealed from her pram with delight when she saw Zoe, and lifted up her arms to her, for they were friends by now.

Nanny Penny frowned, but Zoe had eyes only for the children, the tender green grass and newly budding leaves; for the blue, pale and pure, of the sky, and the delicious, delicious smell of spring. She wanted to run, and jump and leap into the air like a rubber ball. She wanted to shout and sing, and caper about like 'summat not right', as Sarah would have said.

She took Amy's chubby hand and began to run. Helen and Diana, with one fearful look at Nanny Penny, threw caution to the wind and ran after them.

Nanny Penny tightened her lips as she rocked the majestic pram sharply. She called to the racing children to return to her immediately and turned to Lady Pat for support. But like most mothers of her day, and her position, she had little to do with the upbringing of her children. It was Nanny Penny's job to constrain them, and she turned and walked back into the house.

The children and Zoe had vanished by this time, racing like greyhounds round the side of the house, through the rose garden, bare now, pruned back to the black soil, smelling richly of compost; beyond the tennis court they ran, and down to the paddock. The horses cropped peacefully, three fat ponies amongst them. They raised their heads as the noisy group approached, tossing their manes, and flicking their well-curried tails. The ponies began to walk towards the fence in search of apples, and the children, pushing impatiently at their full skirts and numerous frilled petticoats, scrambled up and sat astride, calling and clicking their fingers.

'Come Polly, come, come.'

'Here girl, here Muffin . . .'

'To me, Fliss, come to me, girl . . .'

Zoe stood entranced, the soft fur collar of the coat which Lady Pat had given to her that morning framing her flushed face.

But the exhilarating happiness of the moment was short-lived.

'Miss Helen, Miss Diana, Miss Amy,' said a coldly furious voice. 'You will climb down from that fence at once and come with me.'

The children's excitement drained away as they clambered awkwardly down.

Zoe stood irresolutely. The children had been brought to her room almost every day and she had loved playing with them. She had seen Nanny Penny at the door, and wondered idly why, of all the women in the house, she alone had never come in to talk to her. 'Oh please,' she said bravely now. 'Please don't blame the children. It was my fault. You see, I was so pleased to . . . well, I have been . . .' She bobbed her head shyly.

'I know all about you, Miss,' the old woman said tartly, 'and I'll thank you not to interfere with the upbringing of my children.'

One by one she pulled the three little girls, crying softly now, and fastened each small hand to the handle of the pram. Like a great liner, dragging three small tugs in its wake, she sailed majestically past the tennis court and out of sight.

Zoe stood by the fence, her joy in the day gone.

The ponies nudged her with their soft mouths, liquid eyes gazing at her.

'I'm sorry,' she said abstractedly, 'I haven't got anything for you.' She stepped back nervously from their searching, quivering nostrils, then put a tentative hand to the soft forehead of the smallest. Gently she rubbed and the pony whinnied, standing docilely.

'She can stand a lot of that,' a male voice said gently.

Zoe turned with a gasp, and the pony, alarmed by the sharp movement, shied and backed away, rolling its eye nervously.

A tall man leaned gracefully against the fence, a riding crop in one hand, a check cap in the other. He wore jodhpurs and a pair of glossy brown riding boots, and a jacket was unbuttoned to reveal a mustard yellow waistcoat and cream shirt. His face was tanned, his eyes a dark, soft brown under dark curly hair.

Her face felt frozen. Slowly she began to back away, one hand still on the fence. But the ground was uneven and her coat was long, and as she moved warily, her eyes darting from side to side like a cornered animal, her heel caught in the hem.

She could feel herself going as the man sprang forward, his face full of concern. He put out his hand to her . . . his

. . . Oh God . . . his hand . . . She began to shake uncontrollably.

'Please,' said the man. 'Please don't be afraid. I won't hurt you. Look, I'll step back.'

Zoe clung to the rail, managing to keep her balance as he moved away. He was wretchedly aware that the child was terrified; how could he have been so stupid? Pat had told him her story, and his heart had ached for her, but he had thought her cured. He had seen her at the paddock rail as he had brought his hunter across the stable yard after their morning gallop on the moor, and had strolled casually across to make her acquaintance.

He put out his hand, as though to show her he meant her no harm. It was slim and brown, well-cared for, smooth and hairless. Zoe stared at it as if at a cobra.

Suddenly, her expression changed, and he saw her relax. His hands were like Jamie's hands. They were held out in friendship, not to . . . They were not like . . . his.

'I'm sorry if I startled you,' he said pleasantly, deliberately casual. 'I don't normally creep up on people, but the grass must have muffled my footsteps.'

He leaned across the fence to the ponies, giving her time to recover. They came to him immediately, and he produced bits of carrot and apple, putting the morsels on the flat of his palm, letting them take them, snuffling and blowing gently on to his lean, brown hand. He continued to talk, not looking at her.

'They really are greedy little beasts, and getting far too fat, but they're such pets – everyone feeds them, from the grooms to the gardeners, and my daughters don't ride enough to keep their weight down. Nanny won't allow . . .' He stopped and frowned as though at some tiresome thought, then went on. 'Now then, if you would like to try, I will show you how to make a friend of one of these chaps.'

He turned towards her and she smiled, her face like an opening flower. 'I'd like that,' she said, 'Perhaps I could give them something now?'

Jonathan was enchanted. He felt his heart miss a beat, and took a deep breath. Delicately, as though about to touch a fawn, he placed a piece of carrot on her outstretched palm.

'Like this,' he said, and surprised himself as his voice trembled. 'Just put out your hand, flat, and they will take it.'

He stood back as she timidly put out her hand to the pony and shivered with delight as the soft lips caressed her palm. Her confidence grew, her joy in the day returned. Jonathan watched her lift her head and laugh, the sun glinting on her curls.

She turned to him to smile again, to say thank you for giving me this moment. And though she did not know it, it began then for him.

Chapter Twenty-Three

December 1921

The sound of a slap, flesh on flesh, made the exhausted figure on the bed wince, but the angry wail which followed filled the room, with joy. The midwife smiled at the nurse, who slipped from the room to whisper the news to the housemaid who was lurking, duster in hand, on the landing. She in turn sped down the wide staircase, her duster waving excitedly, to pass on the glad tidings to the footman, and within five minutes the birth of Lady Pat's fifth child was made known to every member of her staff, from Temple the butler, to Albert the gardener's boy.

The tension in the room eased, and the baby was tenderly clucked over, taken from the doctor by the midwife to be washed. The nurse bustled back and opened the heavy, velvet curtains. The fire crackled.

The only still figure was Lady Pat.

The doctor, who had used her private bathroom to wash, returned, sighing with relief.

'A girl, m'lady, and in fine shape.'

Lady Pat turned her head towards the doctor, her eyes sunken to black hollows, her soaking hair straggling across the pillow.

Nanny Penny was on her knees on the other side of the bed, a bowl of warm water, soap and a soft towel beside her, ready to sponge the face and hands of the woman whom she herself had helped to bring into the world, twenty-nine years ago.

'Come, my pet, let Nanny wash you and brush your hair. His lordship is waiting to see you and you want to look pretty.'

Lady Pat would always be Nanny Penny's pet, would always be 'pretty' to her.

Lady Pat touched her hand, her face still turned towards the doctor. Her voice was a whisper of sound in the hushed activity of the room, as bloodstained sheets, towels and dressings were removed.

'The baby, Doctor Blair? Is she all right?'

The doctor smiled. 'Perfect, my dear.' The benevolence on his face hid his anxiety: five children in seven years had taken their toll and Sir Jonathan should be informed.

Nanny Penny tenderly washed the pale hands and face as the doctor continued:

'Sir Jonathan may come in for a moment, then you must sleep. I'm going to give you a draught.'

Lady Pat drank from the glass and fell back on the pillow, her eyes bleak. A daughter, another daughter. Jonty would be so disappointed.

In a moment he was leaning over the bed.

'Jonty,' she breathed. 'Another girl . . . Do you mind too much? Perhaps next time . . .' Her eyes were tormented.

He kissed her pale lips and cheeks for a lingering instant, watched by the sharp eye of Nanny Penny, and looked with compassion into the drowsy eyes.

'A beautiful girl, my love. You have done well.' But his face was sad. 'I'm happy and proud,' he continued softly. 'Now go to sleep.'

Nanny Penny was satisfied. It had been a good answer.

Zoe was sixteen now, more beautiful than ever. As the staff celebrated downstairs, she sat before the nursery fire, holding the child who until this morning had been the baby of the family. She rested her cheek pensively against the bright head, and gazed peacefully into the leaping flames.

She could hear Nanny Penny tread heavily along the uncarpeted corridor towards the nursery, but with relief she heard the footsteps pass on, and down the stairs, and she relaxed, thankful that, for a moment, the old woman was busy with her beloved mistress and the new baby.

Rosemary stirred on her lap and sat up. With restless energy she scrambled from her knee, and chattered to the row of dolls on the sagging old sofa. The other children were colouring with bright crayons which stained their fingers, and smudged the front of their smocked dresses, and Zoe sighed for she knew there would be trouble when Nanny Penny came back. Children should at no time have a spot of dirt upon them, and should they have the temerity to acquire even the smallest, they must be washed and changed at once. Nanny Penny was not an unkind woman. She did not physically ill-treat her charges, but she was strict to the point of militarism, and they were like mice when she was about, almost afraid to speak above a whisper for fear of bringing down Nanny's wrath.

Oh, to hell with it, Zoe said to herself rebelliously, and rocked on, making the most of the peace, her thoughts on the new child. Another girl. Even when Sir Jonathan popped his head in to tell them with a laugh that another girl had joined his harem, it had been clear he was bitterly disappointed.

The door opened, and Daisy came in, plumper and bonnier than ever, looking furtively over her shoulder towards the corridor.

'She wants to see you, just for a minute, so I said I'd sit with littl'uns, but be quick before Madam gets back or she'll 'ave me guts fer garters.' She chortled with laughter. 'Parlourmaids in the parlour, if you please,' and the children giggled wickedly.

Zoe sped down the stairs to the first floor, and knocked softly at Lady Pat's door. It was opened by the nurse.

Zoe approached the bed where Lady Pat lay like a slender, waxen corpse. In a dainty frilled crib by her side a tiny red faced snuffled and mewed, but Zoe had eyes only for the woman on the bed.

She knelt down and gently touched the pale cheek. The

183

eyes in the tired face opened drowsily, and Lady Pat smiled. 'Zoe,' she murmured.

Lady Pat had come to love the girl as she did her own children. She was quick and intelligent, and her extensive education under Joanna Dale's loving care had made her into a young woman of considerable talent and skills. Each day she helped Lady Pat with the estate management, for strangely and suddenly during the past three years, Sir Jonathan had travelled frequently from home: to London, or on what he called business trips, round the country. More and more the administrative work of the estate fell on his wife. Lady Pat, afraid as always that should would one day lose him completely, said nothing, though her heart almost broke, for she was convinced that he had found the love which he could not take from her.

But he always came back, affectionate, kind, and his attitude towards her never changed. In the dead of the night she held his heavy sleeping head against her breast after their disciplined lovemaking, and her eyes never failed to smile at him as he left her again.

What would she do without the child, though? she asked herself, and thanked God for sending her to them. She had become a loving companion to the lonely woman, and their friendship was deep and strong.

'A girl, Zoe. Another girl,' she whispered now. 'And Sir Jonathan . . .'

Zoe smoothed her forehead tenderly. 'Sir Jonathan will love his daughter, you know he will.'

Lady Pat turned away her head, and a tear trickled from the corner of her eye. I know that, I know that, said her beating heart, but will he love me?

'Go to sleep now,' Zoe soothed. She remained beside her for several minutes, watching with reverent love as the face on the pillow yielded to sleep. A touch on her shoulder brought her to her feet. The nurse held her finger to her lips, and gliding across the flowered carpet, opened the door and stepped back to let her through.

As Zoe stepped lightly up the stairs to the nursery, she

remembered that she had hardly looked at the new baby. She let herself into the nursery and Daisy winked at her as she rose heavily from the chair.

'Back to the grindstone,' she whispered, 'and thank God the old battleaxe stopped downstairs. See you later, love.'

Zoe walked to the window and gazed down the long slope to the paddock.

A solitary figure stood at the fence, and the horses jostled to reach the titbits he held out to them. The December sun fell on his bare head, and for an instant a pang lanced Zoe's heart at the utter dejection which seemed to bow his straight back. His hand lifted listlessly then fell back to his side, the apple he had held rolling away. The horses moved off and the quiet figure turned and leaned against the fence, looking up at the house.

As Zoe stood, framed by the shadowed curtains of the nursery window, he saw her and their eyes met and locked together.

She could not look away. She felt an irresistible urge to reach out her hand and smooth the hair back from his troubled brow, as she had done a hundred times for his daughters. A feeling she did not recognise grew in her breast, and her hand at the curtain trembled.

She turned away abruptly, her heart pounding, and sat down with the children at the table. Feverishly she looked at every drawing, admiring, talking cheerfully, laughing at their jokes, the still face of Sir Jonathan engraved on her mind. His eyes had a message for her, unfathomable, in a language she could not yet understand.

'The lady's horse goes jiggety jig and the gentleman's horse goes joggety jog, but the farmer's horse goes . . . gallopy, gallopy, gallopy, all the way home . . .'

The baby squealed with delight, as the strong hands pulled her between slender, silk-stockinged legs. She squirmed on Zoe's lap, her baby cries rising on the warm air, mingling with the muted chatter of the children as they walked sedately across the close-cropped lawn.

Nanny Penny's head rolled gently sideways against the striped deckchair, and she woke with a start. At once, automatically, she began to scold the children, afraid that some misbehaviour she might have missed whilst asleep, should go unpunished.

'Gently, gently, children,' – they could not have managed to walk more composedly if they had been sixty – 'little ladies do not run so vigorously and certainly they do not shout. And Zoe, please do not heave Miss Elizabeth about in that manner. Put her in the perambulator, and if you have nothing better to do than bother us then take her and the children down to the lake and feed the ducks.'

Zoe sighed, and lifted the wriggling baby to her shoulder. Nanny Penny was enough to try the patience of a saint. Little ladies, indeed. They stood decorously, as little ladies should, at least in the presence of Nanny, and Zoe winked. Quickly they smothered their giggles as Nanny sat up; she peered at Zoe suspiciously, for on more than one occasion she had suspected that the girl had set the children off on purpose to annoy her.

She watched as Zoe settled the rebellious baby into the pram, then lay back in the deckchair and closed her eyes. Zoe set off down the slight incline towards the lake, four restrained figures walking beside her. Miss Helen, as the eldest, carried the bag of crusts for the ducks.

June. A white and yellow day.

A day of white dresses and sandals, white satin ribbon and daisies, lacy puffballs of cloud, and the remnants of May blossom, swans on the lake, glistening white picnic tablecloth, and drifts of alyssum edging the lake.

A day of yellow buttercup, mimosa, egg sandwiches and golden slab cake.

The air was delicious, warm, a true English summer's day, and fragrant with the scents of new-mown grass and lavender.

Zoe and the children walked slowly round the south side of the lake, along the path to the trees. The moment they were out of Nanny's line of vision the five figures dashed into the undergrowth like excited puppies.

'Can we paddle, Zoe, can we?' the children demanded, dancing round the pram.

'Yes, but mind your dress, Diana. And watch out for that mud Amy, or you'll slip.'

They adored her with their eyes. Then, with carefree, swinging arms, they ran to the water's edge. They pulled off their shoes and socks, and squealed in delight as the cool mud oozed between their toes, their young voices echoing across the still water.

Zoe sat watching them from the bank, the baby on her lap. 'Do you want your shoes and socks off, too, sweetheart?' She kissed the rounded, pink cheek lovingly and the child crowed. Rising from the soft carpet of grass, Zoe peeled off the little socks and carried her to the clear water. The ripples from the children's splashing sent tiny waves gently to the bank, where they lapped the baby's fat, dimpled feet. Zoe laughed, holding her securely.

An hour drowsed by, the song of insect and bird mingling with the undertone of the children's voices. The baby had fallen asleep on the rug beside her and Zoe watched the pattern of leaves and sun flickering across her plump face and legs. The sounds which floated on the air, fell, like a hymn of joy, on her ear. This was heaven.

Jonathan lounged on the window seat in the study, the early sunshine calling him from the ledger he was studying half-heartedly. From the lake he could just hear the voices of the children.

He sighed. He didn't know why he felt so low, but a niggling feeling disturbed his afternoon. He tried once more to make sense of the names, rents, acreage, cattle, crops, and the figures which must be balanced for the approval of his steward. It was no good. He flung down his pen and strode from the room.

Twenty minutes later he stood quietly in the lakeside

coppice, unseen by the little band of children, drinking in the scene before him. It was enchanting in its innocence.

Zoe lay on the dappled grass beside the lake, one bare arm restraining the chuckling baby as she lay naked in the clear water, flushed with sun and joy. Her buttocks wriggled on the muddy bottom, and her feet kicked tiny fountains into the air.

And the girl . . .

Zoe wore only a pair of cami knickers with a pretty, lace-trimmed camisole top which, as she leaned towards the child, revealed gloriously the perfect, twin, strawberry-nippled fruits of her breasts. Her hair had tumbled from its neat chignon, and the water sent splashing by the baby beaded her rosy, laughing face and flawless neck. It ran in silver rivulets to her breasts, dripping from the soft peaks inside the lacy transparent top.

For an eternity Jonathan had no eyes, no thoughts for anything nor anyone but her beauty. He remembered the first time he had seen her, on the moor, so close to death. But no – that had *not* been the first time. He saw a child dressed in breeches and a vivid red jumper, walking with a boy. They were outside Weston church, and Lady Pat had been riding beside him. He could feel the movement of his horse beneath him, recalled his sudden awareness of the young girl, flawlessly beautiful. Zoe . . .

She had lived under his roof for almost four years. For almost four years he had tried to deny the feelings her beauty aroused in him. Now he acknowledged to himself for the first time that it was his longing for her which had driven him from his home to seek release with a dozen pretty women in his travels about the country. Still she bewitched him. Each time he had returned she had grown more beautiful.

Now she was a woman.

A call from Zoe broke his reverie, and he watched as she produced a towel from the pram and rubbed the baby dry. The little girls came up and she towelled and tidied them all, before dressing herself again, erasing all signs of the enchanted hours they had spent. With wistful backward glances, they all walked quietly along the path, passing within a foot of him. Then they disappeared into the dense summer growth of bush and tree.

Long after they had gone, Jonathan lay motionless on the ground, his face buried in his arms.

Chapter Twenty-Four

During the last week of July, Sir Jonathan and Lady Pat commanded an expedition to Liverpool, which to the children's amazement and delight, included their four eldest daughters. It required two nights' stay in a suite of rooms at the Adelphi Hotel and the party was accompanied by Zoe and Bessy, the nursery maid.

Nanny Penny had fought to be taken too, and was bitterly resentful that Zoe was to go and not herself, but for some reason Sir Jonathan was against it.

'But my lady,' she had said, turning to Lady Pat with a disarming smile, 'how can that . . . how can Zoe manage four children without me, – And as for Bessy – well, she has hardly begun her training. You know how difficult small children can be, particularly when away from home, but I know just how to handle them . . .'

She turned self-righteously to Sir Jonathan, who had rustled his paper angrily, but he turned away, frowning.

Lady Pat looked from one to the other. 'Jonathan,' she said uneasily.

He put down his newspaper irritably.

'Nanny! Miss Elizabeth will not be going with us, and naturally someone must remain with her.'

'But sir, could not Zoe . . .'

He flung the paper on to the table.

'Nanny, you will remain here, and that is that.'

Lady Pat stared out of the window. The old nurse stood for a moment, reluctant to admit defeat. She could not understand Sir Jonathan's intractable opposition, but there was something afoot, that she knew.

She turned abruptly, and left the room, banging the door behind her.

When the travellers returned to Weston Hall, it required three trips of the motor car from the railway station at Chester to transport the boxes which had come in the goods van of the train.

The transformation from diminutive ladies to comfortably dressed children had a devastating effect on Nanny Penny. They wore short-sleeved shirts and skirts, open sandals and ankle-length socks, knee-length cotton dresses. And no petticoats. Brief bathing dresses and loose jumpers, and the hair cuts, oh, the hair cuts. She grieved for the long ringleted curls and huge bows, the straw hats and bonnets, and for the sweet, docile children who were replaced by tomboys and hoydens. She never forgot it, nor could she forgive Sir Jonathan.

Lady Pat, always more than eager to please her husband, was swept along with the new regime and was not unduly alarmed or even suspicious of Sir Jonathan's new-found interest in his children and their activities.

The remainder of that lovely summer passed in a delightful haze of hot sun, picnics on the lawn, swimming, outings in the pony cart deep into the woods, riding and tennis, which Sir Jonathan had decided his children must take up.

Nanny Penny restricted her dominance to the nursery, missing nothing, watching with eyes which were old and shortsighted, but knowing sadly that her day was nearly done.

In all these new interests Zoe took part. She learned to play tennis, for Helen must have a partner. And despite all her duties with Lady Pat, and her work in the estate office, she still managed to spend an hour each day with baby Elizabeth, or Beth as she was called, for the child adored her.

And Sir Jonathan spent scarcely any time away from home now.

Again Lady Pat did not question the change. In her thankful relief, she concluded that the woman in his life was gone, and she did not dwell on it. He was home with her, and it was enough.

But he no longer came to her bed.

'You see, my dear, Doctor Blair thinks that it would be advisable if we . . . He is of the opinion that five children in seven years is enough for any woman to contend with. To tell the truth . . .' he laughed awkwardly, '. . . he made me feel something of a lecher, but I think he's right.'

Lady Pat writhed inwardly with pain. He was telling her that . . . But surely . . . She spoke timidly, bravely.

'But isn't there a . . . something that could be . . . I have heard of some contrivance that may be used to prevent . . .' She faltered at the look on Jonathan's face. 'But, of course, my dear,' she continued hurriedly, 'whatever you think best.'

He took her hand and looked into her face, then away again quickly, for he was afraid she might see the magnitude of the hold the girl had on him.

'You should have a rest for a while, darling. Then, if you feel able, we might . . . well, we'll see.' He smiled cheerfully and left the room unaware of the misery he had inflicted.

Oh Jonty, Jonty, my love, her soul cried. There is no need for this. No need. Passion I want, yes. Your body I want, yes, but to have your love, to have you sleeping beside me, to have your thoughts link with mine, that is all I ask.

During the last week of September, Lady Pat insisted that Zoe have a day off.

'You've been with us for so long, Zoe, and I can't remember you taking any time away, except with Jamie now and again. You should have a regular day off. Why don't you take Helen to Liverpool? She'd adore to have a day alone with you, and you could shop and have lunch at Bunny's.'

Lady Pat's expression softened.

'You're seventeen next week, my dear, and a young woman, now.' Affection shone in her kind eyes, 'Besides, you need a new dress for the party and I absolutely insist that you buy one.'

Helen was thrilled. They took the train from Chester, Zoe's beauty turning all heads in the first-class compartment. The bustle of Liverpool station was exhilarating, and they clung together, thrillingly fearful on their first outing with no protector. Outside, they stopped to look in the window of a large store, and Zoé stepped back to read the name.

Owen Owen, it said; the memory flooded her, and she was walking beside Daly, holding her hand as the child beside her excitedly held her own.

They entered the smart foyer and looked about them, delighted with each other and this fine adventure. Zoe felt happiness envelop her in a warm cloak of protection and safety, and her thoughts for a moment winged to Weston Hall. Home. The word sang in her heart and she felt a wave of joy. Weston Hall was home to her now, and the children were her family. She loved them and their parents. They had been so good to her, so kind. Lady Pat and Sir Jonathan.

A tiny tingle ran down her neck and spine as she thought of him and for a second she felt a strange confusion. She had felt it before. She shook her head, and she and Helen wandered from counter to counter, smiling shyly at willing salesmen.

An hour later they left the store, bemused but delighted with the chiffon dress they had chosen, the colour of pale, pale apricots and the dainty satin shoes to match. The day passed in a spindrift of happiness. They took a tram, sitting on the open seats, their hair blowing about their hat brims, and clutched each other with excitement and shrieked as they clattered round a corner and down to the Pier Head.

As they stood for a moment by the water's edge, Zoe fell quiet. The river lapped gently against the stage and the flotsam heaved in a mass of paper and orange peel, ferry tickets and empty Woodbine packets. The ferry, the *Royal Iris* now in recognition of her fine courage during the war years, when she carried troops across the channel, huffed tranquilly sideways to allow her passengers to disembark. Her rust-spotted black sides touched the huge coils of rope, placed there to cushion her against the impact, and the slatted drawbridge dropped with a clatter across the small space of water, on to the ship's deck. People poured from her, hurrying across the dock, and up the covered, sloping walkways which led to the square where trams awaited them.

It was here that she had boarded the very same boat nearly four years ago. She remembered it as vividly as though it were yesterday. The rain had poured down her face but she had felt she would never be clean again.

Now love had cleansed her, and goodness, and she could think about that day calmly, shrouded as it was in the past.

She shook herself gently, and Helen smiled up at her, her brown eyes warm and glowing, just like her father's. For an instant Zoe felt her heart lift again with the curiously delicious sensation that came over her whenever she thought about Sir Jonathan.

'Shall we go home, now?' she said, and a tiny excitement gripped her, for she knew he would be there.

The train journey was over before they knew it, and there was Ted Richards standing next to the motor car as the train drew in. Helen ran on to show him her brooch and he winked as he bent to admire it.

'You two look as though you've 'ad a good day,' he beamed. 'Lost a tanner an' found a quid, 'ave you?'

'I have, Ted, I have,' Zoe replied. 'I've found a home, that's what, a home.'

They skipped along, one on each side of the chauffeur, and Zoe sat beside him as they drove along the dusty lanes in the deepening twilight. The long days of summer were dying, and autumn, serene and beautiful, touched the trees with bronze and gold. A last trill, faint and sleepy, trembled in the air as the birds settled, and in the fields, knee-deep in lush grass, cattle lowed plaintively, turning towards the sound of the motor as it passed.

The gravel crunched under the wheels as the gleaming vehicle turned between the ornate gateposts of the Hall, and glided smoothly past the lovingly tended parklands and gardens, almost invisible in the purple dark.

Around the house to the stable yard, where welcoming lights shone warm yellow from windows and the kitchen doorway, and Albert the gardener's boy hovered, ready to leap forward and open the car door: he had waited over an hour for Zoe's return.

Someone else lurked in the shadow of the stable doorway, ostensibly settling his new hunter for the night. As the car drew to a halt, Sir Jonathan stepped into the circle of light which streamed from the back of the house, and moved casually towards it, his handsome face smiling a welcome. Albert slunk away as Sir Jonathan gallantly opened the door, offering his arm first to his daughter, then to Zoe. What more natural than for a father to greet his child, as she returned from a day's outing? But the tingle which passed like a volt of electricity between the man and the girl as their hands touched had them quivering like windblown trees.

He ushered them both into the kitchen, and in the laughter and talk which followed, no one appeared to remark the strangeness of Sir Jonathan giving an arm to his wife's protégée or the look in his eyes as he leaned against the dresser, drinking in the sight and sound of Zoe.

Chapter Twenty-Five

The first time was on Black Tor, the craggy peak on which she had first met his wife. With deep irony, it was Lady Pat herself who provided the means by which Sir Jonathan might be unfaithful to her.

Except for Elizabeth, all the little girls could ride, hacking about the estate and the immediate fringes of the moor on their fat ponies. They jogged along the country lanes accompanied by Sam, their diminutive mounts as steady as the nursery rocking horse, but Helen and Diana, seven and eight respectively, were old enough, their mother decided, to be promoted to bigger mounts. They should go on more adventurous rides, and be taught the care and grooming of their own horses. This was how she had been schooled at their age, thrilling to the gallops across the fells of her native Northumberland. She wanted her children to have the same enjoyment.

And, of course, Zoe must be included.

Helen and Diana, the novelty exciting them at first, worked hard for a week or two on the sleek young horses they were given. But the dedication required to become a member of the Hunt was not there, and neither showed the aptitude of their mother. Soon they were back to the gentle, rocking ponies, to the sedate walk and trot.

Zoe, however, adored her new activity. The sensation she experienced as Rowan, her pretty new mare, leaped over rough stone walls, hedges and gates, was exhilarating, and she learned every aspect of horsemanship. Hours were spent polishing the chestnut coat, currying the splendour of her mane and tail, and a great affection grew between the girl and animal.

Lady Pat was pleased with her protégée, resignedly

accepting the shortcomings of her two eldest daughters. At first Zoe went out with Sam, or one of the other grooms: gently through the gate from the stable yard, across the meadow, avoiding the staring cows, over the low, dry stone wall, and then, steadily gathering momentum, pounding the rough path until it petered out, and the moor stretched before her.

For mile upon mile it rolled, and Zoe urged her horse over the springing green turf, faster and faster each day, the wind freeing her hair from its netted chignon until it streamed like a living banner. The groom, at first only a tail's length distant would soon be left far behind. She revelled in the freedom, the emptiness, the silence broken only by the bleat of the timid sheep, and the vivid songs of lark and linnet.

Sometimes, when her duties allowed, Lady Pat would mount her big black hunter, and together they would skim the surface of the rough terrain. Zoe's smaller mount could not keep up, and she would watch as the fearless woman on the spirited horse disappeared over the brow of the hill, and the next, and the next. Zoe would find her on Black Tor, for somehow, in whichever direction they went, they always came back to the high peak on which they had first met.

She began to go out alone. There was nothing to fear on the moor, and she and Jamie, whom she saw less often as he grew into a young man, had come to know every inch of every mile of the wilderness that almost encircled the Hall and village.

Christmas came and went, and the apricot chiffon dress, first worn on her birthday celebration in September, hid a fast beating heart as she danced with Sir Jonathan at the staff party. It seemed through those winter months that all about were blind not to see the feeling blossom between them.

Their eyes would meet across a room and Zoe's breath would leave her. Instantly, as though a signal had passed from one to the other, they would lower their eyes to hide the turmoil there: brown eyes hot with desire, green ones confused, uncertain.

Spring came and Zoe was almost eighteen.

She had raced the eager mare one day until the animal's coat was lathered in a silky foam. Mile after mile she went, trying to escape the wretchedness which haunted her, but the smiling face of Sir Jonathan imprinted itself on every rock and crag. She leaned forward and placed her damp face against the horse's sweated neck, slowing to a walk as she reached the peak.

She breathed deeply of the gorse-scented air, and allowed the mare to pick her way across the small plateau of rocky outcrop. At the far edge she slid from the horse's back, and sank to the same rough, pitted stone on which she had crouched five years ago, hiding from Lady Pat.

Her hand quivered on the rough grey stone, her breath quickened and she closed her eyes as she imagined his mouth, firm and well-shaped. His brown neck was strong and muscled. His hands were beautiful, slender and long-fingered . . .

Oh God, she cried inside her weakened body. Please help me. I can't do this to her. She loves me and trusts me and he is her husband. Help me to be strong.

'Zoe.' He spoke her name softly, and it was as though he had touched her with his gentle fingers. She saw his shadow stretch from behind her. Her eyes filled with tears. She lifted her head, and squared her shoulders, staring through the shimmer of moisture in her eyes. A speck of pink perked beneath her boots, and she bent to touch the tiny ball of clover. She felt his warmth as he sat on the rock, a scant inch from her shoulder.

She turned. She looked into his eyes, and the desolation she saw there tore at her heart.

Gently she touched a finger to his lips, feeling the smooth flesh for the first time. His mouth moved in a gentle kiss, his lips parting against her finger. The months, the years of half-caught glances, unspoken words, of trembling hands and thudding heart, had all led to this moment.

199

Taking her hand in his, he looked down, seeing her young skin against his own, feeling the gentle pulse in her wrist under his thumb. He moved his fingertips across her palm, and the pulse quickened in response. They were drowning in each other's eyes.

One by one he undid the buttons of her thin shirt, watching her nipples rise. Like ripe peaches, her breasts brushed against his hands, and she raised her arms and twisted her hands in his dark hair. As she had dreamed of doing. She pulled his head down until his lips closed on her nipple, and, with a cry of delight, clasped his head to her, straining against him, imploringly.

For an exquisite moment they clung together, his face buried deep in the sweetness of her, and for a wild moment he was tempted to go on. She was lost and she was his.

But slowly, slowly, he gentled her, crooning his love like a father soothing a child. He covered her, tenderly buttoning her shirt, kissing her brow, her cheek but never her lips. He dared not. He held her hands until she looked into his eyes once more, and then he spoke.

'Zoe,' he whispered. 'Zoe, my little love, my robin.' He smiled, and she smiled back at the memory of that first time when their eyes had met, outside the church. She had worn a scarlet jumper, the bright colour a vivid splash against the worn grey stonework.

'Little robin, little robin red breast,' he murmured. 'You know I love you?'

She nodded shyly.

'What happened just now . . .' He broke off, overwhelmed by love and desire.

'Jonathan.' His name for the first time on her lips, without the customary title, made them both delirious with joy. And then the laughter came, and they kissed at last.

It was a kiss like honey. They murmured each other's names, lost, helpless.

'Sweet Zoe, our time will come,' he breathed against her mouth, then tore himself away and sat up, gazing across

200

the empty moors. 'If you have any doubts,' he said quietly, 'If you are not strong enough, and you will need to be strong, darling, you must go now. I will help you leave, to start a new life . . .' His voice broke.

'Oh Jonathan, my love.' She reached out to him. 'I could never leave you. Never.'

She tried to fight back the tears, but could not, and together they rocked in each other's arms. For an hour they sat close to each other, talking quietly, making no plans, but content at last to do away with pretence.

They rose at last and called to their horses.

'You go first, robin. I will follow in a moment.'

The first deceit cut sharply: they must not be seen returning together. Obediently she mounted her mare, turning to look at him, her eyes already sad and lost. He took a step towards her, taking the rein in his hand, and touching her cheek he pulled her head down and kissed her tenderly, chasing the sadness away.

'Smile bravely, little one. Remember, I love you.'

Without turning again, she cantered in the direction of the Hall, then with a wild cry to the horse, she coaxed it into a gallop, thundering between the rocks which scattered the moor like pebbles flung by a giant hand.

Her body throbbed in the rhythm of the galloping horse, tense with awakened longings she had not known existed. She felt a pain start in the pit of her stomach, a hot pain which was not a pain, but a flame. With a soft cry she pulled the startled horse to a halt. Flinging herself from the saddle, she stood, her head bowed against the heaving side of the mare, and she cried out her despair, her longing, and last of all, her sorrow for Lady Pat.

Late that night, as the still face of the moon hung high in the navy sky, she lay in bed, and re-lived the moment when Jonathan's hands and mouth had held her breast. The tell-tale nipples rose instantly. She turned her head into her pillow as her hand found her secret woman's place and her cries of passion were muffled as she came to orgasm for the first time. After a while she wept again, hot tears of desolation as she realised that this was to be her life, snatched moments of love, long hours of loneliness.

They did not deliberately seek each other out, nor did they set out to avoid. Their days and nights continued as before, with one exception. He no longer went to the lake to swim with the children. The sight of her lovely young body, splashing, framed by the crystal chandelier of water, was more than he could bear, and he stayed away, claiming a backlog of work. He swam during the hours when he knew she would be closeted with Lady Pat, cleaving the water powerfully.

His love and longing for her grew with each day that passed. As he watched her from his window, the breath caught in his throat and he yearned to hold her, to caress every secret part of her.

The days were an ache, the nights a torture. He had not visited Lady Pat since the birth of their daughter, but to his shame he used her to assuage his thirst. She came to his room one night, when he called in his troubled sleep, and in the half-waking, half-sleeping state of one just come from a nightmare, he clasped her to him. They lay together, surprise stilling them for a moment. Then both starving, they took each other hungrily.

Afterwards he held her gently as she quivered and cried, her glad heart believing that he was come back to her, but when he slept again he turned from her irritably, as if in sleep his body knew that hers was not the one it sought.

She left him at dawn and stood at her window watching the deep blue bowl shade to pale hyacinth, to milky grey and oyster pink. She heard the dawn chorus joyfully herald in a new day, the high whinny of the stallion in the paddock, answered by the mare. The world was awakening, all creatures greeting the fresh day with joy, but Lady Pat, the hope she always carried in her heart crushed once more, rested her forehead against the mullioned window pane and wept.

Several days later, she received a letter from her father in

Northumberland. He had had a mild heart attack. 'Nothing serious, my dear, so please do not worry, but I would dearly love to see you and those grandchildren of mine. It would cheer an old man up immensely.' The wistful plea had crept through his brave words. And it was an excuse to get away from her own sadness.

Forcing herself to sound cheerful, she spoke to her husband at breakfast, piles of letters on the table between them.

'I must go, of course, and take the older girls, but I'm afraid the baby would be too much for father. Zoe can stay and look after her, and she'll be able to take my place in the estate office, too, so that should work out very well. Besides Elizabeth would fret with only Bessy for company. I shall probably be gone for several weeks, Jonty.' She smiled brightly, 'You won't mind, will you, my dear? The fells will be lovely at this time of the year, and I shall do some riding, and perhaps take father for a short holiday, if he is fit enough to travel. He loves the west coast of Scotland. Perhaps we shall go to Oban.'

She watched her husband's face for evidence of . . . what? Perhaps dismay that she would be away for so long; a sign that he would miss her, but there was nothing. Nothing but kind concern for her father, and a desire to help her on her way. For an instant a tiny spark had glimmered in his eye, but it was gone before she could catch it and decipher its meaning.

'Of course you must go, my dear,' he murmured, 'I'm sure a visit from you will put your Papa firmly back on the road to recovery.' Rising from the table he bent to kiss the top of her head. The hours of passion they had spent in his bed had never been mentioned, but he avoided her eye, and she knew that he regretted them. She caught his gaze and in the dark depths saw there only kindness and something . . . elusive.

It took a week for Lady Pat to make the arrangements to transport her family and all the trappings needed for several weeks away from home, but finally she was ready.

Jonathan drove them all to Liverpool and saw them safely seated in a first-class carriage – magazines and comics, fruit and chocolate already being pounced on by the children, much to Nanny Penny's agitation. She had tried to catch Lady Pat's eye several times, for this was not the way young ladies of breeding should act on a journey, even in a private carriage, but her ladyship had eyes for no one but her husband.

'Have a good trip, my dear.' His face was already turning away to watch the stationmaster, waiting for the movement of the green flag.

She watched his eagerness, barely concealed, and wept inside.

'Perhaps you might get up for a few days?' she tested.

Consternation for the blink of an eyelash, then his face was blank again.

'My love, at this time of the year? You know the work there is to do.'

The pain in her heart was almost more than she could bear.

'Of course, my dear.' Her smile strained the corners of her mouth.

He stood on the platform, smiling at the excited children, willing the blast of the whistle to cut the air.

At last it came, and the great, glass-roofed cavern filled with steam and noise. A brief brushing of cheek to cheek, and then the train moved away, gaining speed slowly. He watched it until it was out of sight, then, whistling cheerfully, his step as jaunty as a boy's, he walked quickly towards the turnstile, and Zoe.

Chapter Twenty-Six

He came to the nursery as she was feeding Elizabeth. The little girl banged her spoon on the table with delight at the sight of her father in the doorway, calling to him for a kiss. Over her head they looked at each other, their eyes grave and loving, for they knew the time had come. He put out his hand as if to touch her cheek, but dropped it instead on to his daughter's curls.

'Papa, Papa! Play horses now!'

His eyes left Zoe's reluctantly, and dropped to his excited child, smiling affectionately at the happy face.

'Just for a little while, sweetheart, and then it will be time for Zoe –' his tongue lingered over her name and she shivered '– to bathe you.'

He lifted the child from her chair, and whilst Zoe cleared the table and prepared her night things, he crawled on hands and knees, small arms wrapped tightly about his neck. 'Wun faster, Papa, wun faster!'

They bathed her together, then put her to bed, her high fenced cot standing next to the bed where Zoe would sleep whilst Nanny Penny was away.

Beth finally slept, and they crept out of the room and into the day nursery. The blinds had been drawn to soothe the little girl, and the dimness cast a light shadow over their faces. Zoe closed the door between the two rooms and stood motionless as he gazed at her, his eyes bright with longing. She reached out her arms, drawing him against her, but when she felt him, hard and demanding, she was suddenly afraid. He felt her slight withdrawal, and turned her face towards him.

'What is it, my love?' he breathed against her cheek.

She moved her eyelashes against his skin, but he raised

her chin and looked into her eyes. They were a deep, dark, drowning green, and the ache of her own need was as great as his own.

'What is it?' he repeated.

'Not here, Jonathan, not so close to . . .'

He sighed, holding her gently against him.

'I know,' he said, 'but we can't leave her alone. If she wakes up and no one is here . . . the servants . . .' He left the sentence unfinished, recognising suddenly that the freedom he thought he had was as ethereal as mist after all. One small child stood between him and his love more effectively than had his whole family.

Drawing her towards the big sofa where all the children, including himself, had played and been nursed, he sat down, pulling her beside him. The room was cheerless with the blinds drawn and the fireplace loomed empty and forlorn, without its usual cheerful glow. He knelt and put a match to the kindling already laid, and as it caught and touched the logs, the room became relaxed and gently warm. An old friend. He felt her tension melt within the circle of his arms, and then she turned her mouth to his.

She moaned, her lips sweet and hot, and her body moved slowly, rhythmically. His hand was at her throat, his fingers light, his nails running exquisitely against the velvet of her skin, and as the remembrance of the day at Black Tor caught them, they shivered as one being.

He tried to go slowly. It was her first time, but she was as eager as he. She trapped his hand, and undoing the buttons of her blouse herself, cupped it around her throbbing breast, the erect nipple burning a circle in his palm He pulled the thin stuff from her, burying his face in her sweet flesh. Her reticence of moments ago was swept away. Her skirt was somehow on the floor, and her underwear, sliding like silk along her thighs. He slipped from the couch to kneel at her side as he flung his own clothes from him, and for a moment stayed her frantic hands as he let his eyes roam her white, gold-tinted body. The firelight played with her thrusting nipples and lapped the dark dimple of her navel. It nuzzled the triangle of dark, bronze curls, and her legs, as the warmth touched them, opened wide, inviting him to impale her.

And they found each other at last. As soft and gentle as a summer's breeze, as wanting as earth needs rain. They moved as gracefully as porpoise beneath the water. There was pain, swift, forgotten, and their rapturous moans; then, like a wave of wild water on rock, they rode the climax together with not a heartbeat between their shared ecstasy.

There was warmth, stillness, silence, peace.

He was the first to return from the far place to which he had taken her. He lifted his head, and looked into her eyes, drugged with joy, dark and bottomless, with a deep glow of love. He whispered her name, his lips brushing her cheek and brow, and his hand cherished her breast, rolling her nipple between gentle fingertips. He felt her stir, her hips lifting slightly as she pressed once more against him.

He laughed out loud. 'You're insatiable, my wanton woman. I'm afraid you'll have to wait.' But she smiled wickedly and he was captivated. As she sat up, her breasts brushing across his face, pressing sensuously against his open mouth, he lifted her to sit astride him and in a vortex of passion took her again.

They slept and played for a while, their soft laughter sighing through the room in which the echoes of a hundred children's merriment whispered from the past. Her eyes sparkled with devilment as she teased him. She wrote 'I love Sir Jonathan' on the children's blackboard in letters six inches high, and hid the eraser as he tried to rub it out, pushing him backwards on to the sofa, making him woo it from her with kisses. As quickly as melting snow, she changed from woman to child, and back again, and he watched her with a love that was almost reverent, as she curled in his arms after their last loving. Her breath was sweet as honey against his lips, and a tendril of chestnut hair drifted like stranded silk across his face.

The baby slept in her cot, her innocent smile curling her soft lips as she dreamed her infant dreams, and her father loved his love in the next room.

. The last wisp of wood ash fell softly in the fireplace, a thread of pearl-grey smoke idling lazily up the blackened chimney. Jonathan slept at last, his cheek against Zoe's tumbled hair.

The minutes, the hours, the days of bewitchment sped by. The loveliness, the joy, the urgent intoxication of being together was a magic potion to be drunk to the full: the cup was brimming, and it seemed as if it would never be emptied. They were children with the child, playing, rippling the waters of the lake like white-fleshed fish, diving and leaping. Elizabeth ran like a fat puppy, chasing the flashing white tennis ball as they skimmed the vivid green of the court like swallows. They swept the surface of the moor, stallion and mare, the little girl cradled against her father's chest as they flew to the top of Black Tor Crag, to rest in loving arms between them, mantled in enchantment.

But at night they were alone, only two, and the love planted in the warm nursery took root, grew and flowered, filling the room and the house with the sweet content that seemed to cling to all who dwelled there. Even the servants moved about their duties as if suspended in the lovers' dream world. These men and women who peopled the enchanted place were not even aware that they were different. They drifted through that somnolent summer as though time had slowed down, and the leading players went unnoticed.

Jonathan and Zoe wandered the far secret side of the lake, the child between them, slowing their steps as she dawdled, her inquisitive mind leaping from one delight to another. The swans stood on tiptoe, their long necks stretched skywards, their wings flapping as though they would fly, their agitation at the unusual sounds dying as the human voices grew quiet and faded away.

The tired baby slept as Jonathan and Zoe held each other in arms of love, their white bodies beautiful, shaded and dappled by the blossoms of the horse chestnut tree under which they lay. Their cries of ecstasy were muted, mingling with the sounds of summer. As passion swelled their voices into a wild clamour, swiftly stilled by mouth on mouth, a sigh, heavy with rapture, winged across the coppice which framed the lake.

Mr Kent, trimming a hedge against the rose garden, lifted his head and listened, but the gentle sound was not repeated. His nut-brown face was expressionless. It was not the first time he had heard a human voice where no voice should be, but it was not his place, or way, to speak of it. Folks must do what they thought necessary, though his thoughts were not worded like that. His were the earthy thoughts of countrybred people, who were used to the ways of animals and their needs.

The players in the drama moved about their small world, seemingly oblivious to the men and women who surrounded them. If the servants thought it odd that the master should spend so much time with Zoe and the infant, they kept their own counsel. Weston Hall was not a place for gossip – and besides, Miss Elizabeth was his daughter, after all, and must miss her mother, poor lamb. It was only natural he should want to be with her.

In the weeks that slipped by, edging the summer into autumn, the gardener missed nothing. The look of shining love which passed between them as their glance met over the baby's head; the protective hand as Zoe slid from her mare; the soft voice fluting across the lake as she called to her lover, thinking herself unheard. His boot-button eyes watched from behind bush and shrub, his old heart lamenting for the lass, for it meant sorrow, but it was none of his business and he said nothing.

In September her ladyship returned.

She stepped from the car onto the gravel drive, followed by the four excited children, and in the chaos which followed Zoe was swept into the warm, loving greetings exchanged between husband and wife; the children and their father, and the children and herself. She stood on the wide steps leading to the open front door, Elizabeth beside her. The little girl was shy with her mother and needed coaxing to run into her arms. She was kissed and hugged for she had been much missed.

The luggage was brought in by a stream of servants who bobbed and smiled.

In the turbulence of talk and movement as the children swarmed about her, Zoe gazed over the eager, laughing faces and saw Jonathan going up the wide staircase, arm in arm with Lady Pat. He was laughing at something she was saying. Suddenly the hall went dark and the pain of jealousy, a feeling she had never known before, pierced her like a sword.

She turned away, stumbling against Helen, chattering of beaches, of the sea, of kites and shells and starfish.

Lady Pat turned at the top of the staircase and called to her. Her face was radiant, flushed and almost pretty in her excitement.

'Zoe? Come up, dear, when you've finished with those noisy monkeys. I want to talk to you.' She looked down at Beth, now clinging to her in an ecstasy of love, and bent to pick her up, laughing into the plump, rosy face. She kissed her cheek, and Zoe alone heard the soft words she spoke into the child's uncomprehending ear.

'And who's going to have her plump little nose put out of joint?'

She put her finger on the soft blob in question, then turned and followed her husband, still murmuring endearments into her daughter's ear. Beth's giggles grew as the man, the woman, and their child entered the bedroom, closing the door behind them.

Heedless of the children, Zoe stood, her face waxen with shock. The words still echoed in her anguished mind.

'. . . nose out of joint . . . nose out of joint.'

Dimly the voices reached her, and she allowed herself

to be tugged up the stairs by demanding young hands, clamouring for attention.

The sword of jealousy turned once more in her heart; and then the hatred came, and she was afraid.

Chapter Twenty-Seven

It was winter now. The gardens were bare, clouds hung heavily, and rain dripped from the great trees.

Nothing remained of the magic land in which Zoe, Jonathan and Elizabeth had spent hours of enchantment. From the lawn where Nanny Penny had dispensed tea and lemonade it was now possible to see through the bare branches to the once hidden path which led away to the far side of the lake, and the children who had shouted and jumped there with the high spirits of youth were trapped in the schoolroom with Miss Rogers.

It was November and Lady Pat was pregnant, and in her pregnancy, her sixth, she was beautiful, for surely this time she would have a son.

Jonathan stayed by her, cossetting and attending to her every whim. He seemed to have eyes for no one but her. He took the onerous duties of the estate from her, insisting that she stayed in bed until ten; that she must not ride – if he had his way she would hardly walk. He watched over her, fussing like a mother hen, soothing her to sleep, and, as the months wore on, checking a dozen times a day that she was content.

One small mystery puzzled her, but blissfully happy for the first time in her marriage she paid no heed to it. He would not work in the estate office at the back of the house. He moved papers and accounts books into the library, saying he found it more congenial, sitting before the open fire, Candy and Floss at his feet as he worked. The steward, and the men of the estate became used to seeing him there, and if Zoe were left unsupervised in the office it did not seem unusual, for she was able to perform her duties without instruction now.

But left alone there, Zoe would sink to her knees and weep where she knelt. Where had the loveliness gone? What had happened to the bright perfection of the summer days? Where was her love? Surely he could give just a word, a look, to tell her she was not abandoned.

In the afternoons she paced the park, and the lanes beyond, her face white and drawn under the brim of her small fur hat, and she clenched her hands, thrusting them deep into the pockets of her russet wool coat.

Now that she was away from the Hall, she allowed the expression of despair to settle on her face. Tears flowed silently across her cheeks, making icy paths to her chin, and dripping to the warm brown of the wool, making dark patches of damp, the size of a sixpence.

Jonathan, she cried silently, where are you? Since Lady Pat came home, you have not even acknowledged my presence, even in the estate office, where you could come innocently. You have avoided the most harmless of encounters, and you are breaking my heart.

The strain began to show in her waxy pallor and drastic loss of weight. The tailored coat hung from her shoulders; the sweet curves were gone. Wearily she trudged the drive. She knew her changed appearance would soon be noticed by others, particularly Lady Pat, but as yet, she was so wrapped up in her husband, and her longing for a son, that she had eyes for no one else.

Zoe's mind cast miserably this way and that as she walked through the open gateway, and into the lane which led towards the village green. She would have to get away, get another job. The agony of living under the same roof, of knowing that Jonathan was always about; that he spent hours in his wife's pleasant sitting room, in her bedroom – oh God, not that – was not to be borne.

Perhaps I could stay with Jamie for a while, she thought one afternoon, as she dragged herself past the row of cottages which lined the lane. He had his own place now, and would welcome her, she knew. But he was courting a young woman from the dock offices, and had his own life: it wasn't fair to involve him in her unhappiness.

She approached the village green and nodded bleakly to Mr Lark, butcher to the Hall. He greeted her cheerfully from the doorway of his bow-windowed shop, before disappearing into the gloom at the back, to report to Mrs Lark 'that there young Zoe do look peaky'.

There were few people about. In their snug cottages the villagers hugged their firesides. Zoe waited impassively at the bus stop outside the inn, stamping her feet against the cold.

At last the bus rattled down the street. Blindly she boarded it, and did not notice the gleaming motor car swerve round the green from the direction of the Hall, and speed past.

Zoe sat at the back of the bus, staring at the winter fields; at the harsh moorland, stripped now of purple heather and yellow gorse. If only she could stop thinking of him, if only her tired brain could rest from the anguish throbbing there.

As the bus drew up outside Chester railway station, where she would catch the train to Liverpool, she rose from her seat, noticing no one, and stepped on to the pavement, pale and beautiful. Numbly she stood on the kerb to allow a shining automobile to pass. But it stopped beside her, and its gleaming splendour seemed familiar now. Then the door opened, and a man's voice spoke tensely from the driver's seat.

'Get in quickly.'

Zoe stared disbelievingly into eyes as agonised as her own. Jonathan's face was thin, pale, wrung with strain. Why had she not noticed? Had she been so concerned with her own heartbreak that the face of the man she loved could grow old, and she not see it? Her flesh prickled.

He tried to smile, to reassure her.

'Get in, little robin,' he said tenderly.

As Zoe had wept for him in her bed, so had he shed inward tears for her. But the knowledge that Lady Pat was carrying his child while he loved another filled him with

215

guilty shame. It had eaten into his soul, filling him with self-revulsion, and he had tried desperately to make up the wrong done to his wife. Like a beloved toy, forbidden as punishment for some misdeed, Zoe had been put away.

She fell back against the seat as Jonathan sped out of the city. Open countryside lay on either side of the road, and still he drove on, mile after mile, never glancing in her direction. They climbed steadily upwards, the moorland harsh around them; the only sign of life the hardy sheep, who lifted empty eyes to watch them pass. As they reached the highest peak, the sun, hidden since the morning, gleamed faintly on the polished surface of the car. As if it were a signal, Jonathan stopped at last.

There was silence and stillness for a measureless moment. Then, turning towards each other, without touching, they both began to weep. With a soft cry of comfort, Zoe took Jonathan in her arms, the crushing band of hopelessness melting from around her heart, as she realised that he loved her still. She rocked him back and forth, smoothing his hair, crooning words of love, until he was calm.

'I couldn't speak to you.' He pressed against her shoulder as if he could not bring himself to look into her eyes, brilliant with love for him.

'I avoided you, I could not bear to . . . with Pat there it would have been . . .' He wiped his eyes as he turned away, and his voice faltered. 'I . . . knew that . . . I must speak with you, but not at the Hall. Then I saw you go today, and I knew that I must explain how it must be, but it was . . .'

It was the first time she had become aware of that flaw; that inclination to avoid the unpleasant, which marred the strength of her lover, but in her joy she turned the tiny spark of doubt away. Was he not perfect, this man of hers?

She interrupted, taking his hand, pressing it to her cheek, her breast, her face radiant.

'Don't, don't, it doesn't matter. Nothing matters, don't you see. I don't care. All I care about is your love for me.

216

You love me. Oh, my darling, if you knew what I have been thinking . . .'

'Zoe, my dearest love.' He caressed her face, rained kisses on her eyes and throat. His hands from long practice and loving habit, found the fastenings of her coat and dress and he uncovered the swell of her breasts, laying his tear-streaked face against them, sucking the engorged nipples, comforting himself, and her, loving her. She responded, her love-starved body and emotions speaking to him without need of words.

With a sigh, regretfully, he drew her dress together, looking into her worshipping eyes, seeing her willingness, her need to comfort, and be comforted.

'No, my little robin, I will not take you here, on the side of the road, like a . . .'

He did not finish the sentence, but held her to him reverently, as if she were delicate porcelain. His voice was sad as he went on.

'I've done you a great wrong. You are only a child in many ways . . No let me finish.' She would have stopped him. 'And I have wronged my wife. You are both good women, and do not deserve such treatment. But does a man choose where he loves? Do you think that I would have chosen to lose my heart to someone who is almost a daughter to me, and my wife?'

He stared into the distance, seeing the hardships ahead. He knew that he should send her away. He could help to find her a job! He had several friends needing an efficient secretary . . .

But how could he bear to part with her?

Zoe touched his arm. 'Jonathan, I know what you're thinking, and the answer will always be the same. As long as you love me, I shall stay near you. I cannot live apart from you, darling.' She faltered. 'Even if . . . if she shares your bed, I must accept it. But please, please don't send me away.'

Chapter Twenty-Eight

1924

Zoe gently brushed Lady Pat's shining, waist-length hair, the rhythmic movement soothing both of them. The room was warm and luxuriously furnished, shutting out the wild January day. The quiet was broken only by the sound of crackling paper as Lady Pat opened another letter with soft white fingers. The lean brown hands of the summer were gone now, gone with the slim waist and trim figure, as her ladyship tranquilly entered her eighth month of pregnancy.

Zoe, too, was content.

The November day on which she had set out to see Jamie in Liverpool, had ended in the soft feather bed of an inn on the edge of the moor near Chester. Though she had been scarlet-faced at the knowing look the landlord gave them, the five-pound note slipped to him by Jonathan had given them a firelit, low-ceilinged bedroom for the afternoon, and the rapture of those hours had dispelled all embarrassment. The months of torment she had known since Lady Pat's return from Northumberland had taught her a hard lesson: every moment in which she and Jonathan could be together must be taken, at whatever price she must pay. And although the opportunities since then had been rare, they were at short enough intervals to make life bearable.

Lady Pat laughed, dropping the letter on to the dressing table and reaching for another.

'Millie Tewkesbury really is a halfwit. She seems to be under the impression that one can ride to hounds in the eighth month of pregnancy.'

She read her next letter, expecting and requiring no answer from Zoe. She was simply voicing her thoughts, and Zoe knew this. The love between them was still deep, though Zoe's position in the household remained an enigma. She was neither servant, friend nor family, she worked in the estate office, was an employee of the Hall, but lived with the family as though she were a daughter.

The close contact she had with them all, more than any member of staff, did not seem to offend any other, with the exception of Nanny Penny. The old woman was almost pensioned off now, living in her own comfortable room at the back of the house. She was slow, and scarcely came to the nursery, where her place had been taken by Bessy – Nanny Bessy now, with a new young nursery maid called Pansy.

Lady Pat lifted her head and smiled. 'Thank you, Zoe dear, that was lovely. No one has such gentle hands as you. I shall write a few letters now, and shan't need you. Go and see if there is anything you can do in the nursery. If not, take Rowan for a gallop. I'm sure she needs it, eating her head off in the stable all day long, and it will do you good, too. I must admit I thought you looked a little peaky a few weeks ago, but you certainly seem better now.'

She smiled again, her kind face thoughtful and caring. She rose from the chair, her bulk seeming not to hinder her, and Zoe turned away, the sadness in her heart making her blink.

'Thank you,' she murmured, guiltily, and left the room.

Zoe and Jonathan had now devised a rough plan which enabled them to live in the same house and yet rarely meet there. They both knew that there was a very real danger that they would betray their feelings for each other, and so, when Zoe was in the nursery, Jonathan tried to visit his wife. When Zoe was helping Lady Pat, Jonathan visited his family, and the problem of the long, difficult dinner hour when the three of them used to sit down together, was solved when Lady Pat declared a desire to eat in the privacy of her room with her husband. Although jealousy bit, it was no worse than when husband and wife shut their bedroom door on the rest of the world at night, and Zoe steadfastly bore the pain.

In this way the lovers felt that there was less risk of a glance, or an unthinking word giving the game away. They were alone together only in the estate office, and though no words had been spoken, they knew instinctively that even here they must act out the part of master and servant, though the temptation to touch and kiss, to exchange loving looks, was enormous. They longed to close and lock the door, to fall to the floor in a passionate embrace, but the presence of Lady Pat stood between them, and they would not dishonour her in her own home. He would come back to work in the office with some murmured excuse to his wife, but, as they looked at each other across a cluttered desk, he often thought that perhaps he should have stayed in the comparative safety of the library.

Zoe turned the corner of the hallway and her thoughts swooped like a lark in the summer sky. Today she knew he was out on the moor with a neighbour's shoot and would not return until dark.

The nursery was warm with the atmosphere of children contentedly playing with a favourite toy, or reading a much loved book, the dismal day shut firmly outside. They lolled or sat about, on sofa and rug, the small girl, Elizabeth talking to herself in the way of young children. The firelight glinted on the polished brass top of the fireguard and caught the gleam of the shining heads of the children.

They looked up as Zoe entered, smiling their welcome. Beth, as she was called now, scrambled from the sagging old sofa on which Jonathan and Zoe had first loved, and ran to her, her high, sweet voice stumbling over itself as she told of some wonderful event which had happened in her uneventful day. Zoe lifted her, holding the small body close. This child of Jonathan's was more dear to her than any other, and she kissed the soft, sweet-smelling neck, nuzzling the tender skin, until the child giggled and squealed with joy.

Zoe whispered to Bessy, asking if she was needed. She

knew that if the girls, especially Helen, heard of her plan to take the mare for a gallop on the moor, they would plead to come with her, and she felt the need for no one's company.

Bessy smiled her acquiescence and drew the little girls' attention with a book, and a square of chocolate. Zoe slipped from the room unnoticed, and raced downstairs to her room to change.

It was not an ideal day for riding, bitterly cold with a keen wind blowing straight from the east, and when Zoe set out she could feel the first touch of snow sharp against her face. She rode slowly through the wood, checking the side-stepping mare, who was fresh and eager to run, coming out at last into the field, where she allowed the horse to canter. Through the opening in the dry stone wall, and they were free, horse and rider, galloping straight into the teeth of the biting wind. The rush of air, the lash of the pelleted snow, made the mare more skittish, and she shied constantly at everything that caught her rolling eye. For miles they went, circling her beloved Black Tor Crag until at last the wind was at their back. She could feel the tension drain from the horse as she tired, and gently she reined her in, slowing until they were walking quietly up the familiar peak.

She dismounted.

The sky above was so low, if she had stood on a boulder she felt she could have plunged her hand into the fat blackberry-coloured billows. The anger of the winter scene was awesome, stretching away across the moor, the clouds a wash of different shades, from the dirty brown of threatening snow to the black which was beginning to open up above her head. Huge, fat flakes big as guineas whipped into her blinking eyes, then as the wind shifted capriciously, floated like feathers in a vacuum, slow, slow, gentle.

She must not stop long.

She let the mare stand, resting for a moment before the ride home. The wind bit through the jacket she wore, tearing at the scarf about her neck, flinging it back like a banner. Her mind wandered back. Here it was that Lady Pat came into my life, she thought. And here Jonathan, Lady Pat's husband, and therefore forbidden, loved me, just as she did. Her face saddened, and shame spread, familiar, tormenting. She loved them both, she did her friend a great wrong, but she knew she could no more think of giving up the man she loved, than she could jump from the rock on which she stood and fly like the crows which wheeled about the bare trees in the distant wood.

The sound of gunshots cracked clearly on the air, carried by the fierce wind racing across the moor. She looked in the direction from which the sound had come, her sharp eyes scanning the murk which was beginning to envelop the landscape. The snow was coming down in earnest now, changing from the sleety rain which had stung her face at the start of her ride. She peered intently across the wintry moorland, hoping to catch a sight of the shoot, but the light was worsening and with a soft, throaty sound, she turned, gentling the mare who was becoming nervous as the light rapidly failed. She leaped, agile as a deer, from the rock, on to the horse's back and with a word of reassurance, urged her across the plateau, down the frozen track and on in the direction of home.

Almost chilled to the marrow of her bones, a small core of warmth in her heart kept her snug. Life is strange, she thought, as the ground flew beneath the mare's hooves. There was no one in the world who gave a damn about me until Daly. Then there was one person. She died, and there was Lady Pat, and Daisy, two people to love. They have multiplied and I have a whole family now. A family to love, and who need me and care what becomes of me. Her face, under the woollen hat she wore, was joyful with her thoughts, loving.

As she clattered into the stable yard Albert ran to take the mare.

'I bin watchin' fer yer, miss. I were gettin' right worrit. Gonna be a bad un afore long, right enough.'

As he had grown, so had his devotion, and seeing no other come a'wooing, hope was strong within him. His

223

hope increased his vocabulary and the sentence was one of his longest.

'You could be right, Albert. I shouldn't have gone, really, not in this.' She indicated the almost solid wall of snow which fell and obliterated the light from the kitchen doorway.

'Give her a good rub down would you, there's a dear.' She patted the heaving side of the mare affectionately.

Albert's heart sang. She had called him dear. He needed no bidding to rub down the mare, it was part of his job, but he bore no resentment at the reminder. In a warm cloud of euphoria, he led the horse into her stable, and as if she were Zoe herself, he cossetted and gentled her, dreaming his impossible dream.

The object of his desires, in a flurry of snowflakes and steaming breath, rose-tinted cheeks and cold-induced brilliance of eye, was stamping her feet in front of the enormous fire in the old fireplace which had never been removed when Lady Pat had had the kitchen modernized. The chaotic bustle which reigned before each mealtime was in full swing. Out of it would come some order, a perfectly cooked and served meal, but at the moment it looked, as Mrs Hart would say, 'like Fred Karno's circus'. Zoe loved it. With appreciative sips she drank the piping hot mug of tea, thrust with loving and possessive kindness into her hand by Daisy, and watched the familiar scene.

The snow which started to fall that afternoon became a blizzard, which raged for three days, howling across the park. The Hall, well stocked against such storms, settled into indoor routines, reading, sewing and playing by the fire. The stable yard was kept clear, the men working turn and turn about, for the horses must be cared for, and the cows, brought in at the onset of the storm, had to be fed, watered and milked. Hens too, were not forgotten, and each day Albert floundered to the hen house behind the stables to collect the eggs, so life went on much as usual.

The children, though, became fractious with the unfamiliar restrictions and Nanny Bessy threatened to report Miss

Amy to her father if she didn't stop teasing Miss Rosemary, after she had reduced her sister to tears for the third time that morning.

All in all, the last days of January were a strain on the household. It was with a great sense of relief that Mr Kent, the head gardener, opened the kitchen door on the third day in February to a mild, almost spring-like morning. It was five-thirty, and still dark, but he could hear the drip, drip, of the thawing snow, and the gurgle of the water as it ran along the gutters and down the rain spouts.

Chapter Twenty-Nine

It started with Bessy's day off.

The snow had disappeared from the drive, cleared as it thawed by Mr Kent and his men. Zoe walked with Lady Pat. Both were glad of the exercise, and the children ran and shouted, their voices ringing in the quiet air.

Lady Pat was pleased when they arrived at the gate to see that the road was clear, and as the red bus to Runcorn passed by the children waved and cheered. They had been isolated for ten days.

And as Nanny Bessy said to Lady Pat the next morning, she had missed two of her days off because of the weather, and if Lady Pat had no objection, would like to have today off instead of her usual Friday, and go to Runcorn to see Miss Webster, who worked in the library, and who had become her close friend.

Lady Pat, tiring of the monologue, was only too pleased to say yes, and see the back of her. She had less than four weeks to go to the expected birth of her child, and she was feeling very weary.

Bessy left in a whirl of last-minute instructions to Zoe, who was placidly spooning boiled egg into the open pink beak of Beth's mouth.

'I'll be back on the last bus.'

'Have a nice day.'

'Nice day, Nanny,' echoed the child.

Zoe and the children spent the day much as usual. Helen, Diana, Amy and Rosie had lessons in the morning with Miss Rogers, and she and Beth took a walk up to the back pastures to see the horses, frisking like children, glad to be away from the stables at last.

Zoe saw Jonathan in the distance, talking to Mr Kent. Her

stomach did its usual somersault at the sight of him, and for an instant she was tempted to call to him, just to see the candle flame of love in his eyes. It was so long since they had exchanged even a word. Perhaps soon, on her next free day . . . She turned away and followed the little girl.

Zoe checked the nursery clock against the tiny watch pinned to her dress front, and for the twentieth time went to the dark window to peer out into the night. It was nine-thirty, and Bessy should have returned half an hour ago: the last bus to the village left Runcorn at seven-thirty. It wasn't like her to be late. Perhaps she had already arrived, and was drinking cocoa in the kitchen. It was extremely unlikely: she'd be sure to check on her charges first.

'I'd best go down and see, though,' Zoe said to Pansy. She didn't want to disturb Lady Pat: she was so very easily tired now, and any worry that could be kept from her, she herself would see to.

'You stay here,' she murmured to the girl, dozing by the fire. 'And don't leave the nursery,' she added sharply. She did not quite trust the new nursery maid, though she could not have said why. She was cheerful and hardworking, and came from Grange Hall, Lady Pat's home and so was very highly recommended. Perhaps it was something about her drifting eyes, which never looked directly at you.

Zoe peeped into each room in turn, bending over the sleeping forms of the children. Reassured that they could be left with Pansy, she hurried down the back stairs to the kitchen.

Cook's head jerked as Zoe came into the huge, beautifully warm room.

'There you are, me duck. What can we do for you? One of the children want a drink? There's cocoa in the jug.'

'No thanks, Cook. Bessy's not back yet and I'm a bit concerned. I can't think what can have happened to her.'

'Nay, don't fret, lass. It's none of your fault if she's gadding off somewhere. Perhaps she's got a chap.'

'Oh, no. She goes to her friend for the day. Bessy's not

interested in chaps.' Zoe laughed. 'But I'll have a cup of cocoa while I'm here, and then I'll go to bed. If Bessy does come back, tell her, will you? Pansy will have to sleep in the night nursery.'

She drank her cocoa and left. Cook stared into the fire, reluctant to leave its warmth. With a great sigh, and a muttered, 'It's no good, Dora, off you go,' she heaved herself out of the comfortable rocking chair. She filled her stone hot water bottle from the steaming kettle, wrapping it in the bit of old blanket kept for the purpose, and made her way along the chilly corridor and up to her room.

Zoe's message was forgotten.

Most of the occupants of the Hall were wrapped in sleep.

In her sparsely furnished bedroom next to the nursery, Pansy shed her clothes until she stood naked in the soft candlelight.

She smiled, a shameless, sensual smile, and ran her hands down her curving body, then unfastened her mass of hair from its pins, and let it fall in luxurious abundance about her face. Zoe's repeated admonishments – that she was to be called immediately should any of the children awaken; that Lady Pat was not to be disturbed; that Pansy must on no account allow the nursery light to go out – had all been forgotten.

A sound from the day nursery, tiny, almost inaudible, widened her eager smile. Opening the door wide, she swayed unblushingly into the room, the glowing fire touching her nakedness.

The footman stood against the door he had just closed quietly behind him. He groaned as Pansy stood before him. What an opportunity. The few fumbling encounters they had enjoyed in the past weeks had left them both eager for more. She stepped closer and licked her lips. Hardly able to contain himself, he tore off his breeches, frogged coat and stockings, until he was as naked as her.

With sighs of satisfaction, they sank to the floor. Zoe not thought to tell the girl that her lover was not to visit her.

*

229

'I'm sorry to disturb you, m'lady. There was a telephone message, and there was no one else to inform. Sir Jonathan left the library some minutes ago, and I'm afraid I don't know where . . .'

Lady Pat cut him off. 'That's quite all right, Temple. I will deal with it. You say an accident? Is Nanny Bessy badly hurt?'

'It seems not, m'lady, but there is no chance that she will be able to return tonight. The bus ran off the road on the outskirts of Runcorn. Apparently the passengers on the bus are being taken to Runcorn Infirmary. Some of them are badly shaken, but Nanny . . .'

'Yes, yes, I see.' Lady Pat leaned back against the pillows. The children must be checked. Pansy would still be in the nursery, of course. She would not leave until Bessy returned, but she was very young . . .

Temple coughed gently.

'Oh, yes, Temple, thank you. You get to your bed. I'll see to things. Pansy will still be in the nursery, I'm sure, but where Sir Jonathan has got to, I can't imagine.'

As the door closed behind the butler she lifted herself laboriously from her froth of pillows, and put on her dressing gown and slippers. Quietly she let herself out of the room.

She was not surprised to see the faint light shining around the frame of the nursery door. Poor child, she must be worried about Bessy, and at the prospect of being left alone all night. She opened the door.

Lady Pat had seen no naked body except her husband's, and then only briefly as he removed his dressing gown to join her in the marriage bed. She was also in the highly emotional state of the last month of pregnancy. At the sight of the heaving bodies on the floor, she stepped back in revulsion. Then she began to moan. She groped for the door handle, and turning clumsily, stumbled from the room, leaving Pansy and her lover to stagger to their feet in horror.

Moving heavily, Lady Pat lumbered along the uncarpeted nursery corridor, one thought in her mind: to get as far as possible from the hideousness defiling her children's nursery, to find her husband and to sob out her distress in his comforting arms.

'Jonty, Jonty!' she cried as she reached the head of the stairs which led down to the first floor and her husband's room. She was shaking as she shuffled awkwardly down the nursery stair. As she reached the bottom, her foot in its dainty mule caught in the hem of her nightgown, and she fell heavily. A pain shot agonisingly through her lower belly as she hit the floor, but she was up in a second, hauling herself to her feet like a wounded elephant, still calling frantically.

'Jonty, Jonty!'

At last she reached his door and flung it open. The room was in darkness. Oh God, where was he when she needed him so? Another sharp pain pierced her, and she doubled up. Where was he? Perhaps Temple was mistaken and he was still in the library. She must find him. He must see to the couple who were . . . she could not bear it. To think of those . . . those . . . and in her babies' room.

Sobbing uncontrollably she lurched to the top of the wide staircase which swooped gracefully to the dimly lit hall. She could see the library doorway, half open, and a light shone from it, encouraging, enticing, friendly. He was there. Jonty was there.

Eagerly she took a step forward and put out her hand to the polished bannister rail. Her foot almost brushed the second step. Almost, but not quite.

Her slipper fell away before her, bouncing lightly from step to step, its pretty white fur gleaming like a snowflake against the dark red carpet. It kept ahead of her as she fell, as though leading the way. She did not go lightly. As she fell into that dark, beautiful hallway, her body twisted and hammered on the stairs and then the carved bannister. And then she screamed. Her head cracked like a pistol shot on a newel post, and the sound bit the quiet of the house.

*

231

Dear God, what was that?

Zoe leaped from her bed, shaking with fear, stumbling against familiar objects. Dear God, oh, dear God . . . one of the children . . .

She flung open her door and ran down the landing. There was nothing to be seen. She heard a door bang somewhere and footsteps, and a woman's voice quavered timorously from a room above. Another door was opened on a distant corridor, and two figures appeared from the servants' rooms. The first was Daisy, her bright and rosy face like paper now in the soft light from the table lamp. Following her, his checked dressing gown only half shrugged on to his shoulders, was George, one of the footmen. Others jostled behind.

'What in heaven was it?' Daisy breathed. As she saw Zoe, her face cleared a little, for her first thought had been for her friend.

Then George moved to the head of the stairs and let out a hoarse shout.

Zoe was the first to move. With her hair flying behind her, her nightgown clasped above her knees, she ran on bare feet towards him and looked down. 'Find Jonathan!' she shouted as she ran down the stairs.

Lady Pat lay like a doll flung irritably away. Her head was turned carelessly in one direction – her body faced the other. Her legs were hidden beneath her nightgown, a deep, sodden crimson, and her feet were turned at a curious angle. Everything, her arms, her head, her feet, seemed to be put on the wrong way.

For an instant which seemed like a century, the appalled servants stood with mouths agape. Then they moved.

Jonathan was found in the stable where he had been peacefully chatting to Sam. He ran before the panting footman and knelt beside his wife, as blood poured from her. Across her body his eyes met Zoe's in anguish.

The doctor was sent for. Water was put on the stove to boil, and hot bottles placed tenderly about the still figure. Her bed was warmed in readiness, and the fire stoked up, and in the kitchen the women wept, for they bustled as though in preparation for a birth, and the shadow of death stalked the house.

On each side of that broken form, Jonathan and Zoe knelt protectively.

'Should we lift her, d'you think?'

Zoe looked up, her face like marble in the soft light from the hall lamp.

'I don't know,' she whispered.

The woman between them moaned, and her head moved. The bright flow of blood spread like a tide.

'Dear God, where's that damn doctor.' Jonathan looked desperately over his shoulder. 'He's had time to get here and back by now.'

A little knot of servants stood like statues in the shadowy hall.

Lady Pat's mouth opened, and a dreadful sound emerged. It was evident that she was in agony.

'We must do something. We can't just . . . sit here.' Jonathan groaned and passed a trembling, tender hand across his wife's face.

'The doctor will be here in a moment.'

Zoe tried to speak reassuringly, but she was deathly afraid.

Then a movement beneath the nightgown caught their attention, and Zoe's face went even paler. She looked round wildly.

'Temple, quickly, take . . . the . . . go to the kitchen at once. Daisy, come and . . . help . . . Daisy!'

In a moment the women came to kneel beside her. Quickly, casting aside all modesty, Zoe threw Lady Pat's nightdress up to her waist. Her legs, still askew, were parted, and from between her thighs came the head and shoulders of her child.

'Dear God, oh, dear Lord, what shall we . . . what . . .'

Jonathan's face was filled with terror, and he shook as if grasped by some giant hand. Swiftly the women elbowed him aside.

Suddenly, in a further gush of blood, the baby was thrust on to the thick pile of the carpet. It was a boy. He lay still, silent, his pitiful, bloody limbs flung this way and that. His chest did not flutter, nor his blue mouth open, and Cook leaned back on her heels, and threw her apron over her head.

He lay, the longed-for son, and his tiny heart never flickered.

From the back door two quiet figures slipped from the house and hurried unseen, across the park at the back of the house. When they reached the shadow of the wall, they crept like thieves along it until they reached the gate. Like two wraiths, Pansy and her lover slipped away into the night.

Lady Pat recovered consciousness next morning. Her body was black with bruises, her wrist was fractured, and she could not see for the swellings round her eyes. She held her husband's hand tightly. He was all she had to cling to as the doctor told her she would never walk again.

Chapter Thirty

'I should have been with her,' he wept. 'I shouldn't have left her alone.'

It was a week later and as Lady Pat slept in the merciful arms of the sedative which the doctor had just administered, Jonathan gave way at last to the tormented guilt which had eaten him since he had held her trembling hand, and the doctor had delivered his death sentence.

Or so it seemed to Jonathan. To lie like some delicate felled sapling, with all her life before her, helpless and dependent on those about her for the smallest task. Never again to feel the horse beneath her, the wind joyously snatching her hair from its neat black bowler, as she thundered across fields, following the high, pealing voices of the hounds. Never to walk with her young daughters across the deer-dotted parkland, down to the lake and the gliding swans, the busy bustling ducks. The moors would call her, like a lover who is keening for one who is lost for ever, and she could not answer. She would never again walk the lovely, ornamental gardens which she herself had designed and supervised so lovingly, and in which she took such pride, or tread the carpeted stairs to the beautiful window, under which he had seen her pause, gazing contentedly at the order around her. Her footsteps would no longer guide her to the library, where they had spent so many companionable hours together, nor run like the wind with Candy and Floss as she threw the stick which they loved to chase.

She might as well be in the grave with her son – and all because of Jonathan. He had made her pregnant. He had made her as she was, clumsy and vulnerable. Though he had loved someone else he had taken her, used her, given her a child, and when she had needed him, he had been elsewhere.

Restless, haunted by images of Zoe, he had gone from the house to the stables, in need of distraction.

He would never forgive himself.

He had spent every possible moment of the last grim week with his wife: hour after hour, holding her hand, dozing when she slept. He was with her when she woke in the morning, and as she fell asleep at night. His patience was endless. He brought her tray from the kitchen, setting it himself. He fed her, tenderly spooning the food into her mouth as she opened it indifferently, for she cared not whether she lived or died. His guilt and grief consumed him and his pity was enormous.

Zoe was there beside him, a pale shadow, waiting for some word or look, some gesture that would acknowledge her presence, her longing to help and comfort, but none came. She would give her life for the woman who had restored her own desire to live again, nearly six years ago.

But Lady Pat needed no one but her Jonty. At last he was looking at her with eyes filled with emotion, giving her the loving attention she had always craved, and she clung to him.

But that night, as she lay in her drugged sleep, watched over by the nurse, he locked himself in the library. Gaunt and pale, he strode towards the table by the glowing fire and reached for the decanter of whisky and a glass. He sat down heavily. The dogs whined outside the door, but he ignored them.

For three hours he drank, ringing only once for Temple to bring him another bottle, and the old man was frightened by the sight of the drawn face, the tortured eyes, and the slurred speech of his master. Sir Jonathan did not get drunk. In all the years that Temple had served the Weston family, not once had he seen a member of it the worse for drink. They were gentlemen and could hold their liquor. They became merry and charming, and always remained polite to their servants. This sodden wreck of a man was a stranger to him.

To whom should he go for advice? The old man stood indecisively outside the library door as Sir Jonathan shut it in his face, turning the key once more. He picked at his lip, and stared at the tapestry on the wall. Then his face cleared and with relief he began to walk sedately towards the staircase. Zoe. She would help. She was almost a Weston herself now, and her devotion to the family, particularly Lady Pat, was part of the weft and weave of life at the Hall. She would speak to Sir Jonathan or at least try. Surely he would listen to her?

The door opened a sliver and Zoe's strained face peeped out.

'What is it?' she whispered.

'It's Sir Jonathan, Zoe,' the old man quavered.

Zoe's face changed, and such a look of loving concern passed over it that even Temple, old and shortsighted as he was, could not have failed to see it, but her back was to the lighted room, and the lamp, which was kept lit on the hall table, was dim.

'He's drinking in the library. Two bottles already and I'm afraid . . .'

Zoe put her hand to her mouth, and the expression on her face changed to one of distress.

Dear God, what next. She stepped away from the door for a moment, disappearing into the room. She crossed to the door which connected with her ladyship's bedroom and opened it quietly. The nurse's head turned instantly and she smiled.

'She's asleep,' she whispered. 'Go and rest, child.'

It took nearly half an hour of knocking and impassioned pleading before Jonathan fumbled with the key, and Zoe nearly fell as she slipped into the room. She took his arm and led him, stumbling and stupid, back to the fireplace, and the dogs, who had whipped in with her as the door was

237

opened, nosed joyously at Jonathan's hand as he sank on to the comfortable sofa.

Kneeling, Zoe lifted a couple of small logs in to the heart of the dying fire. They caught and crackled companionably. The dogs yawned, satisfied now that they had greeted their master, and turned round a time or two before settling down on the rug, their soft noses resting on their golden paws, brown eyes blinking and gazing at him with devotion.

Jonathan was mumbling unintelligibly. His hand shook and whisky spilled on to his jacket. He looked down at it regretfully, the comical picture of a child who has soiled the nice clean shirt Nanny has just dressed him in.

'Tut, tut, tut,' he murmured, and fumbled at the stain.

Zoe's heart ached to see him like this. Where had he gone, her beautiful strong lover, the man who held her in passionate tenderness? Where was the warm look of ardour, of enchantment? Where the gentleness, the glowing, loving spirit of the man? He was sottish, befuddled, ugly. He stank of whisky, and his breath was foul.

'Oh, Jonathan, my love, my love.' Her voice broke. She rang the bell, and when Temple came to the door so quickly he might have been standing on the other side, she ordered coffee and sandwiches.

Patiently, like a mother coaxing a fractious child, she fed the broken man, pouring cup after cup of hot, black coffee down his throat.

It was almost dawn when he began to sober up and she held him in her arms, cradling his head against her breast. He opened her dress and placed his weary face against the sweet curve of her swelling bosom, nuzzling the firm nipples like a baby, and as he had always done he drew comfort from her nakedness. She slipped her dress from her shoulders and held him against her white, velvet, loveliness and rocked him, until at last he was able to speak.

'Zoe, Zoe, Zoe.' It was a litany of despair. 'Oh, God, what shall we do . . . what are we to do . . . How can we help her? I can scarcely bear to look into her eyes . . . the guilt . . . I love you, I love you so . . . but how can I . . . I should not have left her . . . if it wasn't for me she would be . . . and the baby, my son, my son.' He wept, and she crooned to him, holding him closer.

'Ssh, ssh . . . my darling . . . you must not . . . ssh . . . sssh.'

He groaned. 'How can we go on . . . love each other as . . . when she's so helpless. It's got to end . . . She looks at me with such love and pain . . . she doesn't want to live but she still loves me . . .'

At last he fell into a restless sleep, and Zoe stayed beside him, tenderly stroking his face and hair.

The room became light as the wintry day took shape and the darkness slipped away. It was cold, for she dare not leave his grasp to feed the fire. The dogs padded uneasily from the sofa to the door, asking to be let out, but still she did not move, for now he was quiet and she knew he slept.

It was almost midday when he woke up. He smiled wanly and touched her cheek.

'Little robin,' he whispered, 'How I love you. What would we all do without you? You have given us so much of yourself, and now . . .'

He lifted her gently until they could look into each other's eyes.

'You will look after her?' he said, the words of parting he had spoken in the night forgotten.

'Oh, yes. I couldn't think of doing anything else.'

'It will be very hard.'

'For you, too.'

They gazed steadily at each other.

'I love you.' He bent his head and gently kissed her lips. 'I always will.'

'I know. Me too.'

They left the room quietly, and Temple watched them from a discreet distance, as they walked tiredly up the wide staircase. Something in their posture, in the way they moved together, though they did not touch, gave him the first inkling, and his old heart was sad. Could it be . . . ?

239

Was there some . . . ? They rounded the curve of the staircase, and disappeared from his view, but still he stood.

He was the only one of the household to feel the first faint brush of suspicion, but he would say nothing. In the last, terrible days, the only one who had kept her head and strength of mind had been Zoe. If she was . . . if she and the master . . . were . . . He could not phrase it, even in his own mind, but if she were to lead from now on, he would follow.

He turned and made his way to the kitchen, his face unreadable.

Chapter Thirty-One

Jonathan made himself nurse and companion, neglecting his duties on the estate. He talked to his wife for hours, telling her of every small event which took place in the big house, in the village and the scattered farms, and gradually, day by day, she began to respond. She would listen, her eyes on his, waiting for that look of casual affection to replace the warm, loving care which shone there. But it never returned. Always, as her watchful eyes gazed into his, scarcely hearing the words, his eyes would glow with a warmth, a wealth of love that melted the ice of hopelessness round her heart. Time after time he brought her back from despair, and at last she began to heal.

At first she was allowed no pillows and was forced to stare at a spot directly above her. If she wanted to see the person talking to her, they had to stand immediately next to the bed.

The first time Zoe saw her like that she burst into tears, and had to be led away by the nurse, the figure in the bed unseeing, uncaring, the soft rise and fall of the bedclothes the only indication she was still alive.

But the weeks passed and, wrapped now in the mantle of her husband's love, Lady Pat emerged from her protective shell. Pillows were allowed, until she was able to sit up, and a physiotherapist came every day to pull and twist and pound, to massage and exercise until the invalid was able to move her neck and head and shoulders, and then her arms and hands.

Always Jonathan was with her, encouraging, holding her in his arms as she cried with pain. And her strength returned, and with it her sweetness and humour and, at last, acceptance.

Gradually she could be lifted into a chair by the window, and watch the children play, and they would wave. They had been told that Mamma had had an accident, and must not be disturbed, and that they must blow a kiss as they ran down to the lake. They did so casually. Their Mamma was kind, and had always been affectionate as she kissed them goodnight, but Zoe and Nanny Bessy were their mother-figures, now that Nanny Penny's reign had ended. Their Mamma's illness did not especially affect their young lives, and they became used to the sight of the pale smiling face, and the hand that lifted to them as they followed their own exciting pursuits.

The day came at last when they were allowed in to see her. They were quiet at first, awed by the gentle person who had once been their sturdy, active mother. They stood in a neatly dressed line, like soldiers at attention, the toddler, Beth, carried by Nanny Bessy for fear she would run and leap upon her Mamma, and the silence seemed to stretch as they gazed at each other like polite strangers.

Lady Pat looked at her youngest child. She was still plump and soft, still in her baby clothes, and her bright eyes stared curiously at the figure in the chair. She rested her elbow comfortably on Nanny Bessy's shoulder, then said questioningly: 'Mamma?'

Lady Pat smiled and the ice was broken.

'Yes, my darling, Mamma. Put her down, Nanny, and let her come to me. No harm can be done now.' The words were said without bitterness.

The toddler tumbled towards the chair and reached out her hands. Lady Pat took them longingly, then leant forward and lifted her up to sit on her lap.

Zoe and Nanny Bessy gasped, and stepped forward, instinctively, protective, whether for the child's sake or her mother's, neither was sure. Perhaps for both, for Beth was sturdy and her weight might tip the frail woman forward. But Lady Pat looked at them and her smile widened, seeming to say:

'Look, you doubters, I am holding my child. I am able to nurse my daughter, and I will be a mother again.'

The other girls crowded round her. Helen shyly kissed her mother's cheek, and Rosemary tried to climb beside Beth on to her mother's lap. Chairs were arranged, and with some diplomacy the children were seated about her, for there was much vying for the attention of this interesting person who took such an interest in their conversation.

It tired her, that first time, and she soon had to be lifted back to her bed, but each day they came to her she grew stronger, and the time they spent with her lengthened. As they became used to her, to her stillness, they discovered that this Mamma was every bit as nice as the old one, though in a different way. She played games with them: ludo, snakes and ladders, and snap. And, particularly in the case of the older girls, she grew close to them in a way which she had never done before her accident. Now she was always in one place, and could be relied upon to listen to their problems whenever they needed her. She treated them as adults, and listened carefully, woman to woman, and they loved her as they had never done before.

A wheelchair appeared, especially made in London, and at the end of April Jonathan wrapped her up warmly with rugs, and carried her down the stairs, and into the garden, where he tenderly tucked her into it, watched by a cavalcade of hushed children. The whole performance took on the feel of an outing, almost like the day on which Papa's new car came from London, and they had taken their first ride in it. The chair was like a new toy, and they must all play with it, pushing Mama in turns under their father's watchful eye.

Beth was secretly the favoured one now, for she was still a baby, and Lady Pat knew there would be no sons for Jonty. She rode on her mother's knee, plainly delighted with the arrangement. It seemed to her infant mind that she and Mamma were children together, riding in the same pram, and her face was cherubic with glee.

But when the children were in the nursery, or incarcerated with Miss Rogers, Jonathan pushed Lady Pat round the grounds alone, finding sheltered spots to sit in the pale, spring sunshine. He would read to her and hold her hand, and as she smiled fondly, at last able to show him the full extent of her love, he would smile back, and lean forward to kiss her pale lips gently.

He grew even thinner, but his solicitous care for his wife continued.

The doctor came and went away again, shaking his head. Lady Pat was as well as she could ever be, but he had watched with deep anxiety Sir Jonathan fussing around her, and as he sat in his surgery that evening he considered how to tell him that if he did not get on with his own life he would go under.

And so would Lady Pat.

She must be allowed to develop, to find a way to mould her new life; to make it acceptable, livable. If she was to become free and independent, she must learn the ways to do it. Sir Jonathan must be able to see that everything necessary could be done, for the time being, by the nurse who sat idle all day, or by Zoe, who waited and longed to help, but was turned away each time she tried.

Zoe watched Jonathan also, her heart breaking for his weariness, but her timid suggestions that perhaps Lady Pat might be allowed to hold her own book, to read to herself, to brush her hair; to cut up her own food or arrange a few flowers, were met with a coldness which shrivelled her. She loved them so! They were both dear to her as no one had been before – not even Daly. But Jonathan, though he had begged her to look after his wife, begrudged any task she tried to take from him.

For months, since that night in the library, they had barely spoken except in Lady Pat's presence. It was as though he were afraid that if he turned to her at all he would stop caring for his wife. He needed to love, to protect her; to carry her around like a child. He needed it in order to be able to live with himself.

Chapter Thirty-Two

'Zoe, will you obey me just for once and go! I am perfectly able to manage by myself. Jonty is about somewhere, and if I need anything, I have only to ring that bell and a dozen servants will rush to my aid.'

Zoe laughed, and patted the hand lying on the arm of the wheelchair. She got up and walked towards the window and flung it open, gazing into the pale, mauve haze, which blurred the summer's day.

During the past weeks, as Lady Pat had struggled to become a wife, if in name only; to be a mother to her children; and the keeper of her husband's home, Zoe had fought each step of the way beside her. To watch as Lady Pat was at last able to put on and do up her own shoe, to write a letter to a friend, to answer the telephone and comfort a crying child; to tell her housekeeper, her butler, her cook, what should be done, when and how; today, tomorrow or next week, was a miracle, and they rejoiced together.

Zoe had regained the weight she had lost in the first months after the accident, and today, in a simple yellow linen dress, her young figure was more beautiful than ever. Her chestnut hair had recovered its vibrancy, and she wore it in a loose knot at the nape of her neck. Small curls were for ever escaping, softening the severity of the style, but she looked older than her nineteen years, with a maturity which could only have been brought about by suffering. There was a ghost of past sadness lurking in the depths of her eyes, but the shadow of her lovely smile lay about her mouth, ready to shine with the sweetness which had always been a part of her nature.

Lady Pat looked at her with loving admiration. She and

Zoe fitted together like a hand in a glove, and the deep bond of affection grew between them every day. Zoe had come to terms with what had happened: tears would not restore to Lady Pat the use of her legs, but if there was any way she could help her live a fulfilled life she would do it gladly. And her companionship and gentle encouragement had done far more to restore Lady Pat's dignity and independence, than the smothering blanket laid about her by her husband.

'Well, are you going or not?' Lady Pat mocked.

'Oh, I give in,' said Zoe, looking out of the window with a wistfulness which was not lost on the older woman. 'It would be nice to take Rowan out. I haven't been for a ride since . . .' She looked confused, hesitating to finish the sentence.

'. . . since my accident.' Lady Pat finished it for her. 'You don't have to avoid the subject, Zoe.' She smiled fondly. 'I have some wonderful news for you. The doctor has assured me that I shall soon be out of here. I've had an idea for quite a while – to have a small trap designed, a little dog cart which I can manage myself. Don't tell Jonty, will you? You know how he fusses and . . .'

Zoe's eyes filled with tears.

'Don't, my dear, don't cry. I'm not in pain now, and I have so much . . . with you and Jonty I can . . .'

Zoe marvelled at this brave woman. Lady Pat was comforting *her*, begging *her* not to cry, not to be upset. She swallowed back her tears.

Lady Pat watched Zoe's face lighten and laughed shakily. 'Now give me a bit of peace for a while – I'm sick to death of your bossiness. I'll expect you back for dinner and not before.'

She reached for her book and with a wave dismissed her. Zoe walked towards the door. She turned to look back at the woman in the chair, and wondered at the contentment written on her face. She had never seen it there in all the years she had known her.

*

It was like a moving picture run for the second time. The same setting, the same players, even the same lark singing its heart out in the great pale blue canvas of the sky.

Only the words were different.

Zoe rode through the paddock, and along a little-used path taking a different direction to the one which had become the favourite of them all. It was warm, almost humid; the low hills in the far distance looked blue and smoky, as they rose gently to meet the milky sky. On she went, and up. The slopes were gentle here, and in places the turf was so smooth it looked as though it had been recently mowed. Rowan snickered, and Zoe gave her her head. For mile after mile they galloped, the girl's face close between the horse's ears. She whispered to the mare as they flew across the uneven ground telling her of her love and longing. 'Jonathan, Jonathan, Jonathan . . .'

They came to a stream, edged with fern and rough stone, and Zoe pulled Rowan to a halt and slid to the ground. They stood together in quiet companionship, looking out towards the farmland in the distant west: fields disected by neat, dry-stone walls. Then she remounted, and let the mare pick her dainty way, as she daydreamed, stirrup-free and dangling. For an hour they wandered peacefully, Zoe in her own world, where Jonathan made love to her until her breath grew ragged. She moaned softly aloud.

The mare's ears pricked, and she stopped.

Zoe sighed and looked about her.

She was on Black Tor Crag.

His shadow fell across her as she sat on the hollowed out rock, cutting off the warmth of the sun, which caressed her through the thin cotton of her shirt. Her face was turned towards the chimneys of the Hall, shimmering far below, and she didn't see him as he rode up the rocky track behind the plateau.

He stood tall beside her, his thinness was emphasised by the loose fit of jodhpurs and open shirt. His face was weary

247

with strain, but his eyes, as he turned to look at her, burned with love.

She smiled up at him and he sat down, reached for her hand, and tucked it between his, gently stroking the skin with his thumb. For a long time they sat in silence, drawing strength and comfort from each other, as they had always done, and she marvelled that a man so attuned to the needs of one woman, could be so wrong about another. She leaned her head against his shoulder, and he bent to kiss her, tenderly, chastely.

She pushed him gently away.

'We must talk.'

'I suppose so, little robin, though I must say it is remarkably pleasant just sitting here in the sunshine kissing you.' He grinned, and for a moment her heart leapt. He was her old Jonathan again, her Jonathan of the lake, and the enchanted summer, and the laughter. He had called her 'little robin'.

But they *had* to talk. She began hesitantly.

'Lady Pat . . . is better, Jonathan, much better. If I left now, she would manage. She doesn't need me.'

She felt him stiffen beside her.

'Leave? Are you going to leave?'

'Not unless you ask me to.'

He relaxed again, pulling her against him. 'Zoe, don't frighten me so. I never want you to go, never. I couldn't live without you, even if Pat could.' His voice dropped. 'I know it's been hell for you these last months, and I'm to blame. That night, I was lonely for you. I only wandered out to the stables to look at Prince, intending to stay a moment, but Sam and I got talking. I shouldn't have gone, wouldn't have, but I was thinking of you, I wanted you. I had to get out of the house for a bit . . .'

His shoulders sagged. Zoe realised that he was still looking for somewhere to lay the blame; if he hadn't been thinking about her, the accident might not have happened.

The weakness of his endless self-punishment, self-pity, saddened her, but her love did not falter. Her strong,

248

commanding lover was gone but the man who remained still tore at her heart.

She put her hand on his lips, and held him against her.

'Jonathan, you must stop it – all the recriminations, the blaming, the guilt. It wasn't your fault. We must go on, not look backwards. We love each other, we always will. It is part of us now, but we both love Lady Pat. Isn't that right?'

He nodded sadly.

'We must make a life for ourselves, here, with her, but she must never know about us. Never. No one must know. Do you understand what I'm saying? For as long as she needs us, we must be here, and never hurt her, but we must be realistic enough to accept that we too, have needs.'

She stopped, but he didn't speak.

'One more thing. You must allow her to develop, Jonathan.' She took a deep breath, knowing what she was about to say would hurt him beyond measure.

'You must stop smothering her.'

He raised his head, and looked unbelievingly into her eyes. His own became cold, and he sat up, moving away.

'What is that supposed to mean?'

'She wants to be independent,' Zoe replied. 'To do things for herself. You treat her like bone china, wrapping her in cotton wool as though she might shatter . . .'

'Damn it, woman, she broke her back,' he yelled. 'She can't walk – what am I supposed to do? Just let her fend for herself? She's helpless . . . and it's our . . . my fault.'

She heard the swift correction, and realised that she had been right; he *did* blame her as much as himself. Deep down he resented the fact that he had been sleepless that night; had gone to the stables because he could not sleep, because of her. He had suffered a double loss: his wife still lived, but his son had died, and he would never have another.

She said icily: 'You cannot go on working out your guilt on a cripple, Jonathan.'

He recoiled.

'Zoe. Dear God. Zoe, don't, please don't.' His face was ashen.

249

Her heart was breaking as she steeled herself to go on. 'She loves you, Jonathan. She would do anything for you. Oh, my love, don't you see?' Her voice broke. 'You *must* let her go, let her build her world again – around you and the children, certainly, but let *her* do it. Help her. Encourage her. She needs to start her life again, not to sit around and wait for you. She is afraid of hurting you; of letting you see that what you are doing is stifling her, holding her back from recovery.'

The tears welled in her eyes.

There was silence, utter and complete.

Then Jonathan turned to her, desolate.

'Zoe.' He was sobbing now. 'Help me.'

She stroked his hair and kissed his wet cheeks, holding him closer and closer until they lay side by side. She cradled his head on her breast, holding him along the full length of her body.

He lifted his head from her breast and his eyes found hers. She was looking at him with an answering longing. He raised himself on his elbow and looked down at her, his face filled with passionate tenderness.

'Zoe,' he breathed, 'Little robin, I love you . . .'

His mouth came gently down on hers. It was a kiss of thistledown, a mere brushing, but it seared them both to the core.

It had been so long, so long.

Slowly he unbuttoned her shirt, and the sweet white flesh, pink-tinted, thrust its beauty towards him. Her nipples stood like peaks, and his hands and lips reached for them in an ecstasy of longing.

'Zoe, Zoe . . .' His groan of wonder and joy echoed softly on the hillside, but there was no one to hear. And no one to see as they undressed each other, and loved each other, there on Black Tor Crag.

Only the lark, which began to sing again.

Chapter Thirty-Three

Summer 1928

They were a strange cavalcade as they struggled, one behind the other, across the tiny golden beach towards the boat pulled up above the water line.

There were ten of them, their voices rising on the hot, still morning air, echoing against the towering cliffs as they made their way down to the sea.

At the head of the line was a tall, slim girl of about fourteen. She wore a pair of brief shorts and a cotton shirt, and her skin was the colour of amber. Her bare feet kicked up small puffs in the pale sand; she carried a couple of deck chairs which she dropped carelessly, then strode towards the water.

A 'tsk tsk' came from an old woman at the rear of the column.

Four more girls followed, in scanty swimsuits and sunhats, all tanned and laughing.

A handsome man and beautiful young woman walked slowly, carefully after the others. Their hands were clasped together, forming a chair, and they carried a slender woman with greying hair between them. She laughed at something one of them said, and they hugged her affectionately. Her legs, in white cotton trousers, dangled lifelessly.

Bringing up the rear were two women in light-weight Nanny's uniforms and caps, the younger laden with boxes and rugs and a sunshade. It was the elder who had shown her displeasure.

And lastly, another young girl. She was dressed like the first, in shorts and a shirt, and carried a mass of paraphernalia: a picnic basket and two fishing rods, a beach ball, and a rubber ring.

'. . . don't know why I bother . . . not needed . . . I should have stayed at home . . . too old for this . . .' The old woman was grumbling.

They all ignored her. Nanny Penny was harmless enough, and after all she had been with them for so long. She must be allowed some licence in her old age, even though they would have been happy to see her remain at Weston Hall. But for some reason she insisted on coming, though it was obvious she would be more comfortable in her own room, among her own small possessions. She stared now with jealous, prying eyes at the back of the man and the woman who carried Lady Pat.

The first girl reached the boat, and struggled to push it into the sea. She was quickly joined by her sisters: laughing hysterically, they pushed and shoved, and the gulls scattered.

'Wait a minute, Helen!' Jonathan called, 'You can't manage it on your own.' He and Zoe gently placed Lady Pat on the sand and ran towards the girls. 'Now then,' he said, 'Helen and Zoe on that side, and Diana and myself on this, and when I say, all push together. Right? Now!'

The group strained and slipped in the sand, and Diana fell to her knees as the boat moved into the shallow water.

Lady Pat shrieked with laughter, and shouted encouragement, her face bright with love and happiness as she watched her family. Nanny Penny shook her head. With a last enormous heave, the boat was afloat in a rippling circle.

'Jump in, Helen, and catch these bags.'

Jonathan shouted instructions as he lifted the two youngest children into the rowing boat, and with many cries, and much hilarity, the girls were aboard. Turning, Zoe and Jonathan walked back to Lady Pat and lifting her carefully, carried her to the gently rocking vessel and lifted her, seating her in the prow. Jonathan turned to Zoe and held out his hand to her, his love glowing in his eyes like a steady, unmoving candle flame.

Tenderly he helped her into the boat, then, with less

delicacy, he heaved up his eldest daughter. He jumped in after her and shoved off with the oar.

Nanny Penny watched this display with unblinking intensity.

'Okay, darling,' said Jonathan, 'then off we go into the deep, blue briny . . .' He began to sing, 'A life on the ocean wave . . .' The girls joined in. Their voices floated across the water for many minutes as they left the tiny bay, and headed away from the land. The two women on the shore put up their deckchairs. The sunshade was placed above Nanny Penny's head, and after looking about her to see that all was in order, she began to doze.

Peace descended on the cove.

It was 1928, the third year that Jonathan had rented the Cornish house on the cliff top between Helston and Marazion, foursquare to the Atlantic. It stood surrounded on three sides by trees, completely private, and with steep steps cut out of the rocks down to the small private beach.

The house, recommended by a friend one summer, was reached by a mile-long track, built up on both sides with dry-stone walls to keep the cattle from straying on it. It was homely, comfortable. The kitchen was very modern, and the rooms boasted central heating, a feature much coveted on that piece of coastline, where the weather could turn from summer to winter overnight. There were seven bedrooms, three bathrooms, a drawing room, a dining room, and, magnificently overlooking the sea, a completely glassed-in terrace.

From the moment they first saw it, the family adored the place. In their first summer there, Lady Pat became a familiar sight in her little yellow-painted dog cart, Zoe sitting beside her, as they trotted along the country lanes and through the village.

Jonathan had finally let her go.

She was for ever reining in to speak to someone, stopping at cottage doors and farmhouse gates for a word with Mrs Lamb, or Miss Jennett, or Martha Turnbull. She was loved wherever she went, admired for her courage. The folding wheelchair was so placed in the trap, that even if she went out alone she was able to manoeuvre it and herself to the cobbled pavement or country path, and as her independence grew, so did her spirit. She pottered about the estate and talked to the servants, in the park and gardens, the kitchens, linen room and dairy, and her days were busy and contented.

Since that day on Black Tor Crag, the love which bound Zoe and Jonathan together had been one of peace – and separateness – for six months. They had established their love: for the moment they were both content to look after Lady Pat, and help her back to life. They never touched, nor felt the need to.

Until just before Christmas, they suddenly began to avoid each other; when they met they were afraid. Afraid that their love and longing for each other would be seen.

One night, unable to sleep, Zoe left her bed and put on a warm coat over her nightdress. She slipped through the French windows into the empty rose garden, and ran across the frosted grass to the shrubbery. Her feet found the path which she and the children used to walk around the lake and into the little wood at the far side. There was a bright, white moon slipping in and out of the grey, silver-haloed clouds to light her way and she walked, head down, hands deep in her pockets, her love-starved body clenching like a fist.

A figure moved towards her from the tree where it had been leaning.

It was Jonathan. They stared at each other in disbelief.

In a second she was in his arms and with unrecognisable words of love they kissed, quick, moist, open-mouthed, eyes, cheeks, lips, throat, hands clutching, touching feeling, bodies straining like leashed greyhounds.

In the frozen wood, against a tree coated with hoarfrost, he took her, her nightdress around her waist. Pressed face to face, belly to belly, in a minute it was over, their mouths clamped together to silence their cries.

Afterwards they talked, gently, tenderly, shivering with cold and excitement, and within half an hour of leaving her bed she was back there, her feelings in a turmoil she had repressed for months.

They began to meet occasionally on her days off, going to the inn near Chester where they had first taken a room. Not too often. It would not do for Lady Pat to notice that they were both absent on the same day, but as the months passed their need grew stronger: to be together, to have a small part of each other's lives and share it with no other. Jonathan began to look round for a place where they could meet unseen, discreet and secret, and yet not leave the Hall. A private place of their own.

The upper floors of Weston Hall were a maze of attics, divided rooms, cubby holes and extensions, many of them closed and locked up.

Jonathan had keys to them all, and on the pretext of keeping the children from a rare and priceless collection of stamps, he had a new lock and set of keys made to one of them. It was full of his childhood treasures: the stamp collection, cases of butterflies, books, cricket bats, old gramophone records. He had a bed in there, and a spirit stove. His family were accustomed to his disappearances to his 'retreat' now and again – and 'Who wants to look at an old stamp collection, anyway?' said Amy.

No one knew of the key which hung on a fine chain round Zoe's neck.

They managed to spend several hours each week in the cluttered room, and it became a sanctuary, somewhere to fortify their defences against the fear that one day they would be compelled to give up their love, and to comfort each other with the passionate lovemaking which grew more demanding as their love strengthened. When circumstances permitted, they snatched a moment or two in the afternoon, for the servants were very rarely to be found above the ground floor after the morning cleaning of the bedrooms, and the nursery staff on the second floor always used the back stairs. The contentment which they found together, albeit mixed with guilt, seemed to run through the house: it could be seen in the quiet joy in Lady Pat's eyes, for her husband loved her now, and his own serenity gave her peace of mind at last.

Despite her disability, she had never been more content. Now the torment of her passionate longing for her husband was over, forced upon her by her useless body, she accepted the loving companionship which had developed, and their hours together were peaceful and satisfying to them both.

Their children, secure in the harmony which reigned in their home, were bright, cheerful, naughty and loving. And Zoe's strong and sisterly affection which guided them firmly towards young adulthood, was a stable influence in their childhood.

But Zoe had only one intimate friend. Her lover.

It was the last week of August. A perfect English summer's day. The sun shone from a sky the colour of hyacinths. Hot sand. Warm salty sea, gorse flower and buttercup, new-mown grass.

The holiday was nearly over. The girls were due back to the schoolroom in the second week in September, when Miss Rogers would be back from her own holiday in Italy, sunburnt and lean, they looked like gypsies as they half-heartedly began to gather up their bits and pieces, ready to be boxed and carted to the railway station at Penzance. They had spent days on the beach, in the boat, walking the cliffs, cramming into the Daimler for long outings with Jonathan at the wheel.

They said sad farewell to the house, promising a return next summer, as they always did.

The night before they were due to leave, Zoe and Jonathan wandered quietly into the gathering dusk towards the stand of crab apple trees. Lady Pat was tired from the toing and froing of the day's packing; the eternal questions: 'Mamma, have you seen my blue shorts?'

'Mamma, I can't find Binky. He was in his bucket . . .'

'Mamma! Someone's taken my bathing suit!' She had retired to her room and firmly closed the door.

Jonathan and Zoe clambered over the stone wall and followed the cliff path to the rocky track which led down to the next small cove. They climbed down in silence.

The cove was sheltered, still warm from the heat of the day. For half an hour they sat on the sand, shoulder to shoulder, their backs against a rock, watching the sunset.

Jonathan broke the peaceful silence.

'I think this has been the very best, don't you, sweetheart? I don't want to go home at all.' He sighed. '*This* has become home to us, at least a second home. I love it almost as much as Cheshire and I think Pat feels the same. I suppose it's because no one knows her, or wonders about her, or how she became as she is. I've never seen her look so well and happy.'

There was silence again, then Zoe spoke.

'You don't think she knows . . . about us? I've sometimes caught her looking at you, and me as well with a . . . I don't know . . . a quizzical expression, I suppose.'

Jonathan shook his head. 'Don't, I'm sure she doesn't.' He got up, 'Come on, last dip.'

Zoe slipped down her skirt, undid the buttons on her blouse and threw it to the sand. Her brief knickers were next, and then she stood naked, perfect in the faint half-light between day and night. Just coming over the lip of the cliff, the pale, shadowed crescent of the moon caught and reflected in her laughing eyes. Her breasts flaunted themselves, the nipples dark, legs apart, hands on hips, she dared him to snare her.

'Come on, man. Are you game or not?'

Jonathan edged towards her in mock menace, slowly undoing the buckle of his belt. His trousers slipped to his feet and he stepped from them.

'Right, you little witch, you asked for it.' His underpants and shirt were next. She laughed joyously, and turning, ran like a deer to the sea. Immediately he chased and caught her, then released her into the tumbling waves.

For ten minutes they played like children. They sank beneath the surface of the minute, rippling waves, surging upwards, water flowing from their smooth, shining bodies, and plastering their hair to their skulls as if painted there. Their soft muted cries of exhilaration were unheard in the stillness of the bay.

They left the water hand in hand, and in the shelter of the high cliff lay down together in love. It was strong, demanding, giving, almost desperate, as if their bodies knew already what their minds did not. It left them sweat and sand-slicked. Speechless and triumphantly exhausted.

Later, as they crossed the closecut grass, darkened by the night to olive brown, they paused for an instant to look for the last time at the sea now silvered, at the delicate moon mirrored there in a thousand broken pieces. Jonathan lifted Zoe's chin with loving care, placing his lips against hers, a touch as soft and ethereal as a dandelion clock. He kissed the warmth, the soft sweet flesh, and tasted the tang of the sea.

From a darkened window, a still, seated figure watched them.

Lady Pat had been singing to herself on that evening when the blow was struck which ended her life. She did not die, of course, but her life ended as surely as if some intruder had taken a gun from Sir Jonathan's gun case, loaded it, and fired a bullet into her heart.

The last of the packing had been supervised, and her clothes had been put neatly into their boxes. The piles of washing had been sorted into laundry bags, the mounds of suitcases and trunks had been taken to the station to await the train. Exhausted, the children had fallen into their beds, leaving her alone.

What should she do? She did not feel like sleeping and the night was so lovely. The moon cast its frosted rays about the quiet garden, and on the water, she could see the lights of the fishing boats, just out from Penzance.

How beautiful it had all been, and now it was ended.

Tomorrow they would go home. She thought of the graceful parkland, the glorious sheltered gardens, the moorland about it all, and the gracious house. She thought of her little pony, fat and placid, and the trap she pulled so amiably, and imagined herself meandering through it all as the first autumn leaves swirled to the ground, and she knew she was ready to go back.

She trundled her chair across the room and looked out from her ground floor window, gazing raptly at the silvered garden.

And there they were. Like two beautiful statues in the still of the moonlit landscape. Jonathan's hand beneath Zoe's chin, and his kiss soft as the breeze on her upturned face. Even in the strange half light it was all there to see: the love; the easy touch of two who know each other well, who had just come together, and were well satisfied.

It didn't hurt at first.

The silence buzzed around her, getting louder and louder and the dead, shocked core of her was still as a mouse cornered by a cat. She was dead. She knew she was, but her body pulsed, and throbbed, and the blood ran in her veins. For two, three hours, whilst the house slept around her, she sat staring unwinkingly at the spot where they had been.

Like the first, faint return of circulation to a limb, realisation came as dawn painted the sky a wispy pink. Her hands lifted slowly from her lap, clenched into fists, and when she opened them bright scarlet ran from eight tiny crescents where her nails had cut. She placed them, one on either side of her face, and her mouth opened on a great, wrenching groan.

'Jonathan. Jonathan. Jonathan.'

Jonathan and Zoe. Dear Lord. Dear sweet Jesus, she could not bear it. Jonty. Jonty and Zoe. Oh no . . . no . . . no . . . no. She could not bear to think of it. She would not think of it.

But her mind had a will of its own, and the pictures it showed her were cruel.

Jonathan and Zoe laughing in a corner of the library as the dogs bounded up at them.

Zoe shouting to Jonathan as they moved on their horses out of the stable yard, to canter away on to the waiting moor.

Zoe looking up at Jonathan as he had teased her with some childish trick.

Jonathan reaching out a hand to help the girl they both loved into a rocking boat.

The look of shining love had been there, for all to see. And she had seen nothing, had watched them and smiled.

It was not to be borne. She must tear the pictures from her mind.

Her heart was racing, and she felt as if she would suffocate. Then her hand went to the lever of her chair, and she raced for the bathroom.

For an hour she retched over the basin. She shook and trembled and shivered and wept. When it was over, she locked the door and ran a bath. And when she had bathed and dressed herself, her agony was replaced by determination. Bitterness filled her, and desolation, but the courage which had made her fight to take her place as a cripple among the whole, showed in the line of her jaw, and the steeliness which shone from her usually kindly eyes.

He was hers. Hers. She loved him. Had always loved him, and he loved her. She knew he did. These last years he had shown it in a hundred ways. They could no longer be lovers, but they loved. In her pain, she turned the affection which Jonty had given her casually, years ago, into a great and everlasting love – and she had been robbed of it. She forgot the empty years of her marriage; the hours she had waited, longingly, for his indifferent embrace.

Now she could recall nothing but the warm and gentle loving she had received since her accident. She was not prepared to lose it.

She must transfer her agony to the one who had inflicted it on her.

Zoe.

She unlocked the bathroom door, and set the chair in motion, wheeling through the doorway into her bedroom. Her face was fixed in harsh lines and her eyes were like flint.

She dressed herself and brushed her hair, pinning it severely back and skewering it with a tortoiseshell comb.

Chapter Thirty-Four

Zoe's sense of well-being, a legacy from the holiday, lasted for a week.

It was early September, and the glory of summer still lingered, like gossamer in the autumn air. There were crisp mornings and evenings, with hours of gently dying warmth in between, filled with the vague melancholy of the end of summer.

In Liverpool the streets were drab and dusty. Zoe sat in the rattling tram next to an open window, but she could feel her dress stick to her shoulder blades, where they bumped against the slatted wooden seat back.

She was going to see Jamie.

She stared unseeingly at an advertisement for Bisto, her mind churning chaotically. She had known for a week now.

She had suffered it all: the constant running to the bathroom, the obsessional interest in her underclothes.

'I could have sworn I felt it . . .'

An ache in the pit of her stomach: 'At last, at last . . .'

'Tomorrow when I wake up it will have come . . .'

The tram careered round a corner and the passengers swayed. Zoe's blind gaze transferred itself from Bisto to Colman's Mustard, the impassive face revealing no sign of her inner turbulence.

It was no use pretending. She was pregnant.

A sigh escaped her, drowned by the rattle of the tram, and her face relaxed imperceptibly. She was twenty-three now, and the easy years, without grief, without worry; the years of loving, of friendship and affection, had given her strength and repose that had turned her from a lovely, fresh-faced girl, into a strikingly beautiful woman.

Heads turned wherever she went. She had kept the slender, rounded curve of breast and hip; her legs were long and slender, tapering into fine-spun ankle and foot. She had let her polished-chestnut hair grow to please Jonathan: loose, it fell to her waist in a thick, curling cape. She wore it twisted into a dense chignon which emphasised the startling, fine-boned beauty of her face.

With a sigh of relief she saw the familiar outline of Seaforth Hall. She got off the tram, and stood for a moment, watching it whine along Crosby Road.

Jamie lived in Seaforth now. He had worked hard in his job on the docks, and last year had been made a foreman. He had married his sweetheart, and together they had set up home in Cowper Street. It was still in the dockyard area, but it was a far cry from Love Lane.

The houses were terraced and just as close together. They had an outside privy, but one to each household, and a cold water tap inside. And the people were different. The men were in work. The women were houseproud, and cared for their children. They were not dragged down to hopelessness, and Jamie and his Nancy settled amongst them and immediately began to produce a family. They had a son, Andrew, and another baby on the way.

It was cooler here than in the city, and the wisp of breeze from the river smelled of salt and ships, and carried the cries of sea birds. Zoe took deep gulps of the fresh air as she crossed the railway bridge over Seaforth station and walked along Knowley Road to the terraced houses of Cowper Street.

A group of children played under the dusty tree outside Jamie's house. She stopped at the door, and her heart beat faster.

Why was she here? What could Jamie and Nancy do for her now? The damage was done. For five years, she and Jonathan had been lovers, and not once in all that time had she considered the possibility that she might bear his child. Their complacency appalled her.

The children had stopped their game to stare curiously at her, and she was conscious of half a dozen pairs of eyes peeping from behind white, twitching net.

She knocked timidly at the door, and waited.

It was opened slowly, and a slight, palely pretty girl stood hesitantly, one hand on the door latch, the other supporting a young baby on her shoulder. Her stomach swelled gently under her clean apron. She smiled, and her soft blue eyes crinkled with shy pleasure.

'Hello, our Zoe.' They had met only once, the day Nancy had married Jamie. She had been just eighteen.

'Come on in,' Nancy said, and stepped aside for Zoe to pass into the tiny living room. A kettle sang on the bright embered fire, and a ginger cat curled on the rag rug. The range was like ebony, a shining mirror, and the brick walls were a pure, creamy white. An ancient chair was covered in vivid red plush, matched by the tablecloth. Clean nappies were airing over the fire, and a sweet scent of newly-bathed baby, and tasty scouse simmering in a pan, mingled into a smell of home.

Nancy and Zoe looked at each other and smiled. Nancy pointed to the chair and Zoe sat down, looking round Jamie's home with a joyful pleasure. It is what he deserves, she thought.

Nancy put the child down on the rug beside the cat, and reached for the teapot. She placed two china teacups and saucers with ceremonious care on the table, and poured a fragrant cup for Zoe. Then, leaning back in a creaking rocking chair on the other side of the fire, she sipped delicately, savouring the tea and smiling.

She was not a great one for talking, that was plain, but her serenity and calm acceptance of her visitor laid a gentle, healing balm on Zoe's troubled spirit.

The baby lay kicking contentedly, Nancy looked down at him and stroked his bright, ruler-straight hair.

Zoe's fear lightened and at that moment she began to love her unborn child. She had been desperate when she knocked at Jamie's door; even now, she did not know what she should do. But watching Nancy and her baby had steadied her.

She must tell Jonathan. He would have an answer, he was strong and sure.

A prick of uncertainty abruptly caught her, and she felt, strangely, a flicker of renewed fear. But Jonathan would take care of her. Of course he would. He loved her.

She bent to put a gentle finger on the baby's cheek, and he was still, slightly anxious with this strange person who smiled at him with a face that was somehow familiar. She had the eyes of the man who held him in his arms and kissed him lovingly. Reassured, he smiled at her.

'Andrew,' she said, and his eyes almost disappeared into his cheeks.

Nancy sat calmly waiting for her visitor to speak.

Zoe stared into the fire, the creeping uncertainty growing within her. She remembered Jonathan's collapse when Lady Pat had been crippled, remembered her own part, her own strength. It had been she who had supported him; he was strong now. In fair weather, a voice whispered. A proud, handsome man again, sweet, loving, passionate. Tender with his wife and gentle with his children, kind to his servants and animals. But in adversity . . . ?

She let the sentence trail away in her mind, and was fearful. And ashamed. How could she think of him so?

'Would yer like sum more tea, our Zoe?'

The gentle voice brought her back from her bleak thoughts.

'Oh, Nancy,' she breathed.

Nancy leaned towards her and took her hand, her eyes bright with compassion.

'Can yer tell us about it, chuck?'

Zoe blinked back tears.

'You won't tell our Jamie,' she whispered.

'I'll tell no one.'

The small hand clasped hers. It was rough, and a blister had formed on the back of the thumb. Zoe looked down at it, and at her own slim, well-cared-for fingers. She had done

266

no rough work for ten years, and her hands were white and soft.

Looking up into the understanding blue eyes, she said without preamble:

'I'm pregnant, Nancy.'

There was a gentle silence.

'I thought it were tha', our kid.' Without a pause Nancy added, 'Yer welcome 'ere, Queen.'

Zoe's heart swelled with new-found love and gratitude. If Jonathan should . . . If there was nowhere . . . Should the awful possibility that Jonathan might not . . .

Well, she had a haven here.

But of course she would not need it.

She smiled at Nancy.

'Thank you. You are a good person. You hardly know me, and you offer me a home. But you see my . . . baby's father will take care of me. He loves me, and I . . . well,' she smiled shyly and lowered her eyes.

'I wanted to see our Jamie, tell him. But it would only cause trouble. I see that now. I'm glad you know, Nancy, but just for now, keep it to yourself.'

'I will that.'

They kissed affectionately, and Zoe left and walked slowly towards the corner.

She must cast off this dreadful, hopeless feeling which had fallen over her like cloud. Jonathan would take care of her, make it right. He would tell . . . Say the words to . . . find the right . . . Oh God, Lady Pat.

As she reached the road which ran parallel to the river, she turned left and began to walk in the direction of the Pier Head. Along Regent Road, and the overhead railway sang and hummed its own tune as a train rushed past above her head. The huge open gates of the docks yawned on her right, and as she passed them she carefully read the names printed above the gateways, as though she must memorise them for a demanding teacher.

Hornby Dock.

Laughton Branch Dock.

Brocklebank Dock.

Canada Dock.

Shipping lines, the names of which painted emotive pictures in her head.

Dominion Line.

American Line.

Cunard Line.

They were names clearly remembered from her childhood. Names she had heard on her father's lips, but meaning nothing until now.

But it was of now she must think. Now and the future.

And Lady Pat.

How was she to face her? This would crucify her. To learn that her husband, whom she loved above all others, had been loving someone else. And not just anyone, but the girl she had returned to life, ten years ago, had loved and honoured, and made a member of her own family. To learn that she was carrying her husband's child, had deceived her, dishonoured her, degraded her, in her own home, was more than she would be able to stand.

It would cripple her spirit, as the loss of her legs had not.

Perhaps they could pretend that the child was . . . another's. A man from the village, or . . . one of the servants . . . Would Lady Pat believe that Zoe had been carrying on with some casual . . . ?

She sobbed in the back of her throat. Jonathan would not allow it. Would he?

And Lady Pat would not believe it. She knew her too well.

Oh God. Zoe couldn't do it to her. She couldn't tell her, and she couldn't ask Jonathan to tell her. It would be wicked, evil.

She could not be told.

A great groan escaped Zoe's lips, and a man on a bicycle turned his capped head to look at her. He wobbled to the left and his front wheel hit the kerb, as her beauty struck him. He righted himself, and pedalled on, wondering.

Zoe thought her heart would break, but she knew there

was only one path she could take. She must leave her home, and the people she loved, and take her secret with her.

It was warm. She could spend the night in the church, which was never locked, or even walk across the moorland to Chester, and by tomorrow morning she would be back here with Nancy.

Oh God, dear God. Her spirit faltered, and a tiny sound pierced her throat. How was she to do it? How could she leave them with no word? They would think she had run away, that she had ceased to love them, and they would be desolate, but the hurt she would bring with the knowledge that she bore Sir Jonathan's child would be far greater.

This way they would weep and wonder, and Jonathan would be despairing and lost without her. Would he be able to keep his true feelings from his wife? Would he lose control as he had done when she was crippled and his son had died? Zoe had supported his weakness then.

Now there would be no one. Lady Pat would help him, though her own grief would be strong, but could he keep from her the true depth of his feelings for Zoe?

Tears wet her cheeks as she reached the Pier Head, the scene of that last harrowing journey after Arthur. A woman put out her hand to her, saying:

'Are yer all right, chuck?' but she did not heed her. She crossed the gangway and walked on to the trembling deck of the ferry. Her face was still, frozen in sorrow. Her slender figure was straight, and her head was high as she looked up at the Liver Bird, for ever spreading its wings, as if to fly across the river.

She believed in no God, but she prayed silently to some being to give her strength.

Chapter Thirty-Five

Zoe heard Jonathan's voice as she walked up the drive towards the Hall. He was in the paddock, and the cheerful cries of his daughters as they urged their mounts over the practice jumps mingled with his deeper tones.

If she went to the front door and rang the bell, Temple would come, and he would look at her and know that something was wrong. He would ask questions, for he was fond of her, and she would start to cry. No, she must try to slip round the opposite side, and go through the French windows to the dining room. From there she could creep up to the safety of her own room.

She took a hesitant step, and at that moment Jonathan rode round the corner of the house, his great black stallion shying as it caught sight of her. He leaned forward to soothe him, patting his arching neck.

As he petted the horse, Zoe summoned the courage to bring up her hand, to steady her trembling legs and smile lovingly. Even the colour which had drained from her in Liverpool, flooded her cheeks prettily.

As Jonathan's glance found her, the look of adoration which she knew so well filled his eyes.

'Darling,' he whispered. All his love and meaning were there for her to read, and knowing what she must do she looked about her furtively, as though afraid that Lady Pat might be there to see it. At the last moment it might all come out into the open, and the plan she had made be for nothing.

She almost panicked. Her throat closed. The fertile aroma of the horse and the stables from which it had just come was so strong that she could almost taste it. I shall think of this moment from somewhere I have not yet seen. It will be as it always is, as it is now, tomorrow, and tomorrow, and tomorrow, but not for me. This day will return, again and again, but not for me. She heard Jonathan's voice.

God give me strength, make me strong.

'Zoe, sweeting, what is it?'

Rosie's voice called from the paddock.

'Watch, Papa, come and watch.'

He turned his head, and in that split second the course of their lives was changed. The desolation in Zoe's eyes would have told him. With a lover's perception, he would have seen it and known, but in the instant between the turning of his head in the direction of the voice, and back again, the look was gone.

'I'm sorry, dearest, I'll have to go.' He winked at her conspiratorially, and his lips shaped in a small, secret wisp of a kiss. He was about to turn the stallion, pulling the rein. 'Oh, by the way, Pat wants to see you – says it's urgent, and you're to go up as soon as you come back. She wouldn't say what it was.' He smiled, and leaned forward. 'Tonight,' he whispered, and his eyes glowed.

He turned and rode away.

She began to shiver as he disappeared. Lady Pat wanted to see her. Why? Why now?

They had been home a week, and in all that time she had not seen her ladyship since they had carried her up the stairs, and into her own room. She was unwell, and would see no one.

Only Jonathan. Zoe had been relieved, and ashamed to be so, when Jonathan had spoken vaguely of headaches, of backache, of Pat not feeling herself. In the unseeing selfishness of the strong and healthy, whose world is fine about him, he did not notice the pale face and sick eyes which looked out at him each day, or if he did, he told himself it would pass.

With unconscious cruelty, he went about his world of horses and dogs, of the estate and the moor; of Jake Tewkesbury's shoot, for the grouse season was upon them.

And so the two people who loved her most did not see her suffering.

Now, suddenly, Lady Pat wanted to talk to her.

She was sitting in her chair with her back to the door as Zoe knocked and entered. She did not turn at once, but continued to stare across the parkland, drinking in its quiet loveliness.

Zoe cleared her throat and tried to smile.

Lady Pat put a hand to the lever on her chair, and slowly turned it round until she was facing Zoe. For a moment, as her face turned from the light and was in shadow, Zoe thought her eyes were playing tricks, or if indeed it was Lady Pat who sat before her. These were not the familiar and beloved features she knew so well.

Zoe flinched. The face was grey, and ill, the cheeks hollowed beneath piercing cheekbones. The mouth, straight and grim, was set in a line beneath the pinched nostrils, and those eyes . . . Their expression was terrible.

Lady Pat spoke slowly. 'I thought you were my friend . . . to be trusted, as innocent and single-hearted as you appeared. It seems I was wrong.'

For a moment the dreadful eyes left Zoe's, and looked about the room as though in amazement at her own stupidity.

'I have spent the last week . . . not knowing what . . . I loved you. I thought you loved me . . .'

'Please, please, Lady Pat, I beg . . .' Zoe stammered.

'You have lied to me, and deceived me, I can never forgive you. I will say nothing of what has been done for you in this house. The affection you have received . . . from . . . from my children, from the people here . . . from . . .' She laughed, harshly. '. . . from my husband.'

Zoe moaned, and the room darkened about her.

'Please,' she whispered, 'please . . .'

'I don't please,' Lady Pat said flatly. 'I don't please to do anything but see you out of here as fast as it takes you to reach the front door. Jonty is mine, my husband, and he loves me. He is all I have and I intend to keep him. I love him. Oh yes, I know he . . . he . . . that you and he . . . but he will forget. I will convince him of some tale to explain your . . . disappearance. He will not come looking for you, you may be certain.'

She was silent for a long moment, and on her face was a look of utter hopelessness. 'I'm tired. It seems I am never to know . . .'

Zoe took a step forward, aching to soothe away the anguish, but Lady Pat sat up quickly.

'Don't come near me . . . don't touch . . . I couldn't bear it.'

Zoe winced, and waited submissively.

'Take what you need, and go. Don't tell anyone what I have said, and . . . do not try to see Jonathan.'

Her eyes burned. 'Go,' she whispered. 'Go away.'

She turned her chair suddenly away.

Zoe took a step forward and put out her hand. For a moment she stood, silently beseeching, pleading for forgiveness, but she knew it would do no good.

She turned and walked to the door, tears pouring down her face.

'Goodbye,' she whispered. 'Forgive me.'

She did not think of Jonathan as she slipped from the side door and made her way to the drive. She walked through the massive stone gateposts and her thoughts, wild and sorrowing, were on the broken woman sitting lonely in her wheelchair.

She walked, straight-backed, towards the open moorland road. The evening sun glided towards the horizon, painting the bracken golden and darkening the shadows upon the masses of rough stone at the side of the road. A sheep raised its head and skittered away to safety, kicking its heels foolishly, then turned to look at her again. A twitter of birdsong rose for a second into the purple sky in the east, and as she looked, she saw a pinprick of light shine through the night shroud. It was a star, diamond against velvet.

She turned suddenly off the road. Striding now, she plunged into the wild moorland, finding the paths she knew so well, for even in the dusk, the moor was like an open book to her. She walked for an hour, then finding the spot she looked for, she lay down on the spongy moss and sweet-smelling clover. There, at last, she began again to weep.

She slept a little, fitfully, and when the pale, oyster pink of the rising day touched the sky where it met the moor, she got to her feet and began to stumble back the way she had come. She stopped once to rinse her face in a stream, and to drink a mouthful of water. She combed her hair, for her bag was still on her arm. When she reached the road, she began to walk in the direction of Chester.

Chapter Thirty-Six

The young woman pushed the large and ancient perambulator along Aigburth Drive until she reached the gateway which led into Sefton Park. The gates opened on to a fine lawn, and beyond, the terraces were shaded by trees. A giant pine towered, and under its cool shade, a wooden seat was placed, almost hidden from the path by great umbrellas of spiky fern. The woman moved the baby carriage this way and that, until it was in the shade, and with a soft sigh, she settled herself on the seat.

A shout of laughter floated above the trees. Male laughter, followed by the click of wood on wood.

'You 'it the bluddy jack . . .' a voice said. Just beyond the sheltered spot where the young woman sat was a bowling green, and a dozen or so old men strolled about, and considered distances, and mopped their foreheads with white handkerchiefs.

With another sigh the woman reached for the *Liverpool Echo* which she had dropped on to the seat beside her, and picking it up with an air of resignation, she opened it at a page headed 'Employment'. The list of jobs was not long, for the depression had struck and work was scarce.

Not really concentrating, she scanned page after page, until, with a small, agitated movement of her heart, two words leaped like black frogs from the page of the newspaper.

Her own name.

Zoe Taylor.

Her heart was thumping now, for who in this huge sprawling city of Liverpool, would be putting her name in the *Echo*? Jamie and Nancy, the only people she was close to, knew where she was, and would hardly advertise for her. They saw her every day, for she lived with them. Sarah and her Gordon, a pious churchgoer and mealy-mouthed with it, would have nothing to do with her. Indeed Gordon had turned her from their door, when she had called with her child.

Trying to still her trembling hands she read:

ZOE TAYLOR, LATE OF LIVERPOOL. Would Zoe Taylor, or anyone who knows of her whereabouts, please contact Hall, Hall and Fitzgerald, Solicitors, of Dale Street, Liverpool, where news of an advantageous nature may be heard. Expenses will be reimbursed.

She read it twice, three times. After reading the words for the last time, she stood up abruptly. Placing the crumpled newspaper on the light coverlet which shaded the baby's legs from the rays of the sun, she turned the perambulator towards the gate.

Nancy and Zoe hung over the table, reading and re-reading the cryptic, printed message. On the rag rug, the ginger cat struggled to keep its square foot of comfort amidst the tussles of three small children. Two-year-old Andy Taylor, blue-eyed and copper-haired, and the darling of his mother's eye, was the eldest and biggest, and therefore had the most clout, but his brother Christopher, a year younger, was robust, and did not give in easily. They argued amicably, in a language only they understood, their voices high.

The third child, an infant of two or three months, lay on his back watching the bright pattern of sunlight on the ceiling. His dark curls, in which a touch of chestnut gleamed, rioted about his sweetly shaped skull, and fell in damp wisps, about his flat ears. His treacle-brown eyes were bright and wondering, and he murmured a soft flow of baby sounds that fell like a caress on the ears of his adoring mother.

'What can it mean, our Zoe?' whispered Nancy, her pale face awash with colour. She lived from day to day, eking out the tiny wages Jamie brought home: not much now, as the depression bit deeper, and unemployment made even those who were in work uneasy. She loved her husband and her children and fed them as best she could, but the added responsibility of Zoe during the last nine months had placed an intolerable burden on their meagre resources. Zoe was searching desperately for a job, and had deliberately and heartbreakingly weaned her baby early, so that she might be available for employment, but what was she suited for? Nancy asked herself. She was a lady now, and could hardly be expected to turn to in a factory, even though she was willing.

But this in the paper, perhaps, oh perhaps, it meant . . . Nancy could hardly think for excitement.

'I don't know, our Nancy. I haven't the faintest idea, but I'll find out tomorrow. I'll go and see –' Zoe leant over the table again – 'Hall, Hall and Fitzgerald!'

'Eh, our Zoe, will yer?' Nancy was awed and admiring. She had little education and was quiet and self-effacing, and her sister-in-law's spirit was a marvel to her. She'd often heard her weeping in the night, but she left her alone. She knew that was what Zoe would want.

She was rare, was Nancy.

The sorrow and loss were more than she could bear at times. Night after night the pictures came to torture her: Jonathan smiled at her, and held out loving arms, his brown face merry, and alive with longing. Lady Pat called to her cheerfully from the padded seat of the dog cart, her head framed by the halo of the lacy willow tree which dreamed by the side of the lake. Little Beth cried for her, and her friends at the Hall crowded round anxiously, wondering, sad: Daisy and Cook, in the warm comfort of the kitchen on a winter's day.

She ached for the untamed moorland, green and brown and yellow, unending: the sparkling sunshine and caressing air against her face, stretching into the limitless spaces of her mind, and Rowan, fluid chestnut beneath her.

She became gaunt and pale.

But it was not until January, when she felt her child move for the first time that her heart stilled. That night, as she lay in the tiny truckle bed which Jamie had made for her, warm beside the glowing embers of the kitchen fire, she put hesitant fingers on the soft swelling of her stomach, and felt the butterfly touch of her baby. It seemed to respond to her gentle pressure, and she was comforted.

In May, Jonathan's son came into the world, and his mother's eager, waiting arms.

Zoe called him Daniel.

She walked across the patterned marble floor of the entrance hall and stood for a moment before the large notice board where the names of the offices were printed.

Hall, Hall and Fitzgerald. It was on the third floor.

She took the lift, and as it moved upwards, glanced in the tiny mirror fixed to the wall. She adjusted the pale pink wisp of a hat, with the white rose pinned on it; she smoothed the plain white crepe de chine of her dress. She glanced down to ensure that the seams of her stockings – silk, brought from Weston Hall, for she had worn them on *that* day – were straight.

Satisfied that she looked her best, she stepped out of the lift as it came to a trembling stop, and walked down the corridor, following the arrow which pointed to Hall, Hall and Fitzgerald. She knocked on the door.

'Come in,' called a woman's voice. The room was dim and shabby, but the furniture was beautiful, and the carpet soft. The light from a small window fell on the figure of an elderly woman typing rapidly, peering at the paper.

Her look said she did not approve of pretty young women, and her sniff said she was old and lonely and envious.

Yes, Mr Fitzgerald was free, but she did not know if he could spare the time . . . and the name was . . . and it was to do with . . . ?

Zoe was shown into a large corner office, bright with sunshine, and polished surfaces. There were beautiful bookcases, and a small, cheerful fire. Copper firedogs gleamed, and the walls were hung with hunting prints, and country scenes. The desk was a glowing jewel set on a carpet of dull green. Behind it sat a man with greying hair, and steely grey eyes.

Edward Fitzgerald rose when she entered the room, and blinked rapidly. Over the years he had developed a manner of cool professional politeness, which hid his thoughts both from clients and from opponents in court. He was not a man to be distracted from duty by a pretty face, but the lovely young woman who stood before him, had a quality which was rare, disturbing. Her face was smooth and unlined, but her eyes were shadowed. She looked as though she had suffered but shining through was a refusal to be beaten by what she had known in the past.

For a moment, his quick mind was in confusion. He held out his hand, felt the warm pressure of her fingers in his, and murmured conventionally. Zoe sat in the chair before his desk and waited, smiling gently, every hour she had spent with the Weston family showing in the set of her head, the stillness of her hands, and the quietness of her posture. She did not fiddle, nor clear her throat or cross her legs.

Edward Fitzgerald did all these things, and felt sixteen again.

He reached for a file and began to read, the legal phrases he knew so well, steadying him. He looked up at Zoe, and smiled for the first time, and his face changed and became youthful. He was attractive, and his eyes were kind. The steeliness was gone.

'I have received instructions from a client of mine who is interested in your welfare.'

Zoe's eyes questioned his, and a pulse in her temple began to beat faintly.

'I cannot, however, divulge my client's name.' Mr Fitzgerald leaned forward and put both his elbows on the desk.

'I will come straight to the point, Miss Taylor. My client

wishes to make you a weekly allowance of twenty pounds a week.'

Zoe gasped, and her face lost its lovely colour. She swayed in her chair. Jonathan. Jonathan knows and is . . .

Edward Fitzgerald watched as her face crumpled.

'Miss Taylor,' he said nervously, 'Are you all right? Can I get you something?' He stood up, prepared to move round the desk.

Zoe sighed, and she relaxed a little. A faint tinge of colour returned; her head came up, and her anguished eyes met his.

He was transfixed.

'I'm sorry,' she whispered, 'I'm sorry, but . . . please go on . . .'

Edward Fitzgerald sat down again, and coughed.

'My client knows that you have a son, Miss . . . er, Mrs . . . Miss Taylor, and wishes to be assured that he is brought up as a gentleman. To be schooled properly and to live . . .'

Zoe interrupted him harshly.

'He's not to be brought up with a dockie's kids, you mean,' she said. She saw the steadfast and gentle face of her brother, and was filled with anger.

'Yes, if you put it like that. If you accept this offer, you will be able to live in . . . a pleasant neighbourhood. There will be no need for you to work, and you may care for your son without financial worries. Your son will be brought up . . . well . . .'

He sighed gently, and went on. 'I know nothing of you, Miss Taylor, or of your . . . circumstances, but my client was of the opinion that you would be living with a brother. It was known that he worked on the docks, but not where he lived. It would have been easy to find that out, but my client desired that you should come forward of your own volition.'

'What is the name of your client, Mr Fitzgerald?' Zoe asked.

He looked down at his file, then directly at her.

'I cannot say, Miss Taylor.'

'Is it Jonathan Weston?'

'No,' he said, and this time he did not blink.

Zoe leaned back in her chair, nonplussed. Not Jonathan? Then who? Her mind skimmed the years, and the faces of the men and women who had peopled her life. Her father, who had died in the poor house. Daly. Dear God. Daly, perhaps, had left some provision for . . . but then why couldn't this man tell her, and why wait until now? Someone at Weston. But no one there could afford . . . only Jonathan. And Mr Fitzgerald told the truth, she was sure of it. It was not Jonathan.

She shook her head and sighed. She must accept – for Daniel's sake, and for Jamie and Nancy, and their little boys. With this money she would be able to help them as they had helped her. She stood up abruptly, and put out her hand, smiling brilliantly, her eyes starred with tears. Edward Fitzgerald took her hand, and his own shook a little.

'Thank you, Mr Fitzgerald,' she said politely, 'You have been most kind. I will be in touch very soon. I feel I would like a day or two to consider . . .' She left the sentence unfinished.

Edward Fitzgerald hurried round his desk to open the door for her. He watched as she walked along the corridor. A strange emotion made his throat tighten, and he grinned like a schoolboy as she smiled a last goodbye.

Chapter Thirty-Seven

It was a dear little house and she loved it. So did Nancy. Together they stood in the bright, yellow painted kitchen, looking out over the long, lawned back garden and Zoe was transported back nearly twenty years to another kitchen and another garden. Daly had stood beside her then, holding her hand, and she remembered the child who had been speechless with joy. The kitchen had been like this one: airy and warm with sunshine, and the garden had been green with foliage at the height of its mature summer beauty, and high-walled, and there had been a huge tree spreading its protection against the sun.

Nancy was speaking. Her placid face was soft with awe for the happiness which she was to share a little. She could come here whenever she wanted, Zoe had said, and the children were to come and play with Daniel. And Zoe was going to give her some of her weekly allowance.

'It's lovely, our Zoe,' she breathed.

Zoe turned and looked at her lovingly.

'I know, I can't believe it yet.' She turned back to the window and looked unseeingly into the sky, and at the red-tiled roof of the house which backed on to hers. 'I wonder what will happen next? Do you think I'll stay in this kitchen for the rest of my days, or shall I marry a Prince and dash off on a white horse and live happily ever after?'

They both laughed, and then the doorbell rang at the front of the house and Zoe sped lightly along the hall to let in the removal men, and the furniture which she and Edward had picked together.

It was the start of her new life.

*

Edward Fitzgerald was born in Cheshire, not far from the village of Longeaton, and the forest of Macclesfield. He was the second son of a wealthy landowner.

From his first day in the schoolroom, which he shared with his elder brother and sister, he had proved to have a quick and enquiring mind, to be 'something of a scholar', as his father put it – rather disparagingly. He much preferred his elder son who, like himself loved to ride and hunt.

Edward thanked God on bended knee night and morning for the blessing which had been granted him, of being his father's second son. Because of this he was allowed to follow his own inclination.

He chose the law.

When he became a solicitor, at the age of twenty-two, he bought into a small but flourishing law practice in Liverpool. Hall and Hall were father and son, seventy-nine and fifty-five respectively, good, solid, but with no sparkle.

Edward Fitzgerald provided the sparkle.

But only in his professional life. He was a solitary man. He visited his home in Cheshire once a month, mainly to see his mother, of whom he was fond, but the rest of his time was spent in the fastidiously neat flat in Tuebrook, where he read, and listened to music – he loved jazz and Beethoven – and did all the household chores. He went to concerts and the opera, and with a few close friends who shared his interests he had spent ten happy years.

At the age of thirty-three, he thought himself a dry old stick, but the day that Zoe Taylor walked into his office was like the first day of his life. He loved her from that moment, passionately and selflessly and hopelessly. He asked nothing but to serve her; to help heal the tragedy of her life, and make a new one for herself and her son. Like most men who fall in love for the first time at an age when his companions are fathers of a growing family, he was deeply, utterly, smitten.

He smoothed the path of legalities until she could move into the pretty little house in Edge Lane, Wavertree, which he had helped her to choose, driving her and Daniel about the suburbs of Liverpool in his smart little car. He took her to Waring and Gillow's to pick out lovely pieces of furniture; to antique auctions, where his impeccable taste guided her instinctive love of beauty, and he helped with her finances.

Week after week he kept up the pretence of being her legal advisor only, making excuses to call on her.

There came a time when the excuses ran out and he was left with only himself to offer.

Daniel had been bathed, splashing and singing in the large white bath, safe against the curve of his mother's arm. The lovely face above him had smiled and gently trickled warm rivulets of soapy water across his plump stomach, and his baby mouth had laughingly revealed the magnificence of his four teeth.

They had splashed until Zoe was almost as wet as he was and then she had wrapped him in a lovely warm fluffy towel and carried him down the stairs into the gentle, firelit peace of the living room. She sat him on her knee and wiped him dry, and held him in her arms and kissed him.

He had dozed against the soft breast, and she picked him up and carried him up the stairs to his newly-painted little room. She placed him in the white cot, and tenderly tucked the pretty quilt about his chin. He turned his face for her kiss, and then, clasping his teddy bear, he fell asleep.

Zoe pulled a chair up to the cot and watched his soft breath lift the bedclothes.

How she loved him. He was a miniature of his father already. Though he was barely six months old, he sat straight, his curly head held proudly, as four centuries of Westons decreed. His limbs were strong and slender, like Jonathan's, and his smile pierced her, as Jonathan's eyes looked out brightly from beneath his silky brows.

He would be a fine son for . . .

Her chin sank slowly, and a tear fell on to her blouse. Then another, and another, until she ran downstairs for fear of waking him and wept as though her heart would break.

She was so lonely.

She had been in her new home for two months. She had her boy during the day, but when he was sleeping, her heart cried for the loving arms of his father. For a whole year she had lived with Jamie and Nancy in their tiny home and it had been full of singing and laughter, and the cries of children, and she had never been alone, except in the night, when she had wept for Jonathan, but now, for the first time in her life, she knew long, empty stretches of silence, the feel of four walls about her, pressing her in, and she longed to open the door and run through it, out into the night. But she could not. Daniel was upstairs and she could not leave him.

She would walk from room to room as the night wore on, and look first from one window, then another. Her new home was lovely, and she had money to spend, pretty clothes to wear again, and her son would be secure, but she was so alone.

Nancy came and she welcomed her with open arms, and an eager, loving smile, begging her to stay for a little while longer. She petted Andy and Chris, and entreated Nancy to bring Jamie to tea on Sunday, and when she had gone, if it was still daylight, she would put Daniel in his pram, and walk and walk; across Wavertree Park, and the Botanic Gardens, and along the length of Tunnel Road, until she reached Sefton Park.

She loved the open stretches of green lawns and leaf-canopied paths. They reminded her of the parkland surrounding Weston Hall. She would sit by the tennis court as the light failed, and listen to the shouts of laughter, as the players lobbed balls to partners they could hardly see, and the last sleepy sound of the birds in the Aviary, as they settled down for the night.

Jonathan's son would sleep in his carriage, and she would walk home slowly in the cooling autumn air, hating to go back to the lonely beauty of her new home.

Her breath quickened now, and her hand went to her breast involuntarily. She felt the nipple rise against her fingertip and she shivered with need and longing and love.

'Jonathan,' she whispered out loud. 'My love, my love.'

As she moaned, she slipped down in the chair, her body weak with wanting.

The doorbell rang loudly.

She jumped up from the chair, and ran down the hall, certain that it was Jonathan . . . She threw open the door, her face flushed with melting love, her eyes dark with remembered passion, and his name was in her heart, and almost on her lips.

'Good evening, Zoe,' said Edward.

He did not speak nervously, for it was not his way, though he felt it. He was a strong man, and would reveal himself to no one, but his soul was in his eyes.

It had taken all the courage he possessed to come. He had no reason to call: no papers to sign, no financial matters to discuss. All was done. Tied up with legal ribbon and put away.

He stood quietly on the doorstep and waited.

The light went out in Zoe's eyes and he saw it go. He knew who it was she longed for, and he envied and almost hated him.

'I was just passing . . .' he said.

Zoe turned from the door and walked away from him. He stood irresolutely on the doorstep for a moment, then stepped over the threshold and closed the door behind him. It seemed from her indifference that she had no objection. He watched her slump in the chair, and stare at him almost resentfully, all her gentle manners forgotten.

Then he smiled at her, and her own eyes responded to the kindness in his. He was wearing slacks and a casual sweater over an open-necked shirt. He looked young and cheerful, and the premature grey of his hair, which he had not combed into the stiff neatness he affected in the office, was hidden by the thick, heedless wave as it fell on his brow. Everything about him was slightly less than perfect, but the whole was congenial, and somehow, because of the small imperfections, endearing. His tall, spare frame seemed to fill the room, and for the first time she was aware of him as a man.

She sat up and held out her hand.

'I'm sorry,' she smiled. 'You caught me in a daydream and I . . . well, can I get you something?'

He held her hand and she did not take it away. It was agreeable to feel strong male fingers, after all this time of baby softness. He looked at her and his face became serious, and the tension grew. She knew, then, how he felt and what he wanted.

But she was not ready yet. Her body wanted passion. Zoe wanted Jonathan.

'A cup of tea?' she said brightly, and took her hand from his, and he knew he must be patient.

They drank their tea and talked. There were awkward silences, for Edward, though a gentleman, and the son of a gentleman, had no social graces. But in his grey eyes, was a warm fire of hope, and the promise of love.

For almost an hour they sat. Then Daniel cried and she got up and left the room. When she returned, the baby was in her arms.

'I'm afraid he needs changing,' she said apologetically. 'I have some clean nappies airing in the . . .'

She looked about her as if to find a place to put her son, and Edward Fitzgerald, for the first time in his life, held out his arms to a child.

'He's wet,' Zoe warned, and she laughed.

Edward took him and with an expertise he did not know he possessed put him on his knee, and wrapped a protective arm around him.

Later, when Edward left the house, Zoe stood in the doorway and watched as he closed the gate carefully behind him. Every movement he made was neat and showed the order of his lawyer's mind, but she liked it. She like his disciplined actions, and his thoughtful consideration of every side to a problem. He made her feel secure, protected.

He turned and waved.

Chapter Thirty-Eight

The sign read BEECHLAWN and beneath it, in smaller letters, *Preparatory School for Children from Five to Eleven*. It was painted a dark glossy red, the letters picked out in gold, and stood just inside a gateway leading into a large garden. The lawns were green and smooth, the flowerbeds stocked with lupins, peonies, forget-me-nots and wallflowers. In the far corner, a towering beech stood sentinel.

A large white house, serene and lovely, was reached by a circular drive. The front door was painted in the same deep red as the sign, and the brass door knocker – the head of a grinning dog – was spotlessly polished.

A gleaming car drew up at the gateway, turned into it, and glided slowly along the driveway, its wheels crunching on the gravel. When it reached the house it came to a smooth halt, and a chauffeur in dark grey uniform leaped nimbly from the front seat.

He opened the rear door and a boy and a girl spilled out, both clutching books and satchels. They were also in uniform: blazers of the same red as the door of the house, the girl in a red-checked gingham dress, the boy in lightweight grey flannels. Each wore a straw boater with a striped ribbon in red and grey.

The door of the house opened and a woman, simply dressed, elegant and extremely beautiful, stood there smiling.

'Penelope, George, come along.' She beckoned to the children to come inside, stepping back to allow them to pass her. The chauffeur touched his cap and got back in the car. With a swish on the gravel once more, he drove away.

'Put your things in the cloakroom quickly, and then come into the hall. You are late, you know,' she continued reprovingly, 'and prayers are just about to begin. Now be quick about it.'

The twinkle in her eye, and her smile, belied the sternness of her words and George and Penelope darted into a small cloakroom and out again, leaving blazers and boaters askew on pegs, and satchels in a heap on the tiled floor.

From the back of the house childish voices could be heard, singing enthusiastically: 'All things bright and beautiful . . .' and pure and mellow a soprano rang out above them.

Zoe hurried the two children up the wide hall, and ushered them through a door. She placed the two late-comers into line and moved behind the huge desk to join the other adults who made up the community. A small dark-haired boy in the front row smiled merrily at her and his eyelid moved fractionally in what might have been a wink.

'. . . the Lord God made them all.'

Zoe nearly laughed out loud. The face of her son, his bright knowing eyes watching for her reaction, turned away as none came, and she knew he was listening to Rob barking; to the thrush in the laburnum tree at the back of the house; to the call of the summer's day. He loved to be out. Out in the garden, or the spinney which ran behind. He would whistle for Rob, his terrier, and the two of them would cut through the bit of woodland to the country lane beyond. The verges of the narrow road were full of long grass, toad-flax and harebells, and were hedged with hawthorn, blackberry and holly, old man's beard, and honeysuckle. Over the stile and into the field, the white flash of the dog beside him. There were rough bushes to be explored for birds' nests. Ditches full of wild life, field mice and shrews, rabbits and badgers.

He would come back as the sun touched the tops of the oak trees in the spinney, his face pink and dirty, his shirt torn, his arms scratched. His hands would be full of flowers. On his face would be a look of pure happiness, and his tongue would trip and stumble, as he tried to describe to his mother the wonders of what he had seen.

He wanted a pony. More than anything in the world he wanted a pony. His love for horses was only slightly less ardent than that of his love for his dog. He would hang over the gate of the field in which the local riding school kept their stable of hacks, and watch, completely absorbed, his serious face intent on a mare as she flicked her head against the midges. His pockets were always stuffed with bits of apple or carrot and the staid mounts would come to him as soon as he appeared, nuzzling their noses against his shoulder, searching for the titbits he brought them. He knew instinctively the correct way to feed them, holding flat his small grubby hand, letting the gentle mouths take the food.

Once Zoe had come upon him attempting, from the top rung of the barred gate, to climb upon the back of a docile chestnut cob, and had been alarmed at the screaming tantrum he had thrown as she ran to lift him down.

'I could have done it, Mama. I could, I could.'

Now she watched as he sang the words of the hymn, his eyes penetrating the window beside him, flat and unaware, his mind away to the open countryside he loved.

Just like Jonathan, the boy hated to be confined. Just as Jonathan had cherished his fine stable of horses, the feel of his hunter beneath him, the singing of the wind against his face, so did Daniel's young heart, unknowing, unaware of his heritage, yearn to be gone from here.

The singing ended, and the prayers, and the children dispersed to their separate classrooms. Their feet resounded cheerfully on the tiled floor, and their young voices filled the air like birds in an aviary. The teachers followed quietly.

Zoe watched Daniel as he scuffled with a boy of his own age, two heads – dark curls, and silky blonde – together. He laughed, and as his companion slipped on the polished floor, gave a friendly hand to help him up.

He was just five years old.

*

293

She had left Edge Lane when Daniel was two. He grew fast and was beautiful, and she adored him, but he was not enough to keep her lively mind and active body from boredom. She had always been occupied, busy from morning until night, even during those dreadful years when she had kept house for her family in Love Lane! She had scrubbed and washed and cleaned, and sewed the button-holes on Arnie Levy's uniforms. It had helped her, easing her grief at Daly's death, and at the Hall, her every waking moment had been filled. With the children in the nursery, with Lady Pat, with . . . with Jonathan in his estate office.

The idea for the school had come to her on a Spring day when she and Ned and Daniel took a picnic to the other side of the river. The ferry had carried them, car and all, to Birkenhead, and with the idea of crossing the Wirral to the banks of the River Dee, they had somehow become diverted further south towards Chester.

'Let's go further on, Ned,' she had said hurriedly, for memories of Chester set her heart beating and she wanted no reminders.

They had driven peacefully on, through countryside bright with lambs and bluebells, and that special air, soft as satin, that is traditional only to an English spring. They passed through villages: Quarrybank, Byley, Siddington, Wincle.

'We're getting near my own country now, Zoe,' Ned murmured, as they neared the low sweep of hills which swelled beneath the Macclesfield Forest.

It was just as he spoke that she saw it.

'Ned! Do stop – just for a minute.'

The house was in need of repair. The paint peeled from around the blank windows, and slates were missing from the sloping roof, but the setting was so lovely, the gardens, overgrown now, so full of spring flowers, that the shabbiness of the house hardly mattered. An orchard, an enchanting sea of white froth, lay to the right, and tall beech trees stood in their delicate spring finery to the back, the tops waving slightly above the roof, as though in welcome.

They had stopped at the side of the road, and as the hum of the car's engine died away, the sweet murmur of the countryside fell softly about their ears.

'What, darling, what is it?' Ned asked.

For a moment Zoe stood with Daniel in her arms, waiting, listening. Then he wriggled and she put him down and let him run. In a moment he was gone, disappearing into a ditch like a rabbit down a hole.

'Daniel?'

His head popped up, his face ecstatic.

'Look Mamma, look!'

His fingers tenderly clasped a little frog.

'Look, oh look, isn't he bootiful?'

She knew then that this was it. Even before she had set a foot between the crumbling gateposts. Before she had peeped hopefully through the dirt-smudged windows, or walked behind the running figure of her son, around the back of the house, to stare, hand shading her eyes, at the spinney, at the large, overgrown garden, at the small stream, running between.

It was Ned, of course, who bought it for her, though it put back his plans for a summer wedding. His hopes, unvoiced as yet, were set aside, he set the wheels in motion. Her own little house must be sold, of course, and in a way, though she had loved it from the first, she had been glad, for the heavy memories of her early grief had still been about her shoulders when she moved there, and she could not forget them.

Carpenters, plumbers, gardeners. Painters with long ladders, and charts from which she must decide the colour of the front door. Men in white overalls with rolls of wallpaper, and cans of gleaming paint. Furniture, carpets, curtains. School desks and ink wells. Blackboards and pencils. Books and books and books. Lists of the hundred and one things required by young children in the course of a day. Shopping, cleaning, supervising this and that, ordering and re-ordering, until at last it was done.

It took six months. The house was sound. It had only

been empty for a few weeks when Zoe had first seen it, and the warmth and feeling of the family who had lived there still pervaded the rooms like a friendly ghost.

There was a large and lofty kitchen over the cellar, which contained the boiler for the hot water system and the piles of anthracite to fuel it. The kitchen had a huge range and two ovens made of iron. There was a long serving slab, and a hatch through to the pantry. A scullery opened out of the kitchen.

There was a study, a drawing room, a large hall with dark panelling and a sconced fireplace. The airy dining room had a carved Georgian chimney piece. Flat, wide windows looked out over the enormous gardens, greenhouse and kitchen garden; gooseberries, raspberries, plums and cherries, which grew on trees against the wall.

Zoe loved it, and every minute of her life. She was thinking for herself, making decisions, and the twenty pounds which had been hers weekly for four years was returned by Ned at her request, to the mysterious donor.

She was her own person. Zoe Taylor, dependent on no one.

She had interviewed young women, many fresh from training school, and in this she found her own experiences with children with the nursery governess at the Hall, all helped to form in her mind exactly the kind of young woman for whom she searched. Someone young, warm and intelligent, attractive and fun.

A teacher.

Joanna Dale's face came into her mind at the thought. This was whom she wanted for her school. Women like Daly. Kind but resolute. Clever, and able to reach into young minds, to make their pupils sit up with interest, as Joanna had been able to do.

It was a hard task she had set herself, but she had done it, but once more she came to realise that without Ned it would have been impossible.

For a school one must have pupils, and where would they come from? It was to be a private school, for the children of ladies and gentlemen. She put advertisements in the best newspapers.

For three months little happened, and Zoe began to lose heart. But Edward Fitzgerald moved in a world apart from that which he knew with Zoe. He had a brother and sister, and clients who in turn had friends. Friends with young children.

Intrigued by 'old Ned's' enthusiasm, and by curiosity to see this paragon of who he raved, they began to come.

The elegant, well-bred mothers in their chauffeur-driven cars were impressed by Zoe's charm and intelligence. The school was beautiful, the setting superb, and the young teachers they met had the manners, the refinement, and the highest qualifications that could be found in the teaching profession.

They sent their children, and told their friends, and paid the high fees and were delighted and charmed by their progeny's advancement.

In the three years which had elapsed since she had started her school it had exceeded all Zoe's hopeful expectations. And she was content.

But today, perhaps because it was so lovely out of doors, she felt disinclined to go to her small study and get down to work.

The fresh air called her, she leaned from the hall window, for a second the image of a girl astride a chestnut mare flashed across her inner eye. The girl's hair was flung like a banner in the wind, and her body was taut beneath her shirt and jodhpurs. Her face was aglow with happiness and she turned to laugh at the man who rode beside her, darkly handsome. They reined in their horses and dismounted.

Zoe felt the pain strike her before she had time to set herself against it. The sweet memory had slid into her heart of its own volition, and automatically, as she had taught herself during the past five years, she shied away. Now she deliberately traced the expression on the man's face, lingering over his sensual mouth, and the glow of love in his eyes.

In her trance she ran her finger across his arched eyebrow, trailing the tip across the lean flatness of his brown cheek. She placed her hands on either side of his face, and drew his mouth down to hers, pressing her body against him urgently. The school garden disappeared and she lay in a nest of heather, the vast arch of heavenly blue above her, the man's weight upon her. Larks sang their hearts out above them, and the sweet smell of their bed lay like silk against her face.

Jonathan, Jonathan. Sweetness, like honey. The feel of his naked flesh against hers, the strength of him inside her, his mouth, hot and seeking . . .

'Miss Zoe . . . are you all right?'

From the rapture and sadness of the moors, from the erotic, sensuous dream which made her body stretch and move with languor, she heard the voice behind her. Slowly she came back to the present, and her hands trembled a little as she touched her hair, and turned to smile at her housekeeper.

'Yes, yes Glad. What is it?' She laughed, her voice breaking slightly. 'I was daydreaming.'

Glad's face cleared and they spoke for several minutes of menus, and laundry. When she had gone, Zoe stared beyond the window, beyond the garden and the spinney: beyond the miles which lay between her home and Weston Hall, and she let her thoughts dwell sadly on the family who lived there. It was months since she had allowed herself to do so.

Jonathan. Lady Pat. Had she ever forgiven Zoe?

She put her head in her hands and wept.

The summer passed into autumn and that day slipped mercifully from her mind. With the strength and courage which comes to those who bear grief and pain and overcome it, she put the past behind her.

In September she bought a little Austin Seven, and for three weeks Ned sat beside her, teaching her to drive. She set out alone for the first time on the first day of October.

Through Siddington and Goostrey, Occlestone Green and Quarrybank.

When she arrived, it stretched out before her in all its grandeur, immense, glowing with autumn colours, its vast silence filling her heart and mind.

The lovely, lovely, brooding moor.

She parked the car by the roadside and began to walk. For an hour she strode along the sheep tracks, the bracken shoulder-high, bright and sweet-smelling, on either side. The wind blew a little, lifting her hair, stirring her coat about her, caressing her face with the hands of a lover who needs to say 'You have been missed.'

She sat on a flat grey rock, leaning back on her hands, looking westwards towards the rolling uplands, towards the peak which was Black Tor. She longed to go there, but she did not dare.

Walking swiftly, for the autumn day was dying into twilight, she left her memories, and her past, and her love, and knew that she must not come again. Just once she had let her heart rule her head, but her life now was with Ned, with her work, and with the future of her son.

With one last farewell look, she got into her little car and drove away, away from the moor she loved and the family she loved, and her head lifted as she drove, and she smiled.

Chapter Thirty-Nine

Zoe sat at the polished table in her dining room, looking about her with pleasure at the treasures with which she and Ned had surrounded themselves, during the past years. The sense of wellbeing which it gave her every time she entered it, mantled her, and she smiled, as beautiful as she had ever been. Her hair was as vibrant and curling, cut short now, like a cap of rubbed chestnut, her skin was as firm and unlined as the day she had first climbed Black Tor Crag.

She was wearing a plain fitted dress, the colour of honey, and her high heeled shoes, and the handbag which lay on the table, were the same warm shade. Her slim waist was belted, and around her neck in a long creamy rope, was a strand of pearls, their richness glowing against her white skin and the delicate colour of her dress. Ned had given them to her on her twenty-ninth birthday.

The sun was setting and the room lay in a drowsy half-shade. Zoe's eyes closed, and she daydreamed as she waited for Ned.

The familiar sounds of the house carried on the quiet air. She could hear the rhythmic squeak of a tricycle's wheels at the far end of the garden, and Daniel's piping, tuneless song. The lusty chorus of 'There'll be a welcome in the hillside,' which meant that Glad was feeling particularly homesick for the valleys, sounded in snatches from the kitchen.

The open kitchen door was suddenly filled by her ample form.

'Danny, where are you, love? Come and see what Glad's got for you.'

The squeak of the tricycle stopped suddenly. Daniel

leaped off. His voice changed to an excited murmur, as he sped across the narrow lawn to the house. The small West Highland terrier ran at the boy's heels, his ears pricked to the sound of the woman's voice, for it usually meant food.

'Gingerbread men, I bet,' the child was murmuring as he gathered speed, 'or cookies. I hope it's gingerbread men, don't you, Rob?'

The dog moved his pointed ears at the sound of his name and continued his gallop. He didn't care what it was as long as he got some. He followed the boy into the kitchen and watched impatiently as Daniel was folded into Glad's fond embrace. Daniel's likeness to his father was breathtaking; it still tore at his mother's heart.

The little dog barked from the back of the house and Zoe knew that Ned had arrived. Rob always warned off every visitor. The doorbell rang, and Zoe got up and crossed the black and white tiles of the hall. Moving with the grace she had unknowingly inherited from her mother, she opened the front door.

Edward Fitzgerald stood there, the leaping terrier doing his best to kiss his face. He and Zoe smiled affectionately at each other.

'Get down, you rascal!' he bellowed at Rob. 'If I hadn't been the idiot who bought you in the first place, I would recommend most vigorously that you be put down.'

'Ned, you don't mean it. You know you love him as much as we do.'

'Who says so?' he laughed, finally managing to enter the hall.

He kissed the soft cheek which was offered to him, his heart caught in that urgent grip he had first felt five years ago, and his eyes softened with love.

'Daniel?' Zoe called. 'Will you come and get this blessed pup? Poor Ned is being eaten alive.'

The laughter increased as the boy, a half-eaten gingerbread man still in his hand, burst across the hall from the kitchen.

'Rob! Get down, you naughty boy! Come and have a piece of gingerbread man.'

The pup needed no second asking, and the two backed away down the hall and into the kitchen.

Ned turned back to Zoe as the kitchen door banged shut, and a look of impatient yearning and the unspoken question she had come to dread, came into his eyes. It was a long time since he had spoken of marriage: in the regular pattern of his courtship he usually gave her two or three months to 'think about it'.

For weeks, in an agony of self control, he would force himself to remain quiet. He was as much a part of her life now as Nancy and Jamie. Her one true friend, faithful as a dog, loving her, hating her, needing and wanting her, but never giving up hope that one day she would forget the man who still had her heart imprisoned.

He looked younger now than his thirty-nine years. The love which had come late to him had loosened the inhibitions which had hedged him about all his life. His whole body had relaxed and his quietness became almost merry. The strength and purpose remained but the charm was more openly expressed: he had learned that laughter aroused laughter, smiles were returned by smiles, and that as he gave enjoyment, so he received it. Zoe held him high in her affections, he knew, was grateful and though he was not content, he was prepared to wait.

Recently he had noticed signs which gave him hope: she allowed him small liberties, where once she would have drawn back. His goodnight kiss was a trifle longer, a touch more lingering, and on occasions his hesitant hand had been allowed to hold for an instant the trembling swell of her breast and he had felt her relax against him.

He must never again make the mistake that had almost lost her to him.

It was winter. Christmas had come and gone and for the first time he had not gone home. It had seemed to him that she might need him, and though she had gone to her brother's house on Christmas Day, he had stayed alone in his flat in Tuebrook.

On Boxing Day, compelled by his aching love, he walked past her house in Wavertree and the lights were on, and the Christmas tree sparkled in the depths of the bay window. Voices floated, childish, excited, across the freezing whiteness of the winter garden. He saw her lift the child to the mistletoe which hung from the ceiling, and watched as her son placed his mouth against hers.

He turned away, ashamed to be seen peeping, but her quick eye had caught his movement and she came to the window to invite him in. His presence had inhibited Jamie and his shy wife so Edward made a move to leave. But Zoe would have none of it. She let Jamie and Nancy go. When they had gone she put the child to bed, and drawing the curtains, came to kneel before him. Placing her hands upon his cheeks she had drawn his face down to hers and kissed him shyly upon the mouth. A mother's kiss to a sorrowing child. A friend's salute to a friend, the speaking of words without words, to show a bruised heart that she was sorry to be the cause of it.

But Edward, with the exuberance of an alcoholic denied the bottle, and suddenly finding himself in possession of the key to the distillery, lost all control. He took her sympathy for desire, her compassion for a longing as great as his own, and her gentle kiss for an invitation.

He was a quiet man, a good man, a man to be trusted, and had he been in command of his senses his own actions would have horrified him. But Edward was bewitched that night. Bewitched by Zoe's nearness, her softness, the smell and feel of her, and by what he imagined to be her compliance.

Seizing her with arms of steel, he pulled her up from her knees, until her body was locked between his quivering thighs. He strained her against his suddenly thrusting penis, raining kisses about her face and throat, crying hoarsely, and in between, saying her name over and over again, with a gladness which, even in the midst of her distress, tore at Zoe's heart. At first she knelt, amazement paralysing her, allowing his fervent kisses and eager, roving hands. Emboldened, his hands were at her blouse and his eyes on her breasts as he freed them.

'No,' she cried then, 'No, No,' and tried to move backwards, putting up her hands to ward off his.

'Ned, don't, oh don't, please.'

But caution had gone. Diffidence was flung to the wind. Restraint, so long his unwelcome companion, was shown the door, and Edward Fitzgerald, that gentle, kindly man, became for a dreadful moment, Arthur.

Zoe screamed, her head arching back on her slender throat. Her white skin gleamed like pearl. Her pointed breasts quivered as Edward rudely thrust her clothing from her shoulders.

'Edward . . . Ned . . .'

She struggled fiercely, beating her fists against his head.

'Dear God . . . help me . . . please . . . Jonathan, help me.'

It was as though she had touched a nerve.

It was as though she had pierced him with a sword. That name.

As his hands fell from her, she scrambled away awkwardly, like a crab scuttling from a fisherman's net. She was crying now, tears streaking across her creased cheeks, her mouth open, her eyes wide with fear. Her hands trembled about her clothing, pulling and grasping them around her, trying to cover herself from his gaze. She came up against the sofa at the back of the room, and inelegantly pushed herself to her feet, feeling her way along the wall until she reached the door.

Edward's face was red, like port wine, and his hair seemed to stand around his head like a disordered crown. He stared before him unseeingly. His hands hung slackly between his knees. The clock ticked, the fire crackled, the wind of the December night blew against the window, and the curtain stirred, moved by a vagrant draught.

A piece of coal fell in the fireplace and Zoe came to life.

'I think you had . . . you had better leave.'

Edward Fitzgerald's face crumpled, his head sagged forward until his chin touched his chest, and he began to weep soundlessly.

She had refused to allow him in the house for a month. His work slipped through his fingers as clients took their business elsewhere, dismayed by the fumbling, trembling person he had become, but until he swore to leave things as they were before that night, she would not see him. He had agreed, of course, for he could not live without her now.

He had tried to explain how he felt. He wanted to protect her, to wrap her in his arms and keep her from the woes and strife and despair which she had known. He wanted to give her and Daniel the stability of marriage. He wanted a commitment, a pledge, he wanted her to be his in the eyes of the world.

And Zoe, deep down, still yearned for some miracle to bring Jonathan to her. Whilst she was nobody's wife, Daniel could still become his son. If she married he would belong to another, would be lost to him forever.

But Zoe needed Ned, and the longing grew stronger: once more to have a lover, a man who would bind her to him drowning her in passion.

Zoe was to look back on that evening spent with Ned in the relaxed atmosphere of the Quail and Pheasant as another crossroad in her life.

She had thought the desperation of her love for Jonathan had finally loosened its grip on her, as the years with Ned had slipped by. Ned's love had quieted her need and she had been content. She had watched her son grow, uneasy sometimes at his likeness to his father, for it ruffled the smooth tenor of her days, but Ned would come to lift her from her memories, and the disquiet would leave her.

But still, her love returned to haunt her. As Daniel looked up at her she would see the eyes of his father. Every day, as the boy grew, there would be fresh reminders. He would become tall, a schoolboy, a young man, and the likeness would strengthen. His baby voice was leaving him now and the deeper tones of a boy were taking its place. One day it would become gruff and would break and Jonathan would speak to her through his son's lips. She was afraid. She needed forgetfulness, some obligation to take her mind from the past, to tie her to the future.

Ned held her hand, stroking the smooth flesh with his thumb, and his grey eyes were warm and loving. He smiled tentatively, still a little unsure of her, even now.

'A penny for them,' he whispered, and his lips lifted in a gentle smile. He looked ardent and boyish and her heart lifted in her breast.

He was a true man, this friend of hers. He loved her. No ifs or buts. No maybes. No matter what she had done in the past or how she acted now. He loved her. This was her life now – he was her life. She needed a home with a man in it and children. A boy who had Ned's eyes and a daughter to look like her.

As if he read her thoughts he said quietly, 'Marry me, Zoe.'

And she said 'Yes.'

Chapter Forty

The fire was stoked up like a furnace in the large grate, for it was December. The fragrance of pine drifted pleasantly into the warm and lovely room. The velvet curtains were drawn back and the winter light was sharp and white as it fell across the flowered carpet, and touched the uniformed figure sitting at the bedside.

A slight figure lay under the flowered quilt, and a sunken, skull-like face barely dented the crisp white pillow. A sighing breath, slow and hesitant, whispered between pale lips. The eyes opened and gazed feverishly at the woman beside the bed. An arm moved weakly beneath the quilt. The woman in the chair moved forward instantly.

'What is it, m'Lady? A drink? A spoonful of broth?'

The woman on the bed smiled.

'Daisy, Daisy,' she whispered. 'Will you never give up, girl? It's not broth I want, it's . . .'

Her eyes looked sadly towards the window.

'. . . it is absolution.' Her voice was so faint, it could hardly be heard.

'I don't understand, m'Lady.'

'I know you don't, dear Daisy,' whispered Lady Pat. 'You have never done an unkind deed in your life, nor had an evil thought. Not like me.'

Daisy was appalled. She leaned forward agitatedly, putting a gentle hand on her mistress's brow.

'Oh no, m'Lady, never. Not you. You wouldn't hurt a fly.'

'I hurt the one I loved as dearly as my own children. She had hurt me, so I hit back. I did not understand, you see . . . I thought . . . I . . .'

Her eyes closed and in a moment, in the way of those

309

who are near to death, she slipped away into a drugged sleep, and there was silence in the room.

Daisy watched her like a hawk, staring at the delicate rise and fall of the coverlet, willing it not to stop. Her hand hovered near the bell, ready to call His Lordship, should there be a need. He had only just gone to his room, and the strain and weariness would probably put him out for a couple of hours; she was reluctant to disturb him.

The door opened quietly and an attractive young girl slipped inside. She was seventeen or eighteen, and looked as one would have imagined the woman on the bed to have been at her age.

They did not speak, but Daisy took her hand and tears poured down the girl's cheeks. Daisy reached for her handkerchief.

For five minutes the girl kept her vigil, but the inert figure on the bed did not move. Quietly as she had come, the girl left, and as she did so, a nurse entered, her starched uniform crackling, her cap fluting about her dark hair. She came towards the bed and looked down at her patient, then put her hand on Daisy's shoulder, and whispered something in her ear. Daisy stood up and moved slowly away from the bed. The nurse sat down in her place and took up a square of crochet, and with the detachment which comes from many brushes with death began to work the wool with flying fingers.

'Jonty, Jonty,' she whispered, and tried to lift her hand to his face. Her sweet smile lanced him, and he laid his head against hers and his tears fell on to the pillow.

'Please, darling, don't, please don't,' she said faintly.

'Pat, oh, my dearest,' but he could not speak and her agonised eyes watched him as he bent his head to her hand and shook with sobs.

A small frown creased the waxy whiteness of the skin of her forehead and a troubled look misted her already tormented face. Aah Jonathan, my love, it seemed to say, where is the strength you should find when trouble comes?

310

'Pat, don't go, what shall I do . . . Pat?' His cries rocked the bed and she flinched.

The nurse moved forward hurriedly.

'Come, Sir Jonathan,' she whispered fiercely. 'You are upsetting her. Pull yourself together.' She almost pushed him through the doorway, and hurried back to her patient.

Lady Pat looked up at her and a faint sheen of perspiration filmed her face as the pain began to bite at her. The nurse reached for the hypodermic syringe hidden beneath a white cloth on the bedside table.

'No.' The voice was wispy, faint but full of resolve.

'Your ladyship?'

'Not that, not yet. I must see . . . must see Daisy. Send for her, please, at once.'

The nurse turned away, and rang the bell that hung above the bed. A young maid tapped on the door, but was not allowed inside, and a message was given to her.

Within minutes Daisy was at Lady Pat's side.

It took almost an hour. Daisy wept and could hardly write the words, but the woman on the bed bit her lips, and moaned, and feebly tossed her tortured body and finally it was done. Lady Pat lifted her hand, and with her last tiny cache of strength, she signed her name.

When her family came to gather about her, she was serene.

Her daughters kissed her cheek, their young faces contorted with grief, then left to be comforted by Nanny Bessy.

Sir Jonathan was with her when she died.

And Daisy stood quietly weeping by the window. Her tears now were not for her mistress – those had been shed. They were for the girl whose shadow still lurked in this room. In her apron pocket was a letter, and she must fulfil a promise.

If the letter were not delivered, if Zoe should not fulfil the dying woman's request, the Hall would be a cold and lonely place.

*

311

Zoe and Daniel stood side by side on the deck of the ferry to New Brighton. As the *Royal Iris* cleaved the grey waters of the River Mersey and the familiar outline of the Liver Building disappeared in the early morning December mist, she took his hand and he looked up at her and smiled.

It was 5th December, 1934, and tomorrow she was to be married. So many times in the past, she and Daniel had enjoyed this outing. It had almost become a ritual: every Sunday morning they set out on to the *Royal Iris* – for it must always be the same boat – across the dirty river to New Brighton and back. They would stop for lunch – roast pork and syrup pudding in a village inn – and arrive home to Glad and Rob and the warm happiness of an evening by the fireside.

In two weeks' time, when they returned from their honeymoon in Switzerland, Ned would be making the journey with them. Always he would be there from to-morrow on, and she was glad. From tomorrow she would at last 'belong'. She would have her own place in life. She would take nothing that belonged to another woman. She would have her own man, her own husband and home, and they would be a family. A tiny stab pricked her heart and a dark merry face flashed, like a meteor, across her mind.

The boy spoke.

'Will I call him Papa?' he asked earnestly.

Zoe smiled and looked down into the serious brown eyes. She knelt beside him and her eyes were on a level with his.

'If you want to,' she said. 'Ned loves you as though you were his own son. And you'll become his son if he adopts you as he would like to. Do you understand? You will take his name and be his son. Would you like that? You are the one to choose.'

He considered her words as the boat heaved and strained and moved away from the dock.

'Why can't I have my real father's name?'

Zoe's heart shifted and she stood up. Could she tell him

the truth about her love? He was still much too young to understand. He must be told the truth, of course, one day, but six years old was too soon.

A shrieking siren raked their ears across the water, and faintly on the morning air came the merry sounds of a band. Hooters hooted and whistles blew and from against the dock which berthed the great Cunard passenger liners a ship shuddered and began to inch its way from the land.

Diverted, Daniel sprang from his mother's side and ran across the deck.

'Look Mamma.' He climbed on to the lower rung of the rail, and swayed dangerously.

Zoe followed him, putting a protective arm round him. For the moment the crisis had been averted. Perhaps he would forget for a while, become used to having Ned as his 'Papa'.

She gazed at the familiar skyline. Perhaps this time next year she would hold another child in her arms. A child with bright eyes and a fine, pale skin.

A shiver of delight ran through her at the thought, and she leaned forward to touch her son. For a second the old feelings of uncertainty and doubt stole into her heart, and she was suddenly afraid. Then they were gone. She looked at Daniel and imagined another by his side, and her mind settled into peace. This was right for her and Daniel. A husband, a father for her boy, and a brother or sister to play with. And she would keep her school, Ned had said so.

She did not question why she should reassure herself in this way, why should she need to convince herself that what she did was right.

She shook her head. It would be perfect.

Zoe contentedly drove the little black beetle of a car along the narrow lane to the school. She and Daniel had had a lovely day.

Would it be fine tomorrow? How happy Ned had become. Would the lily of the valley be too delicate to match her dress?

She turned in between the school gateposts, and pulled up at the front door. The carriage lamp was lit though the sun had not yet slipped beyond the horizon, and Glad had turned on the lamps in the hall and sitting room. They glowed in welcome. It was half-term and the staff were away for the weekend, leaving only Glad and the scullery maid. Zoe looked forward to an evening of quiet peace with her son. Their last alone together.

As she switched off the engine the front door opened, spilling a soft beam of light across the steps. Daniel leapt out of the car and ran eagerly towards the waiting figure. Glad bent to stroke his cheek, and looked over his head to Zoe.

She seemed to hesitate.

'What is it, Glad?' Zoe smiled as she shut the car door. Was the meat over-cooked? Had Rob made a puddle?

Glad jerked her head towards the sitting room.

'There's someone to see you. I put 'er in the sitting room, see, but I don't know . . .'

'What don't you know?' Zoe entered the bright hall and stopped abruptly. Coming slowly, hesitantly down the stairs was a woman in black. For a space of five seconds, Zoe did not know her.

She was plump with a bosom like a pouter pigeon's. The sturdy legs were encased in dense black stockings and on her greying hair was a large, flat, sensible, black hat. She stopped halfway down the stairs, and her pale face moved, and tears brimmed her soft blue eyes.

She moved down another stair and Zoe took a step towards her. 'Daisy . . .' she whispered.

Clumsily the woman thudded down the stairs, and Zoe's feet carried her across the hall like wings.

Glad and Daniel stood, mouths open, struck dumb and motionless at the sight of Zoe, clasped like a homecoming bird, in the stout arms of the stranger in black.

314

'She died 'appy, Zoe. I promised 'er I'd come an' bring the letter an' it seemed to make 'er – easy in 'er mind, like.'

Daisy's plump, red-cheeked face was composed now.

'D'you know what she said?' She looked directly into Zoe's sorrowing eyes. 'She said I done someone a great wrong once, Daisy. I loved 'er an' I hurt 'er, 'cause she'd 'urt me. That's what she said, Zoe, and she said she wanted . . . absolution.' Her voice cracked.

Zoe's hand flew to her mouth, to force back a cry of grief and remorse. If only, at the end, she had been able to make up for the pain she had given to the woman she loved.

'She were that spunky, our Zoe. Right t't end, she never complained. Cancer, Doctor said.'

Daisy's musings seemed haphazard, but Zoe could feel the tension building slowly, and shivered, for she knew what was to come.

'It were too much fer one woman. But I allus thought, well, she's got 'im. 'E loves 'er, at least she's got 'im.' Her head turned slowly from the glowing fire to Zoe's shrinking figure. 'But she 'adn't, 'ad she, our Zoe? She 'adn't even got 'im.'

'Dear God, Daisy, don't, please don't . . . please . . .'

'When I seen the boy, I knew it was 'is. I guessed, years ago, but when I seen 'im, I knew.'

Zoe lifted her head sharply.

'Oh, yes, our Zoe, I knew. It was me what told 'er. It was me day off – I'd gone to Liverpool, an' I saw yer in Dale Street. You was gettin' on a tram an' I called to yer. Ran after the tram, but yer'd gone. You must 'ave bin six or seven months then, it was in the March. When I got back, I couldn't wait to tell her ladyship. To tell 'er you was all right

– but I should a' known. When I told 'er you were in the family way . . . well . . . she nearly went mad. She swore me to secrecy, an' I never told a soul.'

Zoe wept openly now.

Daisy shook her head, wonderingly. 'You an' 'im. It must a broke 'er 'eart when she found out.'

Zoe rocked to and fro in an agony of grief and understanding. So that was where the money had come from. Lady Pat had scorned to have Zoe in her house, but her kind heart could not let the child grow up in poverty. Though she did not forgive, she had provided for Jonathan's son.

'Why, Zoe, why d'you do it? You loved 'er as much as me.'

Zoe shuddered, and her head hung low. It might have been yesterday, so clear was it in her mind, the dead, cold look of misery in Lady Pat's eyes. If she could just have been allowed the gift of holding her close once more, of begging her forgiveness, perhaps Lady Pat's death would have been made easier.

And yet Daisy had said that Lady Pat had died happy.

Zoe raised her head and looked into the countrywoman's eyes. There was no blame there, no judgement or recrimination. Just sadness and bewilderment. Zoe was her friend; it had been she, young and simple though she was, who had helped restore Zoe to sanity. She had loved her protectively, and like a mother whose child had committed some heinous crime, she could not comprehend, could not grasp the fact. But like a mother, she loved her still. Zoe could see that, and was comforted.

'You said there was . . . a letter?'

Daisy came out of her sad reverie with a start. She opened her bag and produced an envelope.

She passed it to Zoe.

'I wrote it out for 'er so I know what's in it. No one else. It's more 'n you deserve, Zoe.'

Zoe tore open the envelope, took out the sheet of notepaper, so familiar, and began to read:

Dear Girl,

How can I begin? My mind slips away from our last moments together. Your face haunts me. I will not speak of wrong, nor hurt, only of love. I loved you from the first, and I love you at the last. There was love in this house when you were here and it is needed now. I am tired. I would like to say more, but have not the strength.

I understand, at last. Please come.

It was signed, in a faint, trailing, but well known hand, Patricia Weston.

Zoe bowed her head.

For an hour she wept, and it was in Daisy's comforting arms that she at last found release. Afterwards, in the dimming winter's afternoon, they sat, rocking in silence, the calm of forgiveness and understanding between them. Bitterness had been washed away, they were easy with one another again.

Zoe felt the sweet relief settle like a mantle of serenity about her – as though Lady Pat touched her. Or was it Joanna Dale? Sometimes the two would become inextricably bound in her mind – and in a way they were the same person: she had received wisdom and goodness from them both. They had known her for what she was, they had known of her needs, her desperate desire to be loved, and though Lady Pat had suffered from it, both had understood.

But now – her heart surged – now what was to happen? A gladness, a guilty, half-ashamed gladness, began to seep into her sorrowing heart. She was desolate, lost, at the thought that she would never again see the impudent smile nor hear the humour in the voice of Jonathan's wife. But how could she not be glad that she would see – Oh God, she could hardly bear to let the thought into her mind – see Jonathan again.

Jonathan, Jonathan, her heart whispered. Do you remember, my love?

She leaned forward and put some coal on the fire and

317

flames leaped merrily, painting the quiet faces of the two women with glowing colour.

'When did she die, Daisy?'

'On Friday,' Daisy sighed.

'Did she . . . was she in pain?'

'Oh no, the doctor gave her . . .'

'Did she speak of me?'

'No.'

'The girls, how . . . were they?'

'We all loved 'er, Zoe, everyone is sorrowin'.'

Zoe bent her head and stared at her hands, bracing herself for the next question.

'And his Lordship?'

''E's out of his mind.'

Zoe's head came up sharply.

''E can't take it, Zoe. It's like she was . . . well, even though she were the one who couldn't walk, he leaned on 'er. No one can do owt wi' 'im. Vicar's bin, Doctor Blair, an' 'e won't even see anyone. Just shuts 'imself up in 'is room. Drinkin'.'

'Dear God.'

The silence in the room was full of ghosts as each woman conjured up pictures in her own mind of what was happening at the Hall. Servants, rudderless, heartbroken, waiting for direction. The young girls grieving for their mother, longing for comfort, a father's arms denied them.

And Jonathan. The perfect man, handsome, charming, thoughtful and loving, but unable when crisis struck, to be a man.

Oh Jonathan, my love. I love you and you need me.

'I'm to be married tomorrow, Daisy,' she said quietly.

'Who . . . wha . . .' Daisy stammered, and if the moment had been less poignant, Zoe might have laughed.

'I have known – Edward – for several years. He has been good to Daniel and me. Kind. I have no one, Daisy. I needed a – friend. He is the only man I have ever known to give me love and friendship without demanding something of me in return – except marriage. I have held out all these

318

years, hoping, I suppose that . . . Well, I finally said "Yes",
Daisy and tomorrow . . .'

Daisy's hand crept to hers, and she looked with pity at
Zoe's averted face.

'Eeh, what a to-do.' She shook her head. 'The funeral's
tomorrow.'

The funeral is tomorrow. Dear Lord, the funeral is
tomorrow. Ned, oh Ned, my dear. Zoe writhed at the
thought of the suffering she must cause him, but she had to
go. Tomorrow it was the day for which Ned had fought
with all the strength of his love for her, but she must go
back. To Weston Hall, to all those who needed her, to her
friends who grieved, to say goodbye to Lady Pat and to
stand beside her grave – and to be with Jonathan.

'Oh, Daisy, what am I to do?'

She stood up quickly and crossed the room to the win-
dow. The dusk was drawing in and the gaunt winter trees
in the road stood like black skeletons, silhouetted against
the washed pearl of the sky.

Ned had offered her a home with children in it. Peace,
protection. He would look after her and Daniel; he would
give her love and trust, and the surety that from the
day she took his name, her troubled heart would find
peace. Her mind would be calm. She would no longer be
alone.

But Jonathan. Jonathan, Jonathan.

Her heart sang as his name flowed through her mind and
the feeling drowned her, a breathless, painful, delicious
exhilaration. It had been so long. In six years she had not
once felt with Ned the complete, the rounded happiness
she had known with Jonathan. Even if Jonathan did not
need her, no longer loved her, she knew, sadly, that she
could never marry Ned.

She turned from the window.

'Will you stay with me, Daisy? I must telephone . . . I
shall have to see someone . . . before I can leave.' She
crossed the room and opened the door. 'I'll take you
upstairs and you can meet Daniel properly.'

A proud and loving look passed over her face.

'He is a beautiful boy, Daisy. I think Jonathan will be proud of his son.'